CROP BURNER

THE TALE OF FEARN AND THE DEAMHON

Noel,
Beware of
deamhons!

DunDraCon
2022

CROP BURNER

THE TALE OF FEARN AND THE DEAMHON

GAVIN BLACK

Crop Burner: The Tale Of Fearn And The Deamhon
By Gavin Black
©2021 Gavin Black. All rights reserved

ISBN: 978-1-956193-00-8
Book Design & Publishing done by:
Susmita Dutta
Global Book Publishing
www.globalbookpublishing.com

For

Ann, my wife, my first editor, and eternal love. Thank you for taking this journey with me.

Joanne Burnett, the one person I wish was here to read this. I will be forever indebted to you. I hope this is properly numinous.

My father, who introduced me to science fiction and fantasy.

THE FLOWER

Dair teetered on the edge of the wooden chair, staring at the dying flames in the hearth as he tried not to focus on the sounds coming from the bedroom. His callused fingers alternated between tapping rhythmically on the lip of the chair and tracing the outlines of the raised grain in the wood. He was trying to ignore the Crop Burner that sat behind him in the dark. Sweat trickled down his neck at the thought of it. Turning his attention back to the fire, he noticed it had burned down to its last log. The light of the flames barely lit the small, sparsely furnished room. As he watched the flames dance across the oak, the sound of his wife's screams rattled the walls of the adjacent room.

Why did I allow her to bring that into our house? Dair asked himself, though he knew the answer—he would do anything for his wife.

He reassured himself that there was no reason to worry; no child of his would be one of *them*.

The cries of childbirth grew more pronounced. Getting up slowly, the chair creaking as his weight shifted, he moved to the pile of wood next to the hearth and carefully selected a log that would give enough fuel to stoke the fire but conserve the dwindling fuel supply. It had been a harsh winter, and despite spring's approach, the cold still seeped into every nook and cranny at night. Dair had not been able to go out and get fresh wood the last few days. Needing to preserve what they had, he picked up and meticulously weighed the log in his hands, placed it in the hearth, and grabbed a long metal rod, prodding at the embers to help stoke the fire.

He turned back to the table and looked up at the Asinta seated across from him. The man had been there for most of the night. A thick winter cloak was draped over his shoulders and fastened around his neck with a thin metal chain. Under the hooded cloak, the man wore a fine woolen tunic with intricately embroidered golden hands clasped at the wrist over his left breast. The man's face was covered in shadow; just his lips could be seen. Dair surmised the man to be about his same age. To get his mind off of his wife's screams, he gave in and derided the man. "So, Crop Burner, you spend all of your time harassing farmers? Or do you get time to kill their crops as well? I bet you're pretty disappointed that the winter weather has spoiled any fun you might've had killing everything I own before leaving." Dair spat on the dirt floor next to the man's worn leather boots.

The man scowled, pursing his lips together as if to speak. Finally, his face slackened and he shook his head in disgust before replying. "Your wife is the one that summoned me here. I would have been more than glad to have come during the spring. I am surprised we were requested, as you Northerners rarely comply with testing your children."

Grumbling, Dair responded, "I would've been fine if you didn't come at all. She's been sick for the past few months and got it into her head that you had to be here. Oy, Dainua knows I tried to talk her out of it."

The screaming from the other room suddenly quieted. No sound followed, and time seemed to stop. The silence washed over Dair and the stranger like a wave, drowning Dair in fear. Just as he was about to bolt to the bedroom door, a new cry broke the silence. He stared at the door. A moment later, it slowly opened, and the midwife beckoned him into the room. As he approached, she put up a hand.

"The baby is doing well, but I cannot do any more for your wife. I'm sorry." She slid past Dair into the other room with the baby swaddled in her arms. As Dair peered into the room, the strong smell of iron assaulting his senses, he noticed the bedding was dark—almost black in the light of the lantern on the nightstand. Speaking to himself somberly, Dair mumbled, "Oy, the bedding is so dark. How can all of that blood be hers?"

He stumbled towards Lia, who lay on the bed among rumpled sheets. Her rosy complexion was gone, replaced with a pallid gauntness. Her eyes were sunken, peering at him as if within a deep well. The taut skin made her cheek bones flare out like those of a bird about to take flight. The beautiful lips that had been full and vibrant sat flat and pulled back, her gums and teeth showing through her weak smile. Every breath she took contorted her face into a grimace of pain and agony.

"My love, everything will be fine," Dair lied, thinking that she was too pale.

Her lips began to quiver, and her mouth opened as if to speak, but not a single word was uttered. As he leaned closer, she strained to whisper faintly, "Fearn... name him Fearn."

"Shh. Be still, my love. Everything will be alright," Dair replied, trying to reassure himself as much as Lia. The weight of the world seemed to be crashing down on him. Sliding to the floor and putting his forehead to her icy hand, tears started to pour down Dair's cheeks. Her hand moved, reaching to brush away his tears. Looking up at her through bleary eyes, he saw her smile—the same smile he remembered from their wedding day as she said 'I do'. After a moment, her eyes closed, and her pure face showed no more pain. The hand that touched his face slowly fell away. "I will always love you. We'll name him Fearn, after your father," Dair whispered. Pulling himself up, Dair leaned over Lia, his tears raining gently on her face as he kissed her one last time.

Dair stumbled out of the room and slumped back into his chair. Laying his arms on the table, he buried his face and wept. "Oy, Dainua, take me in her place. What did I do to deserve this?"

A faint and muffled cry broke through Dair's sobbing. Sitting up suddenly, trying to wipe the tears from his face and wetness from his nose, Dair looked to the midwife. "O Dainua! The baby! How is the baby?" The midwife walked over and placed a hand gently on his shoulder. Glancing up into her face, he blathered, "Umm... is it... no, I mean the girl... uh, boy... doing alright? Oh dear, if it is a girl, I can't name her Fearn. But I made a promise."

"The baby is fine and it is a boy. Here." The midwife slowly lowered the baby into Dair's arms. The baby was strangely quiet except for a few soft whimpers. Dair asked, "Are babies supposed to be this quiet?" Those he had encountered in the past were always crying over something. The midwife smiled a knowing smile and nodded.

Running his hand over the baby's head, he wondered aloud, "How can something so perfect come from such chaos? Oh, why did she have to die?" A gloved hand reached out and patted his arm. Looking up, he realized he had forgotten all about the Crop Burner. As the Asinta walked around the table, he pulled back his hood. He had closely cut brown hair, a day's worth of stubble covering his chin, crow's feet near his brown eyes, and tan skin weathered from a life spent on the road. Dair recognized a smell that reminded him of his wedding day while standing under the great oak: the smell of the grass beneath his feet and that beautiful flower his wife wore. *What flower was that? Why are memories so hazy?* Dair wondered.

"Are you well enough?" the Asinta asked.

"Eh? Oh, sorry." Dair mumbled as he pulled himself out of his reverie. "Get to doing what you need to do so I can be rid of you," he huffed.

Leaning forward, the man gently lifted the baby out of Dair's arms and placed him on the table. Searching in his robes for a moment, the man finally withdrew a small metal box, opened it carefully, and placed it on the table at arm's length. Searching again in his robes, he pulled out a finely-made pair of silver tongs. Using these, he pulled a flower from the box, one with flawless petals of the deepest shimmering blue Dair had ever seen. The emerald green stem looked as if it had been carved by artisans. As the man quickly closed the box, Dair noticed that there was a second, identical flower still inside. "I never get tired of looking at these," the Asinta sighed.

Reaching down, the man unswaddled the baby until the pink skin of his tiny chest was exposed. The Asinta placed the flower gently on baby Fearn's chest. "This should take only a few moments, and then you can be rid of me."

"Wait! What is that? No, that can't be! He has Telgog's curse," the midwife gasped and shrank away as the flower started to change. The cobalt blue of the petals slowly started to fade. Black veins began to creep up around the petals, the green in the stem seeming to melt as a black hue boiled to the surface. The stem curled, writhing like a snake. The black veins in the petals grew wider and longer, a plague enveloping the blue until nothing but black remained. The once pristine flower that lay on Fearn's chest was now a bright, glossy black reflecting the flames in the fireplace.

A loud crash echoed through the room as Dair desperately tried to back the chair away from the table and instead knocked it over, toppling to the ground himself. Dair continued backing away until he was against the wall. "Get that thing out of here!" Dair screamed. "I won't let this thing mock my wife's death or taint her father's name. It won't be living under this roof. I'm a respectable farmer and won't have some deamhon killing my crops!" Fearn began to bellow. Rushing over, the midwife quickly swaddled him and pulled him up to her chest. Swaying back and forth to try to calm him, she looked to the Asinta and said, "The baby is going to need to feed soon." The Asinta pulled a heavy leather purse from his belt and held it out to her. "Take the boy to the closest wet nurse," he directed. He looked over at Dair, still flat against the far wall. "Better yet, arrange for the baby to be taken care of until it can be weened, at which time the baby will be returned here." Dair started to stammer in protest, then stopped and looked back through the door to where Lia lay.

"I will feed and clothe him, but not for you, Crop Burner. I'm doing this for my Lia," Dair insisted. Standing, he walked over to the chair that lay on the floor and picked it up, turned it to face the fire, and sat down. "Get out of here, both of you," Dair growled. "I've had enough for one night."

The Asinta glanced at the midwife. "You better get going. Wait, though. I almost forgot I need one more thing. Please let me see the baby's shoulder." He reached into his robes, withdrew a small bottle and pulled a knife from his belt. "I will need a sample from him so we can determine where his powers may lie." The midwife did as she was told. Grabbing the baby by his hand and pulling his arm straight, the Asinta slowly carved a small square of skin from Fearn's shoulder and dropped it in the bottle. Fearn burst out crying again. The Asinta pressed his hand over the wound and grabbed the midwife by the arm. Before she could ask what he was doing, a sharp pain shot from the center of her body to the arm he held. Just as she was about to scream, the pain ceased. He removed his hand and, where the small square was cut in the skin, a fresh pink scar had appeared. The Asinta hurriedly picked up the box and tongs, put them away in his robes, and without another word, left the small farm house. Gathering up her supplies and baby Fearn, the midwife followed the Asinta out.

A Deamhon In The Night

A week after Lia's death, Dair decided to travel into town. He pulled on a few shirts and wrapped several blankets around himself for good measure. He carefully arranged the table scraps from dinner onto a plate. After looking at it a long while, he decided there wasn't quite enough food, so he headed over to the cupboard, pulled out a smaller plate, and carefully moved the scraps over.

"Perfect!" he exclaimed to himself. He placed several more logs on the fire and re-arranged the coals with a fire iron. Then, Dair picked up the plate and a lantern and left, walking around the back of his home to the far corner of his property. Dair set the lantern down and, bending low, he carefully balanced the plate in one hand while gently brushing the snow away with the other until there was a hole in the snow just slightly larger than the plate. Gingerly setting the plate down, Dair rotated it one direction, then the other. Still hunched over, Dair picked up the lantern and slowly backed away, covering his tracks in the snow. After a few paces, Dair straightened up, grinned broadly, and turned back towards his stable.

Dair could only really call the stable a stable because there was a horse in it. In reality, it looked as though someone nailed eight outhouses together. The stable was just big enough for his horse, hay and tack, and farming supplies. The horse was his prized possession,

13

given to him as a dowry from his marriage to Lia. He saddled the horse, tied the lantern to the saddle, mounted, pulled the blankets closer around his shoulders, and headed off across the farm and out onto the road that ran parallel to the fields. The road was covered in snow with a thin, oft-trodden track running down the center. He glanced back to make sure smoke was still pouring from the chimney.

"Errr, I hate to having to waste wood on an empty house," Dair grumbled to himself. Just at the edge of his property, Dair steered the horse down a small path that lay on the opposite side of his field. Swinging down and grabbing his lantern, he approached a small patch of ground with only a dusting of snow on a small wooden tombstone. Setting down the lantern and pulling off a glove, Dair traced his fingers across the carvings, which danced in the flickering light.

"O Lia, why did you have to leave? I love you and miss you. The bed is so cold without you." Dair spoke into the silence.

He stood up, wiped a tear from his eye, replaced his glove, and started to return to his horse. A voice called out to Dair. Turning around, Dair saw Lia, or what looked like Lia, standing behind her grave marker. She was translucent and the small snowflakes that fell from the trees above passed right through her.

A soft voice floated through the air: "Hello, my love. I'm sorry I had to leave you. Is our son well?" Lia reached a hand towards Dair. Looking at the ghostly image of his wife through tears, Dair rubbed his eyes, hoping he was just seeing things. He found that she was still standing in front of him. Dair mumbled in confusion, "How can this be? You are dead. I buried you here myself." Cautiously, Dair walked forward a few steps. The woman, whose arm was still outstretched, looked just like Lia in every way. However, there was not weariness and pain on her face, a face that was as radiant as the morning light.

"Are you some sort of deamhon?" he asked hesitantly. "If so, this is a cruel trick to play on a grieving man."

"Dair, it's me, Lia. I don't have much time. I wanted to tell you that I love you one last time. You haven't mentioned Fearn. Did he die as well?" Lia looked around, desperately searching for another grave marker.

"Lia, Fearn is fine," Dair said. "He's with a wet nurse and will be coming home in a few months. Though, I should tell you; he failed the test of the flower. I don't know what to do with him."

Tears filled Lia's eyes and fell softly from her face; as they hit the snow at her feet, they made no imprint. "Please. Don't turn our son away. Raise him. Love him," Lia pleaded. "I was so afraid he was going to turn out like my father and me."

Dair spat into the snow at Lia's feet. "You can't be her. If you were my Lia, you couldn't say that, knowing what those Crop Burners did to my family and your dad." Turning, Dair ran to his horse, mounted, and, kicking its flanks urgently into a gallop, rode away from the gravesite. A faint plea echoed through the trees around him, but as he looked back, he saw nothing chasing him. After about a quarter stone, Dair pulled up on the reins, slowing the horse to a walk. The moment with Lia played over and over in his mind.

The small village was only about an hour down the road, past scorched fields abandoned long ago. Once Dair reached town, he looked around; not a person was out on the road. The village had a surrounding palisade once, but now just a ramshackle fence. Most of the homes that had made up the village had fallen into disrepair years ago, having crumbled in on themselves or been burned by some local kids. The only sign of life was the smoke that poured out of the few still-occupied buildings. Leading the horse through the entrance that once held two large gates and a sign marking the name of the town, Swallow, Dair glanced around and then back over his shoulder.

Dair thought back to when it was full of life and the day that both the village and his life were forever destroyed by Crop Burners.

Winding his way through the town, he passed by the broken ruins of homes and businesses until he came to the small tavern that stood at the edge of the town square. There had once been an intricate sign hanging above the door, Dair recalled, but it had long since been replaced by a crudely inscribed scrap of wood with a mug on it.

The locals just called it "the tavern," while travelers mostly avoided it unless they were coming for market day. Leading the horse around the back of the tavern, Dair tied it up inside an abandoned home now being used as a stable after the old stable's roof had collapsed due to heavy snow a few winters back. After making sure the horse was tied up properly and had fresh hay, Dair walked through the snow back to the front of the tavern. As he opened the door, a hot blast of stale, ale-scented air assaulted his nose and made his skin sting. The tavern was typical of this part of the world, though this one had two fireplaces: one to the left and one to the right of the door. Four rows of tables were haphazardly laid out down the center, and at the far end stood a small bar with two small casks behind it. It was a busy evening, and most of the villagers were there, the adults eating and drinking while the children ran around the tables, playing made-up games.

Dair walked towards an empty seat directly across from the right-hand fireplace. As he passed, several locals raised their mugs in salute. Several greeted him: "Good evening, Teller of Tales." Dair pulled off the blankets and set them out on the table to dry.

"Oy there, Dair!" the tavern owner called out. "Wouldn't have expected to see you out on an evening as cold as this. Make yourself comfortable. I'll grab a mug of ale for you, and if you're interested, I have chicken in the back." Dair looked up at Cromm, a man so thin one could almost look through him. His hair looked as if a family of rats was currently residing in it, and his nose was strangely small for a face that was overly long and narrow. The nose sprouted a bushy mustache that covered his upper lip.

"Cromm, when are you going to realize that until you put on some weight, no one is going to trust anything you have to offer?" Dair said, his lips curling into a wry smile.

"I'm only going to let you get away with that on account of everything you've been through," Cromm replied. "Let me go get you an ale." He turned and headed to the bar.

Sitting down, Dair spread his hands towards the fire to warm them. A clanking sound caused him to turn; Cromm sat down across from him with two mugs. He pushed one to Dair, raised his mug, and declared in a low and somber tone: "To Lia! May her sul rest in the embrace of Dainua." Dair looked down at his mug, ran a finger across the rim to wipe clean a safe place from which to drink, then looked up to see Cromm sitting there, mug in the air, waiting. Slowly raising his mug, Dair clanked it against Cromm's. The ale sloshed over the side of both mugs, into the other mug, and onto the table. Putting the mug to his lips, Dair drank fast and deep, wishing to get lost in his ale and rid his mind of the ghostly Lia. After finishing, Dair realized that he would need to drink the entire keg to even get a little fuzzy.

"You call this ale, Cromm? This piss gets worse each time I come in. Are you just refilling the barrel with water and sloshing it around some?"

Cromm recoiled, looking visibly hurt. "By Dainua, I know you have been through a lot, but keep that up and I'll throw you back out into the snow," Cromm barked. The two men sat there, staring each other down until they suddenly broke into laughter. Cromm grabbed Dair's mug and headed back to the bar. Dair looked around to see who else was at the tavern. At the table across from him, the two Bitveen brothers sat with a man he thought was one of their cousins—a blacksmith, if Dair recalled correctly, though he couldn't place a name with the face. The man had thick arms and a barrel chest.

Cromm returned and sat down in front of Dair again, blocking his view, pushing a full mug and plate across the table. "Here's another mug of ale, though this one ain't free, and a plate of food," he said. The plate held half a chicken, a poor lumpy attempt at mashed yams, and a few pea pods.

"Who is that man with the Bitveens? Is he a blacksmith?" Dair asked as he poked at his food.

Without turning around, Cromm chortled, "Nah, there's no way anyone in that family would breed anyone smart enough to do that; though, I've heard he works for one. Shovels coal for him, by my recollections." Cromm then leaned in closer. "Say, the rumor around here has it your boy failed the trial of the flower. Is that true? I can't recall the last time someone this far north had their child tested."

Lia's words rang out in Dair's head. "I was so afraid he was going to turn out like my father and me."

Dair quickly discarded the idea, then replied, "Ay, the creature is probably the cause of Lia's death. It'll be hard enough tilling and planting the land each year by myself. Now, I'll have to find a way of keeping it busy, so it can't run through the field, killing everything it touches. That isn't even the worst of it. Lia made me promise to name him after her father." Dair tore the chicken leg from the breast and checked that it was cooked all the way through before he took a bite.

"Oy, naming him after such a good man? What a shame, especially after what this village has been through. That kid isn't going to have an easy time growing up. Maybe when he's old enough, you can sell him off to the Asinta." Cromm leaned back in his chair. "Oy, did you hear the Miller's son disappeared? Some are saying that he was last seen heading east into the woods past your farm. Folks believe that the forest deamhons got him."

"Oh," replied Dair. "That explains why the food I've been leaving out hasn't been touched. When did he go missing?"

Cromm ran a couple of greasy fingers through his mustache. "I saw him not two days past, so it can't be any longer than that." Dair seemed lost in thought for a few moments, then suddenly pounded his fists on the table loud enough to bring most everyone in the room to a dead silence and turn in the direction from which the sound had come. Dair slowly stood up, and as he did, the room started to quiet down. Those who did not notice were elbowed or hushed.

With a broad voice, Dair addressed the room: "Ay, so the Miller's son has gone off into the woods, I hear. Well, I tell you this: it had to be one or two nights ago when I was lying in bed. The fire in the next room was just a few coals, but it still lit up the walls with a deep red glow. My horse gave off a loud, startled cry. I sat up in bed and listened intently. A pounding on wood came from my stable as if the horse was trying to get out... or something was trying to get in. It stopped abruptly. I strained my ears and could hear something outside. It was stomping through the snow, the sound becoming louder and louder."

Dair paused and looked around to make sure every eye was on him. "Go on, Teller of Tales," the baker urged. After a dramatic pause, Dair continued. "The sound came right up to my house. I could tell that it was just on the other side of the wall from me. I held my breath but couldn't hear the deamhon and was hoping it couldn't hear me. Then there was a scraping sound sliding down the side of the house, followed by a sound like a blacksmith's hammer on an anvil: *BANG! BANG! BANG!*" With each bang, Dair pounded a fist on the table. A few villagers jumped and spilled their ale.

Dair paused again to take a swig from his mug, then continued: "The noise wasn't coming from the side of the house... but from my door. I was so focused on the wall that the sound startled me. I fell right off the bed and onto the floor! I think I may even have screamed a little."

A small spattering of laughter broke out in the room. The children had stopped playing and now were eagerly listening.

Dair wiped his brow, acting as if the story was straining him to tell, before continuing. "The scraping noise stopped. *BANG! BANG!* My door shook. A low roar erupted like two boulders being slammed together, followed by a sharp but brief, scream. I lay on my floor, waiting for the deamhon to break down my door and carry me off. Not a single sound came. Not from the horse nor a single animal in the forest. I lay on my floor all that night, not daring to move except to pull my bedding down onto me. When I awoke in the morning, I grabbed the poker from my fireplace and slowly pushed my door open. In front of me was a track in the snow, as if something had been dragged away into the woods. The only human footsteps came from the forest directly to my door. I walked around the side of my house, and there—down the side of the wall—were three long, deep scratches. Not a single track could be seen in the snow. I ain't saying that it was the Miller's boy who came to my door that night, but it's a strange coincidence."

Finishing, Dair slowly started to sit down. A drunkard from the back of the room yelled out, "Oy! Dair! Why didn't it break down your door and drag you away as well?" Dair stood up, looking slowly around the room.

"Ay, you know as well as I do why it left me alone, just like most of us in this room. Those that don't believe take heed. It's because we leave an offering out every night for the deamhons. Don't ever forget, not only do they want food but respect as well." As Dair started to sit down again, he heard sobbing coming from his right. He noticed the Miller's wife was sobbing into her husband's shoulder. Standing back up, Dair lifted his mug from the table and out in front of him. "To the Millers and to their son: may he still be out there." The sound of mugs scraping across tables echoed through the room as everyone raised their mugs in response. Dair drank a long draught, and the crowd followed suit.

Then, another voice yelled out. "To Lia! May she forever rest in Dainua's embrace." A murmur of consensus moved around the room. Dair raised his mug again and drank what remained. A feeling of warmth grew in him.

"Maybe Cromm wasn't cheating me out of the good stuff," Dair thought. "This is going to be a good night to get lost in my ale." The muttering and retelling of Dair's tale could be heard throughout the tavern. Everyone from town came and paid their respects, most with a new mug of ale. He even heard folks around him talk of Fearn; Cromm confirmed to another farmer that the child had indeed failed the test.

ᗪAINUA AND ᚦELGOG

S omeone tugged on Dair's pants. Looking down, Dair saw a boy no older than six or seven surrounded by a gaggle of children. "Teller of Tales, tell us the tale of Dainua and Telgog?" the boy squeaked out. "Yes! Please?" the other children pleaded.

"Hmmm, haven't you gotten tired of this tale yet?" Dair asked. The children shook their heads back and forth in response.

"I brought a plate," one of the older kids chimed in, holding it above her head.

"I have a candle!" another child yelled, holding it out proudly.

Dair removed the blankets from the table and gestured to have the kids gather around. The kids crowded around the table or sat on the dirt floor by Dair.

Dair held out a hand to the girl with the plate, took it, and set it down next to his own which now held just bones, yams, and several empty pea pods. He placed the candle next to the plates. Then, with everything in place, Dair began the tale.

"Renar, the all-knowing, left his daughter, Dainua, and his son, Telgog, to attend to other matters. As soon as he was gone, Dainua and Telgog got into an argument about who was more powerful.

"Dainua created around them a perfect blackness and challenged Telgog to create a light to penetrate it. A large circle of light appeared, pushing back the darkness.

21

"Telgog exclaimed 'I name this...' " (Here Dair paused dramatically.)

"Farkor!" the children chimed in.

Dair took a piece of kindling from next to the fireplace and used the fire to light it. Then, with a flourish, he lit the candle and continued the tale.

" 'Come on,' Dainua chided. 'Anyone can do that.'

" 'Fine!' Telgog spat back. 'Give me a challenge!' Dainua reached out in the darkness and created a round flat disc. 'I name this... ' "

"Mehron!" the children responded. Dair smiled to himself and carried on.

"One side was covered in the light of Farkor, the other in darkness."

Dair picked up the empty plate and handed it to a child across the table from him, who then held it up vertically next to the candle. He continued.

" 'Light the other side, brother,' Dainua chided. Telgog reached out to the side that was black and, with his finger, poked a hole in the darkness, leaving a pinpoint of light. He then looked to Dainua and smiled. Turning back, Telgog raced across the darkness, poking at it as he traversed back and forth until the darkness was covered in stars."

Dair stood and fetched the lantern from the mantle above the fireplace. It had a metal plate on one side with holes. He used the candle to light it, then placed it next to the plate in the darkness on the opposite side of the candle.

A child reached out and turned the lantern so the side with metal holes faced the plate.

" 'Impressive brother,' Dainua exclaimed. 'What do you name it?' Telgog replied 'I name it...' "

"Lemall!" the children screamed out.

" ' ...and proclaim that I will be the god of all that resides above Mehron, for I am the creator of Farkor as well. Your turn, sister: I leave you this flat barren disc you named Mehron. Show me wonders that can outshine my creations.' "

Dair plucked the plate from the child's hands and spun it around, showing its emptiness to all of the children around him before setting it down on the table.

"Dainua went down to Mehron and, under the light of Farkor, pricked her finger and pressed it into the flat brown dirt. As her blood flowed into Mehron, grasses, trees, and all matter of vegetation arose from the barren land."

Dair grabbed a spoonful of the lumpy yams from his plate and slopped them onto the empty plate, then dipped a finger into his ale and held it over the plate. He mimed pricking it, letting the drop of ale fall onto the yams, then pushed his finger into them.

Right on cue, a child grabbed a few pea pods and stuck them in the yams to represent trees. Dair went on.

"Telgog looked over the beauty his sister created and wept, not because of its beauty but because he knew she had beaten him. Telgog's tears dug into Mehron and ran across it."

Dair pushed the plate to children to his left who drew rivers and lakes in the yams with their fingers. He grabbed his mug of ale and poured it onto the plate until the ale flooded over the small rivers and lakes.

"Dainua, not wanting the beauty she created to be washed away, pulled up the land so the tears could not flood it. They flowed down the rivers and around the land."

Dair pushed the plate to the kids to his right. They eagerly grabbed more yams from his plate and slapped them on top, pushing the ale off and around them, shaping the yams into an uneven landscape. Dair poured ale around the yams until the lumps were completely surrounded.

"Dainua then created the spine of the world to hold it all together."

Dair grabbed a chicken bone and handed it to the kid who had asked for the tale. The child gingerly placed the bone across the yams.

"In order to remind Telgog she was the better of the two, Dainua waved a hand and formed clouds with Telgog's tears. So, every time it rained, it reminded Telgog of his failure."

Then, Dair poured more ale onto the plate, but this time directly onto the yams, creating small pools and rivers that flowed into the ale that surrounded the yams.

"As the rain fell upon Telgog, he became desperate for Dainua to fail. He looked around and remarked, 'This place is beautiful, my dear sister, but it is such a lonely place. Make us playthings that will run across this land, that will bask in the light of Farkor.'

"Dainua sat and mixed the dirt that her blood flowed through with the tears of Telgog. With this mud, she molded all of the animals and all manner of life, from the smallest insects to the birds that dominate the sky that Telgog called his own."

Dair turned and held his hands out over a child at his feet who had heard the tale many times before. He mimed creating something in the air and lifted his hand slowly. The child rose and as she did, she twisted and turned as if growing from the floor. The other children laughed, a few imitating her moves.

"Looking at the life around him and the birds that now encroached on what was his, Telgog stomped his foot in anger. The force caused Mehron to rotate and the spine to crack."

A small kid elbowed his way past another and grabbed the chicken bone on the yams. As he strained to snap the bone, his face started to turn red and then a deep purple; just when everyone thought his face would pop, the bone gave a satisfying snap. The kid held the bones aloft as if he had just vanquished some imaginary foe. Then with a smile of satisfaction, he placed them back down on the yams, leaving a small gap between them.

Dair, not wanting to inflate the child's ego anymore, said nothing and continued on.

"So, as Mehron rotated, half of the time it dwelt in the light of Farkor and the other half, the light of Lemall. Dainua looked up as the light changed from one to the other and proclaimed, 'Wonderful! Now Mehron and its many creations can marvel in both of yours.'

"Frustrated and angry, with his head held low, Telgog turned and walked across Mehron, plotting how he could best his sister. Eventually, he came across the most beautiful thing he had ever laid his eyes on. Anger flared in him at the thought of his sister creating something with such exquisite beauty, until he realized he was looking at his own reflection.

"Suddenly, the answer as to how to beat his sister came to Telgog. Looking around to make sure she was not in sight, he sat and molded from the mud of Mehron a man who was not quite as pretty as himself (because nothing deserved the perfection of a god, after all). After creating many men, he set them loose upon Mehron, smirking with glee when he saw that they went about killing and eating the creations of his sister. He was especially delighted when they killed the birds that encroached on his domain."

Dair paused, and as he did, the girls at the table ran about, pretending to be different animals with the boys in pursuit. This went on until a boy tripped and fell against one of the other farmers, causing him to spill his drink. After a stern scolding for running and a disapproving look towards Dair, the children returned to hear the rest of the tale.

"One day, while walking in one of the many forests she created, Dainua found a doe of exquisite beauty had been killed and butchered for its parts. Horrified, she searched for what could have caused such destruction. Dainua followed the trail of blood and ruin to find the men Telgog created, gleefully devouring the doe. Trying to temper man's lust for killing and butchering, Dainua molded many likenesses of herself and, unlike her brother, she made the women more alluring and beautiful than she. Once man had found woman, his desire and lust turned to them, craving them above all other things. The women, smarter than the men, used their beguiling ways to temper man's desire and help show him how to cultivate the land and admire Mehron for its beauty, not just what it could give.

"The men and women then started to pair off and make pacts that they would desire none other but the one they were with. Dainua, enthralled by these creations, hid her beauty and radiance so she could walk among them. One day, coming upon a farmer who was harvesting his fields, she stopped to remark on his hard work and asked for the first fruits of his labor. The man spat at her, telling her that a stranger didn't deserve any of his crops, let alone the first of them. Dainua turned and left after telling the farmer that the only fields he would be able to sow were that of the ground and that no fruit would ever come from his loins. Later, in one village that Dainua came across, she found a man who stood out from the others; he was kind, helped injured animals, and always gave more than he took from Mehron."

"Stay away!" a few kids yelled. Dair gave them a disapproving glance and continued the tale.

"Though she knew it was wrong, she gave her heart to the man and, under a willow tree, devoted her life to walking by his side, remaining companions until he died and she would be forced to live with just the memory of him.

"Dainua soon became pregnant and had twins: a boy and a girl. As her husband looked down upon them and started to smile, his face rippled. Suddenly, her brother stood before her.

" 'O sister,' Telgog sneered deviously, 'you may have bested me at everything else, but to these children I give a curse: that one will walk in the light and the other in darkness. The one who walks in the light will live by feasting upon the suls of all that you have created. The other will be cursed to live in the deep dark places, feasting upon the flesh of these humans you have grown to love so much. This leaves you with a choice: do you kill these children? Or watch them grow and become a blight upon all that you have created and cherished?'

"In her anger at Telgog for defiling the two things that were, in her eyes, the greatest creations she had ever made, Dainua grabbed her brother and dragged him to the heavens, trapping him there to spend eternity looking down at the beauty she created. Watching her children from the heavens, Dainua cried, and as her tears fell, they froze and covered the once green and beautiful Mehron in a thick blanket of white snow. Seeing the snow, Dainua created winter as a remembrance of her pain and anguish. Then, she turned to the heavens and rearranged the stars in a likeness of herself weeping. Dainua created the rest of the seasons to commemorate the love she has for us: spring, to remind us of her gift of creation; summer, for the peaceful times she walked amongst us; and fall, for the lost love she had.

"Dainua separated her children. The one cursed to live in light she left upon the doorstep of the farmer who had spat upon her to bless his wife with the child he could never give. They raised Dainua's daughter as their own, giving her all the love for which Dainua had hoped. The one who was cursed to live in darkness was left with a pack of wolves to be raised so that he could learn to hunt and kill animals and not humans. She gave his offspring—those he sired with wolves—the other side of Mehron to dwell in, though it was barren and desolate.

"So, children, every spring, Telgog rises in the east to see new life emerge from the cold grips of winter. We use his coming to know when to plant our crops. He sets in the fall before winter comes. That is when the crying mother emerges from the west to tell us it is time to reap what we have sown and prepare for the long winter months ahead."

Once the tale was done, the children got back to the games they were playing. The boy who asked for the tale stayed behind, looking at Dair.

"What happened to Dainua?" the boy implored.

Looking down at the boy, Dair replied, "No one knows. Some say her father came back and banished her for eternity for trapping her brother. Others say she walks Mehron, looking after us."

"What about her baby she left with the farmer?"

"That child and all of its lineage became Crop Burners, cursed to kill the land they touched." Dair's mind wandered to the past until a tugging at his pants brought him out of his reverie.

"You get one more question and then run along," Dair directed.

"What happened to the other baby?"

"It's said that a few of them burrowed down and out into our world. They are the deamhons that roam our woods. However, that is a tale for another time." Dair winked at the boy.

The boy smiled, then returned to play with his friends.

Turning back to what was left of his mug of ale, Dair lost himself in the thought of his Lia, until a few villagers stopped by thanking him for his tales with a new mug of ale. Once the ale stopped flowing, Dair dragged himself to his feet and headed for the door.

"Oy, you all right going home, Dair?" Cromm called out to him.

"Ay, I'll be fine. I've ale in my belly to keep me warm on the way home. As long as I keep to the road, nothing will bother me," Dair slurred. He fumbled with his blankets before heading out into the night. The cold was even more bitter than before. After retrieving his horse, Dair let it walk him home. As he passed the small path that led to Lia's grave, Dair looked nervously down it but found nothing there.

Once home, Dair found the fire was nothing but embers and the room was almost as cold as it was outside. After stoking the fire, Dair sat at the table, pulled the blankets he wore closer around him, and fell asleep with his head in his arms, dreaming of better days.

GRAVE MATTERS

Fearn was raised like any working farm animal: given just enough food as was needed, expected to work from before first light until last, and given as much love as one has for a tool. At the age of eight, he was taller than other boys of his age, lean but surprisingly strong. His curly cinnamon brown hair hung down, nearly obscuring eyes as green as new spring grass.

Dair forbid him from entering the field of turnips; instead, Fearn had to gather the firewood, take care of the horse, and forage for berries, mushrooms, and herbs. For his work, Fearn was given a place to live and food to eat.

Every two years, an Asinta had come to check on him and then left with a square patch of his skin cut from his left shoulder. The Asinta sent a teacher from a nearby village to teach Fearn the basics of reading and writing.

His favorite days, though, were when he and Dair would go into town for the market or to head to the tavern. He felt certain, however, he was only allowed to come along because his dad was too afraid to leave him alone at the house. At the tavern, Fearn would sit in the back and close his eyes while his dad told his tales, playing out the story in his head while imagining that he was sitting on his dad's lap with his dad's arms wrapped around him. Seeing other kids sitting on their parents' laps made Fearn yearn to have a father that loved him as a son and not as another farm animal.

The other kids treated him well at first, though the older Fearn grew, the more they kept their distance. They were constantly asking him to make a flower burn, but no matter how hard he tried, nothing happened.

The story of Fearn's birth did not come from his dad, because he never spoke of Fearn's mother, but from the tales the other villagers told in the tavern. Some of the stories had deamhons breaking into the house and ripping him from his mother's womb, leaving her to die. Fearn didn't know the exact details because every tale was different, but the common thread in all of the tales was that his mom died and it was his fault. The first few times that Fearn heard the tales of his birth left him in tears. His only consolation was the tavern owner, Cromm, and a mug of something he called "children's ale."

He never spoke to his mom like his dad would when he visited her grave, sometimes spending hours there, often never speaking a word. When his dad did speak, Fearn never knew what was spoken since he was too afraid of getting close enough to hear. On the rare occasion Fearn did visit his mom's grave, he would mostly sit there and daydream of a life with a loving mother and father.

He didn't really believe the tales that his dad told, though his dad showed off the scratches on the side of the house whenever someone visited or stopped by on their journey down the road. He always figured that his dad put them there to give credence to the tales he told; that is, until the day that they buried the baker.

Fearn didn't know the Baker's name and had only eaten the bread from the bakery on occasion in the tavern; he didn't know why or how the Baker had died. Most people didn't tell him the things he wanted to know, especially since he was a kid that no one wanted. In preparation for the funeral, Fearn and some other children were sent to the graveyard to help clean out overgrowth. He was excited to go since it was a few stones south of the village, a direction he seldom went unless he was foraging, and the graveyard was strictly forbidden to children. It was an overcast day and the work pulling the lull weeds was tough; the excitement of getting to go soon wore off as the sweat dripped from his forehead. After Fearn was done, he was ushered off to the far side of the graveyard with the other children so as not to disturb the proceedings.

The baker was brought out, wrapped in a white sheet with what appeared to be straps, or maybe some sort of iron bands, fastened around the body. It was hard to tell from where he stood. Asking a few of the other kids about the baker got him nothing; they either didn't know or ignored Fearn altogether.

Fearn was so overlooked by the others that the older boys didn't even notice he was there. One of them asked another, "Are you still coming back here tonight? Anyone that is brave enough is going to come."

Later that night, while lying on his straw bed on the floor, staring into the dying fire, Fearn looked at the bedroom door and assumed his dad had to be asleep. Creeping across the floor to the outside door, Fearn slowly slid the bar up, turned the handle, and opened the door. The only noise was the sound of the door's hinges quietly protesting. The warm spring air felt refreshing on his face, and starlight illuminated the room. Once Fearn was outside, he realized that the door wouldn't be barred while he was away. He had only left it unbarred before on the rare occasion when he needed to relieve himself. The house had always been in sight, though, and he was never out that long. Being a young and foolish kid, the thought of leaving his house unprotected was quickly displaced with the thought of the looks on the older boys' faces when he showed up at the graveyard. Quietly, Fearn shut the door, walked along the house, and peered around the corner towards the forest's edge where his dad left the plate out every night. Not seeing anything, Fearn turned and headed eagerly towards the road. Upon reaching it, he realized he hadn't brought a lantern, but afraid that returning would wake his father, Fearn cautiously started down the road using the starlight to guide him. He first thought about cutting south through the woods, but Fearn then thought better of it, in case the stories his dad told were true, so it took him longer than he expected to get there. As he approached the graveyard, he strained to hear voices but heard only the wind through the trees and the rustle of the underbrush.

As Fearn drew closer, he realized why there were no sounds: the boys had brought along some of the local girls, and they were kissing. They had brought lanterns with them and the place was eerily lit up, with shadows dancing across the trees on the far end of the graveyard.

"They must be trying to make babies," Fearn rationalized to himself, but this seemed like a strange place to be doing it. As Fearn drew nearer, one of the boys who didn't have a girl to kiss, or maybe didn't want a baby yet, noticed him and called out, "Oy, who's there?" Fearn stepped into the lantern light so the boy could see him.

"Ay, it's Fearn," he replied shakily.

"Oy, guys! Look who decided to come out tonight: Fearn the Fearful!" At this, the kissing stopped, and they all turned to look at Fearn, the boys visibly upset that he had interrupted them. Fearn's face turned bright red. He hated when they called him "Fearn the Fearful."

"Ay, it's, um, me. Sorry to be bothering your baby-making," Fearn blathered. The older kids looked at Fearn queerly, then glanced at each other before bursting out into laughter.

"Baby-making?" one of the girls replied between fits of laughter.

"Ay, the kissing," Fearn stammered out; although, now that he looked at their faces, he realized he may have been wrong about something.

Lowering his head, Fearn quickly circled the older kids and headed to the other side of the graveyard, feeling foolish for coming. He hoped he could slip into the woods from there and double back around without them noticing. As soon as Fearn had left the group, they quickly forgot about him and returned to talking amongst themselves. After getting about midway across the graveyard, Fearn tripped and fell flat on his face. Rolling over, Fearn noticed he had stumbled over a low mound of dirt; luckily, the dirt was soft. Scrambling quickly to his knees, Fearn looked back at the older kids to see if they noticed while he wiped the dirt from his face.

"Hello," a voice called softly from behind him.

Great, another kid has come to make fun of me, Fearn thought.

"Go away," Fearn replied, almost in tears, wishing he was back home on his straw mattress by the fire.

"You're not disturbing me. I was just thinking it would be nice to have someone to talk to, is all," said the voice. Fearn realized it wasn't a male's voice.

"Why don't you leave me alone and just go back to kissing one of those boys?" Fearn hurled back in frustration. Pulling his knees to his chest, Fearn started to cry, wanting even more to be back home.

"Well, I don't think any of those boys would be interested in the slightest in kissing me. You're Dair's boy, Fearn, right? Haven't seen much of you. You were always sulking in the corners at the tavern. Don't ever recall seeing you come round my place." A cold, thick chill fell over Fearn like a blanket, causing him to squeeze his legs to his chest to try to stay warm. It hadn't been that cold when he left, he thought.

Then, something deep in the recesses of Fearn's brain clicked, and he realized something wasn't right. That wasn't a girl's voice but an adult's voice. Why wasn't she scolding the other kids or himself, for that matter, for being out here at night? Wiping his eyes on his shirt, Fearn slowly turned around. Standing over him was the baker. Strangely, he could see right through her. Everything in his body screamed to run away, but fear pressed down on him like a great weight, causing Fearn to sit there instead, staring up at her, his mouth agape. No matter how hard Fearn struggled internally, his body was rooted in place. Fear welled up in him as he yearned to either flee or have the soft earth beneath him swallow him whole.

"I thought the Baker died," was all that Fearn could muster as a response. The woman just laughed and smiled, "Oh, you were expecting my husband? No, my lunk of a husband couldn't bake a loaf of bread even if Dainua blessed him. I went to bed one night and woke up here. Didn't take me too long to figure out I was dead, considering I could see right through myself." The woman lifted her hands, seeming to admire their transparency.

"I'd been meaning to lose some weight. Just didn't expect it would be like this." The woman broke into laughter at her own joke and, for some reason, that laughter eased Fearn's fear and convinced

33

him that, at least for the moment, she wasn't going to eat him, or whatever it was the dead do to the living.

"Oy, Fearn the Fearful, what are you laughing at? Or have you finally gone mad?" one of the boys called out from across the graveyard.

"Oops, forgot they were there," giggled the woman. "You just sit right there and I'm going to have a bit of fun." At that, the woman walked straight through Fearn, causing a sharp chill to run up his spine. It wasn't until the woman was a few paces away that one of the older kids finally noticed her. Fearn heard a sharp yelp from one of the girls and then a loud 'Boo' from the baker. The other kids turned to see where the sound had come from, and that is when utter chaos erupted. Every single kid ran off in a different direction, including into each other. Eventually, they started getting organized and headed off in the same direction towards the village.

Fearn had what he felt was a brilliant idea. He screamed after them as loud as he could: "Don't leave me! She ate my legs, and I can't run!" He added what he felt would be the appropriate sounds someone with their legs just eaten off would make.

The baker returned to Fearn a few moments later with a very wide grin.

"I don't think I had that much fun when I was alive. I need to head home and try this out on my husband. I can't wait to see the look on his face." The woman burst out laughing again. Fearn looked at her in despair.

"My dear, why such a long face? You do know that I'm not going to eat you, right? I mean, I lost all of this weight; no need to put it back on."

Fearn tried to hold back tears as he glanced up at her.

"I enjoyed you scaring the kids more than you can know. Maybe now they will stop picking on me. It's just that I suddenly thought of something: is this what it is like to have a mom?"

All of the joy on her face drained away as she replied, "Oh, dear, well, every mom is different, and I can't say that I was always the best at it. I know you have had a rough time, but I know that your dad must love you." The woman reached out and tried to wipe away the tear that was rolling down Fearn's face, causing him to twitch as he felt the chill of her ghostly finger. Unexpectedly, a warm feeling arose in him as he felt motherly love for the first time. Fearn even thought that the tear moved just a little.

"How can someone love the person who killed their mom?" Fearn replied between sobs.

The woman honestly didn't know what to say. She stammered, "Well, it's late. We better start heading back to the village. We can talk on the way." Part of her was scared of the boy and his destiny as she remembered what it was like when the Asinta stormed through their village burning houses and killing those who stood in their way, as the ground at their feet withered and turned black. Helping the boy couldn't hurt; after all, she was already dead, and she couldn't think of anything worse that could befall her.

"You should grab one of the lanterns those kids left behind to help light your way since it's becoming overcast." Fearn did as he was told and fell in beside her as they headed towards the village.

"Look, Fearn, I can't tell you why one person loves someone and why they can't love someone else. We must trust in Dainua that the path she lays before us is the one we must follow. I know that you feel like your dad doesn't love you, but I'm sure he does in his own way. If you want, I can swing by your place and tell him in my scariest voice that 'By Dainua's will, ye must love this child!'" The woman's voice grew deep and she raised her hands as if they were claws about to strike.

That put a smile on Fearn's face. No one had ever asked to do something so nice for him, though he didn't want someone to force his dad to love him.

"No, thank you," was all Fearn could think of as a reply. They walked in silence for a while. Then the Baker piped up, "If we get to my place and my husband is trying to bake bread, he better be using my recipe."

Fearn suddenly stopped and looked up at her, worried. "Wait, won't he burn it?"

The woman just smiled, "He does have our three children to help, and our oldest daughter really seemed to have a knack for baking, which was something that always came naturally to me. He helped me come up with new ideas and did all of the deliveries for us. You see, we don't have enough people in our village to bake for and we are lucky the village to the west doesn't have a baker and won't as long as we keep up with the demand. They have a very busy tavern. I just hope my husband can cope with everything now that I'm gone." The woman's shoulders sagged as she frowned, and Fearn wished he could hug her and tell her it would be all right.

The woman started walking again, and Fearn fell in beside her. They were about a stone down the road when she exclaimed, "Oy, I'm feeling a bit peculiar. And that is saying something since I can't feel a thing." Fearn looked over at her and noticed she seemed a bit more see-through than she had been before. The farther they walked, the less of her Fearn could see. The Baker seemed to be noticing this as well, as she suddenly stopped and looked at Fearn.

"Well, before I disappear altogether, you listen here. I'm sure your dad loves you, and if those kids give you a hard time, remember to tell them that you fought off a deamhon and won your legs back. If you see my dear husband, tell him I love him and to make sure the bread is kneaded exactly five times on each side."

Fearn nodded before he responded, "It was nice meeting you, and thank you again for the help." Turning, Fearn continued to walk towards the village. He stopped and looked back a few times; each time he did, she was still right where he left her until she faded into the dark and could be seen no more.

Fearn approached his house with caution, worried about the door being unbarred for so long. Warily, he pushed open the door and smiled with relief—no deamhons had gotten in. Turning in the doorway, Fearn stared out into the night, thinking about everything that had happened. Suddenly, his dad's tales started to play out in his mind. *Maybe they weren't just tales, after all*, Fearn thought. The world suddenly seemed to have gotten a lot bigger and stranger. Thinking of the long deep scratches on the outside wall, Fearn hurriedly shut and barred the door, hung the lantern, and went to bed.

A Tale is Told

Shortly after Fearn fell asleep, he was awakened by his dad. Groggily, Fearn rolled over and covered his face from the bright light of the fire that his dad had started. After getting his bearings, Fearn got up, wrapped himself in his blanket, grabbed the lantern his dad handed him, and headed out to do his chores, grumbling under his breath about how tired he was.

It seemed as dark as it had been when he had arrived home earlier that night. The chores consisted of feeding the chickens, which his dad had newly acquired through a trade a few weeks back, along with cleaning out the stables and giving the horse new hay. The horse was Fearn's only companion on the farm; his dad never gave the horse a name, saying a working beast didn't require one. As Fearn brushed the horse's mane, he would often talk to him. The horse would always turn his head and gaze back with his large brown eye, as if really listening. That morning, Fearn slowly brushed the horse, waiting for his dad to disappear into the field. Once the bobbing light from his dad's lantern was all Fearn could see, he turned to the horse and recounted everything that had happened to him the night before.

Fearn kept thinking back about how nicely the baker had treated him. Then, it dawned on him that he had never gotten her name.

"Well, I hope that Dainua gives her a big kitchen to cook all the bread she wants; that is, if they cook there," Fearn said to the horse. As Fearn continued to brush the horse, he started daydreaming about his dad's tales, and instead of being stupid old tales his dad told to get free food and ale, they started to take on a mystical quality.

After taking care of the horse, Fearn went to gather firewood. Before taking the long way around the house to the front door, Fearn looked around and saw his dad was still a ways off. Holding up his lantern to the house, Fearn looked at the scratches, running a finger against them, feeling how the cuts were shallow, deepened, and then grew shallower again. Fearn walked the length of the house, looking up and down the wall, but couldn't find any other evidence of the deamhon. Finally, Fearn hurried back inside the house, grabbed a small hatchet, and headed to gather some wood. He didn't venture very far into the woods. They seemed a lot darker and more foreboding than they were the day before. Every crack of a twig under his feet or the sound of an animal in the distance made him jump and freeze in place. Working as fast as he could, he looked for branches that could easily be chopped off or a dead tree that had fallen over that he could cut up. After gathering an armload, Fearn hauled it to the edge of the clearing and then headed back for more, continuing until he had enough wood for the next few days. Once he was satisfied, Fearn picked up the pile he had made and moved it to the woodpile, sorting it by pieces that were dry enough to burn and others that needed to dry out. Farkor was up by the time Fearn finished and his stomach was feeling very empty. Between all of the walking the previous night and the work from that morning, he felt as though he hadn't eaten in weeks.

Heading inside, Fearn left the door open so they didn't have to rely on the fireplace or a lantern to provide them with their light. He placed the hatchet back on the wall, then blew out his lantern, and, when he went to put it back on its peg, he found that there was already a lantern there. Fearn was perplexed as to how another lantern had appeared. Suddenly, it dawned on him that he had forgotten all about the lantern he took from the graveyard. As Fearn hurriedly looked for a place to hide it, a voice came from behind him.

"So, our lanterns have sprouted a third one, I see," his dad jested.

Turning around with lantern in hand, Fearn didn't know what to say; he never was a good liar. Finally, Fearn held out the lantern to his dad, who took it, placed it down on the table, and went back to the pot in the fireplace to finish making that morning's porridge. Sitting down at the table, Fearn stared at the lantern, trying to come up with a tale about how he had found it. After Dair was done, he scooped the porridge into two bowls, sat at the table across from Fearn, pushed one across the table to him, and then started eating. After a few minutes of silence, hunger won out and Fearn dug in.

After they both finished, Dair finally spoke up: "I bet there is a tale to tell about this lantern, and it better be good."

Fearn sat there trying to decide where to start and what he should leave out. He was saved by the sound of galloping horses outside.

"Stay there," Dair said, holding his hand out to keep Fearn from standing up. Dair walked to the door and stared at the riders coming down the road. Right when Dair thought they were going to pass them by, the leader pulled up short and led the horse right up to Dair's front door. The other five riders stopped behind him.

"Oy, Farmer," the lead rider said as he dismounted and held out his hand. Dair recognized the man; it was the tanner from a village to the south. Dair walked out and grasped the man's wrist.

"Ay, Tanner," Dair replied. Looking over at the other men as they dismounted, he observed the baker's husband from his village, the farrier from a village to the north, and three other farmers from his village. Dair called out in greeting, "Ay, Baker, Ferrier, Farmers!" then approached and grasped wrists with each.

The tanner behind him spoke up, "Farmer, we have bad news."

Dair glanced furtively into the house, and seeing that he couldn't make out Fearn in the dim interior, turned to the Tanner.

"What news is that?"

"Well, as you may have noticed, your son is missing."

Dair didn't reply, simply nodding his head and glancing again into the house.

"The kids from our villages decided it was a good idea to head out to the graveyard last night; apparently, your son came along as well. The story my son told me was that the Baker appeared as a deamhon and tore the legs off your son. He said he tried to stop her, but she tried attacking him and the other kids. I rode at first light to the graveyard and found these men there." The tanner gestured to the other men.

"They had similar stories to tell. We searched and found no sign of the deamhon or your son—just a few lanterns that had been left behind."

Listening in rapt amazement from just inside the door, Fearn forgot all about his troubles with the lantern. Before Dair replied, he looked back into the house, and Fearn thought he had the same expression he made when he grew a particularly large potato or radish.

"Well, men," Dair said with a wry look of amusement on his face, "I think we should have my son come out and explain this himself." The men looked generally awestruck.

"Well, get out here, boy!" Dair called into the house. The men looked even more dumbfounded when Fearn didn't crawl out the door.

"Boy, I think this is a good time to explain what happened last night," Dair prompted.

Fearn had never had this much attention all at once; he wasn't sure what to say, so he told the truth—all of it. Once he was done, he could tell that they believed what he said. One of the farmers asked Dainua for a blessing because he was sure Fearn was cursed. He hastily mounted his horse and left. The remaining farmers glanced at each other, backed up a few paces, jumped on their horses, and galloped away as well; keeping an eye on Fearn until he was out of sight.

Once the cloud of dust blew away, the Baker's husband turned to Fearn. "Did you really see my wife?"

"Yes, and she told me to tell you to make sure to knead the bread five times on each side. Oh, and she loves you."

At that, tears welled up in the man's eyes.

"By Dainua, bless you and thank you." With that, the baker's husband turned and left.

The Tanner, who had just been watching this, turned to Fearn. "Glad you're safe, boy," he said, then grasped Dair by the wrist. "You need to come by the tavern and tell your tale. I'm sure there'd be some free ale in exchange. Bring the boy along. Everyone would love to see how he has grown his legs back!" A deep throaty laugh erupted from the Tanner, who mounted his horse and rode off.

Dair turned Fearn around and led him back inside to go about cleaning up breakfast. The only thing Fearn could do was stand there and stare at his dad. His dad had never beaten him, but if there was such an occasion when he deserved it, this would be it. As he watched his dad, Fearn noticed Dair had more of a spring in his step than he did the day before. As he scraped the meager remains from the pot onto a plate, Dair looked up. "What's wrong?"

Fearn stuttered, "W-w-w-well I thought for sure you would beat me for going out at night and leaving the door unbarred!" Fearn stepped back, not sure if his dad was toying with him; instead, his dad laughed—actually laughed—a real honest-to-goodness laugh. Fearn had heard his dad laugh before, but this was different. It made all of the laughs that had come before seem fake.

"No, I think what happened to you last night was enough to make sure you don't ever do it again. Maybe you will listen to me more when I tell you to be careful in these woods and to heed my tales for what they really are: a warning."

Fearn couldn't hold it back anymore. He had to timidly ask, "Dad, do you make babies when you kiss?"

Without even pausing, Fearn's dad replied, "As long as your tongue doesn't touch hers, you will be fine, boy." Dair turned away, suppressing a laugh, and hurried to look busy cleaning the porridge pot.

The relationship between Fearn and Dair changed after the ordeal with the Baker's deamhon. Dair showed no additional love for his boy, but a kind of friendship started to grow between them.

The other kids, in both his village and the surrounding ones, treated Fearn differently as well. A few were awed, but most feared him. Instead of calling him "Fearn the Fearful", the children avoided him completely, gossiping when he wasn't around that not only was he a Crop Burner, but he also consorted with deamhons.

Fearn's dad started having him stand up in front of the villagers in the local taverns and tell the tale of the baker's deamhon. After each retelling, his dad would suggest adjusting parts to make the tale more frightening, or how to tweak the ending so it gave a warning to others, or places he should pause for dramatic effect. At first, Fearn felt guilty about changing the story since the baker was so nice to him, but he went along with it because his dad had never given him attention like this before. The more he told the tale, the more he understood why his dad loved telling tales so much.

The next time he told his tale, he was confused why no one tried to correct him when it was different than it was before. On occasion, someone would blurt out an addition as if he had been there. As Fearn's dad continued to tell his tales, Fearn paid more attention, doing everything he could to remember them. He even recited them when he was alone doing his chores.

****

One night, a couple of years later, Fearn and his dad were late in heading to the tavern. Dair needed to harvest the rest of the vegetables for the following day's market and refused to let Fearn help.

When Fearn insisted and swore that he had never shown any powers, Dair grabbed Fearn by his shirt and yelled, "Get away!" before pushing him to the ground and heading back to the fields. Brushing himself off, Fearn headed back to the house where he crumpled to the ground in the doorway and cried. Fearn thought he had finally gotten his dad to love him; he didn't understand what more he needed to do.

On the way into town, Fearn walked a few paces behind his dad in sullen silence. They hadn't brought the horse because his dad had had to work him in the field all day and he was needed to carry the vegetables to market in a neighboring village. Dair noticed a change in Fearn and tried to explain that their crops were their livelihood, and he couldn't risk the boy spreading his curse. Fearn didn't pay attention; he just stared at the road, nodding when he felt his dad wanted an answer.

Once they reached the tavern, they found it packed with villagers, forcing them to find a seat at a table in the back. Fearn was still lost in thought when something pulled him out of the pit of despair he was digging for himself. He caught bits of a tale and, as the tavern quieted down around him, it dawned on him why the tale was so familiar: it was his tale being told. Looking up from the table, Fearn saw that the man telling the tale looked familiar, but he couldn't recall from where he knew him. Looking over at his dad in confusion, Fearn saw that his dad was staring back at him, smiling.

"Who's that?" Fearn asked his dad.

"He's a farmer from a neighboring village," his dad replied.

"Oh. Which one?"

"The one to the east? Now, let's listen and see how your tale has changed," Dair whispered gruffly.

Indeed, the tale had changed; as a matter of fact, there were now several deamhons that appeared in the graveyard. Apparently, they were arguing over which limb of the boy they were going to tear off first. Suddenly, the baker appeared and rescued him because he had fended off bandits who ambushed her on the way to sell her bread when she was still alive. The boy in the tale was successful in fighting off the bandits; however, it was too late for the Baker. She died from a knife wound suffered during the attack, her limp body falling dramatically into the boy's arms. It was genuinely melancholy and Fearn felt himself caught up in the story, eager to find out what happened next. When the tale came to an end, the villagers around Fearn cheered and toasted to the boy's deeds.

In turn, a few more villagers stood up and told tales. Some Fearn recognized, others he didn't. Later, someone called out to his dad to tell one of his tales. Fearn watched as his dad played the crowd, pretending he didn't want to tell the tale, riling them up until they were begging for him to stand and tell a tale. A few even offered free ale if only he'd agree.

Once Dair knew he had the crowd to a point that they were about to give up and move on, he stood up and said, "Well, my mug is empty, so I guess I could tell a tale or two." The crowd cheered. With that, he went into telling his tales. He worked the crowd well that night. His mug was never empty; he had even gotten someone to give them a plate of mutton, which was better than a week's worth of ale to Fearn. All they ate was porridge for breakfast, occasionally with an egg baked in, though his dad preferred to sell the eggs rather than eat them. They had stews or vegetables for dinner, with the rare chicken, but only when they found one dead in the coop. Every now and again, Fearn's dad would say the stew had mutton in it, but the meat had a suspicious taste and never looked like the meat Fearn saw at the market or tavern. The real mutton that night just solidified Fearn's suspicions. Since his dad was so busy with the crowd and his ale, he didn't notice that Fearn had way more than his fair share of the mutton.

On the way back home that night, Fearn asked his dad why he allowed other people to steal their tales.

"Once you have told a tale to someone else, that tale is no longer yours," he responded. "Plus, there is no greater compliment than hearing your tale told by someone else."

"But if everyone else tales your tale, why would they still want to hear it from you?" Fearn asked quizzically.

"Ah. That's when they want to hear it from you even more. For them, it's just a tale being told, unless they hear it from the person who started it. Then, to them, the tale gains truth, and the teller gains credibility. When they hear a new tale from that teller, they will say to themselves that it too must be true."

Fearn walked along in silence, thinking this over. "So, is that why they give you free ale and food?"

"Fearn, you'll learn as you get older: our life is a hard one. People go to the tavern to escape, even if it's for just an evening. They're willing to pay for a mug of ale if that's the cost of forgetting life outside the doors of the tavern."

Fearn thought of his long days of work and how they never took a day off because they always had something to do around the farm. Sure, in the winter there were days they had to stay inside because of the cold, but those days were just as miserable in their own way. He always looked forward to going to the tavern because it wasn't his life on the farm; moreover, the people there felt like part of his family, in a way. Suddenly, a thought struck him. "Oy, Dad! All of our tales are about the villages around here and the people in them or the people that used to live here. Why don't we talk about what's outside of that? The baker told me that she remembered the village before the Asinta came and burned the ground. I haven't heard anyone ever tell that tale. Is it true?"

As Fearn and Dair walked on, Fearn could see his dad was lost in thought. Finally, Dair stopped and turned to Fearn.

"It goes back to what I said before. We go there to get away from our life. We don't like to tell tragic stories that don't have a happy ending because those remind us even more how hard life can be. Tales rarely come from other places, especially here; people rarely come through this way anymore."

"Why don't people come this way, Dad?"

"There was a war. Long ago, we had troops come through here from both sides of the battle. Neither side cared for our land or its people. They took what they wanted and burned the rest." Dair scowled, and then his expression turned to one of pain and sadness.

"The armies had Asinta with them. The worst of them were Crop Burners. They came into the village, killing the trees and the ground to feed the power within them. It wasn't enough power for them, though; they went to the surrounding farms and killed every plant, every blade of grass, every seed. All that was green withered and died as the Asinta passed, leaving the village barren and dead: a scar on the land for all to remember. The vegetation grew back in some places but in others, like the town, the ground never recovered. People tried to plant and rebuild the village. A few were successful, but most gave up and built elsewhere. Now, we must hurry along and get back home. It's getting late. You also need to start thinking of a new tale to tell."

Fearn nodded and didn't say a word. He just followed along behind his dad. Later that night, when Fearn was alone on his bed, pictures of angry Asinta ravaging the land filled his vision.

Am I really someone who will kill the land? Fearn wondered. The vision changed. He was walking through the market, all of the vegetables and food turning to ash as he passed. He understood now why his dad could never love him, even if his dad was teaching him how to tell tales. Fearn decided his next tale needed to be so great that his dad would continue to want him.

THE TILLER

About mid-morning on one of the early days of spring, Fearn sat by the house watching his dad in the field. A cloaked rider on a chestnut brown horse appeared down the road. As he drew to a stop in front of Fearn, a large patch depicting two hands clasped at the wrist became visible on the man's cloak. The only people Fearn had seen wear these were the Asinta. His cloak was dusty and worn, the burnt umber color faded by the sun. The rider who wore it looked to be in his twenties with dirty blonde hair, gray-green eyes, and a long face, grimy from the road. Under the cloak, the rider wore a basic tunic over dark brown pants, which were tattered at the hem and draped over weather-worn leather boots. After the man dismounted, he gathered a few things from his pack, placed them inside hidden pockets in his cloak, and pulled a piece of cloth from another pouch on the horse to wipe his face.

While waiting for the man to recognize his presence, Fearn looked at his left shoulder and ran his hand over the four scars. The largest and darkest was at the bottom with each one above growing smaller and fainter. He had one for every two years of his life. The man eventually finished tidying up, turned to Fearn, and reached out his hand.

"Uram the Tiller, at your service," the rider proclaimed.

Fearn stood slowly, and after some hesitation, reached out and grasped Uram by the wrist. "Umm, Fearn the Farmer," Fearn quizzically replied. The previous Asinta he'd met were never this nice; on one occasion, a gruff old man had never given his name during the process of cutting a square from his skin.

Fearn took Uram's horse by the reins and tied it to a post in front of the house. Gesturing to the woods, Uram asked Fearn if they could take a walk. This was a great relief to Fearn because he was always nervous when the Asinta came. Dair would eventually wander up from the fields and glower at the Asinta until he was gone, never saying a word.

This time, as Uram and Fearn walked away from the farmhouse, Dair looked up from his work, waved a hand in recognition, and then returned to his work.

Fearn guided them south into the woods. It was a warm and beautiful day. The sky was a deep shade of blue, and the sound of birds filled the air. After a quarter stone, they come across a fallen tree in a clearing. Fearn stopped and looked up to admire the blue sky above them. Spring was always Fearn's favorite time of the year.

The Asinta sat down on the fallen tree and motioned for Fearn to do the same. As Fearn approached, he noticed that the tree must have fallen over recently; the dirt still hung in big dark brown clumps from the roots. The tree's branches that weren't broken off still had green leaves. Fearn sat next to Uram, who then asked him the normal questions the other Asinta had asked about his powers, or lack thereof in this case. After that, he asked Fearn to give him his arm and then cut the fifth square into his skin, leaving him now with a row of squares going from his shoulder to his elbow. However, Uram didn't use his powers to heal him this time. The Asinta normally used the energy inside Fearn to turn the wound into a bright pink scar, which always left Fearn tired for a few days after. Instead, Uram took out a white cloth and bandaged up the wound.

"I am not a Mender, like those who have come before," Uram said to Fearn. "I am a Tiller, or as you and the commoners in the North incorrectly call us, a Crop Burner."

Fearn was taken aback. Uram didn't look like someone who would burn and kill the land. Fearn always pictured them to be a foot or two taller and at least three feet wider, riding around on black horses, laughing gleefully as the land burned around them. Instead, Uram looked like any other villager Fearn would see at one of the local taverns, though Uram smelled a lot cleaner. Fearn pondered a moment about when he washed last before asking, "What's a Tiller? Is that what I'm going to be?"

Uram smiled warmly and replied, "Let me answer your last question first. When we take your skin, a Mender will go through a process to preserve it, with each new piece taken sewed onto the last piece. Our imbiber will then pass a hand over the skin and feel how the power grows with each new piece. From this, he can discern what powers that person will manifest. This process normally requires between five and six patches; though, on occasion, they can detect it at four. Our imbiber has determined that you will be a Tiller."

A vision of an enraged and disappointed Dair flashed in Fearn's mind. Fearn thought, as panic started to take hold, *There is no way my dad will ever love me now. Will he even let me live at the farm once he finds out?* Backing away slowly from the Asinta, Fearn turned and ran, not caring in which direction he went. All he felt was a need to get as far away as possible and that if he got far enough, everything he had been told would go away and wouldn't have happened. He crashed through bushes and stumbled over rocks and roots, not heeding the scratches and bruises he suffered. Little by little, Fearn realized he didn't recognize the woods, and the farther he ran, the greater the sense of being lost overcame his desire to flee. Eventually, he stopped to catch his breath.

There wasn't a sound in the forest around him; the only thing he heard was his breath as he panted. The trees here were thicker, and the light from the sky only broke through in a few places. This part of the wood seemed older and untouched, as the dead wood from the forest floor hadn't been cleared for firewood and there were no hatchet or saw marks on any of the trees. Every tree seemed taller than the trees closer to the farm.

To his right, he noticed a clearing; carefully, he made his way there, listening for the sounds of Uram's footsteps or for the call of a bird, but the only sound was the crunch of dead detritus under his feet. In the clearing, he found a massive blackened mound crowned by large standing stones. It smelled of decay, like when Fearn would find a dead animal in the woods. Having seen nothing like it before, Fearn crept closer to the blackened earth and realized he could not see a single blade of grass or weed anywhere upon it, though the ground vegetation from the forest grew right up to its edge. To Fearn, it looked similar to the blackened patches of ground in and around the village, but this was darker, and the light from the sky did not illuminate it. The stones on top looked to have been arranged; they didn't have the random appearance of the stones and rocks Fearn had seen elsewhere in the forest. If there was a pattern to them, however, Fearn didn't recognize it.

Looking up, Fearn noticed that Farkor was just behind the stones. He turned his back to the mound and slowly turned completely around again, using the light of Farkor to figure out his location. Judging that it wasn't midday yet, Fearn surmised he had run east into the forbidden part of the forest. Even his dad wouldn't venture this way. There were occasions when Fearn would walk in this direction to gather wood, but he always kept the farm in sight, never daring to go any deeper into the dense forest. Quickly, Fearn looked around for deamhons and surveyed the mound again. A cold chill ran down his spine.

Is this where they dwell? Fearn thought. He couldn't see any doors, but he could only see a portion of the mound. Out of nowhere, a hand with an earthy smell clapped over Fearn's mouth, followed by a strong arm which wrapped around his chest and lifted him into the air. Kicking his feet out and arching his back, Fearn squirmed, trying to free himself.

A voice whispered in his ear, "Shhhh, be still. This is a cursed place. We must be away at once. If I let you back down, do you promise not to run off again? I know this is a frightening situation for you. I promise to help you through it as best as I can."

Fearn stopped struggling, thinking over his options. He looked at the mound and the unknown terrors that may be lying in wait beneath. Fearn decided that if he went with Uram, at least some of his questions might be answered, so he let his body go slack. Uram slowly lowered him down.

"I'm going to remove my hand. Do not say a word. Mirror my movements," Uram whispered. Fearn nodded his head in agreement. Uram removed his hands and turned Fearn around. He put a finger to his lips, eyes darting back and forth as if searching for an assailant that he could not see, then turned and headed west into the woods.

Fearn followed, noticing that Uram was careful in where he placed his feet as he quietly made his way back. Fearn realized that if whatever was living in the mound could scare Uram, he would be wise to follow as quietly as he could. Fearn pretended the Asinta's steps were like tracks in the snow and carefully placed his own feet where Uram's had been. They walked this way for about a quarter stone; the farther they traveled, the more sounds of the forest started to return. When Uram finally returned to a normal pace, not caring about the sounds he made, Fearn ran up to walk beside him.

"What was that mound and is anything in it?" Fearn asked, staring up into Uram's face.

Uram was still scanning the area around them, a look of fear and concern in his expression. Finally, he looked down at Fearn, smiled nervously, and spoke. "That is a relic from the old war. I do not know if anything dwells beneath it, but let us be glad it wasn't night or we may have unwittingly discovered its purpose. The king has burned the written accounts of what happened—at least, he burned the accounts he didn't want told. Mounds like that are an old way of burying a powerful Asinta—those that twisted and abused their power. There is a lot to tell; however, my time today is short. I promise that when I come back, I'll be able to tell you more. For now, I need to start preparing your path to learn our ways. Just be sure to stay clear of that place," he warned. Uram managed to lead them back to exactly where they had been sitting by the downed tree.

"Before I go, it might be best if I give you a small demonstration. It may help do away with your backward thinking of Tillers and what we do," Uram said as he untied a small bag hanging from his hip. He reached inside and pulled out a seed, then tied the pouch back into place. Kneeling, Uram cleared the underbrush away while constantly looking from the ground to the sky like he was trying to puzzle something out. Once Uram seemed satisfied, he dug a small hole in the ground and planted the seed. He closed his eyes and reached an arm towards the downed tree while keeping his other hand in the dirt next to where the seed was planted. A strange rot started to spread across the bark of the downed tree, black tendrils creeping and wriggling back and forth like a spider's legs trying to gain purchase on a slippery surface. The bark nearest Uram's hand started to crumble and fall away; not like ash from a burning log but more like when an old tree rots and falls apart. The wood beneath the bark was just as black and rotted. This went on until the blackness covered almost the entire tree. When the blackness looked like it was about to spread to the ground, Uram stopped. The tree started to fall into itself, looking less like a tree that had fallen over yesterday and more like a tree that had been there for many seasons, decaying and returning to Dainua, though without the moss or insects normally seen.

Fearn looked over at Uram. His face was strained, as if trying to hold in something which caused him great pain, then contorted into intense focus. The ground beneath Uram's hand shifted, and a small sprout emerged. It grew and changed, and Fearn soon realized it was a tree. It was growing in moments but should have taken months or even years. The tree twisted and moved, seeking the light coming through the branches of older trees around it and, as it continued to grow, the trunk enlarged, causing its bark to split and widen, the pattern in the bark ever-changing. Uram slid his hand away from the tree to give it room as it grew. Finally, Uram lifted his hand, wand the tree stopped growing. It was now poking its top branches out of the canopy and crowding out the neighboring trees. Uram looked up at Fearn and smiled broadly. "I'll never get tired of that. I have a little power left, and I think it is enough. Please step closer and close your eyes."

In awe of what just happened, and not even considering the consequences, Fearn approached Uram and closed his eyes. While still kneeling, Uram placed his outstretched hand onto Fearn's chest. A sudden rush of energy coursed through Fearn, creeping through him like it was desperately seeking a way out. He could feel the rot of the tree as it moved to his arms, then up his neck; his face became hot as the energy flooded his head. He was overcome with intense smells—smells of leaves on trees, fruit, grass, and the open air. The rot and decay of the downed tree overwhelmed Fearn, causing his stomach to lurch. Coming to his senses, Fearn tried to struggle but his chest felt like it had become part of Uram's hand, like they were now one person. When the energy reached Fearn's eyes, the darkness engulfing him ripped away to reveal the air, trees, and ground around him, though they changed. They were now faded outlines of trees and plants, allowing him to look through everything around him. They all had an energy that rushed around inside. In the trees, it flowed from the roots up to their branches. That is when Fearn noticed that the air seemed thick, like he was standing in a clear lake but still able to breathe. As he gazed around in amazement, he noticed the energy ebbed and flowed in a rhythmic pattern. Looking down, Fearn saw two powers surging through him: one was flowing out of Uram's hand and into his chest, and the other churned through him. As he saw the energy flow from Uram to his feet, it shot through his boots and into the ground. Under the ground, there was a power that flowed like a river, crashing into the energy of the trees' roots and swirling around them in a rhythmic dancing motion. As Fearn looked closer, he could see that the power from the ground occasionally attached itself to the energy in the trees' roots, and when it broke away, the power in the ground left some of itself behind.

"Keep your eyes closed," Uram said in a soothing tone before he pulled his hand away from Fearn's chest. Fearn noticed that the power inside himself moved and flowed like that of the trees, and though it didn't dance and flow with the power of the ground like the trees' roots did, it rippled around him like a stone dropped into a pond.

"Fearn, everything you see around and in you is that creation's sul. Below us is the power of Dainua. You can see her giving life to the trees, and if you look up, you can see them giving some of their power to Telgog's realm." Looking up, Fearn noticed the leaves sending a lesser energy into the air around them like a breath on a cold winter's night.

"Now, look to the fallen tree whose sul I partially removed to give life to the seed I planted." As Fearn focused on the fallen tree, he again saw the same dance of energy, but this time, the tree was giving its energy to Dainua.

"When things die, their energy returns to Dainua, helping give new life to something else. The trees give off power to Telgog to balance the power between his realm and Dainua's."

A strange burning sensation suddenly flared around Fearn's feet, which felt like he had placed them against hot coals in a fire. Opening his eyes, Fearn dropped to the ground, feverishly trying to remove his boots in the hope that he could find some way to quench the pain. As he did this, he noticed that the image of the suls vanished, returning his vision to the way it was before. Once the boots were off, though, the pain seemed stronger, like he had stoked the fire beneath them.

"Don't worry. Stand up, close your eyes, and focus on the ground. Feel Dainua as she courses around you," Uram said reassuringly. Desperate to get the pain to cease, Fearn quickly stood up, closed his eyes, and looked down. The images of the suls returned as soon as his eyes closed. Focusing on the ground around him, Fearn saw the energy in himself reach out and touch the power of Dainua. As it did, the pain ceased immediately. Fearn relaxed, realizing he could feel the power of Dainua rush past him. He could now sense the suls of the things around him; even the air had a strange power and seemed to thicken near his skin, though it did not interact with the power of Dainua. Keeping his eyes closed, Fearn let the power of Dainua rush around and past him, soothing and calming him in a way he had never felt before.

"Going barefoot for awhile will make it feel better, until your sul is balanced with Dainua," Uram remarked. "Now, open your eyes." As Fearn opened his eyes again, the suls disappeared, but he could still feel his new connection to Dainua.

Uram turned to the tree he had grown, looking up at the branches and then to Fearn. Finally finding the one he was looking for, he said, "Now, close your eyes and concentrate so you can see what I am doing." Fearn closed his eyes and focused on Uram, seeing that he was manipulating the sul of the tree. He created a barrier in a branch, then split off a portion of the tree's sul, trapping it in the branch. Uram reached up and broke the branch free. Fearn opened his eyes to see Uram run a hand across the branch which shifted and straightened. The leaves, smaller branches, and bark fell away before he handed it to Fearn. Fearn placed it beside himself to see how tall it was; it was the perfect size for a walking stick. He glanced at Uram, then back to the stick, not sure if he was supposed to do something with it. Uram sat down in the shade of the tree and gestured for Fearn to do the same next to him. Fearn went over and sat down, laying the stick across his lap. He could feel the power in the ground in every part of him that touched it.

Uram reached down and picked up two green leaves, saying, "When we use our power to manipulate things, that object's sul is weakened. Close your eyes and take a look at this first leaf."

Fearn closed his eyes and looked at the leaf which had a very small amount of sul. He saw the sul of Uram flow around the leaf, then attach itself as Dainua had with the trees' roots. The sul slowly moved down the leaf and flowed into Uram.

When there was just the faintest bit left, Uram stopped. "Now, open your eyes," he directed. Fearn looked, and the leaf was no longer bright green but grey and brown, dried out and crumbling in Uram's hand.

"When we take the sul out of something, we kill it. You should only draw the sul out of things like that fallen tree. When you get powerful enough, you will learn to harness a sul to help you do powerful deeds." Fearn's hand reached up and touched his scars above the bandage, thinking of the times that his sul was used to heal himself. Seeing this, Uram smiled. "Ah, you are very bright! That was done by a Mender and they use the sul in a different way.

Now, back to this other leaf. Close your eyes again and look." Fearn saw the sul flow from the leaf and enter Uram, but instead of leaving any sul behind, Uram took all of it, leaving an inky black patch like the empty night sky. When the sul of Uram drew near the blackened leaf, it recoiled as if his sul had been burned.

"As you see, we can take all of the sul out of something, to the point it is just a husk. This leaf will never decay but remain as a blight to Dainua and the gifts that she bestows. This is something that you should never do. Ours is the power to take death and create life. That mound you saw today was a result of doing this kind of damage to the land. Nothing will ever grow there again, and those that created it scarred their suls doing so. You can take the power from Mehron, but be careful: this is Dainua's sul. Never take too much."

Fearn opened his eyes and looked at the leaf. It looked decayed like the first leaf, but instead of a greyish-brown color, it was deep glossy black. The leaf, though strikingly beautiful in its own way, was a sharp contrast to the world around them.

Uram continued, "So, back to your stick. We call it an oska. This is the first thing you will master. You must keep it by your side. It will be a place you can store suls; if you don't store suls in it, it will die. Anything you store in it will eventually seep out and return to Dainua. You must keep it alive until I return. To do that, you will need to be a Tiller of the land around you. You will take the suls of the decayed and dying things and store them in your oska." When Uram spoke the word *oska*, he pointed to the stick in Fearn's lap.

"This oska will give you a place to store energy to use when you need it. What you want to do first is to feel the sul flowing back and forth between you and the ground. You will be able to feel the decaying things that lay on and beneath Mehron. Use that power first. Try to never use Dainua's sul. Focus on the sul that flows in you. Then, like an arm, try to reach out to the suls of the things around you. Go grab a leaf and try, but make sure to take it slow and be careful." Uram waited and watched.

Fearn nodded, picked up a leaf from the ground, closed his eyes, and focused on the ebb and flow of the sul inside himself and the leaf in his hand. He realized that, when he closed his eyes, he had what could only be described as another body; he was looking out of his sul, not his eyes. It was a body he couldn't see but feel, tethered to his real body, using it like an anchor. As Fearn focused, he could feel the suls of the worms, insects, and decaying things beneath him. Fixating on the leaf in his hand, Fearn manipulated his sul so that it flowed out of him and into the leaf. He expected to easily grab the leaf's sul, but instead, it floated atop his sul, bobbing up and down like a boat. The leaf's sul exuded a small amount of energy, like the heat given off by a match. As Fearn concentrated more deeply on the leaf's sul, it started to flow out of the leaf and into himself. He felt it creep up his arm, starting to swirl around his own sul (though the two never became one), and he could feel the leaf's sul inside him before flowing down his body and out into Dainua. Fearn opened his eyes and looked at the dry, brittle leaf in his hand. Smiling, he looked up at Uram and exclaimed, "I think I got it, but it's making me awfully hungry."

Uram smiled. "Here, eat this," he said. Uram pulled from his robe a small paper package, unwrapped some dried meat, and handed a piece to Fearn, keeping a small bite for himself, which he then put away. The meat tasted wonderful to Fearn. It was smoked and had the perfect amount of salt. He devoured it eagerly. Uram went to the tree he had grown and walked around it before reaching up and picking an abellio from one of the branches. Fearn had been so focused on Uram, he never realized what kind of tree now stood before him. Uram tossed him an abellio and then picked one for himself. It had a bright bumpy red skin, and when Fearn bit into it, it was firm, crispy, and sweet. It was the best abellio he had ever eaten, although he had only had a few of them in his life.

"Sure beats packing a basket of abellios to bring with you," Uram called out while patting the pouch on his hip. While Fearn ate, he noticed the dirt under his feet felt softer. He looked down at a small circle around him in which the ground appeared as if his dad had tilled and fertilized it. He was amazed, never having seen anything like it before. Fearn jumped up and sprinted in a circle, digging his toes into the soft earth. It felt amazing. Fearn closed his eyes and saw his feet now splashed into the power of Dainua. Falling down, Fearn let his sul flow out and into Dainua, letting her power turn and twist around him as it rushed by, enveloping him on all sides with her power. It was a joy that he had never before felt. After a while, Fearn pulled his sul back into his body, opened his eyes, and looked over to Uram. A huge grin broke over Fearn's face before he rushed over and embraced Uram, tears filling his eyes.

"Thank you, Uram, for giving me a mother," he cried. Uram knelt and gently wrapped his arms around Fearn, speaking softly, "You're welcome, Fearn. Treat her well."

"Time for your second lesson," Uram stated as he stood back up. "Now that you have pulled the energy from something, I want you to hold it inside and then move it into your oska. This is a lot harder than it sounds."

Fearn ran over to a branch lying on the ground and picked it up, holding it in one hand and his oska in the other. He closed his eyes and focused on the sul in the branch. He was easily able to take part of its sul, but as the sul flowed into him, Fearn found he had a hard time grasping it, as it desperately wanted to reunite with Dainua. His tenuous grip on it suddenly failed, and it slipped down his leg and into Dainua, where it swirled until her power absorbed it. Fearn kept at it all day while Uram gave him pointers. When they got hungry, they ate dried meat and abellios. When Farkor started to set, Uram decided it was time to call it quits for the day. They could pick up again in the morning. He reached for the oska he had given Fearn, held it for a while, then handed it back.

"That should keep it alive until morning," he said. As they walked back, Fearn could feel that many small suls swirled inside.

When they got back to the farm, Dair was still in the field. Fearn turned to Uram and asked, "Where are you going to sleep tonight? I can talk to my dad about you staying in the house. I sleep on the floor, but there is plenty of room for the two of us." Uram turned his head to the east. "I had planned on staying in the woods, but after the events of this morning, I don't think that would be wise. I will head into town and find a place there. It will be safer for both of us. You should make sure you are both inside before nightfall. I would avoid going out tonight if at all possible," Uram warned. He untied his horse and mounted.

"Be safe. I will be back mid-morning." He turned the horse and started towards town. As Uram rode off, Fearn saw a walking stick with intricately engraved animals blending into one another strapped just behind the saddle.

VISITOR

O nce back in the house, Fearn started cutting vegetables for dinner, then took the pot and headed to the well that sat midway between the house and the field. After filling the pot, Fearn called out towards the field: "Dad! Putting on dinner, and you need to be inside before last light!"

Dair looked up and wiped the sweat from his brow with the back of his hand. He looked down at the pile of lull weed in his cart; it had been a long day. Thinking to himself that he could really use some help in the field, he considered how irritating it was that Fearn was useless; the boy hadn't shown any signs of being able to kill the crops, but he had to be kept away to be certain of it because this was their livelihood. Wiping his hands, Dair considered the cart and the fields covered in lull weeds. Maybe Fearn could work in the north-eastern field, just to see what would happen; Dair never could get anything but lull weeds to grow there—worst case, the boy would kill the weeds. He really was a good kid, and Dair realized he had grown fond of the boy, despite his fears. Abruptly, Fearn's words echoed back. He realized Fearn had never before asked that he be in by last light; something must be wrong. He glanced up at the changing sky: blood-red offset by purple ribbons. Fearn had been with the Asinta most of the day, he recalled, so something must have happened. The boy would have a tale to tell.

✳✳✳✳✳✳✳✳✳✳✳✳✳✳✳✳✳✳✳✳

Fearn stoked the wood under the pot of water before adding the vegetables. He picked up a handful of cut radishes, thinking that if he left tomorrow and never saw another radish so long as he lived, he would be more than happy. As his thoughts drifted back to his lessons, he considered the cut radishes in each hand. Closing his eyes, he looked at the radishes and saw their sul flowing out of them and slowly into his hands, his body, trying to find a way to Dainua. Hesitantly, he let his sul flow into the radishes in his left hand, then tried to move part of their sul to the radishes in his other hand by wrapping his sul around it and concentrating on moving it to his right hand. The radish's sul grew brighter, but as he tried to force the sul from the left-hand radish into it, it felt like pushing on a wall. A loud crash came from outside, startling Fearn and causing him to pull his sul back quickly, accidentally pulling the remaining suls from the radishes as well. Fearn's stomach sank as he opened his eyes; the radishes were now black and empty like a starless night. The firelight reflected off the surfaces of the radishes, mocking his lack of control. Fearn glanced at the doorway but saw nothing but Farkor setting. He momentarily wondered what had fallen outside, then threw the radishes into the fire.

****

Dair had finished in the field and gone to the well to draw water so he could clean up some before dinner. He threw the lull weeds from his cart onto the burn pile and headed to the side of the barn to store the cart. He tripped as he came around the side of the house, running the cart into the wall. Cursing Dainua and too tired to move the cart again, Dair decided to leave it where it lay. As he neared the doorway, about to call out to the boy, he stopped, frozen in his tracks. Fearn stood with eyes fixed on what appeared to be radishes in his hands. Then, suddenly, the radishes changed: the white of the root clouded, becoming dark like an approaching storm until the radishes became a sickly black. Dair jumped back and pressed himself against the outer wall, stomach twisting, his worst fears realized. What was he going to do? Fearn couldn't work in the field now. He turned to look at the lush greens in his field and imagined his livelihood wilting away. Sighing, Dair couldn't bring himself to scold Fearn, for what good from Dainua would that bring? Wiping a tear from the corner of his eye, Dair steeled himself and walked into the house.

Dair spotted Fearn tossing the blackened radishes into the fire. Fearn turned, a look of shock and horror on his face, and backed away like a dog waiting to be beaten. Dair's heart dropped; he wanted to rush over and wrap the frightened boy in his arms, but he quickly pushed the thought away. Squaring his shoulders and pretending like he hadn't seen a thing, he closed and barred the door.

"So, I see that you and that accursed Asinta were in the woods all day. Does that have anything to do with having to come inside before last light? Better be straight with me—you know I can tell when you are lying." That was a lie in itself. The more Dair taught him to be a better teller of tales, the more the boy could lie and look honest or be honest and look like he was lying. He was raising the boy right, he thought.

Fearn mulled over his dad's request and decided it would be best to just stick with what happened at the black mound. He glanced over at his straw bed to make sure his oska wasn't showing, looked back to his dad, and told his tale. "We were far from the farm and Uram was teaching about how Dainua feeds the trees. I really needed to water the ground but was embarrassed to do it so close to Uram. I went around a few trees until I was out of sight. When I was done, I heard the hooting of an owl, so I went to see where it was. I wasn't able to find it and realized I didn't know my way back. I was ashamed to call out, so I wandered off in the direction I thought I should travel. I noticed that I couldn't hear any birds or animals. I started to get really scared, Dad, but that is when I glimpsed a clearing and decided to go and find Farkor, just like you taught me, to point me back to the farm. When I reached the clearing, I saw a massive hill as black as coal with standing stones arranged like a crown on top of it. As I turned to leave, Uram grabbed me and told me to follow him quickly and quietly. Uram was really scared of it. Do you think that is where the deamhon lives?"

After he finished, his dad sat there for a while thinking it over. The black radishes he had seen earlier told him Fearn wasn't telling him the entire tale.

"Hmm... Well, I've always known there was a deamhon in these woods. We now know where it lives and how to avoid it." Dair suddenly wondered if one was sitting across from him. No, he decided. He knew the boy and would know if it wasn't him. He continued, "This has all the makings of a good tale, and it should be yours to tell." Rising, Dair went to stir the vegetable soup, adding a little bit of spice and trying to find and pull each vegetable to the surface to see if it was black.

Fearn sat in silence, mesmerized by the spoon as it went round and round, up and down in the pot. The black radishes were at the forefront of his mind as his eyes wandered from the spoon to the fire. He studied the fire for any remains of the radishes and wondered if they could burn without a sul or if he would find them when he cleaned out the ashes. Dair seemed satisfied with the outcome of the soup and started dishing it out. They ate in silence like they did most nights, until Fearn broke it: "Oy! Dad, how are we going to leave food out tonight? It's too late to take it to the edge of the wood!"

"Don't worry. We'll leave a plate outside the door," Dair replied. After he finished his bowl, he stood and partially refilled it, unbarred the door, and slowly peeked out. A faint bit of light illuminated the horizon, but he saw nothing in the creeping darkness. He set the bowl outside the door, then hastily closed and barred it. Thinking of the blackened radishes again made him wonder if he was locking himself inside with a deamhon, so Dair grabbed the hatchet from the wall and the sharpening stone from the dish cupboard and placed them on the table. He lit the lantern from the fire with a piece of straw and set it on the table. Sitting down, Dair picked up the hatchet and started to sharpen it with the stone while he warily eyed Fearn.

Fearn saw his dad grab the hatchet and wished they had time to get the ax from the stable; even without the ax, however, he was grateful that his dad was there to protect them. Seeing his dad tense and ready to strike put Fearn at ease. They would be safe. He laid his head on the table and stared into the flames, playing back the day's events in his mind. He smiled at the thought that he was a Tiller, not a Crop Burner. He thought, "Maybe if I could create a tale about what Tillers do, people would see us for what we are—protectors of the land." He imagined working the field with his dad and walking back to the house after a long day, his dad's arm over his shoulder, which made his smile widen.

Hmm... Now, how to tell that tale, Fearn pondered.

Time had passed quietly, Dair sharpening the hatchet and Fearn mulling over his new tale. Suddenly, a chilling screech came from the horse, which brought Dair's slow methodical sharpening to a stop. Fearn's head rose quickly from the table. He locked eyes with his dad briefly, and then they both stared intensely at the wall behind Fearn's chair, the pops from the fire being the only sound as they held their breath. Something pressed hard against the wall. The boards creaked and groaned as it passed by each one, slowly making its way to the front of the house. Dair and Fearn followed the sounds, turning little by little as the thing outside moved. The groaning of the wood called out a warning, which grew louder and more earnest the closer the thing got to the door. After what seemed like an eternity, it finally reached the door. A scuffling came from the lintel, sniffing as though a dog was searching. A sudden silence was followed by the distinct sound of something ceramic being moved around, hitting the wall a few times. Dair turned to Fearn, put a finger to his lips, and mouthed, "The bowl of soup." He slowly stood up, hatchet in hand, looking to the door and then back to Fearn, petrified at the possibility of being cornered between two deamhons.

BANG! The door bowed in, but the bar kept it from exploding inward. Fearn fell backward from his chair into the dirt, then rolled over and studied the door, sensing something. Closing his eyes, Fearn looked and saw a tattered shapeless mass with parts billowing out behind it. It didn't look like anything else he had ever seen. It was a sul without a vessel, and as he focused, he saw another sul inside it, moving back and forth erratically as though desperately trying to get away. Zeroing in on the second sul, Fearn saw that the larger sul had clamped down on it. It faded as if being feasted upon by the larger sul. A mass at the top of the deamhon rippled like water, and two eyes appeared, staring straight at Fearn.

BANG! BANG! BANG! BANG! The deamhon became enraged, doing everything it could to get into the house. Dair turned and looked at Fearn. "Apparently, it didn't like the soup," he stated solemnly. "Help me turn the table over." Then Dair dashed to Fearn's side and started to pick the table up.

Fearn opened his eyes, scrambled to his feet, and helped his dad lift the solid wood table. The bar rattled in its housing as the metal braces on each side started to bend and strain under the force of the blows. They moved the table to the door and up-ended it; then, Dair threw himself against it, struggling to hold it against the door. He yelled at Fearn to do the same. Dair realized the deamhon was even stronger than the two of them together. The table shifted forward with each new blow against the door, and they could hear the braces start to crack. Fearn decided that he needed to do whatever he could to save his dad since the deamhon seemed to want him. Fearn closed his eyes, reached out, and felt the presence at the door, then pushed his sul down into Dainua, flowing with her underneath the deamhon until he was behind it.

Fearn flowed out of Dainua and entered the deamhon, quickly grabbing the sul it was feeding on, desperately wanting to distract it from his dad. He pulled the partially devoured sul towards Dainua. The deamhon was taken by surprise and turned its attention towards Fearn, clamping down on its prey just as the sul was about to slip from its grasp. The smaller sul was now trapped: part of it in the deamhon, the other in Dainua. As Fearn struggled with the trapped sul, tugging and grasping for control, it swirled around him. Flashes of a mill, a blackened hill, and a shovel raced through his mind until the deamhon pulled hard, forcing part of the sul back into itself. Fearn pulled harder, the power of Dainua strengthening him. Again, images flashed through his mind. This time he saw trees, feeling panic and fear. Then, he saw what looked like his farm. Fists in front of him that weren't his pounded on the door. Something pulled him back into the freezing snow, and he could see hands clawing at the ground wildly attempting escape. As the memory faded, Fearn felt Dainua's energy swirl around the trapped sul, trying to absorb it, wearing it thin, which caused it to rip in two. The deamhon leapt back from the door and dashed to the woods. The ripped sul that Fearn still held onto turned into boiling rage as it screamed in his mind. He felt the sensation of being pinned down, his arms slowly being pulled from their sockets, muscles and tendons tightening before they ultimately snapped. He was dragged by his legs away from home. A sharp pain shot through his stomach, and looking down, he saw his steaming entrails pulled and dropped into the snow. A bottomless, biting cold entered where the warm entrails once stood and flowed towards his head as his sul was slowly ripped from his body. A sharp realization overcame him: pain would be the only sensation he would ever feel again. As the ripped sul thrashed about, it caused Fearn to relive being pulled apart over and over again, until he let go and watched as it flowed away in Dainua's energy. Struggling, Fearn pulled his sul back into his body. He gasped for breath before he threw his body forward into the dirt, echoes of pain and anguish reverberating through his head until an intense blackness swallowed him.

Fearn suddenly awakened on something soft, but it wasn't his bed. He reached down and gingerly prodded himself to ensure he was still in one piece. His head felt like an anvil, heavy and beat upon. There was no light in the room. He fumbled out of bed, collapsed onto the floor, crawled a few feet, then passed out again. The power of Dainua beneath him felt like a warm blanket on a cold winter's night.

Fearn awoke again, feeling like he had slept for days. Carefully, he pulled himself off the floor, felt his way to the door, opened it, and found himself in the main room of his house. It was quiet. No fire burned, and not a single lantern was lit. Cautiously, he shuffled across the room, running into the table which had been placed back where it belonged, as he headed to the door. He couldn't feel the door bar so he reached for the handle and slowly opened the door. A bright light illuminated the cracks around the door, which he swung wide open to reveal a calm mid-morning. His body ached, but sleeping on the dirt had helped refresh him. He glanced down, and in the dirt, a shiny black line trailed from where he had cowered with his dad to just outside the door where the deamhon must have stood. He looked around for his dad and saw him down in the field pulling weeds. Then, he noticed that Uram's horse was tied up at the stable door. Fearn tried to locate Uram, but the Asinta was not in sight. He went back into the house, dusted the dirt from his clothes, found his oska, and headed to the abellio tree in the hopes of finding Uram.

At the abellio tree, he found Uram resting in the shade, patiently waiting for him. Uram saw Fearn, and a broad smile crept across his face as he stood to greet him.

"Fearn! Glad to see you survived the night's events. I spoke with your dad this morning, and he filled me in on what happened. He said after you threw yourself down, the wraith left. Please, tell me your side of the tale," he requested. Fearn recounted how he fought with the deamhon outside the door and how the sul ripped in half.

"That's very impressive! Very few Asinta can pull a sul like that, let alone from a wraith as powerful as that seemed to have been." Then, Uram patted him on the back and returned to his seat beneath the abellio tree.

Fearn sat next to him, asking, "Will the deamhon, or whatever you called it, return tonight?"

"I doubt it. I suspect that it is a wraith. Think of it like a sul without a body that possesses powers like us. Everyone is born with a sul. Some are born with powers strong enough to become Asinta, if they are discovered, which is why we do the test of the flower. We can teach them to harness their suls correctly. Some folks have suls that give them innate abilities, like a farmer who always knows exactly when to plant and what the crops need. They are harnessing the power in their sul to know these things, though most aren't aware of it. People with powerful suls can come back briefly and walk the land until they become one with Dainua again."

Fearn suddenly remembered. "I met the Baker's sul a few years ago, just after she was buried. She was very friendly, though. Not like last night."

Uram nodded, then continued. "Those suls that do briefly come back are as friendly or horrible as the person they were when they lived. That hill we saw yesterday was blackened to keep whatever was buried there locked away. Their bones and sul are cut off from the energies of Dainua. These are the suls we call wraiths. Apparently, this one has found a means of escape. I have heard from elder Asinta even older tales of a time when powerful members of our group were buried in this manner so they could come back and teach. It was said that they feasted on suls so they could stay with the living. I believe that your attempts to pull apart what this wraith was feasting on will keep it from coming back. However, I will need to leave sooner than I hoped to consult with the imbiber to see what he wants to do."

Fearn turned his oska over in his hands, looking over the patterns in the wood while he listened, then looked up at Uram. "So, what will happen to *me* when I die?"

"I suspect with a sul as powerful as yours, you will be able to walk this world for a short time, if you wish, though Dainua will quickly embrace you, returning you to her."

Uram spent that day and the next three days teaching Fearn. Each night was quiet with no sign of the wraith.

As they walked back to the farm on the last day of lessons, Uram gave his final instructions: "I may not be back until next spring. You must keep your oska alive until then. I'll know if you try to replace it. I hope to be back sooner, depending on what the Imbiber decides to do in regards to the wraith." Fearn did not want Uram to go; he had never had a friend, and he felt like Uram was as close as he was going to get to having one.

"Uram, is there any way I can go with you?" Fearn pleaded. "I am sure my dad will be fine with it, especially after he finds out I am a Crop Burner. First, I killed my mom, and now this."

Uram stopped and turned to Fearn. He appeared weighed down, carrying a burden Fearn had not seen before. Heavily, Uram knelt and took Fearn's hands, reaching out and entwining his sul with Fearn's. The power between them ebbed and flowed. Fearn looked up and smiled as he felt the connection to Uram's sul. It felt so different from what he had felt with the wraith, plants, or tree. It embraced him as Dainua had. He looked into Uram's eyes and saw pity.

"Fearn, I know your life has been hard, but I cannot let you come with me at this time. You need to do your growing up here before you come with us to finish your schooling and learn the finer points of harnessing your sul. Your fight with that wraith means there are great things in store for you. In the meantime, take care of your oska and be patient."

They walked the rest of the way to Uram's horse in silence. Before Uram mounted the horse, he reached out his hand, and Fearn grasped him by the wrist.

"Goodbye, Fearn the Tiller," Uram said as he smiled widely.

Fearn smiled back, "Goodbye, Uram the Tiller." With that, Uram mounted his horse and left.

THE TREE

The rest of spring followed like any other spring Fearn had experienced. He would do chores in the morning, followed by any errand his dad needed. Then, he would sneak off and practice harvesting suls, making sure his oska didn't die.

Fearn spent all his free time under the abellio tree after filling his oska. One day in mid-summer, while leaning against the tree, eating its fruit and relaxing, Fearn noticed a thick grass growing in the spot he and Uram had tilled during their lessons, and an idea struck him. He stood, digging his toes into the ground and focusing on the dead leaves, seeds, insects, and animals all around him. He pulled their suls; then, instead of harvesting them, he pushed them back into Dainua. As her powers swirled around them, he pulled the mixture of the two back, letting it flow through the dirt beneath his feet. He paced back and forth across the clearing until all of the soil had been touched. He returned each day, carefully tilling the ground until the soil was a deep rich black; each day, he had to walk farther into the woods to find the dead things to harvest. Once the soil was ready, Fearn turned to the green patch of grass and poured the suls he found into it, causing growth to spread rapidly. Deciding his work was complete, Fearn stood at the edge of the clearing, admiring the emerald oasis he had created. Closing his eyes, he saw the rush and flow of Dainua had become stronger in the clearing; like rapids in a river, energy crashed into everything, splashing up from underneath the ground and over the grass, lapping against the tree. When the flood of Dainua's sul reached the clearing's border, it flowed back down into the ground. The grass emitted a faint power that flowed into Telgog, making the air thicker. Fearn laid down in the thick lush grass, feeling the power and love of Dainua flow around him.

As the harvest season approached, Dair made a deal with a few of the local farmers' sons: they would help harvest his field in return for a portion of his crop. Even though the boys had once been scared of Fearn, after the incident in the graveyard, he quickly discovered their fear had waned. They called him names when his dad was out of earshot and occasionally would throw rocks when he got too close.

One morning, after doing his chores, he grabbed his oska and headed into the woods to gather some firewood. The oska had become his constant companion. After gathering some wood at the edge of the forest, he started towards the abellio tree. He harvested suls to fill his oska along the way. Once there, he lay against the tree, finding peace as he reached out to Dainua and closed his eyes.

****

From the clearing's edge, a pair of eyes watched. The boy had been working for Fearn's dad and slipped off earlier that morning to relieve himself in the woods. As he was finishing up, he spotted Fearn bending over and picking up what looked like a freshly dead rabbit. The boy thought little of it until he saw the rabbit change. Its fur whitened and the body collapsed in on itself before Fearn dropped it and headed deeper into the woods. Being careful where he quietly placed his feet, the boy walked over to where Fearn discarded the rabbit and crouched down to examine it. Confused, the boy looked for a second rabbit; the one at his feet looked like it had been dead for days, or even a week or more. A sudden fear washed over the boy. He knew that Fearn was a Crop Burner; however, he hadn't heard they could do this to animals. Looking up at the direction Fearn had gone, the boy slowly crept after him until he got close enough to see what Fearn was doing without being noticed. It looked as though Fearn was aimlessly walking through the woods until he came upon a moss-covered cracked stump. As the boy watched Fearn and the stump, he saw it change. The decay and rot grew darker and spread like poured water until part of the stump split further and fell away. Thinking about his family, his friends, and the tales he had heard, he knew for certain that Fearn was a threat to them. He had to do something, but what could he do against that kind of power? Instead of going back to the field for help, he decided it would be best to follow Fearn so he could give a better account of what he saw to his dad. After following Fearn for a ways, he saw him enter a clearing with the greenest grass he had ever seen. As he drew nearer, something seemed off; the clearing didn't feel like the rest of the forest. Something peculiar hummed throughout it. Fearn was lying next to a huge tree that stood almost at the center, his eyes closed. As the boy turned, determined to tell the others at the farm what he had seen, he noticed a large rock by his feet. He looked from the rock to Fearn. "That's a deamhon, not a boy," he told himself. In his thoughts, he saw images of a toast made to his heroism in the tavern followed by the tale of how he vanquished a deamhon. He picked up the rock, tested its weight, and, satisfied, carefully placed one foot in the clearing. Feeling more strongly the strange power of the place without ill effects, he continued. He held his breath and stepped lightly, hoping the deamhon wouldn't open its eyes.

****

Suddenly, a sharp pain struck Fearn in the side of his chest. The force of the blow rolled Fearn onto his side. He looked up and saw one of the boys who had been hired to help his dad standing above him, a rock held over his head in trembling hands, a wild look of determination upon his face.

"I saw what you did to that rabbit, you deamhon!" the boy bellowed, spittle flying from his mouth, before he kicked Fearn in the stomach again.

"I knew you were up to no good. I saw what you did to that tree stump. I saw it wither and die." He let fly another swift kick, this time to Fearn's ribs; Fearn felt one crack, and searing pain coursed through him as he gasped for breath.

"I'm going to tell everyone in the village, and they are finally going to see you for what you are, you deamhon," he hissed as he brought the heavy rock down onto Fearn's face. Fearn's nose collapsed, exploding in a bright red stream of blood. Tossing the rock aside, the boy grabbed Fearn by the throat.

"I think I'll do everyone a favor and kill you. Tell them how you tried to kill me first. I'll be a hero, and tales will be told." The boy's hands tightened around Fearn's throat. Fearn desperately reached out for his oska but it was too far away. His vision blurred. Closing his eyes, he felt the power of Dainua all around him. Reaching out, he let his sul flow into his attacker and then pulled the boy's sul into himself. Fearn felt the boy's fear and desire to kill rush through him as his strength returned, but it wasn't enough; as his vision started to blacken, the primal desire to kill took over and Fearn lost control. He instinctively pulled harder on the boy's sul while feeling for the roots of the tree in the ground beneath him, then pushed the sul of the boy into them, feeling the tree grow and change as the sul entered it. Fearn urged the tree to grow, pouring the boy's sul into it, feeling almost one with the tree. The boy's screaming snapped Fearn out of his trance, and he felt air returning to his lungs. He struggled to open his swollen eyes until finally a hazy image of his attacker materialized. The boy was now old and wrinkled, his skin blotchy and hanging limply from his face. The boy stared at his hands and arms in horror.

"What've you done to me? You deamhon!" the boy wheezed, then started coughing. He was still sitting on Fearn's chest, while Fearn struggled to get out from underneath. Upon feeling him trying to escape, the boy focused again on Fearn, punching him in the face, though this blow was weaker than the ones before. Noticing this, the boy reached for the rock he had dropped. Panicking, Fearn knew that he had to do something quickly; he pulled on the boy's sul again, and directed it into the tree, urging the branches above the boy to grow downward and around the boy's neck, twisting and turning until they lifted the boy off Fearn. Opening his eyes, Fearn

73

now saw an old man. His toes were scraping at the dirt for purchase, trying desperately to get enough leverage to push himself up, while his hands clawed futilely at the branches encircling his neck, nails breaking in the struggle. The rage that had been in his eyes turned to panic and fear as his eyes bulged in his head; his face started to turn blue, and his lips swelled. Fearn watched as the boy struggled for air, not knowing what he should do. The boy went limp, except for the occasional spasm.

Fearn crawled to his oska and pulled in some of the suls he had stored. This rush of energy helped clear his head; the fear and rage he felt from the boy finally started to dissipate. Fearn's face and shirt were a bloody mess as blood continued to flow from his nose. He stared into the sky, pain shooting through his chest. Closing his eyes, he waited for Dainua to take his sul. After a while, he lifted his gaze to the old man—no, boy, he reminded himself—who was hanging from the tree. His eye that wasn't swollen shut searched around the clearing. Despite what happened, he could still feel Dainua as purely as he had earlier that morning. He closed his one good eye and imagined her embrace was his mother's. Tears welled in his eyes and ran down his face. He would give anything to be able to see his mom standing there. He blinked away the tears as his head swam with pain.

Using his oska to pull himself to his feet, Fearn was able to gain his footing, though an intense pain shot through his chest and stomach, which caused him to stumble. He headed home. It took him twice as long to get there as it normally would. He forgot his shoes in the clearing, and the ground seemed sharper and more hostile than it had on the way there. Finding himself out of the woods, he could see his dad and the other boys in the field still working. He tried to cry out, but only coughed up blood, so he stumbled across the farm until he reached the edge of the field. Afraid to step foot in it, panic started to set in. He didn't know what to do. He saw his dad coming towards him, so he gave into the pain, slumped into the dirt, and fell onto his side, closing his one good eye and letting the world slip away.

****

Dair busily pulled lull weeds. It had been a particularly bad year for them, and it looked like some of his crops wouldn't make it due to being crowded out. One of the boys had walked off earlier that morning and didn't return. He wasn't going to pay the boy's dad for work that wasn't being done; moreover, he'd see about forcing the kid to put in a few days' work free. One of the other boys called out and pointed behind Dair. He turned and saw Fearn limping across the farm, clutching his walking stick as he walked right up to the edge of the field. As Dair ran to prevent him from entering the field, he noticed something was wrong as Fearn collapsed. Fearn's face was covered in blood, his nose was bent at an odd angle and still bleeding, and the places that weren't bloody were purple and bruised. His shirt and pants were splattered in dark red. Images of Lia lying amid blood-soaked sheets rushed through Dair's head. He yelled at the boys behind him for help, though he didn't know what they could do. He carefully gathered Fearn in his arms and told one of the boys hovering over his shoulder to get help.

Dair rushed to the house, opened the door and laid Fearn on the table, then grabbed a shirt from his room. When he got back, one of the boys stood in the doorway.

"Grab the pot and go get some water," Dair demanded. The boy didn't question him; he simply did as he was told. Another boy appeared in the doorway. "Go get your dad and any men who are free," Dair barked. The boy raced away, calling the other boys to help him get the men. Dair snatched a knife from the cupboard and cut off his boy's shirt. There was a huge bruise covering Fearn's right side. Dair lightly ran a hand over it and could feel Fearn's ribs grind against themselves. The first boy reappeared with the pot of water from the well. Dair tore off a piece of the shirt, dipped it into the water, and started cleaning Fearn, whose nose was broken. Dair grasped it between two fingers and snapped it back into place, though it remained slightly crooked. Dair then delicately cleaned off his boy's face and chest. The right side of Fearn's face was swollen, a deep purple. The right eye looked like it had been stung by a hive of angry bees. From the corner of the room, Dair picked up Fearn's only other pair of pants, wrapped them firmly around Fearn's chest to keep his ribs in place, and then gently carried him to his room, laid him down on the bed, and looked back at the door. When he didn't see anyone, Dair bent and gently kissed his son on the forehead. Then a few words came from Fearn, raspy and weak: "Boy... old man... attacked... "

Dair waited a few moments longer to see if his boy would utter anything else, then returned to the main room where the last boy waited. Dair ordered, "Head to your dad's, grab him and any weapons he might have. Tell him a person attacked my boy. Grab anyone else you see on the way."

The boy started to run away, then pivoted on his heel to look at Dair. "How do you know a person did this? Couldn't it have been a deamhon?"

"I've seen enough bar fights and animal attacks to know which is which," he replied. "Go, and hurry!"

Then, Dair remembered the boy who wandered off that morning and yelled out to the boy as he was leaving the house, "Tell him another boy may have been attacked as well."

Dair ran over to the stable and grabbed the ax, then paced between the bedroom—where he could keep an eye on his boy— and the main room, where he stared out the door waiting for help to arrive.

Several men arrived an hour later, carrying lanterns and various weapons: axes, hatchets, and a hoe. Dair told them what little he knew, then recognized one of the men as the father of the boy who took off that morning, confirming Dair's worst suspicions: the boy hadn't come home.

"We have to go find my son!" the man exclaimed. "You have any idea where the attacker might be?" Dair knew his son went south into the woods every day, so he said, "Let's head south. That's the direction my son came from," Dair directed. They all checked their lanterns one last time, then Dair led them south into the woods. There was a clear path that looked to have been used quite often, so Dair followed it. They got about half a stone in when they came upon the most beautiful clearing any of them had seen. It was a verdant spring green, with a huge abellio tree in the center; an old man hung from its branches. They all stared at the sight, and then looked to one another in wonder. None dared enter the clearing. It felt like a sacred place. They all felt a strange presence here, but it didn't seem to come from the body. Dair spotted his boy's shoes by the tree and gingerly took a step into the clearing. The grass was soft and lush, without a single lull weed. After feeling no ill effects other than the "presence" around him growing stronger, Dair bravely walked up to and around the body to see if he knew who it was.

He was an old man, at least twice the age of Dair. The dead man's eyes were open, bulging out of his head, his face a deep purple with lips puffed and swollen tongue sticking partway out of his mouth. The man was a stranger, yet Dair couldn't help but think he looked familiar—maybe a traveler or merchant. Since Dair was not struck down by some unknown force, the other men slowly stepped into the clearing and approached the body. After they reached the tree, one of the men piped up in confusion, "Those clothes he is wearing are my son's, I know for certain. My wife made them herself." The man turned away, tears streaming down his face as he realized it was unlikely he would find his son alive.

"Oy, look how he's hanging!" one of the other farmers exclaimed. They all looked up; it appeared as if the tree had reached down and strangled the man, its branches completely surrounding the man's neck. There was no way to free him unless they cut the branches, which they were hesitant to do.

"Well, what do we do? Do we leave him here?" Dair asked the other farmers.

"I'm not touching that tree with my ax," came a reply. The others nodded vigorously in agreement.

Dair looked to the sky. "It's going to get dark soon. This isn't a place I think any man should be at night." They unanimously agreed as they hurriedly left the clearing, heading back to Dair's farm.

Once they were clear of the woods, the father of the missing boy spoke up: "What am I going to tell my wife? I need to find my son." He looked to each man pleadingly.

Dair was the first to speak up: "Let's meet here at first light. If Fearn wakes up, I'll ask if he saw your boy and where he might be." They all agreed except the boy's dad. He didn't want to leave his boy alone at night if he was still out there; he reluctantly grasped wrists with everyone else and headed home, examining the woods as he rode away, hoping to find his son.

Dair went to put the ax away. As his hand left the handle, he thought it might be better if he had it with him that night, considering what he had seen in the woods. Wearily, he headed into the house to check on Fearn.

The Field

Fearn slipped in and out of consciousness for days, sometimes waking up from fever dreams, screaming about trees, suls, a boy, and an old man. The thing about which Fearn screamed the loudest, which sent a fear deep into Dair's bones, was when he pleaded for his mother, causing Dair to relive again and again the night he saw Lia at her grave marker. He pondered whether the ghostly image was really her and considered the last words she had spoken: raise him and love him.

Regardless of what Fearn screamed, Dair sat by his side, trying to pour water down Fearn's throat when he was awake enough to drink and placing a wet rag on his head to try to keep the fever down. When he wasn't by his side, he was pacing the room.

On the morning of the eighth day, Fearn awoke. He felt weak. The events under the tree seemed far off, forgotten like a vivid nightmare that once seemed so real, but the memory faded quickly into a haze as he awakened. His dad was there by his side and helped him to the table in the main room. Dair opened the door to let in some light and warmth. The breeze felt good on Fearn's face, and the porridge his dad made was even better. Dair had to make another pot to keep up with his appetite. Fearn was aware something had changed; his dad had never fretted over him like this before. As he finished his third bowl of porridge, his dad eagerly asked him, "You want me to put on another pot for you?"

Fearn, feeling like he should have stopped at two, declined and continued to stare at his dad. Fearn then reached up with both hands and felt his face. His fingers traced scabs that ran across it, and the right side was swollen. He paused for a moment, then felt his nose which was still very tender and had a slight crook to the left.

Fearn, not knowing what to say, broke the silence and asked quietly, "Dad, what happened?"

His dad explained as best he could how Fearn and the missing boy must have been attacked by the old man hanging from the tree in the clearing. The other villagers surmised that the older boy was killed first for his clothes and that Fearn must have been an unwilling bystander who came along after the murder or stumbled upon the act itself. The part of the story that everyone focused on the most was the hanging tree. Many had ventured out to see it, making sure it was at least midday when they did. All stopped at the edge of the clearing; only a few fearless kids dared to venture into it for a closer look at the tree. No one tried to cut the man down, for fear of the tree turning on them. Despite the heat, the man's body didn't appear to decompose. The smell was so awful, though, it felt like it crawled up the nose and took residence, tainting everything smelled or eaten for days.

Everyone who claimed to be intimately familiar with the woods swore they had never seen the clearing before. A few even said they walked through there the morning of the attack and saw nothing out of the ordinary. Out of all of the explanations, the one that gripped the community and seemed the most plausible was that Dainua herself had arisen as a tree to seek vengeance for the killing, leaving the tree there as a reminder against such crimes. People were coming to the tree to pray to Dainua despite the smell, and unlike most tales, this one was starting to spread farther than just their part of the world.

Fearn stared in disbelief, not knowing what to say. He wanted to tell his dad the truth, but instead hesitantly replied, "I was walking back after foraging and heard a scream echo through the trees. I cautiously crept through the woods and, just as I rounded a tree, I found the boy's body. Then something struck me from behind. When

I awoke, I found I was surrounded by thick grass, and a large tree loomed over me. My vision was foggy, and all I could think of was getting back home. I don't recall seeing the boy as I left." Fearn felt light-headed, his side still hurt, and he didn't want to be questioned.

"Dad, I need to lie down," he said. Fearn arose, went to his straw bed on the floor, and collapsed; he reached out to Dainua, letting her power flow through him.

Dair sat on the chair and stared at his boy; something wasn't right with the tale. He didn't recall seeing a bruise or wound on the back of Fearn's head. Dair concluded that ever since the Crop Burner came, things had changed and not for the better.

Fearn awoke that night and found a cold stew on the table, his dad asleep across from it. While eating it, Fearn stared at his dad, wondering if he should wake him. Looking down at his spoon as it scraped the side of the bowl, images of the clearing came to him. From what his dad said, it didn't sound like it would ever be just 'his clearing' again. Tears welled up before spilling down his cheeks. The only peace he had ever found was tainted and gone. Suddenly, the emotions he felt when pulling on the boy's sul flooded back, causing Fearn to grip the table briefly to steady himself. For a moment, he wanted to lash out at anything and everything. Pushing back from the table to get up, Fearn twisted and felt something like a hot knife stabbing his side. Looking down, he touched his ribs and found them very tender and painful. His lips were dry, and a sudden thirst came over him. He cautiously walked to the door, pushed the bar up, and slowly opened it, all the while watching Dair's even shallow breathing. It was a cool night, and the cold air felt refreshing to his face. Leaving the door open, Fearn walked over to the cupboard, grabbed a mug, and then headed outside, closing the door as silently as possible behind him.

At the well, he drew a bucket of water and dipped his mug into it. The water was so cold it sent shivers through him that caused his ribs to echo back in pain. He glanced around in the starlight and noticed the field looked strange. It was hard to make out, but it looked like the forest had overgrown it. How long did his dad say he was out? Remembering the wraith, he quickly finished the rest of the water and ran back inside. Seeing his dad still asleep at the table, Fearn gently placed a hand on Dair's shoulder.

"Dad, it's time for bed," Fearn said softly.

Dair stirred and groggily looked up at his boy. "What's wrong?" Dair slurred.

"Nothing, Dad. Time for bed."

Dair grabbed Fearn's arm to help himself stand and let his boy walk him to his room. After getting his dad into bed, Fearn left for his own. When he got to the bedroom door, his dad called out to him in a daze, "Did you see your mom at the tree? Is she well?"

Pausing, Fearn thought of his mom, or what he made her out to be, which made him think of Dainua and the first time he felt her presence.

Not knowing why, Fearn replied, "Yes. She saved me." As Fearn closed the door behind him, he could hear soft sobs coming from Dair. As he lay down, not knowing if he could sleep, Fearn realized he had never heard his dad cry before. As soon as his head touched his straw bed, he was fast asleep.

Awaking refreshed the next day, Fearn looked for Dair but found the house empty. He opened the door to find it was midmorning. Dair was in the field, back bent deep, pulling lull weeds, as the entire field was thick with them.

Fearn found his shoes and oska and headed down to see his dad. Examining the oska, he noticed it was cracked and dry. Fearn's heart sank; he wasn't sure if he could breathe life back into it. When he reached the edge of the field, his dad called out: "The lull weed has never been this bad before! Other farmers have been fighting it as well. I don't know if we'll get anything out of this harvest. I'm afraid we may lose the crop completely." Dair's shoulders sagged as he looked around him at a task he knew was pointless. "I don't know what we will do for food this winter or how we will afford the oil for the lanterns," he groaned.

The weeds had grown over most of the crops, crowding them out, causing them to hang limply. The green leaves were turning brown, and some had already fallen off. Fearn had never seen anything like it before. He thought that if he hadn't gotten into the fight with the farmer's boy, none of this would have happened.

"With you being attacked, and the other boy killed, the other farmers wanted to keep a closer eye on their boys. So, I haven't been able to find any help; couldn't very well keep up on the field and take care of you. I'm not sure what I can salvage, but I think I can pull enough to give us some food for the winter. If we can get some rain soon, it may help what's left. I guess we'll have to see if Dainua blesses us. Things have felt more like a curse lately. Your mom would've known what to do," Dair said in dismay.

Fearn thought over the things that had happened: his mom's death, the wraith, the clearing, the boy's death, and now the crops. Deep down, he knew he was the cause of it all. His dad sighed, "Well, I better get to work or we definitely won't have anything to eat." With that, Dair turned to his work, calling over his shoulder, "If you're up to it, the stable needs to be cleaned out and we need more wood."

Fearn eyed the stack of firewood next to the house; it had grown nearly as tall as Fearn and reached almost the entire length of the house. He was sure his dad was asking him to do this chore just so he was kept busy and out of the field.

"Ay, Dad, I'll be fine. I'll get to it," he replied.

Cleaning out the stable was a lot harder than Fearn expected, especially with his ribs hurting, but by mid-afternoon, it was done and he desperately just wanted to lie down and sleep. His mind, however, continually drifted to the clearing; his feet in the grass, the warmth of Farkor on his face, then the joy melted into anguish as the hanged man's face appeared. Standing between the house and stable, looking from his home to the woods, Fearn finally decided he needed to see the clearing one last time and headed south towards the woods.

As Fearn neared the edge of the forest, a sudden fear gripped him. Staring into the woods, the shade of the trees appeared darker to Fearn, menacing and haunted. He gripped his oska tightly, closed his eyes, and reached into the ground to feel the power of Dainua. He let Dainua calm him until he felt his heart slow down. Opening his eyes, Fearn took a shallow breath and stepped into the trees.

Coming to the clearing, he found a woman kneeling on the outer edge with her head bowed. He walked up as slowly as he could, so as not to disturb her, and looked towards the hanging tree, which looked the way it always had, except for the corpse hanging from it. The smell was rank. It smelled as if someone had dumped a bloated animal carcass in the outhouse at the tavern after a particularly bad night of Cromm's cooking. The corpse didn't look all that decomposed, except for the fact that something had chewed and dragged off the legs, leaving torn tissue and protruding bone of brilliant white.

The woman noticed Fearn, sat up from her prayers, and addressed him: "Isn't this a wondrous sight? What a blessing Dainua has given us! Have you come to pray to her as well?"

Fearn was taken aback; it *was* a beautiful place, but the corpse hanging there and the smell made him think that it would be the last place Dainua would want to visit. Fearn noticed the woman wasn't from his village. She wore a clean blue dress with green embroidered flowers across the bodice. Her blond hair draped down her back in a tightly woven braid, and her lips were a bright red, like he had seen on some of the richer women in the neighboring villages. Fearn wondered briefly if this was a sign of wealth before he replied, "I don't understand how you can see this as a blessing. There is a dead man hanging from the tree and it smells awful!"

She stood up, reached out, and took Fearn's arms. "Look again— the meadow is lush, not a lull weed or flaw in sight. It's Dainua and her example to us, showing us the perfect path in this life. That man is us: our flaws, our wickedness, blights to her perfection. The tree is the power that she wields, and the branches are her lifting us up and bearing our burdens, showing us her perfection as an example by which to live." Fearn wanted to ask why Dainua held us up by the neck so that our back was turned to her perfection, but instead he looked one more time. Closing his eyes, he saw it was exactly as she had described. The field was perfect; there were no flaws or dead things to be seen, and the power of Dainua rushed through it, feeding the tree's sul, which in turn flowed rhythmically. As the tree's sul touched its leaves, the tree breathed out into Telgog, mingling the two energies, causing small ripples in the air like waves. However, like a plague against perfection, the sul of the corpse, or what Fearn had left of it, remained. It flowed and danced with the tree's sul. Each time the two partners came together, the tree took a bit of the dead man's sul, handing it off to Dainua when it chose her as its next partner. Tears came to Fearn's eyes, so he turned, and, avoiding eye contact with the woman, he left.

After wandering for a bit, Fearn came across a shady spot at the edge of the woods near the farm and he sat down on a tree stump, reflecting on what the woman had said. He knew that Dainua was in and around everything. He had seen it and felt it, but it wasn't until now that he finally understood it. As he looked into the field and saw his dad struggling to pull weeds almost as tall as he was, a thought struck him, and he realized what he must do to right the wrongs he had created. Before anything else, he needed to focus on repairing his oska.

Fearn closed his eyes, reached out and gathered the suls of the dying things in the dirt around him—and even found a little energy in the stump he was sitting on, though he didn't take much in fear of the stump crumbling beneath him. He turned his attention to his oska; instead of being whole, he could see what appeared to be grey cracks running through the wood. When he poured some of the gathered suls in, part of the oska sprang back to life, but the cracks were like holes in a bucket and the suls poured straight back into the ground. Fearn focused more on the grey cracks and could see that they were like a wound in the wood. Carefully, he pushed a sul in and, with great effort, was able to move the sul in the oska to the crack on which he focused. He swirled the sul around the crack, scrubbing the grey wound vigorously, much like the porridge pot after it sat all day. As he scrubbed, the grey started to vanish. Fervently, he continued to work on the single crack until he could only see a thin grey line where the wound had been. He then poured another sul into the oska and went to work on the next wound. He continued like this for some time, until he was able to pour a sul in without it leaking out. He opened his eyes again, wiped the sweat from his face, and noticed the oska looked like it had just been cut from a tree; in the places where the cracks in the wood had been, he found intricate swirling patterns. He was already exhausted, but he knew that he had a long night ahead of him. By morning, everything would be right again.

Fearn and his dad ate in silence that night. Fearn could tell his dad was in a sour mood; the weed pulling didn't go well, and Dair was visibly troubled by it.

Fearn lay awake on his bed later that night, waiting anxiously until it was safe to slip out. Once he heard a few snores coming from his dad's room, he quietly grabbed his oska and a lantern, then headed to the door. Cautiously, he peeked around for any signs of the wraith, but he knew he couldn't worry about it. He had work to do.

As Fearn walked to the field, his heart raced. He had never stepped foot into any field before. Strange fears grasped him: what if he burned the crops? What if he made a bad situation worse? Slowly, he took off his shoes and gingerly stepped on plowed soil. He examined the ground intently with the lantern, but nothing changed. The lull weeds were thick, and the sharp barbs on the stems pulled at his clothes. Fearn closed his eyes and reached out in front of himself, then stretched his sul out as far as he could in a straight line, going from weed to weed, draining each one until there was just the faintest amount of sul left in them. He stored the energy in his oska and bottled up the rest inside himself, fighting to keep the suls from rejoining Dainua. When he couldn't store anymore, he used his oska to knock down the lull weeds. Most had crumpled on their own, but there were a few that had to be beaten down. Fearn was surprised to find it was more work than he expected and wondered how his dad did this every day. He returned to where he started, placed the oska on the ground, and dragged it behind him. As he went, he pushed the stored suls into the crops and soil. Once the row was done, Fearn headed to the next to start the process all over. He quickly realized that going barefoot was a bad idea. He considered putting on his shoes, but they dulled his senses when he tilled, so he pushed on. He finished a few hours before daylight. He knew his dad would be up soon but he had one last thing to do. He ran back to the edge of the field, put on his shoes, grit his teeth against the pain, and ran south into the woods.

When he reached the clearing, he peered around and was grateful no one was in sight. He slipped off his shoes and walked onto the grass. It felt wonderful under his feet, but he had to cover his nose in order not to experience dinner for a second time. A few paces from the corpse, he raised the lantern and looked around. Confident he was alone, he placed the lantern down and went to work. He started by pulling some of the sul from the corpse, using it along with suls in his oska to loosen the branches holding it, and then willed the tree to grow—not a branch but many vines. This was a lot harder since this wasn't a thing the tree did on its own; Fearn had to envision the vine in his head while his sul was connected with the tree and show the tree what he wanted. After a few aborted attempts at teaching the tree about vines and their movement, a vine slowly emerged from one of the branches. Fearn grew and multiplied it, intertwining them around the corpse to cover it and turn it around. Something about the shape and pose of the corpse didn't seem right, so Fearn moved the vines to bring up one of the arms and bend it askew, as though he was asking you to follow him. He covered the head in vines so the face couldn't be seen. Fearn stepped back and picked up the lantern to admire his work; it was almost perfect. Feeling uncomfortable with what he was about to do, Fearn knelt and prayed. He had never prayed before and wasn't sure what to say, so finally, he decided to keep it simple: "I'm sorry, Dainua, for what I have to do. Please forgive me."

Hoping it was enough, Fearn stood, reached out, and pulled all of the sul out of the corpse. It was a lot harder than he expected, as the last remaining bits were tough to pull, like pulling weeds by hand instead of by pulling their suls. Once he was done, he slowly opened his eyes, afraid of what he might see. In the lantern light, the corpse was now a shiny black statue with vines woven around it following his form until they trailed on the ground. To Fearn, it looked like the tree had grown a man, and the light from the lantern glinted off the black statue as if the fire was dancing between the vines. Exhausted but ecstatic with his night's work, Fearn hurried to the edge of the clearing, winced in pain as he put his shoes on, and headed home.

SHRINE

air shook Fearn awake. Fearn looked up from his straw bed; the light shining through the door told him it was early morning.

He looked up and saw that his dad was glowering at him. "What have you done?" he demanded. Fearn tried to put on his most innocent face and replied, "I don't know what you are talking about." His dad gave him the I-wasn't-born-in-the-stable-yesterday look and pointed to the floor. Fearn followed his gaze and there on the floor were partially bloody footprints leading from his shoes by the door through the dirt to his bed. He pulled his legs free from the blanket and realized his feet were a bruised and bloody mess.

"I was trying to help, Dad," Fearn explained. "Uram taught me how to be a Tiller. Crop Burners aren't bad!" Fearn pleaded. Dair turned and paced back and forth, each time pausing to look out the door into the field.

"No, Crop Burners burn fields," Dair argued. "This is something different. Dainua must have changed you when you were attacked by that old man. I have seen what Crop Burners are for myself," Dair explained. Fearn was confused; if his dad had seen what they could do, then he should know that they are caretakers of the ground.

"Dad, you saw them grow crops and take care of Dainua?" he implored, hoping to convince him.

Dair spat on the ground.

"You are young and easily swayed by these Asinta. They're murderers and mean to lead you astray. I should've told you these things a long time ago, but I hoped that once you saw them, you could see them for what they are: destroyers of lives." Fearn had never seen his dad this angry. He cautiously looked up at Dair, whose face was bright red, his brow like a newly tilled field.

Fearn cautiously asked Dair, "What should you have told me, Dad?" Dair continued to pace, then abruptly stopped and sat at the table. After a few moments, he began to speak, but it wasn't the voice he used to tell tales. This voice was full of anger, anguish, and terror. Fearn felt a chill run up his back and his skin prick up in fear.

"When I was about your age, this was a place of peace. The village was whole and thriving. Life was still hard but my dad showed me that a good harvest could bring meat to the table, clothes on our backs, and a roof over our heads. I was in the village selling eggs when riders in cloaks appeared from the South. When they passed through the town gate, we all knew them for what they were: Asinta. Very few came through these parts, but tales were told of them growing crops in a night or making carts move without horses. But unlike my tales, these were lies." Dair paused and looked up from the table, out the door towards his field, then to his boy before he continued on.

"So, when the Asinta entered the town, everyone came to see them. I tried using my small size to push through a sea of legs, but I kept getting blocked. I don't know what started it, but as I was fighting forward to get a better look, screams pierced the air. People turned and fled towards me. A man picked me up and threw me over his shoulder. I didn't know who it was—just that he had blonde hair and smelled like sawdust. I looked behind him as he ran. The crowd was thick, running in every direction. I could see the Asinta. They were off their horses and had sticks like the one you carry around now." Dair's eyes narrowed as he studied the boy and then the stick that lay beside him. Fearn was one of "them," but something tugged at the back of his mind. The boy must have changed.

"The Asinta raised the sticks high above their heads. I noticed that the oldest people in the crowd were at the back of the mob—easy pickings for predators. But then I recognized a young man I knew, and he aged before my eyes. I can still see the skin sag and the hair fading to a winter white. Then the Asinta slammed down their sticks in unison, causing bodies to be cast into the air. Buildings burst into flames around us. We ran around a corner and I lost sight of the Asinta. The man carrying me just kept running. We got to the edge of the village, and he set me down and told me to run straight home to tell my parents. He said he had to get his family and ran off. I scrambled through the woods, frightened and not sure if what I saw was real. I don't know how I managed to get home, but I did. I ran into the field and told my dad what happened. He asked me to repeat myself over and over again because I was crying and talking too fast. He told me to run to our house to get my mom and he would be there shortly. I ran to the house and could smell the stew she was cooking. I told Mom what had happened, but before she could respond, Dad appeared in the doorway with an ax in his hand, ushering us outside. There were people on the road running towards our farm. Mom screamed and pointed. Above the trees rose a thick black pillar of smoke, coming from the direction of the village. Dad told Mom to take me into the woods. Mom begged him to come too, but he refused, saying he had to help the other farmers. She finally gave in and led me away. We got partway into the woods, just where it started to get dark, when we heard a sound behind us. We stopped and looked back. There were Asinta on horseback coming down the road. Dad looked towards the woods to where he expected we were hiding, and then stepped onto the road. A few of the Asinta didn't even stop. One struck dad with the stick he carried, but instead of falling in the road, he was sent flying into the air. When he hit the ground, he crumpled like a rag doll. Mom didn't hesitate. She ran out of the woods to Dad. All I could do was stare because I felt rooted to the ground like the trees around me. I watched as Mom ran to Dad, bent over him, and turned him over. Not caring about anything but him, she didn't see one of the Asinta come up from behind her. He didn't even have to touch her;

91

she collapsed on top of Dad. As the Asinta walked by our house, it burst into flames, just like the houses in town. I noticed other Asinta in the field, and as they walked through it, the crops withered and died around them before bursting into flames. When they were done destroying everything I knew, they got on their horses and rode off. I sat there and watched as the house and crops burned, and my parents lay still in the road. I wasn't brave enough to leave those woods. I sat there and watched my life burn.

"I stayed in those woods all night, and some local farmers found me in the morning. They said the Asinta had ridden eastward. They helped me bury my parents, then took me to a farm—this very farm we're at now." Dair tapped the top of the table with his finger for emphasis. "A great man named Fearn had broken his leg in several places in the attack and would never walk right again. I worked his field for a roof over my head and food on the table. Your mom was his daughter and she became a fast friend, the only person after the attack I could talk to who really understood me. Her dad died a few years after the attack, and her mom followed a few years later from a broken heart. They left us this farm and the horse. Most families that could afford to leave had left the area and went west looking for security and a place to settle again. I don't know if they ever did find a decent place to live. There were a lot of folks like your mom's parents that couldn't leave. We did the best we could with the scarred land that was left behind." Dair finished his telling, his eyes focused afar, as if looking at something that wasn't there. He sighed, stood up, and turned to leave.

"Mom's dad was named Fearn?" Fearn asked, confused why he had never been told this.

"Yes, he was a better man than you will ever be. You bring shame to him by carrying his name. I was a fool to listen to your mother." Dair turned in disgust and headed out the door.

Fearn called out, wanting to explain what a Tiller was, but there was no reply. He grabbed his oska and tried to stand, but the pain in his feet made his head swim. He leaned against the wall and slid back down onto his bed.

Fearn thought about Uram, the clearing, and the crops he saved the night before. Why would someone burn the ground on purpose, especially a farmer's land? Why didn't Uram tell him these things? Was this part of the tales that the king had burned? Fearn was confident his dad wasn't lying to him about this, but he couldn't reconcile the two tales in his mind.

After clearing his head, Dair returned with a bucket of water and set it down at Fearn's feet. "I don't know what you are," Dair said, "but you can't be a Crop Burner if you managed to do what you did to the field last night. Dainua must have changed you in that clearing. However, people are going to question how it happened, and we better quickly find a way of explaining this." Dair headed back to the bedroom, then returned with some cloth he had used to soak up Fearn's bloody nose. It appeared to have been rinsed really well and didn't smell of blood or rot.

"Here, bandage your feet with this. Stop hurting yourself or we'll run out of clothes to wear." He handed Fearn the cloth along with a knife and then started to head outside. He stopped as Fearn pleaded with him: "Dad, you said yourself that Asinta were known to have grown crops overnight. I don't know why they attacked, but I've given you proof that they can do good."

"Those were just tales," Dair said. "You have seen for yourself how a tale can change. Believing a tale and seeing the truth are two different things." Dair paused and rubbed his chin, contemplating something before continuing, "Maybe there are special Asinta blessed by Dainua. There's always a truth in every tale." Dair hurried out the door.

Fearn cut the cloth and used part of it to clean his feet. He found a few barbs he had to pull out. Once they were fairly clean, he wrapped his feet with the dry pieces of cloth and then tried to stand again. It was still terribly painful but he wanted to go outside in the daylight to see the work he had done. Fearn used his oska to support his weight, then grabbed a chair with his other hand and dragged it outside, set it down, and slumped into it. The pain radiated from his feet to his legs. He wasn't going to go much farther than this. The field was now an intense green, with no signs of sickness. The only brown he noticed was the dead lull weed peeking from beneath the crops. Out of the corner of his eye, he noticed his dad down the road, talking to several people. After a while, they all headed towards the farmhouse. As his dad approached, Fearn could hear him talking in his teller of tales voice: "As I was saying, I was awakened last night by a strange crashing sound, and when I went outside, there was my boy wandering through the field. When he touched the weeds, they withered and died while the crops gained life and grew stronger under his feet. See? There are his feet bloodied by the work he has done for Dainua. Think of his sacrifice to help bring her back to this place." Dair made a grand gesture to everything around them before pointing again to Fearn's feet.

"Oy, Fearn, don't be shy. Show them your feet." Fearn slowly raised his feet. They looked a lot worse than they were since they were wrapped in something that was already once soaked in blood. Fearn recognized the men as local farmers. They stepped back and conversed in low voices, looking at the field and Fearn as they talked.

Finally, after coming to some conclusion, one asked Fearn, "Oy, boy, as you know, we have all been plagued by this lull weed. Do you think you can do what you did here for the other farmers?"

Fearn didn't know what to say, he just stared at them and then back to his dad, hoping he had an answer for him. Before Dair could reply, one of the other farmers piped up: "So did this blessing of Dainua make him mute as well?"

"Ay, no, he is not mute, just in pain from the ordeals he has suffered." Dair gave an odd sort of side wink to Fearn that the farmers couldn't see. Fearn knew where his dad wanted him to go with this.

"Ay, it is my feet. The pain is so bad that my mouth is clenched shut because of it," Fearn replied, as if on cue. The farmers nodded to him as if they knew exactly what he was talking about.

"Dair," said one man, "once he is recovered, we will need to meet at the tavern to see if he can at least try to help the other farms. Dainua's blessing shouldn't be kept to yourself."

Then a farmer in the back who hadn't said a word yet spoke up. "We also need to make sure this isn't some trick of the deamhon.

We know the boy has conversed with them in the graveyard. I don't think he should be trusted."

Holding up a hand, Dair replied, "Ay, I agree we should see what he can do for everyone else and confirm this isn't some trick. However, have you seen the grove that Dainua has planted in the woods? I find it doubtful a deamhon could dwell so close to such a sacred place."

Thinking of how the grove made his sul feel, Fearn added, "I think my feet could heal better if they were in Dainua's grove. Besides, if I were a deamhon, I wouldn't be able to walk in her presence." Fearn smiled at his dad, hoping this would ease the tensions.

"How do we know what a deamhon can and cannot do?" a farmer asked. "None of us has seen one. Is this what they spoke to you about in the graveyard?"

Before things got out of hand, Dair bent down and picked up Fearn, then led the way into the forest, acting as though he hadn't heard the last comment. When they got to the clearing, it was encircled by villagers from all over, most kneeling and praying in silence. Fearn had only seen a few people pray in his life and most of those in the past few days. He looked up and into the tree. There was the hanged man, but now he looked like he was carved out of a black glossy rock. Vines flowed to the grass below so that he looked like a man made of stone and wood. His gesture ominously beckoned the worshippers to come closer.

Dair walked Fearn right up to the clearing and gently set him down on his feet. Fearn used his oska to help balance himself. The feeling of Dainua flowing in the ground helped ease his pain. He took a few steps forward and noticed he was the only one standing in the clearing. Those around him who were not praying gave him threatening glances.

One person reprimanded, "How dare you set foot in this sacred grove!" Then, there was a scream off to the left, and everyone turned. Those who were praying looked up to see what the commotion was about. The woman whom Fearn had seen the day prior was running towards him, yelling, "Dainua's child is here!" As she drew closer, he noticed her face was streaked with tears. She still had on the beautiful dress she wore the day before; however, it was now dirty and tattered from her knees down, a few rips in the fabric showing a white undergarment. Her lips were no longer bright red. She fell to her knees in supplication in front of Fearn, her lips kissing his bandaged feet. Fearn looked up from her and noticed every eye was on him. He tried backing up a few steps, but the woman clung to his ankles, not letting him move. Fearn stared down at her, afraid to say anything. Finally, the woman let go, sat up on her knees, and turned to address the crowd. "This is the boy who I saw enter the grove last night. He walked up to the tree, and, as he held his lantern aloft, I saw the tree move. The hanged man turned, vines sprouted and grew and, finally, the man turned to stone. I learned this morning that this is the same boy who was saved from that very hanged man. This boy is the one that Dainua herself grew a tree to save." As the woman finished, she raised her hands above her head, then pressed her forehead into the grass at Fearn's feet. Some of the people around the edges of the clearing dropped to their knees in prayer, bowing in Fearn's direction. Others ran into the clearing, falling at Fearn's feet while begging for blessings or to be healed. Fearn tried to get away, but as he turned, he found the mass of bodies was so tightly packed around him, he couldn't flee. He looked up at his dad, hoping he could save him. Dair looked confused and uncertain what to do. Another voice rang out, "Isn't that Dair's son, the Crop Burner?" There was a loud consent amongst those who knew Dair. The self-made priestess near Fearn spoke up on his behalf: "We have seen what Crop Burners do. Is this the work of one of those creatures?" A voice broke through the din from Fearn's right. It was the farmer who contradicted Dair earlier. He asked, "How do we know this isn't some sort of trick of a deamhon who wants to gain access to our crops to poison them, leaving us to starve this winter?!"

This led to further outcries against Fearn, and the voices grew louder and more panicked. The followers around Fearn stood and hurled insults back at those they claimed were not true believers of Dainua. When Fearn couldn't hear one person over the other anymore, his dad finally stepped forward, pushed through the followers around him, picked him up, and hurried back to the farmhouse. Dair didn't say a word to Fearn all the way home. As Fearn looked back at the clearing over his dad's shoulder, he remembered his dad's tale of looking over the shoulders of a stranger, running from the Crop Burners. Fearn finally understood Dair's fear and hatred.

As the shouting faded behind them, Fearn wondered if the crops were safe to eat. The abellios hadn't poisoned him, though Uram made that tree and grew it from another tree. He had grown the crops with the suls of lull weeds. Would the sul of the weeds poison whoever ate the crops? Fearn thought back on the boy and how the boy's emotions had tainted him. He wished Uram was there to help straighten everything out. He wished he could be a normal kid and didn't have to deal with any of this.

Once they got back to the farm, Dair walked into the house, sat Fearn down at the table, lit a lantern, and went out. He grabbed the chair and brought it inside, then went to the stable for the ax. Finally, he closed and barred the door. He pulled the whetstone from the cupboard, then sat at the table and sharpened the ax. The silence in the house seemed louder than the voices in the clearing.

"Are they going to come for us, Dad?" Fearn asked, realizing he was more scared now than he was the night the wraith had come.

"With you out of there, things should simmer down," Dair replied.

Fearn was confused and scared, not knowing what to say or do. Everything he had done had made their situation worse. He didn't want people praying to him, but he also didn't want them thinking he was a deamhon. He sat there, staring as his dad sharpened the ax.

Dair finally spoke up. "Do you think that you could do for the other farmers' fields what you did for ours?"

Fearn watched as his dad stopped and gripped the handle of the ax. "Oy, Dad, I could help out," Fearn responded, eyeing the ax nervously.

Dair stood up. "Good. I need to go talk to the other farmers. I'll be back later. I'm taking the ax. If something comes up, the hatchet is on the wall." Dair paused a moment, then added, "Or do whatever

it is that you do if that can protect you. Bar the door behind me."
Dair then unbarred and opened the door, looked around, and shut the
door behind him.

Fearn hobbled to the door and replaced the bar. He spent the
next few hours sitting by the lantern light worried about what was
happening outside and if his dad would even come home.

Dair returned later that night. "I sent word out that we're going
to meet in the tavern in two nights," he told Fearn. "We'll see which
farmers want you to help, then try to reassure the rest that you aren't
a deamhon. I still don't understand what's wrong with you. I won't
lie; you frighten me. When the Asinta comes back, we should discuss
you leaving with him. In the meantime, we need a good tale to tell,
to explain what happened to you. I'll tell you the tale and you'll
need to remember it, exactly how I tell it. I don't care about the truth
of it. Our lives may depend on this." Dair then sat down at the table
across from Fearn and told him the tale, making Fearn repeat it back
to him over and over until the early morning. "You'll need to go
over this in your head and remember it exactly," said Dair, who then
went to bed, exhausted.

The next morning, Fearn still couldn't walk very well. Dair
told him to stay inside, as it would probably be good if no one saw
him; his absence might help people calm down. Fearn decided to
lie on his bed all day. He preferred not to light the lantern. It felt
good to lie in the dark, trying to figure what to do. Two days ago,
he would have felt excited about going and helping all of the other
farmers; however, today it felt like a burden he didn't want to carry.
He reminisced about Uram and wished he could have left with him.
No matter where he turned, he was unwanted and had no place to go.
If the Asinta refused to take him when they came back, what would
his dad do? Fearn had expected Uram to return to investigate the
wraith, but so far no one had come back. Fearn spent the afternoon
reciting the tale Dair told him, trying to find the right places to pause
and give inflection.

Dair came home that evening and complained about people
coming by to look at the crops or using the farm to get to the clearing.
The upside was that the work Fearn did ripened the crops early so

they had a fresh vegetable stew that night. Dair watched Fearn eat first and waited a while before he took a bite himself, not caring that the stew had grown cold. After dinner, Dair made Fearn tell the tale back to him over and over until he felt it was sufficient and then they went to bed.

The next morning Fearn's dad had him do his chores around the farm but forbade him from going into the woods. Fearn's feet felt better but they were still a little tender and raw. Fearn had to come inside about midday and rest to be ready for the walk into the village that night.

TRIAL

D air brought out the horse for Fearn to ride into town so he didn't have to walk. He packed up vegetables in a few sacks and tied them onto the saddle. As Fearn was mounting the horse, he noticed that his dad had tied the hatchet to his belt under his cloak.

The walk into town was quiet until Fearn found the courage to talk. "Dad, will things go well tonight?" He eyed his dad in the fading light of Farkor, looking for any sign of trepidation.

"Well, Fearn, things don't look good. People in these parts don't like things that can't be explained. Either you are a Crop Burner or you have been changed by Dainua and both of these things are trouble. You would be wise to make the villagers feel safe and do what you can to prove you aren't a Crop Burner. We can only hope that we can convince them that Dainua has blessed you. If we can, then they may be too scared to do anything." Dair looked up at Fearn and patted him on the leg. "I know from what I've seen that you aren't bad. Only the hands of Dainua could have blessed our field."

Fearn met his dad's eyes and saw fear and doubt, which caused his heart to sink. He wondered if he was riding to his own funeral.

When they arrived at the tavern, they had to tie up the horse outside of the stable since there was no room inside. Dair untied the bags of vegetables and helped Fearn dismount. Fearn's feet throbbed in pain the moment they hit the ground. He winced but forced himself to walk with Dair to the rear door of the tavern. Dair knocked heavily. Cromm opened the door and Dair hurriedly passed him one of the bags of vegetables. Cromm gave them a wry wink and shut the door. The ruckus coming from within the tavern made it clear that a big crowd had gathered. Dair and Fearn walked around to the front of the tavern. When Dair opened the door, all Fearn could see was a wall of bodies. He had never seen the tavern this full before, even during harvest days. They had to push their way in; people recognized who they were and parted quickly for them. Whenever Fearn looked up, he saw a face that was either angry or scared. He looked around for a smile, but noticing none, he looked down again and followed his dad's feet. When Dair stopped, Fearn looked up just enough to see the room in his peripheral vision. He saw that the tables had been moved. Instead of four long rows, they had been set up so there was a table in the middle of the room with the rest arranged in a circle around it. There were not enough seats, which caused the majority of the people to stand, balancing plates and cups in their hands. At the center table sat the tanner, miller, baker, and two other farmers. There were two empty chairs, and Dair headed towards them. Fearn felt the walk from the outer tables to the center table took longer than the walk into town. He was glad his dad gave him the outside chair; he could run off if things got ugly.

After Fearn sat down, he rested his hands on the table and stared down, feeling the rough grain of the wood beneath his fingers. Ale spilled long ago felt smooth and sticky. Cromm placed bowls of stew in front of them.

"Here. This is on me," Cromm said and smiled, which made it feel like Farkor had broken through the clouds on a cold, gloomy day. Fearn could only manage a weak smile back as a reply.

As the villagers around them started to eat, the atmosphere seemed to lighten. Fearn even noticed laughter breaking out, like birdsong in the forest. As Fearn's heart slowed down, he realized he was clutching the fork like it was the last thing he owned. He loosened his grip and started paying attention to the conversations around him. His dad was talking about the vegetables in their field and had pulled examples from his bag and placed them on the table. One of the farmers kept picking them up and looking at them like he had never seen a vegetable before. Fearn turned back to his stew. The vegetables were good and soft, the meat tender. He looked at the vegetables on the table. Maybe this harvest would allow them to have meat in the stew more often. Having eaten, Fearn felt even more relaxed, so he gazed up and around the room. It appeared the entire village came, along with folks from the neighboring villages. Then, he noticed the woman from the clearing sitting in the back. She was staring right at him. She wore a clean blue dress, and her lips were blood-red again. As soon as she noticed his gaze, she held her hands together in front of her as if to pray and bowed her head. Others surrounding her mimicked her actions. This didn't seem like a good turn of events. Fearn patted his dad's leg under the table, and when Dair turned to look at him, Fearn nodded in the direction of his unwanted following. This caused Dair to groan and mutter under his breath, "This may make things more difficult. Try to ignore them."

Once everyone had eaten, or at least appeared to be done with their meal, the tanner stood up. He wore a fine leather jacket and pants. He had brown curly hair that covered an already short forehead, with a round nose that just seemed to stick out just far enough for him to be able to breathe. He raised his left hand, which only had four fingers, and the room quieted down.

"Now, we all know why we are here. Dair has asked us to come so we can talk about what happened these past few weeks." The tanner gestured to Dair. "We need to decide what to do next. Now, please let these gentlemen and me talk until we call on you. If you can't be respectful, we will kindly ask you to leave." He waited for any dissent, and when he didn't hear any, he continued. "So, we all know that Fearn failed the test of the flower when he was born, but these past ten years, he hasn't caused any problems."

"What about the baker's deamhon?" someone called out.

The Tanner raised his hand again. "Let me clarify. He hasn't done anything to show that he is a Crop Burner or harm any of our crops. He has been to the market every year. We talked to the local sellers that he has purchased from and none had seen anything happen with the fruits and vegetables he touched or purchased. He's handled food at home, and Dair hasn't seen anything amiss. We all know Dair and know that he'd be forthright with us. We've also talked to the villagers who have witnessed the events of the past few weeks. From what we can determine, it started with the arrival of the Asinta after Fearn's tenth birth year. Is that correct, Dair?" Dair, who had been intently watching the proceedings, nodded his head in agreement. The tanner then continued. "We've had very few fail the test of the flower here—of those who have had their children tested. Fearn is the latest to fail that we know of. We spoke to the families who have had one grow up in their homes, and most found their powers when they were between ten and twelve." There was a loud murmuring from the crowd, villagers looking towards the families that the Tanner was referring to. The tanner raised a hand, and after the murmuring quieted down, he continued. "Several farmers were very generous in helping Dair deal with the lull weed we have all been plagued with. Some farmers have many hands that can help them out and were gracious to spare a pair to help one who did not. We are grateful that they chose Dainua's path and will be blessed by her for doing so."

The self-made priestess called out, "All hail Dainua and her son Fearn!" The crowd around her erupted into yelling and bickering. A few men came to blows and had to be dragged out of the tavern.

Once order was restored, the tanner continued. "As I was saying, some farmers were kind enough to lend a hand to Dair. Sadly, while one of the boys was helping out, he was attacked and killed. Fearn here came upon the attacker and was attacked himself, according to Dair. No one else has heard Fearn's account of this meeting. So, Fearn, we would like you to stand and tell us what happened that day." All eyes in the room shifted to Fearn. He felt his stomach lurch before it dropped to the floor. His mind raced and he looked at his dad then timidly glanced around the room. He breathed out slowly, stood, and spoke.

"This all started a few days before the attack. Dad and I were eating a vegetable soup not unlike the one we had tonight. When it was time to leave a bowl for the deamhon by the woods, I opened the door and noticed that all of the sounds in the forest were gone, and the night seemed blacker—the stars dimmer. Dad pulled me back inside just in time. He had seen a deamhon come by the farm before and knew what signs to look for. He grabbed the bowl in my hands and hurriedly placed it outside our door, shutting and barring it behind him. Dad put his fingers to his lips, and we stood there in silence, each of us not daring to say a word or move from the very spot on which we stood." Fearn paused and looked around. Every eye in the room transfixed on him. He glanced at his dad, who gave a curt nod, and Fearn continued on. "I noticed that I was holding my breath, but right when I was about to let it out, our horse let out a horrible squeal. We both thought for sure it had been attacked. Then, we heard something large outside the walls. Its footsteps shook the house. The house started to shift as the boards strained. It was trying to push the walls in. A few boards along the top of the house cracked, but the house did not give. Then, suddenly, nothing. We couldn't do anything but wait and listen. We heard the bowl being picked up. A great slurping sound followed—then the sound of pottery shattering. The deamhon hurled itself against the door. Our cross bar shook under its immense weight. My dad, being quick, grabbed our table and urged me to grab the other side. We picked it up and pushed it against the door and braced ourselves against it. It was great thinking on his part or we wouldn't be here today.

"The deamhon smashed against the door over and over, but, luckily, it didn't give. We sat there, straining to keep the table in place, and after what felt like days, it finally gave up and left.

"We didn't dare move in fear it would return. I looked at my dad and told him that I had been telling him for years that his soup wasn't good enough for the horse and I finally had proof that it was definitely not good enough for a deamhon." Fearn paused. The laughter he wanted came but not as loud as he hoped. He glanced at his dad, who was sitting there smiling, before continuing. "We both slept against the table that night, and a long night it was.

"A few days later, I was in the woods gathering firewood. I had to go further in since the pickings were slim and I didn't want to damage the trees I had trimmed any further. As I walked, the light in the forest dimmed as though evening was coming, but I knew it to be mid-morning at that point. I slowed down and crept further in and noticed there wasn't a single sound in the forest—not the sound of a bird or even an animal scurrying through the underbrush. The air was still and smelt stale. I thought of the deamhon at our house and turned to head back when I heard a blood-curdling scream. I looked at my hatchet and made up my mind: I had to help.

"I crept closer to where the screams came from and then, just as suddenly as the screaming had broken the silence in the woods, the silence flooded back like a weight pressing around me. I walked around a tree and saw the boy lying there in the clearing, his body naked in the dirt. One leg was bent across his back, an arm was torn off, and his head turned completely around, staring blankly at the sky above him. I could tell from his face that it was the farm worker I had seen helping my dad. Above him was an old man, one that I couldn't imagine having the strength to do the terrors that had been inflicted.

"The man stared down at the boy as he dressed himself in what I assumed were the boy's clothes. I began to turn away to get help, and as I did, a branch snapped under my foot. It broke the silence like a hammer on an anvil. I slowly turned around and the old man who had been about fifteen pebbles away was suddenly right there behind me. I have never seen anyone move that fast or silently before. I didn't have time to run or scream for help. I knew I was his and the fate of the boy in the clearing was soon to be mine. The old man picked me up and threw me across the clearing. When I landed, I hit a rock and a loud crack erupted from my chest. I struggled for breath but no matter how much I gasped, I couldn't find any. I lay face down in the dirt, clawing at it, trying to crawl away. A heavy foot pressed against my side and rolled me over. I looked up at the old man and pleaded for my life between gasps of breath. He sneered, and as he did, his face contorted until he looked like a feral dog about to strike. He stomped my stomach, and the little air left in me raced out. I groaned and tried again to implore him to stop but was unable to breathe, which left me light-headed and blackness started to envelop me. I struggled to breathe in so I could beg him to stop or just end it quickly.

"The old man bent down. I could smell his breath; it smelled of rotten meat. His nose twitched as he sniffed me. He stood up in surprise and started to laugh, a laugh that sounded like two stones being ground together. He danced around, pointing at me, seeming as spry as a man half his age. He stopped and dropped to his knees, his face hovering just above mine. 'You're the boy from the farm I visited the other night with that horrible soup. You aren't safe now, are you?' he rasped. His head tilted back as he laughed again, then licked his lips with a tongue black as soot. He swung his head forward into mine, smashing my nose and causing blood to spray out onto his face. That long, thick black tongue slowly slid out of his mouth and licked my blood from his cheek. He seemed to savor every last drop of it. This gave me enough time to catch my breath and finally speak. 'You don't look like a deamhon,' I said. 'You're but an old man. The deamhon that came knocking had the strength of a man twice your size.' He didn't say a thing. He just looked at me as drool dripped onto my face; it was hot and thick and clung to my cheek like a snail as it slowly slid. He then spoke, slowly and quietly: 'Boy, this is how we look during the day. We blend in so we can befriend you, telling you how we are lost and only need a place for the night, only to transform into our true shape to kill you in your sleep, to drink your blood, and feast upon your bones. I think you will be especially tasty tonight.' He stood and, as he did, the air around me felt fresher. Grateful I could breathe in the cool forest air, I turned to face him. As I did, I saw his foot coming right at me. The force whipped my head back. Then, it kicked again, and my vision blurred and darkened, pain searing through me. I felt like meat on a hot pan. The only thought I had was to plead for Dainua to take me because I couldn't bear the anguish any longer. As Dainua entered my thoughts, the ground shook beneath me. I heard a loud cry from the deamhon. I turned my head and looked from my eye that wasn't swollen shut, and I could see a tree lifting from the forest floor, its branches moving like arms and lifting up the deamhon. It struggled and kicked, clawing at the branches, until the deamhon finally slowed and only the briefest twitch could be seen. I felt a soft sensation under me like I was being lifted up in a blanket. Grass was growing all around me. A sudden peace overcame me; I collapsed, waiting to be borne away by Dainua. When that didn't happen, I struggled to stand and managed to find my way home. The last thing I recall is seeing my dad's face briefly, then a sweet darkness that bore away my pain." Fearn finished, hoping that all of the hard work he had done with his dad would pay off, and sat back down. His dad reached over and patted him on the knee. "Well done, boy," he whispered.

The tanner stood up after Fearn was seated. "Well, that matches what your dad told us you said to him." He looked at the other men at the table and they all nodded in agreement. Then, he turned to the rest of the room. "Anyone here have any questions for Fearn?" The mother of the boy who was killed stood up, sobbing, "What happened to my son? Why didn't Dainua save him?" She slumped into her chair. Fearn slowly stood up, not sure what to say.

"I don't recall seeing him when I left the clearing, I'm sorry. I was eager to leave and find help."

"This is proof that Dainua has been angered by our lack of faith and given us a son in her name to lead us. Fearn, tell us what we must do," the self-proclaimed priestess called out.

Another voice rang out: "This is the reason we cannot trust strangers. I have told my wife for years that we have deamhons living amongst us."

Dissent broke out in the room, some calling for Fearn to stand and preach to them, while others yelled that he was a deamhon mocking Dainua and was actually there to lead them astray.

With help from a few men, the tanner was able to restore order.

"Now that we have calmed down, let's get back to the business at hand. We know what happened in the forest. Now, please, Fearn, tell us what happened to the crops and turning the deamhon into stone."

This part was the easy part. Dair really didn't have an explanation for it, except that Fearn couldn't be a Crop Burner. Fearn stood and addressed the room again. "I don't recall anything that night except for a dream where I awoke and found our door wide open. A beautiful lady stood in the doorway. A brilliant light seemed to glow off of her, so much so I had to avert my eyes. I knew in my heart it was Dainua. She beckoned me to follow, so I fell in beside her and we walked. When we got to our field, she turned to me and kissed my forehead before stating in a motherly voice, "You will have the power to grow and not burn crops." She directed me to wave my hand, and as I did, the lull weeds shrank and the crops grew. We then went to the tree where the deamhon hung." This was where Dair wanted Fearn to stop—to tell the room that that is when he woke up. However, something struck Fearn, and he looked towards his unwanted followers, hoping this next part would appease their desires and they would leave him alone.

"She showed me the clearing and explained that the grass was a representation of herself, pure and unblemished. The tree was the world where her powers flowed, and the man is us, blemished, hanging by the neck to represent our frailty. She showed me how she is there to support us. That is when I was awakened by my dad." Fearn looked around the silent room, trying to judge whether or not they believed his story.

"Proof that Fearn has been called from Dainua! She has given him the power to heal crops for his unwavering devotion and showed him the path back to her!" the self-proclaimed priestess yelled. She pushed herself into the open space and fell at Fearn's feet, raising her hands above her head. "Fearn, show us the way!" she insisted. Then she bowed until her forehead was touching the dirt floor, arms stretched out in front of her. The other followers chanted, "Fearn, son of Dainua," then rushed forward to join their priestess, kneeling beside her.

A group of drunken villagers started yelling and pointing to Fearn. "Liar! Dainua would never speak to a tainted son of Telgog, he must be a deamhon!" One of the men threw a mug in Fearn's direction, hitting the table in front of him. The followers stood and turned on the group. A brawl broke out, cups and dishes hurled in both directions; a few folks picked up chairs and tried using them as clubs. Most didn't care who was who and swung at the closest person to them. Dair stood and kept himself between the brawlers and Fearn as best he could.

After some time, the rest of those in attendance managed to break up the fighting and ushered the brawlers out of the tavern, many of them cursing Fearn until the tavern door shut behind them. The self-proclaimed priestess was knocked unconscious during the fight; her followers lifted her and left as well. Fearn looked around the mostly empty tavern covered in broken bowls, plates, and chairs, with food scattered across the floor in puddles of spilled ale. He turned to his dad and asked, "Why is it that no matter what I do, I can never do anything right?"

"Boy, I told you to keep the tale of the tree out of this. If you would have just listened," Dair said.

Not knowing what to say, Fearn just stared at the table.

"Well, this night could have gone better," the tanner remarked as he stood in the middle of the room looking around. "Dair, I think you better keep Fearn out of sight for a while until things simmer down. I do have two final questions to ask Fearn. The first is: do you think you can help the other farmers' crops like you did with your dad's? It may help ease the tensions." Fearn shrugged. "I don't know. It was a dream. I can pray to Dainua and see if I can have another dream to help the other fields."

A farmer stood. "How do we know that it actually healed the crops and didn't poison them? We are just going off of his word. How do we know we can trust him?" The farmer then looked quickly around, hoping he wasn't starting another fight but finding that he said the one thing that everyone seemed to agree on.

As if on cue, Cromm stepped forward with the bag of vegetables that his dad had given him and held it up. "Dair gave me two bags of vegetables. I used one of them to cook the stew you just ate." There was an audible gasp from everyone in the room. Some stood up and yelled that it wasn't his right to test the vegetables out on them. Others proclaimed how wonderful the stew was and how they felt closer to Dainua while eating it—only they were afraid of saying it out loud before. A new fight seemed to be brewing, and the tanner yelled for everyone to quiet down. An uneasy silence blanketed the room. Then, the tanner pointed to individuals and let each one have their say, making the rest sit quietly and listen. After some time, it was agreed upon that since no one in the room was dead, they were more than likely blessed from eating the stew.

"This last question is the most important one of all, Fearn, and you need to answer it honestly. Are you a Crop Burner?" Fearn felt conflicted. He looked back at everything that had happened since Uram arrived and gave him his powers. He hadn't burned any crops, but he felt like he had burned everything else around him, including the friendship with his dad. Knowing he needed to put out the fires he caused, he looked over to the tanner. "I don't know. Dainua said she blessed me. All I do know is that when the Asinta come back, I will be leaving with them. If they won't take me, I'll leave on my own."

The tanner scratched his chin for a bit and then addressed Dair. "When do you expect the Asinta to return?"

Dair quickly replied, "They usually come before the planting, but this last time, they came when summer was almost upon us." The tanner sat down and conferred with the other men at the table; after a bit, he stood and addressed the room. "We feel at this moment that the village is safe. We request that Fearn stay at the farm until the Asinta return, which includes trips to this village and any of the surrounding ones. If there are any more issues between now and then, one or both of you will be hanged. Is everyone in agreement?" Everyone in the room yelled out "Ay!" Fearn had never heard of anyone in town being hanged before but there had never been issues like this either. He looked to Dair, whose face was pale, but he refused to look back at Fearn.

Now that the proceedings were done, everyone turned back to drinking and talking amongst themselves. It was quieter and more subdued than normal. Dair grabbed Fearn's arm and told him it was best if they left.

They stood without saying a word and departed. Once outside, Dair directed Fearn to wait while he untied the horse. When Dair returned, he lifted Fearn into the saddle and turned towards home.

ᛁNTO THE ᗡARKNESS

The sky was overcast, not a single star to be seen. Dair lit the lantern he brought and held it in front of him while he led the horse down the road. Once they were outside of the village, Fearn spoke up: "You only gave Cromm one bag of vegetables. Why did he say you gave him two?" Without looking back Dair replied, "I knew there was no way I could sell those vegetables unless everyone thought they were safe. I convinced Cromm that they were and told him he would get a portion of the money made in selling them. Honestly, I think he went along with it just to see everyone's faces once he told them what he had done."

"But why not just make a stew of the vegetables if he thought they were safe?" Fearn asked.

"Because, despite cutting him in on the deal and the fact that I told him we had eaten them, he still didn't trust feeding them to the entire village," Dair replied. Fearn frowned in confusion. Dair continued, "By the way, Fearn, adding the soup to the tale was clever."

As they neared home, they noticed a bright light in the distance. Dair stopped short and looked back at Fearn. "That's a bad sign. Get off the horse in case we need to flee into the woods." Dair reached into his cloak and removed the hatchet from his belt. Fearn slowly climbed out of the saddle, his heart racing, and untied his oska from the saddle, then crept over to his dad who hadn't moved.

111

"Dad, what's wrong?"

"That's a fire in the distance. A big one by the looks of it. Better take it slowly from here."

Dair opened his lantern and blew out the flame. They moved cautiously down the road in the dark. Fearn had to lean on his oska since his feet still hurt. The glowing in the distance grew brighter as they crept closer. When they had gotten a quarter stone down the road, they realized it was their house and stable in flames.

Dair held out a hand to stop Fearn. "Whoever set this more than likely hasn't seen us yet." Dair looked around closely, and feeling safe they weren't being watched, knelt in front of Fearn. "Boy, I need you to stay in the woods. I will sneak down the road myself. When it is safe, I will come back and get you. No matter what happens, don't leave the woods. Now, get going." Fearn looked from his dad to the farm, then nodded and headed for the woods to the north. Just as he was about to enter the trees, his dad called in a hushed voice. "Fearn, remember to stay in the trees, no matter what, and... " Dair paused, and Fearn turned to look at him. Dair was struggling to say something. "Never mind. Just be careful, and stay out of sight." Dair turned and, without looking back, crept towards the farm. The clouds parted and starlight lit Fearn's path. He whispered a thanks to Dainua before slipping quietly into the trees. He stayed far enough back so as not to be noticed from the road but near enough to keep an eye on Dair.

From the cover of the trees, Fearn kept pace with his dad, who was leading the horse slowly to the house. As he walked past the path his dad created, Fearn looked to his left at his mom's grave, shrouded in darkness, causing a sudden chill to run up his spine. He looked back towards his dad. They had gotten about halfway down the length of the field when suddenly his dad staggered and dropped to his knees. Dair looked down at his chest, but Fearn couldn't tell what he was looking at. Fearn could hear him gasping loudly. Dair pulled the reins in his hands, trying to lift himself up, and looked into the woods, making sure Fearn couldn't be seen. Without warning, the horse reared up on its hind legs, the reins pulling free from Dair's hand. The front hooves of the horse kicked out and made contact with the back of Dair's head. A loud crack erupted and echoed back from the surrounding trees. Dair collapsed forward in a heap, his body jerking strangely as it went down. The horse cried out again, spun in a circle, stumbled, and fell over, its legs kicking out in front. It struggled to stand up but collapsed with bleats of anguish. Fearn began to cry as he noticed two arrows protruding from the side of the horse. He suddenly felt very vulnerable. He crouched down as fast as he could without making a sound and closed his eyes. He saw his dad, whose sul was dripping out like blood into the ground. Fearn was pretty sure he was still alive. There was another smaller sul jutting out from his dad's back; he realized the sul was an arrow. He looked over the horse whose sul was flowing out as it continued to flail about. Through the weak glow of suls in the field, Fearn concentrated on locating the suls of those who attacked them. Off in the distance, he could faintly make out what he thought were people hidden in the field nearest the house with the fire to their backs, but didn't see anyone closer. Glancing back at his dad, Fearn knew he had to do something. The tale his dad told of his parents, of how Dair stood in the woods and watched his parents die, crystalized in Fearn's mind.

Fearn didn't hesitate. He dashed out of the woods and slid sideways across the road next to the horse. He patted the side of it, which was slick with sweat and blood; it seemed to calm down some, then quickly struggled to get up again. As Fearn looked at the wounds, he saw that each time the horse strained, they bled more. He closed his eyes and focused on his oska, pouring the suls he had inside into the ground. Fearn ran his hand down the back of the horse, trying to calm it while he pulled its sul into his oska. The horse stopped struggling, each breath becoming shallower than the last. Fearn watched as the dark brown hair on the horse turned silver in the firelight, and he stopped pulling only when there was a faint breath of sul left, which quickly seeped out into Dainua. Looking over the top of the horse, Fearn saw the men hadn't moved, though they had to have seen him when he ran across the road. Fearn crawled around the front of the horse's body, keeping it between himself and the attackers. He peered around the other side and tried to judge the distance between himself and Dair. The gap seemed immense, even though it was only a few paces. Quickly, he crouched and dashed to his dad's side, sliding just before he got there; unfortunately, he misjudged the distance and crashed into Dair, causing him to groan.

Relief washed over Fearn; his dad was still alive. A loud swooshing noise sped past Fearn's head. When he glanced back, an arrow was sticking out of the dirt. The attackers had seen him. He waited for the second arrow while worrying about his next move, but nothing happened. Looking towards the farm, he could see that they were creeping closer. Dair's face was covered in blood and mud from the road. As Dair breathed out, Fearn could hear bubbling and sucking noises coming from the wound in his back and noticed that not only did he have the arrow through his chest but there was another shaft broken off. Fearn didn't know where it had hit his dad. The back of Dair's head was a mess of blood and hair. His eyes fluttered open, and he tried to lift his head out of the mud to look at Fearn.

"I told you to stay away," Dair croaked out, each word sending pain radiating through his chest. Dair lifted his arm and reached out, groping, and Fearn grasped it. Dair squeezed tightly. He moved his head, trying to focus on his boy, then weakly whispered "Son... I'm sorry. I was too stubborn to see it. Your mom was right; Fearn was the right name." Dair's eyes closed, and his head dropped back into the bloody mud, his hand limp in Fearn's.

"No, Dad, please don't go! I don't know what to do without you!" Fearn blurted out, tears now streaming down his face. Ignoring the whistling of an arrow as it flew past his head and hit the horse behind him, Fearn closed his eyes and looked for the attackers' suls; they were much closer. Anger and hatred welled up inside him. He reached out and could feel the closest man's sul; he yanked with everything he had and a brief scream emanated from the darkness. The distance was too great and Fearn was only able to pull a small portion of the sul. Hatred flared briefly in Fearn as the sul entered him, but not wanting any part of the man, Fearn let it slip from him and into Dainua. The hatred quickly dissipated.

"Back up! Don't wander too close or he'll kill you," someone called out. Fearn watched as the men backed up, then he saw two small suls rushing at him. Quickly, he rolled away, both arrows hitting the ground where he had just been. Dair coughed up blood, causing spasms to rack his body. Fearn crawled back to his dad and grabbed his dad's hand again. Sobbing audibly, Fearn understood there was only one thing he could do for him. As he slowly pulled his dad's sul out and pushed it into his oska, a feeling of guilt and sadness washed over him. He watched his dad age before him, something his dad would never get to see Fearn do. Leaving only a small bit behind, he watched as it bled into Dainua and flowed away with her.

"Dad, don't leave me. I don't know what to do," Fearn whispered, as tears stained his cheeks.

Realizing he had little time, Fearn grabbed the hatchet from where his dad had dropped it, turned, and leapt over the horse. A few arrows flew overhead as he landed in the shelter of the horse's body. Looking up, he saw more men coming from the west. He wouldn't be able to kill all of them, so he turned and ran for the woods. He didn't hear or see any arrows as he disappeared into the shadows, Fearn hid behind the nearest tree and closed his eyes. The men were grouping, their leader making sure they kept their distance. Fearn hurried through the woods towards the house, not even noticing the fresh cuts to his feet. He stopped and looked back out at the road, waiting for the men to dash across it. The leader finally emerged from the field and walked up to his dad, stabbed something into the body, then looked down the road directly at where Fearn was hiding in the trees.

"Boy, I know you're out there, and we'll find you! Come on boys, let's get the deamhon!" The leader yelled in an accent that was not familiar to Fearn. The other men stepped from the field behind the leader. Thinking fast, Fearn looked at the house, where the flames had started to die down.

Fearn ran away from the men while remaining parallel to the road. An insanely mad idea struck him then, and he stopped and looked back at the men. Doing this would more than likely kill him, he thought, but maybe he could kill the men in the process. He dashed out into the road near the house and stopped. He looked straight at the man nearest his dad and lifted his oska and hatchet into the air.

"Come get me!" Fearn yelled, then turned and sprinted towards his house and into the thick smoke surrounding it. His eyes burned and, in the haze, he stepped on a rock, lurched in pain, stumbled, and fell. He rolled over, grateful he hadn't landed on the hatchet. Fearn squinted through the smoke to glimpse the men walking down the road towards him. He pushed himself up and ran on, hoping his feet wouldn't fail him. After only a few paces, an arrow hit the ground off to Fearn's left; he turned right and then left, hoping that if he weaved like a rabbit, he would be harder to hit, especially with the smoke between them. He stumbled again and saw another sul flying as he dove to the right, trying not to fall on the hatchet as he hit the ground. The arrow grazed his calf, pinning his pants to the ground. He turned and pulled at his pant leg, trying to rip it free. He closed his eyes and saw the leader was getting closer; he might be able to kill one, but the others would be on him too soon. Instead, he yanked harder until his pants finally tore free. Not having enough time to weave, Fearn dashed to the tree line. The man yelled behind him, "We can track you all night, deamhon. No matter where you go, we will find you!" The rest of the group laughed in response.

Strangely, Fearn hoped they could track him or what he was about to do would be in vain. After a few paces into the trees, Fearn tried to judge where the clearing with the hanged man was; he used that to gauge the direction he needed to go. He headed east, stopping now and again to see where the men were. They had lit lanterns and were still on his track, keeping their distance from him. As Fearn ran on, the men called out to taunt him. It felt like hours had passed, and he was about to turn to go a different direction; he thought he must have miscalculated and gone the wrong way. Suddenly, he stumbled out into the clearing, and there in front of him was the blackened hill.

The sky was an infinite black; the stars had disappeared behind the clouds. If Fearn didn't know there was a hill in front of him, he would have thought he stumbled upon an endless nothingness. Closing his eyes, Fearn looked at the hill. It looked as empty as the sky above him and acted like a dam to the powers of Dainua when they reached its edge. The energy splashed against the hill and flowed around its perimeter. Not a single sul could be seen in the blackened earth. Fearn looked back, and the men were drawing nearer. Taking a deep breath, Fearn climbed up the hill, feeling like he was rising into the heavens. Fearn closed his eyes briefly partway up and felt that he was in a void. Not being able to feel or see Dainua, he began to realize how quickly he had come to rely on her constant companionship. The feel of the oska in his hand reassured him; his dad was with him. Once he was at the top of the hill, Fearn ran into something solid. He realized it was one of the standing stones on top of the hill he had seen when he was here previously. Cautiously making his way around it, Fearn tripped over something. Slowly reaching down while staying alert for any movements or sounds, he picked up the object. It felt like a shovel head with bits of broken wood protruding where the handle should have been. Crouching down, Fearn discarded the shovel, set the hatchet down, and felt around to see if there was anything else he could use. His hand came across a hole; nervously, he felt around. The hole felt perfectly square and seemed just big enough for him to squeeze into. Tilting his head, Fearn listened for any sounds coming from within, but it was eerily silent. Kneeling, Fearn crawled to peer around one of the large standing stones to see where his pursuers were; he could see the lanterns just through the tree line. Being careful of the hole, Fearn searched around again, desperate to find something, anything, that could be used as a weapon. His hand brushed a strange round stone. He picked it up; it had odd holes in the front and was smooth on top. It felt familiar, but he couldn't place it. Just as he was lifting it up, the clouds broke, and there, illuminated by starlight, was a skull staring right at him. Fearn gave a sharp yelp, dropped the skull, and scrambled backward, almost falling into the hole. He knocked his hatchet down into it, and as he scrambled to keep from falling in himself, he listened to the hatchet bounced off of unseen walls until he could only hear a trickle of dirt. A few moments later, when no noises came from the hole, Fearn noticed every muscle in his body was tense, and he was holding his breath. Slowly, he relaxed and breathed out, glancing back to where he had dropped the skull.

What am I doing here? Fearn thought. *I have to get off this hill.* He scrambled to his feet, making sure to avoid the hole. He glanced around the standing stone again and saw the lanterns at the foot of the hill, muffled voices drifting up. He looked behind himself, hoping he could get down the other side of the hill without being noticed. One of the lanterns started up the hill, the others headed left and right; the hill would soon be encircled. Fearn was trapped.

"What am I going to do?" Fearn asked himself. The ground underneath him shifted and he fell, not down the hill but into it, hitting something hard, dirt and rocks raining down on him. The floor shifted again, and he fell even further than he had the first time, crashing into another floor, with large stones and dirt strewn around him. Fearn's heart raced as he looked up. The small amount of starlight above briefly illuminated the walls that ran straight up around him. A scraping sound came from somewhere off in the darkness, echoing off the walls, making it impossible to determine where it was coming from. As it grew closer, it sounded like an animal's claws trying to find purchase when desperately trying to scale a wall. The sound became clearer the closer it got, now like the sound of a knife being dragged across stone. Fearn tried to back up, but the dirt, rocks, and stones around him prevented him from moving, so he grabbed the nearest rock and flung it in the direction of the sound. It didn't deter whatever it was; it kept coming towards him. Abruptly, Fearn realized he didn't have his oska. He flailed around until finally, his hand fell on it; he grasped it tightly and pulled it to his chest, comforted that he'd have his dad with him when he died.

A cold chill fell over Fearn. Something icy grasped his leg and pulled him closer to it.

"*The wraith!*" Fearn's mind screamed.

The coldness ate into him until his bones shivered as the wraith slowly crawled on top of him. A voice, deep and guttural, spoke: "Trying to steal from me? It will be the last thing you do." The wraith then paused; Fearn, too afraid to close his eyes and look at it, forced his eyes to stay open as his teeth started to chatter.

"I know you," the wraith hissed out at him. The wraith pushed down, pressing the oska into Fearn, which reminded him why he was there.

"Please, help me first before you kill me. They killed my father, please help," Fearn squeaked between chattering teeth. The wraith paused as faint footsteps echoed off the wall of the pit from above. Suddenly, it pushed Fearn down and sped up the tunnel away from him. A few moments passed; then, primal screams tore through the forest and down into the pit, piercing into Fearn's skull as he wondered what was going to happen to him. A horrible ripping noise, like a chicken's leg torn from the carcass, came from the edge of the pit above, followed by pleading, and then gurgling. Fearn wondered what noise he would make before he died as he lay there wondering what to do. He knew he couldn't climb out of the hole, but maybe there was another way out. Getting to his feet, Fearn headed in the direction the wraith had come, arms outstretched, feet shuffling across the floor to avoid tripping. Finding a wall of stone as smooth as ice to his left, Fearn followed it deeper into the hill. Stopping briefly, Fearn felt the floor slick beneath his feet and noticed it was made of the same stone.

Why would someone waste perfectly good stone for a floor? he thought as he stood and continued searching, using his oska to sweep around to find any hidden obstacles. Fearn finally came upon another wall. He was about to start moving to his right to see if he could find another tunnel when he heard scraping sounds coming from behind him. He clutched his oska and turned, pressing his back against the wall. Parts of it were jagged and bit into his skin. As the wraith drew near, the scraping sounds changed to the sound of cloth being dragged across the floor. The air grew colder as the wraith approached; it stopped a few paces away from Fearn. The swishing sound came again, then nothing. Fearn hugged his dad—no oska— to his chest and waited for the inevitable.

BARROW

The wraith finally spoke mockingly. "Why did you come here, fool? To have me kill those men and then expect me to pity you and let you live?"

Fearn stared into the darkness, not being able to see the wraith. He breathed in slowly and bravely closed his eyes. There, floating in blackness devoid of Dainua, the wraith seemed more ominous. When Fearn had fought the wraith at the farm, he was only able to get glimpses of it. Indeed, it was a sul without a vessel. It ebbed and flowed like a sul but didn't seek out Dainua like every sul he had seen that had escaped its corporeal husk. It also had a faint resemblance to the silhouette of a man. At the top of the wraith's shoulders, part of the sul flowed behind it like a cloak that went all the way to the ground. Its arms were faint and ragged, and the hands were claws instead of fingers. There were no legs—just the torn cloth of the cloak which shifted back and forth across the floor. All of the suls that Fearn had seen were clear; yet, this one looked like a storm cloud just before lightning. Inside the wraith's chest was a fresh sul that fought vigorously to get free of the four ghostly fangs that held it in place. Fearn shrank back as he realized the wraith was feeding on it. Fearn slowly shifted his eyes to the wraith's face which manifested as a thick mist; then, like a stone dropped into a pond, a menacing grin rippled across it before fading away into placid stillness. As

Fearn caught a brief glimpse of the wraith's eyes, they seemed to bore into him. It didn't speak a word. Fearn looked down at his dad clutched to his chest, his sul flowing and intertwining with that of the horse's sul inside the oska.

Fearn, finding comfort in having his dad close to him, summoned the courage to speak: "Those men out there killed my dad." As the word 'dad' left his mouth, Fearn hugged the oska closer to himself. "I hoped that if I came here, you would kill them before you killed me." Fearn took a deep breath and opened his eyes so he didn't have to see it coming. Then, with the last bit of courage he could muster and the comfort of knowing his dad was him, Fearn bravely concluded, "I'm ready."

Fearn held his breath, waiting for his sul to be ripped from his body, but nothing happened. Then his strength and will faltered and he started to cry. "Why are you torturing me?" Fearn blurted out, tears streaming down his cheeks.

The wraith finally spoke, not noticing or caring for Fearn's emotional distress. "There was an Asinta that visited my barrow, and I felt its strong power. When I went to seek it out that night, I mistook the power I sensed at your farm for him. When I realized you were not that Asinta, but one just blossoming, I decided to have you as a snack before my feast." The word *feast* came out wet and hissing. "I misjudged your power, though." Fearn could hear it move, the faint noise of its cloak swishing back and forth rhythmically.

"I let my guard down and almost let you steal the only power I had. It was a terrible mistake, which left me weakened and unable to continue my hunt." The wraith paused for a moment, contemplating its next words carefully. "Very few could have done what you did that night. There is a power in you that you have yet to realize." The teeth in the wraith's chest bit down harder on its prey. He continued, "A power I hunger to taste... " The wraith paused. Fearn thought back to the day he stumbled upon the hill with Uram. Why hadn't the wraith sensed him? Fearn didn't keep his guard up and spoke openly, expecting that he was to be killed once the wraith was done playing with him.

"O, you must have felt Uram," Fearn said." He was my teacher. I was with him when we accidentally came across your home. He hadn't shown me my powers yet." The rhythmic sweeping stopped, and the wraith's voice became friendlier and sweeter. "This Uram you speak of—I knew a man of that name. What was it that he taught you to make you so powerful and strong?"

Fearn thought back on Uram's lesson as he stared into the darkness. There is nothing he could say about the teachings from Uram that the wraith surely didn't already know; plus, maybe, if he told the wraith everything, it may let him go. Fearn recounted the details of that day, not closing his eyes, but instead feeling more comfortable speaking into the darkness, almost like he was talking to himself. The wraith didn't interrupt once during Fearn's retelling of that day.

Once Fearn was done, the wraith spoke, urging Fearn to tell more. "What do you know of the men who attacked you tonight?" it asked. Fearn shrugged, "I don't know who they were. We had a meeting at the tavern about what to do with me after everything that happened, so they were probably some of the men that were there." Fearn paused. He wasn't sure what to tell or not to tell it. Sitting in the dark, speaking out loud about everything that happened to him seemed cathartic, like a weight he wasn't aware he had been carrying was lifted from his shoulders. The wraith didn't say a word, only waiting for Fearn to continue. Fearn then poured out everything that had happened to him since Uram arrived. There was no telling of tales—just the truth. When Fearn finished, he leaned his head against the wall; it felt wonderful to tell someone or something the truth, instead of hiding who he was.

The wraith spoke up. "This is the Uram I knew. I am sure of it."

"Who were those men? Were they men from the village?" Fearn asked, hoping to get some answers in return.

"That does not matter. Your sul is mine now." The wraith drew closer, and cold enveloped and flowed around Fearn as if he was plunged into an icy river. Something sharp slowly moved up Fearn's chest to his neck. The cold grip of the wraith felt like a metal rod left out in the cold of winter as its hand clutched Fearn's neck and slowly started to squeeze. Fearn struggled, but the wraith was too strong and the cold sapped his strength. Suddenly, the wraith stopped and its hand relaxed, but it did not withdraw.

"I could use someone with your power if it was bent to my will and honed with my knowledge. What do you say, commoner? Is it death or servitude?" The wraith's voice had a hint of mirth: it was enjoying playing with its prey.

Fearn shook, but he wasn't sure if it was from the cold or the fear that gripped him. His mind raced with what to do. He desperately didn't want to die, but he wasn't sure what servitude meant. It surely couldn't be any worse than life on a farm, he tried to convince himself. Maybe he could find a means of escape if he agreed. So, he steadied himself as best he could and replied, "I choose servitude."

The wraith cackled, "That is a wise decision. First, introductions: I am Airnin, the keeper of the Asinta, or I was before I was betrayed." Airnin retracted his hand from Fearn's neck but didn't move back.

"My name is Fearn the Tiller. What is it that you want? You also never said who those men were who attacked us."

Fearn heard Airnin slide away from him a bit, and the cold he felt subsided some. After a long pause, Airnin replied silkily, "Those were the king's men that pursued you. You serve me, and in return, you will get the information you seek. I can tell you everything you need to know about the Asinta and teach you what you need to avenge your father's death. Also, you will get something far more important than knowledge. I will show you how to harness suls to do great and powerful things. In return, you will help me regain my throne." Fearn mulled over Airnin's words in confusion, then said the first thing that came to mind: "So, you aren't going to kill me?"

"As I have said, I have a use for you, and I have learned that useful things should never be discarded. Would you throw away something that was useful?"

"Well, no, I guess not," Fearn said, still unsure what Airnin really wanted him for.

"Ah, wisdom at such a young age, and from one that is so dull-witted; how refreshing. I suppose you are going to want something to sleep on and food to eat. I have never had the want or need of a pet, but sacrifices must be made, I suppose. You just better be worth the effort. It is still early enough. You stay here and I will get you what you need, but nothing more. Do not think of wandering off or I will run you down and gut you from belly to neck before I pull your sul from you," Airnin warned.

Fearn, still not wanting to look at Airnin, just stared into the dark. *What should I do?* he wondered. The images of the sul torn in half raced through his mind, and he could taste bile as he recalled the sensation the sul gave him of its stomach being ripped open. It was something he would do anything not to experience himself. What other choice did he have?

"I will stay," Fearn responded shakily.

"Good," Airnin said proudly. "Stay here. I will be back. I will also look for any other men who are seeking you and draw them away from here." The swishing noise faded away. Fearn looked around in the dark, wishing that he could see. He hated the dark; he had always had the faint light from the fireplace to keep him company. His mind drifted back to Airnin; what did he want with him? Servitude started to feel like something he did not want. Suddenly, Fearn heard Airnin approach.

"Fearn, here is a lamp to stamp out the darkness of this place." The echo of metal rang out through the room before Airnin continued. "Oh, if you do run, please make it a challenge; it has been so long since I have had such fun," Airnin said sarcastically. Fearn closed his eyes and looked into Airnin's face, not seeing any anger or malice ripple across it. It was calm and emotionless.

"If I stay, do you promise to protect me from... " Fearn paused, then wondered if there was anything outside of this place that he could fear more than the wraith. Before he could find the words, Airnin interrupted.

"I suppose that if you are to serve your purpose, I cannot have you cowering like a beaten dog all of the time. I will make this one promise. You do as I ask, and in return, this will be a safe place for you. You will have no need to fear me or anything outside of here, understood?"

"Yes," Fearn replied, though he didn't think he would ever feel safe again.

"Good, now I must hurry; I must be back before first light," Airnin said as he turned and left.

Fearn groped around in the dark until he found the lantern that Airnin had set down; there was a dent on one side as if it had been dropped, and next to it was a stone and iron to light it. Fearn lit the lantern, and the warm glow relaxed the tension in his body.

He peered around and noticed he was in a large room; the floor, walls, ceiling, and a large rectangle in the center of the room were all made from the same glossy black stone.

Fearn stood, clutched the oska in his hand, and thinking of his dad's sul inside, carefully leaned it against the wall, then put his hand to the stone. It was unlike any rock that Fearn had seen. When he closed his eyes, there was just emptiness. "How could something block me from seeing suls or Dainua?" he wondered. Fearn looked closer and saw the stone resembled objects after their sul had been removed, but stone didn't have a sul; he was sure of it. As he ran his hand across the stone, he noticed some of the stones had corners as sharp as a knife's edge. How had someone managed to make this? Fearn was perplexed. He grabbed his oska and slowly made his way around the perimeter of the room. Everywhere he looked, it was the same stone. Even the only tunnel in or out of the room was made from the same stone. Fearn walked through the tunnel into the large circular room that had vertical walls running straight up all around him. He glanced briefly to the clouds above before scanning the walls and finding no way out.

Fearn returned to the inner chamber and walked to the large rectangle in the middle of the room. These stone blocks were smooth, and each fit together perfectly; not a gap nor mortar like he had seen in the chimney back home could be found. His mind drifted to home, a place he thought he would never miss if he got the chance to leave, but now he longed for it. As he walked around the rectangle, several of the stones were lying on the floor. He couldn't tell where they were missing from, so he bent down to investigate, noticing a large hole at the bottom of the rectangle. He held up the lantern and peered inside. A pure white leg and the foot bone of a skeleton peeked through fabric that had rotted and clung to the bones like moss on a tree. He thought of the skull he saw on the hill. Did it belong to this skeleton? He couldn't see anything else and was too afraid to reach in to feel around. He stood up and looked around again, realizing that he must be in a crypt like the ones in the tales his dad told; however, those were always full of treasure. Remembering his dad brought tears to his eyes again. Quickly wiping them away, he held his oska and told himself, "He's still with me."

Fearn walked through the tunnel again, certain there had to be a way out. Back in the circular room, Fearn went to the walls and looked closer; they too were made from the same perfectly placed stones with the occasional razor-sharp edge. He felt a breeze and looked up, noticing that some of the stones on the wall opposite him were recessed, giving someone what they needed to climb out. He looked up at the opening above him and estimated it had to be about three times as tall as his dad had been. As he stared up, the clouds parted and the stars shone brightly down on him, reflecting off the stones and surrounding Fearn in starlight. It was the most amazing thing he had ever seen. He turned in a circle, imagining that this had to be what it was like to be amongst the stars. Sadly, as suddenly as they appeared, they were gone, hidden once again by the clouds.

Fearn walked over to the handholds, set the lantern down, started to reach for the first gap, and then paused. "Where am I going to go?" Fearn asked himself. "I have no other home, and I can't go back to the village. The tanner said if there was another incident, I would be hanged." Fearn was quite confident this qualified as another incident. He had nowhere else to go. He dropped his hand in defeat, looked up one last time at the stars, then headed back down the tunnel.

Fearn walked around the crypt in frustration, certain he had missed something, but there was nothing else was to be found. He thought back on what Airnin had said. Did he say that the men who were after him were the king's men? Why would the king want him dead? He paced back and forth. He started getting tired, so he sat in the corner of the room across from the tunnel and blew out the lantern. He had reached the point of exhaustion, and comfort didn't really matter anymore. His head bobbed a few times until it slumped forward and he drifted off into a troubled sleep.

Fearn awoke abruptly and could hear something in the room. "Hello?" he called out, cautiously.

"It took me a few trips, but I have some supplies for you along with some food," Airnin grumbled. Fearn lit the lantern and looked up. In the light and with his eyes open Airnin was a cloaked figure shrouded in fog with a hood that appeared to hang in the air and only mist where his head should be. He appeared to float above the floor, except for the tattered cloak that dragged behind him. Next to Fearn, along the wall, were a bedroll, blankets, and pillow. There was also a plate with a mix of different scraps of meat and a bowl with some sort of soup inside.

"I was able to find the soldiers' camp, along with these supplies. I am certain they are better than what you had in your hovel. Do not ask for anything else, understood?"

Fearn just nodded his head in agreement, unsure what a hovel was.

"The camp I found had enough tents and supplies to house at least thirty men. The only soldiers I saw were those that attacked you tonight, along with the villagers who aided them." Fearn looked at the supplies and then back to Airnin.

"Thank you. Did you get the food from the camp as well?"

"No, I grabbed the food you stupid commoners leave out at night."

"Wait?! I thought you ate that?" Fearn asked in surprise. Then, he closed his eyes to look at Airnin.

Airnin shook his head in disgust. "I couldn't eat it even if I wanted to." A brief look of longing quickly rippled across Airnin's face.

Feeling foolish, Fearn muttered, "Right, it's for the deamhons. Sorry, I forgot."

Airnin broke out into mocking laughter. "Oh you fools. The animals in the forest eat the scraps you leave out. Do you think that some leftover food would appease a deamhon that could break into your home and feast on something far more delectable?"

Fearn stammered, not sure what to say, leaving his mouth agape. He had never really considered that. He thought back to the tales that his dad and other Tellers of Tales had told, and timidly replied, "Really? Are you sure?"

Airnin's laughter died, and his face rippled as he glowered at Fearn. "The only thing you had to fear around here was yourselves until that stupid boy came snooping around and freed me."

"Which boy was that?" Fearn asked, fear creeping into him as he thought back to the vision and the sul's fate he had seen.

Airnin sighed heavily, "This is the last answer you get tonight. Morning will be here soon. We both need our rest. This place you see around you was built to keep my sul from joining Dainua and to leave me tormented for eternity, the cruelest torture you will find in these lands for an Asinta. I was lucky, though; a foolish boy about your age came here, looking for treasure, I expect. After digging around and finding the entrance, he climbed down here. The only thing he saw was my tomb, so he must have decided that that was where the treasure was buried and broke into it. Once opened, I was free though powerless. When he looked in and saw only bones, he turned to leave. That was when I struck, pouncing on him, hoping that he had the powers of the Asinta. Telgog smiled on me that day, for the boy did have power, but only faintly. I stabbed him and was able to pull enough of his sul to gain some of my corporeal form back, but was too weak to subdue him. He managed to throw me off and escape. I chased him to your farm, following the tracks he left in the snow. I found him pounding on your door, but no answer came. It gave me the time I needed to attack and remove the rest of his sul. I dragged his body back here to the top of the hill, hoping someone more powerful would come looking for him. He was too young, and his powers were limited. I waited for one stronger so that I could finally regain my full power. That is where you and Uram come in; the rest you already know. Go to bed. We have long nights ahead of us. I have a feeling I am going to have to beat the lessons into you." Then, like a morning mist in the light of Farkor, Airnin faded from sight.

Fearn waited for something else to happen, and when it didn't, he grabbed the bedroll and noticed it had a soft down filling. He rolled it out in the corner opposite of the tunnel. He blew out the lantern and then lay there, staring at the ceiling.

Well, the bedroll is an upgrade from the straw one, at least, Fearn thought. He hoped he had made the right decision to stay. He noticed a faint glow out of the corner of his eye; he turned his head and watched as the light from Farkor's rising reflected off the walls in the tunnel. It reminded him of the fireplace at home. He closed his eyes and clutched his oska, grateful to still have his dad with him. He quickly fell asleep, but his dreams immediately turned into nightmares.

ꟼMBIBER

Fearn awoke to absolute blackness. He was unsure where he was at first, but the events from the previous night slowly trickled back as he rubbed the sleep out of his eyes. He reached out, and the lantern was where he had left it. He lit it but kept the flame low, not knowing when he would be able to refill it. He looked around and didn't see Airnin, so he called out, which didn't elicit a response. He looked down at his oska and closed his eyes.

"Wait, that can't be right," he said to himself. His dad's sul should have shrunk and dimmed as it slowly returned to Dainua, but it seemed to be as full as it was the night before. Maybe he didn't recall it correctly. A swishing sound startled him; he looked up and saw Airnin coming out of the tunnel, his face rippling with satisfaction.

"Good evening, or I guess I should say, good morning. These will be the hours you will be keeping from now on. I see that you made the wise decision to stay and not make me have to hunt you down."

"Well, I don't really have any place to go that would be safer than here," Fearn mumbled.

"Fearn, I promised that you would be safe here. I will not let any harm come to you that is not deserved. Here, I brought some food." Airnin's clawed hand held out a sack. As Fearn neared the wraith, he could feel Airnin's icy presence; he quickly grabbed the bag and backed up into the warmth of his corner. He sat down on his bedroll and opened the sack. There was a fresh but deformed loaf of bread, a few slices of meat, and a small chunk of cheese. He held the cheese to his nose and inhaled. He had hardly ever eaten cheese but loved the way it tasted. He put it aside to eat last, ripped a piece of bread and took a bite, then dug into the meat. Everything was delicious. He looked up partway through his dinner—no, breakfast, he reminded himself. Airnin hadn't moved, so Fearn closed his eyes and saw a look of longing that rippled into jealousy. Fearn looked down at his meal and felt guilty that Airnin had brought all of this food and he didn't even offer to share any. Fearn looked at what was left, reluctantly held out the cheese, and wished he had eaten it first.

"Airnin, here. I'm sorry, I wasn't thinking," Fearn said glumly. Airnin put up a hand and waved it away.

"I appreciate the offer. Despite having a corporeal form, eating is something I will never be able to do; though, it is something I sorely miss, especially after seeing you savor that piece of bread." Fearn looked sheepishly down at his food and thought of an eternity without being able to eat. He recalled the long winter nights when food would get scarce; stomach grumbling, he would have given anything for the meager rations to double or triple in size.

"I'm sorry, Airnin. I had forgotten. You told me you couldn't eat last night. I can turn around if you would like me to."

"No, that is quite all right. I need to go and set up our lessons. You finish eating, then meet me outside; make it quick." Airnin floated down the tunnel. Fearn put some of the bread and meat back into the sack to eat later. Looking at the cheese, a selfish part of him was grateful that Airnin couldn't eat. Raising it to his nose, he inhaled deeply before biting into it. The tanginess mixed with a hint of sweetness made his eyes roll back in his head in delight. He fought the urge to eat the last bite; instead, he placed it into the bag for later. Silently, he thanked whoever left it out and hoped Dainua would bless them. An odd thought struck him, and he burst out laughing. *I am the deamhon who eats the food!*

He got up, worried he had already taken too long. He picked up his oska, looked at it closely, then placed it back on his bedroll. *If this place is keeping my dad's sul from draining out, best to leave it here*, Fearn thought. He grabbed the lantern and headed out.

When he got to the ascending shaft, he looked up; the sky was full of stars and the air smelled wonderful. He went to climb up and then realized he couldn't with his lantern in hand. After staring at his hands for a bit, the horse came to mind, and with it, the solution. He put the lantern handle into his mouth and climbed up. The climb seemed a lot farther than his fall down was the previous night. Once he got to the top and peered down, he wondered how he didn't break anything. He backed away from the hole and looked around. He couldn't see Airnin, so he closed his eyes and looked again. Down at the foot of the barrow, he saw a large grey sul. It had to be Airnin, so Fearn headed in that direction. Once he reached where he thought Airnin was, he closed his eyes and walked over. Airnin seemed closer to the ground than he had before. In his hands was another sul that was slowly seeping into Dainua. Fearn opened his eyes and saw that it was a dead rabbit.

"Fearn, you need to be quicker next time. Now, sit."

Fearn did as he was directed and then closed his eyes. He saw that he was almost at eye level with Airnin. He looked at the sul in his chest; it was thrashing back and forth, but the smoke-like fangs continued to hold it in place. Fearn thought back to the sul vision he had experienced and wondered if a sul could feel pain after the body died. Airnin reached down, and with his finger, started to cut the rabbit. As he did, he turned it around. Fearn noticed that it had been gutted already. After about three turns, Airnin grabbed both halves and pulled the rabbit apart. Fearn saw that the sul split evenly with it. Airnin then skinned the bottom half, and before he skinned the top half, he grabbed the head. With little effort, he ripped it clean off. Fearn saw that the head had an equal part of sul as well, though fainter, before Airnin tossed the head behind him into the undergrowth. Once that was done, Airnin laid all four parts out on the ground in front of him: the two pelts and two chunks of meat.

"Fearn, what do you see in front of you?" Fearn looked at the rabbit and then back to Airnin.

"Four parts of a rabbit?"

"Yes, that would be obvious to a small child. Now, think," Airnin scolded. Fearn leaned closer.

"I see that the sul didn't stay in one part but is shared based on the size of what was left."

"Good. Now, watch." Airnin took the two skins and trimmed a side on each one straight with his finger, then took the two sides and pushed them together. As Airnin did this, Fearn could see the two suls in the pelt join back together and, as they did, so did the pelt. Airnin then lifted the pelt to show it was now one piece.

"Fearn, this is what a Mender does. With the help of a Tiller, more can be accomplished. Please, pull the suls out of the meat and push it into the pelt." Fearn could only push a little more sul into the pelt until it couldn't hold anymore. Fearn stopped and looked at Airnin, who was grinning.

"As you see, each piece can only hold so much. Now, let us work together. You push into it and I will mend it." Fearn pushed again and this time, the sul started to slowly flow in. As it did, he noticed that the pelt's sul changed; it grew more opaque.

"Here, take it. Tell me what I did," Airnin directed. Fearn took the pelt and looked. He could feel the sul inside, and it felt strong. As he turned the pelt one way and then another, he noticed that the sul inside wasn't seeping out like all of the dead things he had seen previously. It appeared to be perfectly locked away inside; that was, until he held the pelt closer and saw the sul escaped as a faint mist, almost like the leaves or grass.

"It feels different and the sul only escapes as a mist," Fearn remarked.

"That is correct. Menders see things slightly differently than Tillers. Menders can't pull and push the suls, but they can meld them together and then use the power of that sul to lock it in. They can change the way something acts depending on what sul they bind to it. What you saw me do is very basic. This pelt, once turned to leather, will last a lot longer and be more durable." Airnin floated back to his normal height.

"Leave the pelt here and follow me." Airnin pointed to his side as if directing a dog to heel.

Fearn stood and followed Airnin into the forest. Fearn inspected his surroundings. It seemed wilder, and the undergrowth thicker, than back at the farm. After about a half stone, Airnin finally stopped.

"Look here." Airnin pointed to the ground.

Fearn stooped and looked. There was a small animal track, and suspended between two bushes hung a small circle of rope.

"This is a snare made to trap animals. You have to learn how to make these so you can survive on your own. I am not going to coddle you, understood?" Fearn nodded his head in agreement.

Airnin made Fearn sit down and went over several different types of snares and traps, making Fearn create each one. Whenever Fearn screwed up, Airnin would remark, "Fool. Do it again." Once they were done, Airnin led Fearn deeper into the woods. As they walked, Airnin showed Fearn how to tell one animal track from another, having Fearn set a specific trap for each animal.

"Fearn, this is going to be part of your routine each night. Do not neglect it."

After all of the traps were set, they headed back to the barrow. Fearn finally felt the courage to ask a question about the lessons. "So," he said, "are you a Mender?"

"No. I was what they call an imbiber. It is a very rare power to get as an Asinta. In life, it allowed me to attach my sul to another Asinta and either mimic their abilities or boost them. If an Asinta dies and becomes a wraith, their abilities change; as a corrupted imbiber, I now have the power of both a Tiller and Mender. However, I must have the sul of an Asinta in order to keep my corporeal form and powers. I also cannot pull suls like you. I have to cut them out." Airnin's hand made a quick movement like he was gutting an animal as a gleeful smile rippled across his face. Fearn shrank back as Airnin's gaze fell on him. A whisper escaped from Airnin's lips, "Good." They walked the rest of the way to the barrow in silence, then went to bed without saying another word.

Fearn awoke suddenly, covered in sweat. His nightmare of being hunted in the forest by dozens of wraiths felt real until he got his bearings. Daylight shone brightly in the tunnel. Fearn reached out and clutched his oska, closed his eyes, and looked at his dad's sul. It was still intact and whole. A sudden determination gripped Fearn, and before he could change his mind, he picked up his oska and slowly crept out.

He got to the ladder leading up, then remembered something; he knelt and started searching through the rubble until he finally found what he was looking for. He picked up the hatchet, placed it in-between his belt and tunic, then slowly climbed out of the tunnel, balancing his oska across his arms. At the top, Fearn peered over the edge, checking to see if anyone was around before climbing out. Farkor seemed brighter than normal. Panic started to set in as he thought of Airnin hunting him down. "I'll be fine as long as I get back in time," Fearn told himself before he cautiously walked to the foot of the barrow. He glanced back briefly before he set off into the woods. It seemed quieter than normal, but when he got far enough into the woods, he could hear the birds in the trees and the occasional animal scurrying about. He walked hunched over and moved from tree to tree, hiding behind each one as if he were being pursued. He closed his eyes on occasion and searched the ground until he found an acorn. He continued on until he reached the edge of the woods. The sight shocked him. There was almost nothing left of the house. Like a burnt corpse with its ribs showing, a few charred posts and the chimney were all that remained. He surveyed his surroundings and slowly crept over to the house, finding only ash drifting back and forth in the breeze. He hurried over to the road and looked towards the village. His dad and the horse weren't there.

"They are right here," he told himself, as he gripped his oska tightly. He looked both ways on the road, then hurried across into the woods on the other side and slowly made his way towards the village through the trees. His panic felt stronger, which made Fearn glance over his shoulder constantly, expecting each time to find Airnin there. He looked out at the field as he walked along. It had large burnt patches at the edges. Whoever set the fire apparently couldn't get the lush green of the field to catch. The unburnt crops looked ready to be harvested. Fearn continued forward until he found the small path his dad had made. He quickly stepped off the path and examined the clearing. Once he felt he was safe, he stepped forward and looked down at the fresh mound of earth at his feet. Someone had been buried next to his mom. There was a crude wooden grave marker that read:

— ᚦᚪᛁᚱ —
— ᛗᚪᛋᛏᛖᚱ ᚩᚠ ᛏᚪᛚᛖᛋ —

Fearn studied his surroundings again and, feeling confident he wasn't being watched, knelt down. "Hey, Mom, I have to make this quick. I have Dad's sul, so you two can be together again. You don't have to worry; I have a place to stay. He's not the kindest person, but he says he will protect me." Fearn chipped at the dirt around the grave markers with the hatchet and then carefully removed them, dropped the acorn seed into the hole his dad's marker left behind, and covered it. Fearn closed his eyes, placed his hands on the ground and focused on his oska. He carefully pushed the suls into the seed, which started to grow. A small sprout emerged from the ground which rapidly grew and expanded. Fearn could feel the flow of the tree's sul and its eagerness to reach the open sky above the forest canopy. Fearn drove the roots deep into the current of Dainua's energy. When his oska was empty, the tree's eagerness to grow overpowered his emotions, so he hurriedly went to the surrounding trees and pulled most of their sul until they were weak and could easily be pushed over. He poured them into the tree, rejoicing as it shot upward and through the forest canopy, making the surrounding trees look like saplings in comparison. The trunk widened in the process, pushing over the nearby trees from which Fearn had pulled suls. When Fearn had just a little left in his oska, he grabbed each grave marker and placed them one at a time on the side of the tree. He pushed the trunk out and around them. Standing back, Fearn realized he had created the biggest oak tree he had ever seen. It had grown way bigger than he expected; the bottom branches just brushed the tops of the nearby trees. The euphoria from the tree's sul still coursed through him. He smiled ecstatically, sure that his dad was with his mom once again. Fearn spun and danced around the tree until his jubilance waned and exhaustion took hold. As Fearn slumped against the tree, his head started to swim with memories of his dad. He slid to the ground, tears filling his eyes as he wept for his loss until he curled up and fell asleep.

Fearn awoke from a dreamless sleep, startled to find himself surrounded by darkness. Panicking, Fearn looked up and saw starlight twinkle through the canopy above. He scrambled to his feet, grabbed his oska, ran around the tree, and deciding it was best to risk running on the road, tried to make it back to the barrow in time. As Fearn left the small path his dad had made and entered the road, he skidded to a halt. Airnin stood in the middle of the road looking up at the massive oak tree. Startled, he dropped his head to look at Fearn, arms stretching out and claws ready to strike. Fearn stared into the black mist of Airnin's head, too afraid to close his eyes, and slowly started to back away. Fearn focused on the peripheral of his vision, hoping to find some means of escape. As Fearn stepped back into the edge of the woods, Airnin rushed forward, hand outstretched, and struck Fearn in the chest, pushing him off his feet and throwing him backward.

Fearn landed hard on his back and made short wheezing sounds as he tried to catch his breath. Airnin was on top of him in a moment, hand pulled back with his index finger pointed at Fearn's chest. Just before he struck, something caught his attention and he looked past Fearn at the oak tree behind him. Time seemed to stretch as Fearn stared at Airnin's hand, waiting for the final blow, but Airnin didn't move.

Finally, Airnin looked down at Fearn and dropped his hand to his side. Airnin rose, and as he did, he reached down and grabbed Fearn by his shirt, pulling him up with him. "Tell me why you disobeyed me," Airnin demanded in a low voice.

Fearn glanced over his shoulder, and by the faint starlight, saw his parents' grave markers in the tree.

"Look at me and answer!" Airnin roared before shaking Fearn violently. "Out with it!"

"I had to bury my dad." It was all that Fearn could think to say as he tried to focus on Airnin.

Airnin just stood there, holding Fearn tightly in his grasp.

"I promise, I was going to head back, but I fell asleep," Fearn pleaded.

Airnin let out a heavy sigh, dropped Fearn, and began to walk away. Without looking back, he called "Come!" Fearn looked back at the oak tree one last time before following Airnin.

LEATHER

After they reached the edge of the forest near the burned-out farmhouse, Airnin turned to Fearn. "I am going to get things ready for our lesson. I will give you one more chance; I allow you to continue on alone. Do not disappoint me." Airnin melted into mist and was gone.

Fearn looked around, hesitant to continue on and not sure what to do. Reluctantly, he started into the woods towards the barrow.

Upon arrival, Fearn heard his stomach growl. As he ran up the hill, he hoped he had enough time to grab some food. Once he reached the edge of the tunnel, he sat down, hung his legs over the edge, and looked at his empty oska. Fearn tried to hold it back, but tears started rolling down his cheeks as he realized his dad was now gone. Everything he had had was gone. A scream he wasn't aware was in him boiled to the surface and burst out. Fearn looked into the pit, his hands grasping the edge as his knuckles turned white. He wanted nothing more than to push himself off the ledge. His life was gone and it was his fault. He had ruined everything, starting from the time of his birth. He pushed himself up with his arms, feet pressed against the side of the wall, and leaned forward; a terrible fear engulfed him. Fearn scrambled away from the pit, slumped over, and stared at the fate he so desperately wanted but he just couldn't muster the courage to follow through. His vision blurred as tears poured from his eyes. "I can't even do this right," Fearn groaned.

139

Too afraid of what Airnin might do if he was late, Fearn decided to go without food. He stood, dusted himself off, and wiped the tears away. Looking down the hill to where he was certain Airnin lay in wait, Fearn sighed, clutched his oska, and trudged to his lesson.

"About time you got here. Not only did you take your time, it looks like you spent your time crying like a suckling pig. I will only say this once: I do not ever want you to show weakness again. I do not tolerate weak things—those which powerful Asinta crush under their heels. You will be a powerful Tiller by my teachings. You will bury your emotions. Is that understood?"

Fearn nodded vigorously as he stammered, "I'm sorry."

"Someday you will understand what a privilege it is to have one such as myself teaching a lowly commoner such as you. People in my station do not muck about in filth; however, this is a unique circumstance." Airnin paused, thinking for a moment. His tone changed. "Now, as to that tree you grew. That was excellent work, and you should be proud of it; unfortunately, it will arouse suspicions. It will make this area even more dangerous during the day. You will have to stay here in order to stay safe, understood?"

Fearn nodded his head again, "I won't head out again, I promise."

"Here is some food for tonight." Airnin dropped a bag at Fearn's feet.

The smell of fresh bread wafted from the bag as Fearn opened it. He sat and scarfed down his food. As he brushed the crumbs from his face, Airnin laid out the rabbit pelt from the previous night.

"I am going to show you how to tan leather the Mender way. I gathered the things we will need ahead of time, including the lantern." Airnin placed the pelt on a large flat stone on the ground in front of him.

"Now, look," he directed. As Fearn watched, Airnin brushed a hand over the skin slowly, and as he did, the fat and muscle still attached to the pelt fell away.

"As a Mender, we can see more than a sul—we can see how a thing is made. Then, we can then disassemble it into its parts."

Flipping the pelt, Airnin passed a hand over it again. This time, the hair fell away.

"I can see the skin, isolate it, and remove everything else," Airnin explained. He picked up the skin and handed it to Fearn, who observed that it was smooth on both sides, not a blemish to be found, before handing it back. Airnin placed a small bucket between Fearn and himself.

"This is a bucket of oak bark and water." Fearn saw the swirling mixture of suls from the oak bark churn in the water. Airnin then placed the skin into the water and held his hand over it. Fearn watched the suls from the oak bark flow into the rabbit skin. The suls from the bark swirled around the leather's sul in a tight formation, much like a dance, though neither touched the other. Airnin lifted the skin out of the water, and when Fearn opened his eyes, he observed it had taken on the dark brown color of the bark water.

"This is something that would take months or even a year to accomplish for regular men, Fearn, but a Mender can complete it in a span of moments. This is a prime example of how superior Asinta are to commoners."

"Can a Tiller do anything else other than make stuff grow?" Fearn asked.

"Yes, but before you are able to harness those abilities, you have a long path ahead."

"Fine," Fearn grumbled.

Airnin lifted a hand as if to strike. "What did you say to me?"

Cowering, Fearn meekly replied, "I understand."

Airnin dropped his hand, but his unseen gaze seemed to bore into Fearn. "I show you these things so your simple mind can slowly grasp these powers."

"Now, back to the lesson. Here, take it." Airnin held out the leather to Fearn. Fearn ran a hand over it; it was soft and supple, but nothing could prevent the sharp chill from Airnin's presence seeping through.

"To show you my generosity, the leather is yours. Give me your oska."

Fearn hesitantly handed it over.

"Close your eyes."

Fearn did as he was told. Airnin took the end of the leather and pressed it against the oska, about a palm's distance from the top. Airnin then slowly wrapped the leather around the wood, the two melding into one. When he finished, Airnin handed the oska back to Fearn. Fearn opened his eyes and ran his hand over it. There was no seam; the leather and wood were now one.

Fearn had a realization. "Airnin, where are you getting all of these supplies?" He closed his eyes to be able to look Airnin in the face. It was placid and still; then a small smile rippled across it.

"I hid some of the supplies from the soldiers' camp and the rest I took from sheds and homes. I take enough for your needs. After all, these villagers are the reason you are here. Should they not pay a price for the hardships they have placed upon you? They killed your father and that beautiful horse. They left you homeless. Just think: where would you be if you had not been so lucky as to have found my generosity? Lying dead in the woods, forgotten except for the animals that picked at your bones."

Fearn still felt a pang of regret that Airnin had to steal for him. However, Airnin's words began to sway him.

"Besides," Airnin continued. "I have to keep you alive and teach you these skills so you can be a better Tiller. How else would I do it?"

Fearn felt like something wasn't right but couldn't puzzle it out.

"I need you to go check the traps we set last night and reset them," Airnin instructed. "I have errands and will meet you back here."

As Fearn trekked into the woods, he wondered why Airnin hadn't killed him. Airnin made him feel like he was a burden, just as much as his dad had said he was. He checked the snares and traps, finding two rabbits and a fox. He reset the traps before returning. He filled his oska with the suls of the dead and decaying as he went along.

Airnin was waiting for him with a knife in his hand. Fearn froze in his tracks.

Airnin turned the blade around and offered the hilt. "You need to learn how to clean and skin the animals you catch."

Hesitantly, Fearn approached and took the blade. It was ice-cold to the touch and finely crafted; he had never known his dad to own anything so well made.

"Don't worry, Fearn. I took that knife off one of the men who tried to kill you, along with these." Airnin motioned to his left, and there, leaning against a tree, was a bow and quiver. Setting down the rabbits and fox, Fearn walked over to the tree and examined the quiver. He pulled out an arrow, but it seemed different from the arrows that were fired at him. Closing his eyes, Fearn saw the arrow had an opaque sul. He looked back at Airnin.

"A Mender made these, right? The arrows they shot at me didn't look like this."

"I found those at their camp. They are very expensive, and I am sure the soldiers did not want to waste them on commoners." Airnin forced a laugh. "If they knew how powerful you were, they would have reconsidered."

Finally, unable to keep his curiosity in check, Fearn asked "Why you do call us commoners?"

A deep, rumbling laugh burst from Airnin. "I was born a prince. Everyone knows those in royalty are closer to Telgog and Dainua. People below us are called commoners, and their purpose is to serve. Fortunately, because you are an Asinta, you are one step above them."

Fearn suddenly understood. "Oh, so that is what servitude is? You spared me so you could have someone serve you?"

There was a long pause before Airnin replied. "Being an imbiber taught me equality. Calling you a commoner is an old habit I was never able to break; I apologize. If you were here solely to serve, I would not be teaching you. For is it not the teacher who serves the student? I am giving you knowledge very few Asinta attain. The only thing I ask from you is your obedience and absolute loyalty to me."

Fearn looked down at the arrow in his hand and then back to Airnin. Something about Airnin being nice to him seemed off-putting, but he still nodded his head in acknowledgment.

"Back to that arrow. A Tiller can push and pull an arrow in flight; however, its sul is weak and not easily guided. An arrow such as these in the hands of a trained Tiller would allow them to hit someone hiding in a stand of trees.

Fearn turned the arrow in his hands, then walked towards the lantern to take a closer look. The arrow's head and nock were made of bone. He looked up at Airnin, but before he could ask, Airnin answered his question: "That is the bone of an owl. You will learn certain things work best when crafted by a Mender. You could make that arrow from the bone of the rabbit or fox you caught tonight, but it would not fly as true or have the same control as making it from a bird of prey. Now, put it away. I need to show you how to clean the animals you caught."

Airnin taught Fearn how to gut, clean, and skin the animals. Next, they went through the same process as with the rabbit pelt but left the fur on the fox pelt. Once they were done, Airnin taught Fearn how to carve up the meat. Any time Fearn messed up, he would flinch, waiting for a harsh rebuke that never came.

As the lesson came to a close, Airnin said, "I know it is hard for you to understand why I steal from the villagers. Just know I do it for your benefit. Take all of this back to the barrow. I have an errand to run and will be back shortly." Airnin turned and left, gliding swiftly through the trees like a bird in flight, weaving around them until he was out of sight. Fearn picked up the bow and put it over one shoulder and the quiver over the other. He noticed a belt with a small scabbard for the knife Airnin had given him. The belt was a little too big and sagged once the knife was in its scabbard. Fearn poured the bark water from the bucket, placed the animal meat inside, and covered it with the leather they had made. He picked up the bucket in one hand, the oska and lantern in the other, then headed for the top of the barrow. Fearn was just reaching the top of the hill when Airnin returned.

"Quickly, Fearn, hurry inside." Airnin grabbed the bucket in Fearn's hand and dove into the barrow. Lantern in his mouth and the oska balanced across his arms, Fearn hurried down the handholds as fast as he could, his heart racing, with visions of soldiers surrounding the barrow. About halfway down, his right hand slipped and the wall seemed to slowly fall away. As the stars above him came into view, a strange peace overcame him. He waited to hit the rubble floor below; instead, he felt like he plunged into a lake in the middle of winter, then was quickly placed on his feet. His jaw hurt from clenching down on the lantern as he fell.

"Stay here, Fearn," Airnin commanded before he flew back up and out of sight. Fearn glanced up, frustrated, then walked down the tunnel to his bedroll and plopped down. The emptiness and disconnection with Dainua in this place still unnerved him. He felt like he was floating with no connection to the ground. He paced back and forth; then, getting bored, he slowly worked his way back up the tunnel, grabbed the bucket, and brought it inside. He stacked everything against one wall, and seeing the small stack of earthenware dishes, hoped that Airnin would return them, or the villagers would run out of things on which to eat.

Airnin finally returned shortly before first light. "It is now safe here. The soldiers I saw were moving through and appeared not to be searching for you. To be completely safe, we will need to be careful the next few nights. Morning is almost upon us. I am going to turn in for the day."

"Wait, Airnin, why are soldiers looking for me?"

Airnin stood there for a moment then his hand raised and pointed at Fearn's arm. Fearn looked down at where Airnin was pointing and saw the six square scars.

"The king knows how powerful you are and intends to snuff you out. I think it is time to tell you who I am. Tonight," he promised, then faded from Fearn's sight.

Fearn sat down on his bedroll and leaned against the wall, waiting for the first rays of morning. The tunnel slowly started to lighten, and even though it didn't bring physical warmth, the sight of it warmed his heart. He laid down and fell fast asleep, wondering what tales Airnin would tell.

AIRNIN

Fearn awoke and watched as the light in the tunnel faded from red into pink, then was swallowed by black. After a while, the air shimmered and Airnin appeared.

"Morning, Fearn. I am pleased that you made the wise decision to continue to stay. Did you stray at all during the day?"

"No, I stayed here as you asked," Fearn replied.

"Good. Your dad must have been proud of you, listening and obeying so well. I will take the bucket of meat from last night and place it where we have been meeting outside. Head that direction with any other food you want and tinder. We will cook the meat tonight." Airnin removed the leather from the bucket, picked it up, and left. Fearn stood; straightened his bedroll; grabbed the last of the bread, the lantern, and his oska; and headed out.

Fearn arrived where he had met Airnin previously and found the bucket but no Airnin. He closed his eyes and looked around but couldn't see Airnin's grey sul. Fearn placed everything down except his oska, then searched for firewood. After his second trip back, Airnin breezed past him.

"I scouted and I did not see any soldiers or anyone that might see our fire. Go ahead and start it. While you cook the meat, I will tell you the tale of how I was betrayed." Fearn nodded and got to work kindling the fire. Once there was a steady blaze, he took a stick and whittled it straight with the knife Airnin had given him, then skewered the meat and started cooking it.

"I sense great power in you, Fearn, and am trusting you with my life in telling you my tale. I am King Cial's brother—his twin to be exact. He was born first; I followed soon after.

"We had a wonderful childhood, full of hunts, sword fighting, archery, and learning, the latter being the one I liked most. My brother and I not only became fast friends but also each other's biggest rivals. If one of us centered an arrow at 100 pebbles, the other needed to do it at 150 pebbles. If one of us could disarm the other thrice, then the other had to do it four times. Others may have thought this would tear us apart, but I found that it forged us together. Our father loved us deeply, never favoring one over the other, always praising the one who had faltered that day, not the victor. I cannot think of a better or kinder man.

"When we had our tenth birth year, we were given the test of the Asinta. The flower did not wilt for my brother Cial. For me, sadly, the blackened flower I held was the beginning of the end, though I did not know it at the time. My father could not have been prouder of me than when he saw the flower wilt in my hand. He made sure that the best Asinta in the kingdom were sought to teach me. My brother's and my teaching changed: I took the path of the Asinta and staff while my brother learned the things of king and crown. I continued to learn through books and was taught the basics by the Asinta until my powers were revealed. My brother learned how to be a tactician, politician, and steward of the kingdom. Our bond did not waver; we still hunted and caused mischief with the maidens of the castle. That all changed in my thirteenth year, when I was told I had the powers of an imbiber.

"This was the first time someone from royalty had had this power. My lessons changed quickly after that, teaching me how to be a steward to the Asinta, to lead and guide them, to help decide those whom we would help or which land we would till, creating items like horseless carts to help ease the life of commoners. My most important role was as counselor to the king, for the kingdom is ruled by not only the crown but the staff as well. My brother's teachings became mine; I needed to know the battle tactics of those who came before us, learning from their faults and finding ways to improve upon their accomplishments. The hardest lesson was how to avoid being biased, so I could give the king a balanced counsel in disputes.

"Being brothers, we continued to strive to outdo one another. I do not know when it changed, and maybe it was always there, but my father started to favor me over my brother, Cial. I did not notice it until I was older and looked back upon how the favors he heaped equally onto us slowly shifted to favors he only bestowed on me. It is hard to see when something is amiss when you are not the one lacking. I do not know my brother's mind, but I suspect the day everything changed was the day he overheard my father counseling Foiden, the current imbiber of the Asinta, and my great and noble teacher. Father and Foiden discussed whether or not turning over the kingdom to me would strengthen it, binding the staff and crown together. It would solidify our powers and help give pause to our neighbors, especially Soyer in the south with whom we had skirmished, though peace was always found before war broke out. The staff exists in both kingdoms, helping balance the powers and preventing war from breaking out.

"I do not know if my father's thoughts on this were a passing whim or something he truly considered, or if the meeting actually occurred. I only know of it because my brother later told me.

"I also was not aware at the time that, though I thought I was the better tactician, my brother was toying with me. He wanted me to let my guard down and be unprepared for the treacherous plans he had put into motion. Again, I only know of these things because they were told to me before he sealed me alive in my tomb.

"My brother, Cial, went to Foiden and planted small and easily acceptable lies that then slowly grew. My brother began by telling him how he and I overheard the conversation Foiden had with my father concerning me being king. He also said our bond had eroded as I became more power-hungry at the thought of ruling the kingdom myself. He feared not only for his life but also for those of Foiden and Father. He went to the council of the Asinta—those who had been groomed to take the lead before my powers were revealed. When the Asinta do not have an imbiber, they are led by a council until one is found. A few of these men believed me a young upstart whom they did not feel had the wisdom or knowledge needed to rule.

"After my brother found the allies and followers he needed, pacts were created, complete with the promise of great rewards. When my brother and I were in our twenty-fifth year, Cial confronted Father about the conversation he had overheard almost five years past. I will not go into detail on what was said between the two, because I cannot believe Cial on what was said or if it was true; I refuse to tarnish my father's name and legacy on hearsay. What I do know is that, in rage or planned attack, Cial killed Father. He left part of a torn Asinta's robe in my father's hand and the rest he placed in my room.

"After my father's body was found, a tip was given to search my room, pinning the murder on me. The lies expertly crafted in Foiden's ear left no doubt in his mind that I was the one who had killed Father. I left the morning after the murder but before my father was found, luckily avoiding capture. I traveled with a party of Asinta to help cure a bad outbreak of lull weed. My father's men rode out to take me back. I was fortunate, for the leader was a close friend and knew that I could not have killed my father. He let me go to give me time to unravel the treachery and bring justice to the real killer. Sadly, for that loyalty, he and every man who rode with him that day were killed.

My men were loyal and trustworthy, or so I thought. They swore to stick by my side as we rode hard south, then east while we looked for a place to hide. We finally hid deep in the woods; my men risked their lives to go into the town dressed as beggars to get information and find my brother, Cial, foolishly thinking he could help.

"One of my men found my brother. He had swiftly gathered the army and Asinta and ridden after us. We soon realized his betrayal and moved quickly by night, at times hiding within pebbles of the soldiers searching for us. My brother became desperate and paranoid, thinking farmers and villagers were aiding us; he started to burn every town and crop he came across to deter anyone from helping us.

"Trying to save his own neck, one of my men slipped out at night while we were close to a camp of Asinta who were searching for us. He gave them our location in hopes that he would be pardoned. We awoke the next morning to find that, at about 150 pebbles from our camp in every direction, the land was blackened for almost one stone. On the opposite side sat the Asinta loyal to my brother Cial.

"I was a fool and did not fight right away, not knowing their ranks were too few to hold the line. This gave Cial time to rally the army. Once there, my brother was content to starve us out rather than fighting.

"After a few days, our meager supplies were depleted giving us no choice but to fight. We could not gather any suls from the blackened land so we had to take what we could from the small oasis in which we camped. Before we got close enough to strike against my brother's men, they unleashed a volley of arrows, which took down a large number of us. Regardless, we pushed onward and gave to Dainua our share of men. Though we fought bravely, our numbers could not sustain the attack, and we had to withdraw. In the middle of the following night, I tried one last desperate attack, sending out men in one direction to try to get Cial's army to gather there so the rest of us could push through the other side. Even their limited numbers were still too great, and I lost half of the men I had remaining.

"We waited, hoping to draw them in so we might have the upper hand; however, before that could happen, my men decided that turning me over would save their lives. As I slept, they knocked me over the head and cut off my eyelids, which prevented me from using my powers. Then, they bound me and led me to my treacherous brother, who was smart and knew the men I was with could never be trusted.

"He incapacitated them and removed their eyelids as well, then tied me to a stake where I was forced to watch. They tied my supporters between two horses and, one by one, pulled until their arms, legs, or both ripped free; then they tossed the parts into a pile, not caring if the men were still alive before burning them. The entire time, Cial had someone next to me wetting my eyes so I could clearly see and smell everything that had happened.

"Cial argued with Foiden for a while on what they should do with me and, against Foiden's counsel, Cial built the barrow. Once ready, they bound me and sealed me in my tomb alive, leaving me detached from Dainua, never to be embraced in her arms or to finally see my father again."

Fearn was taking the meat from the fire as Airnin finished his tale. He stopped and closed his eyes. Airnin's face was a storm of emotions; anger, frustration, and sadness crashing into each other like waves. His facial expression finally settled into one that broke Fearn's heart to look upon. Fearn knew it well; this was how he felt when he used to long for a father and mother who truly loved him. Thinking of Dair caused him to reminisce about the nights spent in taverns telling tales. Tears welled in his eyes as he longed to have his dad sitting in Airnin's place. It made Fearn furious that Airnin had experienced the real love of a father and had it ripped away.

Suddenly, it dawned on Fearn that the man who was responsible for the death of Airnin's father was responsible for Dair's death as well. He cried harder, not sure whether he was crying for Airnin or himself. He now understood why the revenge that Airnin sought was his as well.

Airnin didn't say a word, not even to rebuke Fearn for showing weakness. Wiping his eyes, Fearn closed them and looked at Airnin. "Why don't you kill your brother now that you are a wraith?"

"My bones are here and I can only travel about three stone away from them. If I was close enough, I would have tried, though with the number of Asinta he surely has surrounding him, I do not know if I could succeed."

"What can I do?" Fearn asked eagerly.

"Stay and train with me. It will be long and hard, and even then, I do not know if the two of us together can do it."

"The two of us together?"

"We will find a way of getting me there. For now, eat up; then, go search the traps you have set. We still have hours left before daybreak, and there are other lessons I want you to begin."

Fearn finished his meal, then left to search and reset the traps. He returned with only a single rabbit this time. Fearn gutted the rabbit himself, and then, with Airnin's help, tanned its pelt.

After they were done, Airnin had Fearn grab the bow and quiver he had brought from the barrow. Airnin taught him how to draw it back, which he could almost do.

"No, Fearn, your feet need to be wider apart. Equal with your shoulders," Airnin snapped before hitting Fearn's legs with his oska. He continued to have Fearn draw the bow over and over again to start strengthening his arms.

"When can I shoot an arrow?" Fearn whined.

"You cannot nock an arrow until you have mastered this," was all Airnin said to Fearn before hitting him again. They kept at it until Fearn couldn't draw the bow anymore and his legs felt like they were covered in welts. Airnin then had Fearn switch hands and try with his right hand. Fearn fumbled more this time, most times unable to draw at all. Fearn was exhausted to the point where he felt like both of his arms were hanging to his feet and going to fall off. His legs were numb from the pain. Airnin finally called it a night, and they made their way back to the barrow.

When they got to the tunnel, Fearn looked down in fear, not sure if he could climb down. Airnin took the supplies and remarked before heading down, "You are not some commoner. You are an Asinta."

Fearn slowly worked his way down the handholds, feeling at any moment that his hands would slip and he would fall into the blackness below. Every step made his muscles twitch and ache as he strained to hold on. His right hand finally gave out and he fell straight down. His heart raced as fear overwhelmed him, but before he could react, his feet crashed into the ground and he stumbled backward. He then realized he had only fallen two handholds. A sense of euphoria swiftly overtook him and he laughed out loud. He tenderly walked down the tunnel. Airnin had already turned in for the day. Fearn lay down and waited for Farkor to show itself in the tunnel as he tried to rub out the aches in his arms and bruises on his legs. He finally closed his eyes and fell asleep from sheer exhaustion.

CRAINING

Fearn awoke to find Farkor had already set. His legs ached and were covered in deep purple welts. After getting up and eating food left by his bedroll, he met Airnin in their usual spot. Fearn's arms still felt like they were going to fall off, and he breathed a sigh of relief when a bow wasn't to be found.

"Fearn, we will do the bow training every three nights. Tonight, I will show you how to use the powers of a sul, but first, you must go and check the traps."

Fearn slowly got up, grabbed the lantern, and gingerly headed off into the woods. His legs screamed in pain with every step he took. He returned with two rabbits and a badger.

"Place the animals on the ground. Do you have room in your oska for the suls of those rabbits?"

Fearn closed his eyes and focused on his oska, watching faint wisps of suls whirling around each other. There was still plenty of room for the rabbit's suls.

"Yes," Fearn replied, looking up at Airnin.

"Good. Instead of skinning this first rabbit, I want you to take its sul and store it."

Fearn focused on the first rabbit and pulled its sul into his oska. As he did, the rabbit's skin hardened, the fur started to slough off, and its body collapsed in on itself. It now looked like it had been sitting in the woods for weeks, not just a day.

"Now," Airnin instructed, "I want you to take the rabbit's sul, pull it into yourself, and hold it there. Do not let it flow into Dainua. Once you have it, focus on your sul and absorb the rabbit's sul into it."

Fearn nodded, eager to do whatever Airnin asked so he could head back to bed and forget about the searing pain that coursed through his legs. He isolated the large sul of the rabbit from the others in his oska and pulled it into himself, grasping the sul tightly so it couldn't flow out and into Dainua. He focused on his sul, stretching it out, and wrapping it around the rabbit's sul. It wriggled out of his grasp and he had to grapple with it before it could race down to Dainua. Fearn tried again and again, failing each time. As he tried to figure out how to hold the sul, he thought of Airnin and the sul trapped in his chest. Figuring it wouldn't hurt to try, Fearn changed his sul's shape so it had fangs like Airnin's and bit hard into the rabbit's sul. As they sank in, its sul melded into his and he felt a rush of energy course through him. Suddenly, he had a vision of running along a path, the underbrush and trees looming large and out of proportion above him. As he ran between two large trees, something pulled him backward. He struggled as he felt it tighten around his neck. He wiggled back and forth, trying to free himself but whatever had ahold of him tightened even more when he struggled. Finally, gasping for breath, he collapsed, and the world dissolved to black. The vision faded, and Fearn realized his eyes were still closed because he could see an energy running around him and through him. It didn't look like a sul, but more like lightning during a storm. As Fearn looked up to Airnin for guidance, he noticed the air around himself shimmered; he could feel its power like he could usually feel Dainua's beneath him. Strangely, he felt cut off from her now, the power creating some kind of barrier.

"Airnin, I absorbed the sul and I feel really odd, like I am being chased or someone is watching me, but I can't see them. I also saw..." Fearn thought back on the vision. "I saw the rabbit's last moments before it died. The air also has a power to it that I have never felt before; it feels like Dainua but different."

"You have taken a sul and turned it into a power you can wield. That power has connected you to Telgog, whose power flows around us. We can only tap into it once we have consumed a sul. Stand up. Focus that energy towards the ground and see what Telgog's power does," Airnin directed eagerly, a sneer rippling across his face.

Fearn stood, shaking a bit, heart racing and palms sweaty and cold. He noticed that the pain in his legs seemed to have eased some. He focused on the energy and gathered it like a sul, then pushed it down through his feet. As he did, the energy around him reacted and lifted him off the ground, like someone was pushing him up from below. Looking down, he could see that he wasn't standing on the ground anymore; instead, the energy in the air shimmered and looked like a small platform holding him up. Suddenly, Fearn's feet felt like they were on ice and he had no grip on anything. He threw his arms out for balance, flailing them back and forth, trying to gain purchase on the invisible platform. Finally, he slipped backward. The stars in the night sky spun in and out of sight as he crashed to the ground on his back. The fall didn't hurt; luckily, Fearn wasn't as far up as it had looked. Loud laughter filled the clearing, and as the fuzziness lifted, he noticed it was coming from Airnin.

"That never gets old. Oh, how I miss torturing the initiates! Now, I want you to try again. This time, instead of using your weight to hold you in place, shift the energy back and forth to hold you up."

Fearn got up, dusted off the dirt, and shook it out of his hair, then glowered at Airnin. "That wasn't funny. You could have told me how to use the energy before I fell."

"I have been kind to you so far tonight; does that need to change?" Airnin retorted.

Fearn ignored Airnin and steadied himself to try again. He noticed that the power flowing around him was weaker. He focused on pushing it down as he did before and felt himself rise again. Fearn's feet slipped out again, but this time he was expecting it and pushed some of the energy behind him. This created a sort of wall of energy he could lean against; however, he pushed too much energy in that direction, and it shoved him forward. He flew forward, not thinking of using the energy to stop himself. Fearn managed to get his hands out in front of him just in time to break his fall as he landed face-first in the dirt. He looked up, scowling at Airnin who was howling in laughter. Brushing the dust from the front of his shirt, Fearn squared himself and pushed again. He focused this time. It wasn't just a downward push; he pushed down and then to the side of him in all directions. This created a circular barrier that forcefully pushed upwards, which didn't feel like the sensation of slipping on ice but like someone held his legs and lifted. He managed to rise about half of his height into the air when the energy depleted and he came right back down. Fearn stumbled forwards then backward, but, thankfully, did not fall down this time.

"Good. You are getting the hang of it. Now, take one of the smaller suls you have in your oska and do the same thing."

Fearn squared his shoulders and planted his feet first before absorbing a small sul and pulling it into his body. He had more difficulty getting this one to meld with his sul. It was harder to bite into, but, once he did, he received the same rush of power he had before, though it lessened right away. No vision came this time, only the brief sensation of insects crawling all over him. He pushed the energy down, and it dissipated without even slightly lifting him.

"Airnin, it didn't work that time."

"Correct... why?"

Fearn scrunched up his face in concentration. Pulling in another smaller sul, he tried again and got the same result. He paced back and forth, concentrating on what to say, not wanting to give the wrong answer. He finally consumed several of the suls until he felt a power almost as strong as the rabbit's. He was able to lift himself into the air again. Another ungraceful landing, but he managed not to fall. He looked towards Airnin, as a slight smile rippled across his face.

"The amount of energy I get from it depends on the size of the sul," Fearn replied, hoping it was the right answer.

"Correct. Now, let us tan this rabbit and badger hide before we continue your lessons."

"Airnin, why are we tanning all of these hides?"

"Can you not think of a reason why we should be doing this?"

Fearn thought for a while before he replied, "To learn how to make better leather?"

Airnin gave a muffled grunt. "Are you incapable of anything other than a basic thought? When I ask you a question, think. Remember who serves whom. You will need other supplies, especially when winter comes. Do you expect me to provide everything for you? You will need something to barter with to obtain those supplies." Airnin pointed to his chest, saying, "I do not use this power lightly."

"Wait, I'm going to go into town? I thought you wanted me to stay hidden and not leave?"

"I do," Airnin sighed, exasperated. "You cannot stay hidden forever, and we will make a disguise for you. You will need to come up with a new name and a backstory. Do you think you can do that?"

Fearn grinned. "Ay, my dad taught me how to be a teller of tales. I can think of something."

"Good. Back to our lesson—go fill up your oska and return."

Fearn hurried off and filled it with dead and decaying things both in and above the ground. When he returned, Airnin was where he had left him.

"Fearn, I want you to practice pushing yourself up."

Fearn nodded, then focused on moving the suls from his oska and absorbing them. When he had gotten to the second one, he felt an icy blow from his side. It didn't hurt him but he lost his concentration and the sul slipped from his body and into Dainua.

"What are you do—" Before Fearn could finish, Airnin hit him from the other side, this time a little harder.

"Do you think that when you get into a fight with another Tiller, they will wait for you to absorb the energy you need first?" Airnin's hand pushed out and hit Fearn square in the chest, knocking him back and into a tree.

"I am not going to stop until you can... " Airnin grabbed Fearn by his shirt and swung him around, shoving him in another direction. Fearn stumbled backward trying to catch his footing. "... get enough energy in you to push back." He came at Fearn again. This time Fearn was waiting for it and ducked under the blow then ran around the nearest tree. He pulled the next sul into himself. Airnin came rushing around the tree a little too fast and ran headlong into Fearn, sending him sprawling backward. He tripped and hit his head on a tree root. Dazed, angry, and without thought, Fearn quickly grabbed a portion of the tree's sul that was almost as large as his own and bit down on it. He felt his blood slow to a crawl and thicken to sap. He felt Dainua flow around his feet; his arms stretched out, his fingers feeling the flow of Telgog. The vision left as quickly as it came. The immense power made him scream out in pain as the energy seared through and around him, muscles contracted, vision narrowed, and he barely saw Airnin rushing towards him, his hand held out.

Wanting the pain to leave, Fearn pushed all of the energy directly at Airnin. There was a sharp crack like thunder as the air around Fearn solidified and blasted forward. It hit Airnin hard, pushing him up through the canopy. A second large crack came from the tree above Fearn; it had rapidly decayed and the trunk couldn't support the weight of itself any longer. The branches started to break and fall to the ground. Fearn began coming to his senses only to be startled as dead leaves and branches rained down. He tried to roll to his right but was stuck in-between two large roots. The branches fell first and pinned Fearn in place; then the tree split down the center and toppled over, knocking him out.

TRAPPED

F earn awoke and couldn't move. No glimmer of light, not even a single star, could be seen. He struggled back and forth, something cutting into his back. Finally, he went limp.

"Help! Help!" he screamed. He waited and screamed some more. Still, no answer came. His heart raced. He noticed the back of his head was wet; he reached up. It was soft and sticky. He could feel it running down the sides of his face. Immediately, something stung his finger and then his hand. He panicked and tried moving his hand back and forth, reaching up with his other hand to try to get rid of what was attacking him. It started attacking that hand as well, then his neck and back.

"Help! Help!" he screamed again, then a sharp stinging pain bit into the side of his face. Realization dawned and panic subsided; he stopped moving and lay completely still. He was still stung a few times, but the attacking tapered off. Afraid to scream, he lay there trying to figure out what to do. He reached around slowly but couldn't find his oska. He closed his eyes and reached out; he could see little suls all around him. He slowly went to each one, pulled its sul out, and consumed it. It became harder to breathe and he slowly turned his head to try to get more air. A sharp sting hit his lip; crying out in pain, he pulled all of the sul from the bee.

"Ha! You are blackened and can't return to Dainua," he said to the bee with satisfaction. He continued to pull the bees' suls until he felt like he had killed most of them, then reached out to the tree around him. He had only taken about half of the tree's sul before. He was more careful this time, taking just a little before consuming it, until he hoped he had enough power. He thought about how big the elm and oak trees were around the barrow, then decided to consume more of the tree's sul. The energy crackled through him and hurt, but not to the point of discomfort. He squared himself and pushed up on the tree. This instantly shoved him right into the ground. He coughed and spat out dirt, muttering to himself, "Great. Now, what are you going to do?"

"Airnin, you out there?" he yelled. Again, no reply. Holding the energy in him was starting to hurt. He pushed down a bit to get rid of it, and when he did, it pressed him up and against the tree above him. He stopped, then spread out his hands and legs as much as he could and pressed down, creating as much space between himself and the ground as he could. He gradually pressed up against the tree. Pushing the energy in both directions created a cushion of air around him. He pressed up harder and heard cracking and creaking; as he felt the energy start to drain away, he pushed as hard as he could. The wood finally gave way and exploded up and to the sides. Daylight poured in as some of the debris rained down on him. It wasn't too heavy this time, and he was able to claw his way out of it.

Once on top, he could see that only a small portion of the tree itself had landed on him; it was mostly branches that had held him in place. A large portion of the tree stuck up, its ends jagged and rotted; only a few broken branches hung limply. The rest of the tree was piled around it in a rotted heap. Farkor was shining down, and it felt amazing on his skin. He paused to take stock of his situation; his hands were covered in small red bumps, his shirt was torn, and in every place where skin was exposed, he could see more stings. Reaching up, he could feel his head was covered in honey and wax. He struggled through the branches until he made it back onto the ground next to the tree. His shirt and pants hung from him like rags. His skin burned and itched. He could see the barrow from where he stood; he was just a short distance into the trees. He looked around and headed in the direction from which Airnin said he had gotten the water. He went to lean on his oska to help him walk and realized he didn't have it. He turned and closed his eyes, searching back and forth. The sul of the tree obscured his vision some. He spotted a clump of suls, so he started to move branches and work his way down to them until he pulled the oska free. He was relieved to see that it wasn't damaged. Leaning on it and walking a few paces, he stopped, dropped to the ground, and pulled off his boots. The energy from Dainua felt good, so he pulled some of her up and into him, the energy flowing around his sul and body before rushing back into the ground. It helped soothe the pain. He stood and stumbled northwest for a bit, then heard the sound of running water. He turned east and followed the tantalizing trickle. Finally, he came to a small brook and stepped into it; the cold reminded him of Airnin. Panicking, he scrutinized the land around him, then glanced up at the blue sky. *Must be in the barrow*, he thought. He remembered pushing the energy away from him and Airnin disappearing into the trees. Realizing there was nothing he could do now, Fearn pulled off his shirt and pants and slowly slid into the brook. The welts on his legs were now covered in smaller, tinier welts. He splashed water onto his face to numb the pain. He stayed in the frigid water until his lower half was numb from the cold. He bent over and dunked his head into the water to wash out the honey, wax, and dead bees. Feeling sufficiently numb, he crawled out to get dressed. His right pant leg was ripped to the knee, and the left was almost completely missing. He looked at his shirt; it too was torn so badly he couldn't tell how it went back on. After struggling with it for a bit, he gave up, dropped it, and headed back to the barrow.

Once at the entrance, he cautiously made his way down the rock wall and into the tunnel. Finally, happy to be "home," he collapsed onto his bedroll.

"Airnin, are you in there?" Fearn called out into the room. The only answer was his own voice echoing back at him. He laid back on his bedroll and looked at the light of Farkor reflecting in the tunnel. Smiling to himself, he closed his eyes and fell asleep.

That night Fearn awoke, cold and sore. Every part of him ached. He reached for his lantern and realized he had forgotten it in the woods.

"Oy, Airnin, you there?" Fearn called out, but there was no reply. His stomach growled. It had been two nights since he last ate. He rubbed his arms and chest, trying to warm them. This didn't help; it just made all of the bee stings itch even more and the scratches sting.

"I want a warm fire," he grumbled. "Oy, my tinder box is next to the lantern. Why didn't you grab them?" he said, irritated with himself. He stood, and every bone and muscle screamed in pain. Stooping to grab his oska and cursing at the pain squatting caused him, Fearn reluctantly made his way out of the tomb.

When he got to the rock ladder, he looked up and stared at the bright stars above him. A cool breeze flowed down and seemed to flow right through him. Shivering, he slowly and painfully made his way up the handholds. Flopping onto the ground once he reached the top, he rolled over to stare at the stars. *If Dainua is below and Telgog is around me, then who do the stars belong to?* he thought. Another cool breeze swept over the hill, motivating him to move on. He tried to sit up, but it hurt too much, so he tried rolling down the hill; however, there was a standing stone in his way. As he pushed himself from his stomach to his feet, he noticed something white gleaming in the starlight against a standing stone in front of him. Using his oska to push himself up, he walked over and picked it up. It was the skull he found his first night there. He had assumed it had fallen in with the rubble and was crushed so never felt a need to look for it. He peered closely at it, then closed his eyes. A whisper of a sul was all that was left in it. Tucking it under his arm, he walked down the hill.

He was relieved to find the lantern, tinder box, and knife where he had left them, but noticed the skins they made the night before were gone, along with all of the meat. "At least whatever took them left the bucket," he thought. He went to the tree he knocked down the night before and gathered some wood that was probably too green, along with some dry wood he found along the way. The fire started right away with the dry wood; when he added the fresh wood, it smoked black and hissed and popped but eventually flared to a wonderful warmth that he wished he could wrap himself in.

He studied the skull. It was pale white, cracked, and dried. He turned it around and noticed that the jaw bone was missing. Placing it in his lap, he reached his hands out to the fire to warm up.

Glancing down at the skull, Fearn remarked, "If it weren't for you, I wouldn't be here. I don't know if that's a good or bad thing. Well, I guess it's bad in your case," Fearn told it. His stomach growled. After he felt sufficiently warm, he gently placed the skull down, added a few logs to the fire, picked up his oska and knife, and headed out to check the traps.

He was freezing by the time he returned but had two rabbits under his arm. Fearn sat by the fire, gutted and cleaned the rabbits, then found a stick on which to skewer the meat and started cooking. As he watched the light of the fire reflect off of the skull, Fearn wondered where Airnin was or if he had killed him. At that thought, a sense of relief overcame him.

After the meat seemed charred enough, he pulled it from the fire and started to eat. Partway through, he noticed the woods around him grew quiet. He stopped, closed his eyes, and looked around. Through the trees, he saw Airnin's foggy outline gliding towards him. His stomach sank. When Airnin finally stopped in front of him, he could see an expression of fatigue ripple across his face.

"Are you all right, Airnin? Was worried when I didn't see you when I got up," Fearn said. Airnin's face looked vexed.

"I am fine. Had to find a new sul since you almost killed me last night."

Fearn's head dropped, and he looked at the skull, realizing there was now another out there. *Where is their family?* he thought. *How are they going to feed themselves?*

Airnin noticed Fearn staring at the skull at his feet and remarked, "I do not like to kill, Fearn, but you forced it upon me. If you were not so careless with your power, this would not have happened." The light in the fire started to reflect off tears building in Fearn's eyes. "This is the cursed life my brother forced upon me. Every death at my hands is not yours but his. Besides, I make sure to kill the Asinta who betrayed me."

Fearn unconsciously picked at a bee sting on his face as he pondered. *Is that true?* he wondered.

"I brought these along. I figured you would need them when I saw what you were wearing before I left this evening." Airnin held out one of the nicest shirts and pair of pants Fearn had ever seen; sitting on top of them was a wide-brimmed hat with a belt inside.

"I don't want a dead man's clothes, Airnin." The thought disgusted Fearn deeply.

"I understand. However, he has no use for them, and if you do not wear them, you will be no better off than he is currently." Airnin pushed the clothes towards him. Fearn looked to the skull and then back to Airnin. He reluctantly reached out and took them. He stood to get dressed.

"Oy, what is all over your skin?" Airnin asked, seeing the red marks in the firelight.

"A beehive fell on me last night," Fearn said glumly. He felt embarrassed by it but didn't know why. Looking from the clothes to Airnin's face, he saw a wide grin spread across it before quickly dissipating; then, like drops of rain, his face rippled until Airnin burst out laughing. His face looked like a puddle in a rainstorm with a wide smile breaking through on occasion.

"I am sorry, but that is pretty funny." Trying to choke down the laughter made Airnin laugh even harder. It was a loud and grating laugh, something Fearn would have feared and run from before. Now, it felt infectious for some reason, and a smile spread across his face as he started laughing as well. Gazing down from Airnin's face mid-laugh, he saw the skull glaring back at him, which sobered and grounded him.

"Why didn't you help me last night?"

Airnin quieted down. "Well, you took me by surprise and shot me through the trees like an arrow. After I crashed down, the sul I had in me was ripped and drained. It took all I had to focus on my bones in order to find my way back. The energy in me was depleted;

I needed to rest immediately so I could use what was left of the sul to find another. When I got back to the tree, I feared you were dead; however, I could make out your sul through the debris and felt it was a fitting punishment to leave you there until tonight. How did you manage to free yourself?"

A chill ran through Fearn that not even the fire behind him could warm. Looking down at the clothes in his hands, he slowly dressed as he told Airnin about the bees and how he managed to free himself. The clothes were too big, but once he rolled up the shirt sleeves and pant legs they fit adequately. The pants had a few loops sewn into them. He looped the belt through these and notched another hole in it with his knife to make it snug enough. Folded in the pants were a nice pair of leather boots. These were also a tad big, but Fearn had worn worse. Once dressed, he felt surprisingly warmer. He grabbed the hat last and put it on; it fell over his ears and covered his eyes. Frustrated, he set it aside.

"Fearn, I think we will take a rest from lessons tonight. I do want to commend you on your efforts last night. Do you see how great you are already becoming already under my tutelage? Uram could not have taught you to do that in twice the time. That lesson was a fight not meant to be won; it was given to show you the importance of keeping a large sul with you at all times. Though, apparently, having a strong sul at your back is just as good," Airnin finished with a chuckle. "You consumed that sul last night quickly. You should be proud of yourself, taking me off guard twice. I will not let it happen a third time."

Fearn smiled weakly. Thinking of the man who died because he couldn't control his powers didn't make him feel very proud. "Thanks," he finally said.

Fearn looked down at the skull. Thinking for a moment, he finally picked it up and looked around for some soft dirt, which he found near a tree. He dug a small hole with his hands and then gently placed the skull in it.

"May you find your way to Dainua," he prayed, then covered the skull and returned to the fire.

Airnin shook his head and muttered, "So weak. If you continue to show weakness, your enemies will have defeated you before you have even begun the fight."

Luckily, the next weeks and months passed uneventfully. Fearn progressed far enough to be able to start shooting arrows and became quite good at it. Consuming suls became second nature, as well. The end of summer turned to fall, and winter fast approached.

MARKET

Fearn awoke and saw his breath in the air, grateful for the furs that Airnin had helped him make by mending several together to cover Fearn's bedroll.

He felt groggy. This was the first time in months that he was getting up in the actual morning.

He pulled on the cloak Airnin gave him a few nights past. As he did, guilt filled him; he hoped there wasn't another person dead or cold because he needed some warmth. Airnin said he had stolen it, and Fearn hoped it wasn't a tale. After stuffing a small fur into the wide-brimmed hat Airnin had given him a few months back, he placed it on his head. It felt big but shaded his face.

He carefully piled the leather and furs and tied it all together with a long piece of leather, careful to leave enough excess so he had something to hang onto once it was slung over his back. Putting the leather over one shoulder and grabbing his oska in his other hand, he headed out, glancing at Airnin's tomb as he walked past.

"See you tonight," Fearn called towards Airnin's tomb, then tapped his oska against it. He walked through the tunnel until he got to the stone ladder. He pulled in and consumed one of the suls in his oska, then jumped, pushing down with the sul's energy, flying up out of the tunnel and landing lightly on his feet next to one of the standing stones. Fearn smiled as he recalled all of the times he had landed on his face trying to master that jump. Farkor was bright overhead and Fearn had to squint in the light even under the wide-brimmed hat. Turning towards the farm, he thought of home.

"No, that isn't home anymore," he told himself.

Fearn walked through the woods as carefree as he could muster. Airnin had told him not to sneak, saying suspicions would arise if someone saw him. When he arrived at the edge of the woods, he looked over at the old farm; the house appeared as it had the last time he'd been there, a black and grey corpse amongst weeds and grass. Fearn leaned his oska against a tree and set down the leather and furs. Running his fingers through long hair that now hung past his shoulders, he pulled some hair in front of his face to partially hide it. Then, for good measure, he knelt down and rubbed some dirt on his face. Picking up his oska and pack of leathers, he turned right and headed for the road.

As he approached the field, he noticed browning lull weed had taken over, and there were no vegetables in sight. It hurt to see something that his dad spent a lifetime caring for withered away. He turned his eyes to the right and caught sight of the massive oak tree that loomed over everything around it. It felt like the day he planted it had been many seasons ago, not just that past spring. He stood, his mouth agape; he had forgotten how large it had grown. Most of its leaves were gone, a sign winter was approaching. The exposed branches were as thick as some of the neighboring trees. Walking over to the tree, he saw that his mother and father's headstones were still firmly embedded in it; offerings of now rotten food had been left at its massive roots.

"Oy, Mom and Dad, I miss you," Fearn whispered as he ran a hand across the bark, feeling the tree's sul. Not knowing what else to say, he stretched his back, adjusted the leather bundle, and headed towards the village.

He passed a stone marker to his right. *One more stone till the village*, he thought. He was nervous. What if they recognized him? The road felt longer than he remembered, and his anxiety escalated with each step.

Finally coming within sight of the village, Fearn realized nothing had changed. It was still the broken husk of a once-thriving community. *You can do this,* he whispered to himself as he passed the now-defunct gates. He began to relax as he neared the tavern, memories of telling tales flooding his thoughts. The village was full; people were bustling about, moving to and from the village square. Slipping behind someone, Fearn did his best to blend in.

He saw familiar faces everywhere, peering around as often as he could without looking suspicious. Thankfully, he didn't see a single soldier. Fearn picked a spot between two farmers and got to work unpacking, setting out the leather and furs he had brought. Once he was done, he noticed two men waiting for him, eyeing him queerly.

"Oy, you not from these parts?" one of the men asked.

Fearn tried to deepen his voice as he replied "Ay, Father and I recently moved into the woods east of here. We don't like the village life but we needed some supplies." His voice seemed to draw even stranger looks; maybe Airnin's idea of being a mute was better.

"From the east, you say? No one comes from those parts, deamhons that way," the other man replied.

Fearn suddenly recognized the men; he had seen them in the tavern. They were farmers who lived off in the woods, southwest of the village. The Bitveen Brothers, if he recalled correctly. They stayed to themselves mostly. His dad had told him that they came from the west when he was younger. The brother on the left had a deep scar across the cheek, and the other had eyes that always looked in opposite directions. When they were at the tavern, the tales of deamhons always seemed to get them riled up. That gave Fearn an idea.

"You're right. It's crawling with deamhons. We've found a way to avoid them." The man with the lazy eye stepped closer.

"How you do that?" Lazy Eye asked.

"See this leather and fur? My grandfather found a way to make it so that when you wear it, the deamhon will think you are that animal. We all know that the only thing they will eat is human bones, so when we wear them, they crawl right on by and leave us alone," Fearn said with all the confidence he could muster.

"How we know you not lying?" Lazy Eye nudged his brother knowingly.

"I'm standing in front of you as proof," Fearn replied, squaring his shoulders to look bigger than he was.

"Hmmm, that you are," Lazy Eye replied. Scar finally stepped forward and lowered his voice. "The deamhon take the food I leave out before. Now, they take my plate and bowl. Will this leather fix that?"

"Just cut a piece from this leather and place it under your bowl or plate," Fearn directed.

The two men stepped back and talked between themselves, but Fearn couldn't make out what was said. Lazy Eye bent down, picked up one of the rabbit furs, and held it up in front of himself.

"How do I hide behind it?"

"You buy enough to cover yourself, and you will look like the biggest rabbit the deamhon has ever seen. It will avoid you altogether."

The men nodded and started talking to each other again. Scar spoke up: "What you want for leather? We have dried meat for trade." Fearn stood back and scratched his chin, trying to look deep in thought.

"Sounds like a fair trade," Fearn replied.

The two men went off and came back with a bundle of dried meat. Judging by the size and thinking back to what his dad would buy, he expected it to last a few months, as long as he rationed and continued eating what he caught in the traps.

"This is what we offer for furs in equal weight," Scar proclaimed.

Fearn nodded and all three headed to the middle of the square, where a man stood next to a set of scales. The men placed their meat on one side of the scales, and Fearn placed the furs on the opposite side. The furs clearly outweighed the meat, so Fearn removed a fur one at a time until the scales balanced out. Fearn was surprised by how few furs it took. Noticing this, the brothers started to haggle, asking for additional furs. Fearn had seen his dad go through this every year.

"No more furs. You can see that the quality is the best you can find. That is why it weighs so much." It was a similar line to what his dad always said. Before the men could respond, he did what normally had worked for his dad.

"I see that the meat is a good quality and you must be fine and upstanding men in this community." The man at the scales sniggered at the comment. "I will give you another fur," Fearn continued, ignoring the man.

"Two more furs," Scar countered, holding up two fingers.

"Done," Fearn groused, trying to appear like he wasn't getting a fair trade as he reluctantly stuck out his hand. Scar reached out and grasped Fearn's wrist. Fearn fetched the meat and headed back to his stall. He was setting the dried meat off to the side when he heard a comment from the farmer to his right.

"Do those furs really hide you from the deamhon?" Fearn knew the man; he was one of the farmers with whom his dad had done a lot of business. He felt bad about lying to the man but needed to trade his goods.

"Ay, they have helped me," he said, reluctantly. The farmer came over and picked up one of the furs, turning it over in his hands.

"This is excellent work. You know, you look awfully familiar. There was a farmer east of here that had a son about your age. The farmer was killed, but his son was never found. Some say whoever did the killing made off with him; others say he did the killing himself. Personally, I think Dainua took him. He had been blessed by her. You may have seen the tree that Dainua grew in the farmer's honor, not far off to the east of here. You can't miss it—biggest oak you will have ever seen." The farmer paused and stared at Fearn. Fearn didn't know what to do. He wanted to run, but he had to get the goods he needed, so he just stared back at the farmer. The farmer looked back down at the fur.

"Dair was never a hunter nor did any tanning... told some mighty fine tales though. Guess you couldn't be his son. Say, would you be interested in trading for some potatoes?"

"Sure," Fearn blurted, a little too eagerly. They went to the scales at the center of the square and Fearn traded one fur for fifteen potatoes. He returned and placed the potatoes next to the meat, picked up a few furs and leather, and went to look around for the rest of the supplies he needed. He pulled the brim of his hat down and hoped no one else would recognize him.

He walked past various vendors, most of them farmers selling different vegetables or the occasional fruit. He hurried on past each until he found the vendor he was searching for. There in front of him was a man about a head taller than Fearn with tufts of brown hair, bushy eyebrows, and a round belly under a white apron. He stood behind a crude table piled high with wheels of cheese. It was the dairy man, who Fearn knew kept to himself, except for when he went to the surrounding villages on market days. Fearn had begged his dad to buy from him on occasion, but Dair had strongly felt that cheese and milk were frivolous things.

Fearn walked up to the table and gawked at the different colored cheeses. The aroma was heavenly. "Oy, looking for some cheese, young man? I can also arrange to have milk brought to you, depending on where you reside, of course." The portly man placed his hands on his hips and smiled broadly.

"We live too far away for milk, but I would like to trade for some cheese," Fearn responded as he stepped closer. "I don't know anything about cheese. Do you have one that would survive the winter?"

"You will want a hard cheese." The man stepped forward and started picking up a few rounds of cheese, then stopped, eyeing the leather and fur in Fearn's hand. "Is it leather or furs you are looking to trade or something else?"

Fearn held out his goods. "Yes, the finest you will see around here." The man took the furs from Fearn.

"I don't know about the finest around here; there is an excellent tanner in this village. He tends to stay away from furs, though." The man ran his hand back and forth across the fur and then pressed it between his fingers. "Don't normally have any use for furs; however, this one is nicely crafted." The grazier fiddled around with the cheese on the table, then held up one of his smaller wheels. "Not interested in trading by weight, but if you are willing to part with this fur, I will make you a straight trade." Fearn nodded, "I'll accept that trade." The man reached over his table and handed the cheese to Fearn. "Should last you the winter as long as you keep it in a cool, dark place. If anything green grows on it, just cut it off. Hasn't hurt me any." He patted his stomach and gave a small chuckle.

"Thank you, and I hope you enjoy the fur." Fearn stuck the cheese under his arm and went off, looking for the rest of the supplies. Everywhere he looked, he saw someone he knew. Keeping his head down, he hurried on before anyone could recognize him.

By the end of the day, he was able to get a few woolen shirts, a thick winter cloak, a couple of pairs of pants, oil, enough foodstuffs to hopefully help him get by for the winter and a small hand cart to bring it home in.

Fearn got about a stone away from the village, and his eyes started to droop from fatigue. He pulled a few suls from his oska into himself and consumed them. The power instantly perked him up, but the suls were small and the energy didn't last. He kept this up until he ran out of suls in his oska and desperation set in, knowing he was only about halfway to the barrow.

Fearn closed his eyes and looked around for anything bigger he could use. The only suls he found were small and faint, then something caught his eye. It was the power of Dainua that flowed through the ground beneath him. Airnin had been goading him to use her power for weeks but he had refused. Uram had forbidden him from using her power. Now, he was exhausted and felt she would understand if he used just a little. He pulled her into himself and let her flow through him and back into the ground. It helped some, but not enough to get him back to the barrow. Fearn glanced up and down the road to make sure he was alone, and, feeling confident he was, he contorted his sul and bit into the power of Dainua. The power was like a lightning bolt hitting him. He fell to the ground and his body seized as the energy erupted around and through him. He struggled to cut off the power, but her energy continued to flow from the ground into him. The energy almost filled him completely; he felt like he was going to erupt from the inside out. Out of instinct, he reached out a hand to pour energy into Telgog. It wasn't enough.

The world around him grew black as he seemed to fall into a dark tunnel. The energy abruptly stopped, and Fearn tried clawing his way out, his strength fading as he slipped further into black until the void consumed him.

Air rushed into his lungs. Fearn sat upright and felt sweat stream down his face. Dazed, he tried to take in his surroundings; his cart and supplies were still next to him, judging by the sky above, not too much time had passed. He had had no visions from Dainua's power but was overwhelmed with the feeling of disappointment. A strange sensation of disconnection overcame him as well, like he was floating above the ground. He could not feel Dainua. He looked down and, in a large circle around him, the land was as black as a starless night and utterly dead. In front of him for about fifty pebbles, lay a straight row of trees blown down when he had released Dainua's energy.

Fearn stretched out his arms and legs; they were cramped and sore. Slowly standing, he moved back onto land that wasn't scarred, letting Dainua flow through him again; however, her power didn't seem to course through him as it had before. In fact, it seemed to recoil as it drew near his sul. Thinking it was just his mind playing tricks, he ignored it, breathed in and out a few times, stretched out his hands, and flexed his fingers. Closing his eyes, he focused on Dainua's energy and let it flow through him, trying to reconnect himself to her, though again, she felt fainter and more distant. He panicked that he had lost his connection to her. As a reflex, he closed himself off from Dainua and then had her rush into him again.

"What was that?" Fearn asked himself. He closed his eyes again and focused on Dainua's power, and as he did, he realized he could choose to open or close himself to her energy. He had never done that before, and he wondered how this ability might help him in his lessons.

Looking back at the downed trees, Fearn knew that he should probably get going in case someone came to investigate. He pushed his cart and hurried down the road. As he walked, he practiced opening and closing himself to Dainua.

Once Fearn arrived at the barrow, he stood in the treeline and slowly let some of Dainua into himself, then cut her off and pushed the part that was in him into his oska. He slowly pushed the cart up the hill.

Fearn pulled the sul from Dainua in his oska and consumed it. The power crackled around him and was stronger than any of the suls he had consumed before, but it didn't cause discomfort. The feeling of disappointment was even stronger this time; he felt like he had been caught stealing. He tried to shake the feeling by focusing on the task at hand. He unpacked the cart, then jumped into the black pit, pushing down and around himself to slow his descent. Once on the ground below, he set down the load of supplies. It was dim, so Fearn crept down the tunnel and retrieved the lantern. Holding out his hand, Fearn concentrated on the energy in him and rubbed his thumb and forefinger together, focusing the energy in the air just above his fingertips. A few moments later, a small flame began to hover in the air, and he used it to light the lantern. Fearn thought creating fire had to be the best thing Airnin had taught him so far. He walked back, set the lantern down, and jumped to the top to get the rest of the supplies.

After emptying the cart, Fearn placed it next to a standing stone and jumped back into the barrow. The energy from Dainua still had not been depleted. Fearn stared up the tunnel above him. The light of day was starting to fade. Holding his hand in front of himself, Fearn concentrated, moving his fingers back and forth until the small flame appeared. Slowly, as he concentrated on the flame, feeding it the energy it needed to stay lit, he moved his other hand around it, then moved the flame from one hand to the other. As he poured more energy in, it became a large ball of flame. His arms and face started to sweat from the heat; however, the energy that he poured out protected his hands. He lifted the flame and, as the energy waned, he flung the fireball up the tunnel, pushing the rest of the energy behind it. He watched as it flew out of the tunnel and faded as the energy that created it dwindled and died.

Fearn happily got to work moving the supplies from the tunnel to his bedroll. As he finished, an icy cold filled the air.

"Glad to see you made it back safely. You seem to have done well in trading the leather and furs," Airnin said behind him. Fearn closed his eyes, turned around, and smiled at him. "I'm exhausted. It's been a long day. I had to use the power of Dainua to get back here." Airnin's face rippled and a gleeful smile appeared.

"So, you finally gave in and used the power that is every Tiller's birthright?"

Fearn felt ashamed but recalled how exhilarating it felt to have Dainua's energy course through him. A part of him was eager to do it again. He pushed the feeling of disappointment into the recesses of his mind.

"You will take a nap. I will scout the area and wake you when I return. Now that you have taken the step to use Dainua, we can progress with your training."

"I'm tired and want to go to bed. Can we do this tomorrow, please?" Fearn pleaded.

"No. Do as you are told. You need to practice and, if I let you sleep tonight, you will be up tomorrow. Get some rest, and I will be back." Without giving Fearn a chance to whine anymore, Airnin left.

Exhausted, Fearn lay down and fell fast asleep.

DAINUA

An icy cold jab awoke Fearn; the chill sank into his shoulder and slowly spread. He recoiled from Airnin, yelping, "I'm awake!" Fearn rubbed his eyes. "Just let me go back to sleep," Fearn begged. He rolled over, glaring and ready for a fight, but found that Airnin had already left. Sighing, he stood up and pulled out the knife he kept on his belt. He walked over to the supplies he purchased and laid them out one by one until he found what he was looking for. He grabbed the round of cheese, cut a small triangle, and pulled back the waxy outer shell. He held it up to his nose and inhaled deeply, then took a small bite, rolling the cheese across his tongue. It was a tad bitter but had a sweetness that came through at the end. It was amazing. He wished he had traded for more than one wheel. After carefully putting the wheel of cheese away, he grabbed his oska and sleepily left to meet Airnin while holding the remains of the slice of cheese.

Fearn reached the tree where they held their lessons; Airnin was waiting. Fearn stopped, leaned on his oska, and took another bite of cheese. Airnin didn't move or speak. Fearn closed his eyes and looked at Airnin's face. It was placid and still.

"Oy, are we going to do something, or can I just go back to bed?" Fearn challenged with disdain. Airnin replied in a low, soft whisper, "Sit properly and give me the respect I deserve." Fearn stood there, contemplating how much he wanted to push Airnin. After a few moments, he replied, "I don't want to sit. Can we just do the lesson so I can go to bed?"

There was a grey flash. A sharp cold stung Fearn's chest, and his feet lifted off the ground as he flew backward. He landed on his back, gasping for air, tears forming in his eyes. He forced his eyes to close, holding back the tears. Digging his fists into the dirt, he waited for the pain to ease so he could catch his breath. He made himself relax, slowly breathing in the cool night air before opening his eyes. He wiped the tears away with the back of his hand as he sat up. Airnin was still standing in the same spot. In the dirt a few feet in front of him lay the piece of cheese. Eyes transfixed on the savory treat, Fearn bellowed, "I hate you!" Airnin continued to stand, making no response. This made Fearn even angrier. He thought back to when he pushed Airnin through the trees; he reached out and opened up to let Dainua rush into him. Her flow was weak like a brook and not the rushing river it had been earlier that day. Fearn, being outraged, didn't register the change and grabbed her to take as much of her energy as he felt he could muster. He paused, closed his eyes, and focused on Dainua, letting her energy calm him.

Fearn opened his eyes, stood, and cautiously walked over to Airnin, ignoring the cheese. He retrieved the oska, then sat, crossing his legs and placing the oska across his lap.

A few moments passed, and Airnin finally spoke: "Now that you have decided to act like a man, we can continue. Unlike other suls, the power of Dainua is unique; she is infinite, yes, but also limited. You must become like a miller's water wheel, letting her energy flow by you, giving you the power you need. As you learned today, though, her power is limited to one place, while you must be constantly moving in order to stay ahead of your opponent. You may have noticed that the more of her you use, the more distant she becomes until she shuns you completely. This will only last a few days, but beware of it. Use her only when you must."

Fearn finally showed some interest and spoke up. "What?" he said, confused, and then opened himself up to Dainua and focused on her as she flowed into him. Her power seemed timid and drew back when his sul reached out to her. Panic started to set in. Thinking that he had lost the only mother he knew, Fearn blurted out, "What do I need to do to get Dainua back?"

"Stop babbling like a child and listen. If you had paid attention to what I said, you would have heard that she will return. Consuming her power taints your sul with the energy of Telgog. In a day or two, your sul will balance itself. Like I said, be careful doing this. Not only will her powers stop flowing through you, but using the suls of everything else will give you diminished powers, as well. We must be balanced between Dainua and Telgog to harness the power most effectively."

Something seemed off and suddenly Fearn realized why. "Why is our sul not tainted when we consume the suls of everything else?"

"Ah, so you *are* paying attention. Every other sul contains a lot less power than Dainua. However, if you consumed a lot of suls, the same effect would happen. Have you not wondered why we only train some nights consuming suls? If we did it every night, then you would be cut off." Airnin walked around Fearn. "Stand in front of me," he commanded.

Fearn stood and did what he was told, grumbling about how tired he was; if Airnin heard, he didn't remark.

"You have learned to use the oska as a storage device for suls, but it has a more important purpose. Give it to me." Fearn stepped forward and handed over his oska, then stepped back. He closed his eyes to watch. Airnin had only shown mending, and Fearn was eager to see what else he could do.

"Step to my left, Fearn, and concentrate on the oska," Airnin directed. After Fearn moved to Airnin's left, he watched as the sul Airnin had trapped in his chest shrank, turning into pure energy. As it did, Airnin turned a lighter shade of grey; power moved around and through him as he gripped the oska in his right hand. He swung it behind him and swept it forward. As the oska came forward, the energy surged down into a small rock on the ground. The energy discharged, causing the rock to shoot up and sail straight over the barrow, reflecting briefly in the starlight. Airnin handed the oska back to Fearn.

"That is just a small portion of what you can do. With the right gestures, you can throw fireballs or bolts of lightning—or even encase yourself in a wall of protection."

Fearn grasped the leather on the oska tightly. "What do I need to do? Just swing it?"

"No. As you swing, you want to push the energy like you have before but then hold it at the tip of the oska. Just before it comes in contact with what you want to hit, release the energy into Telgog."

Fearn walked over to a small rock and kicked it towards the center of the clearing. He closed his eyes, consumed some of the smaller suls in his oska, moved the oska back, and held it there, concentrating on the energy. He gingerly moved it forward as he pushed the energy down his oska and attempted to hold it there. The energy felt like a large weight he was trying to hold by the tips of his fingers. It didn't help that Telgog was trying to pull it away. Fearn's eyes looked to the top of the barrow, expecting to see the rock sailing away. Confused, Fearn glanced down and noticed he missed it completely. He turned to Airnin for guidance.

"Maybe you should practice swinging at rocks, first?" Airnin critiqued.

Fearn spent the next hour either hitting the rock but having lost all of the energy or concentrating so hard that he missed the rock completely. Each time, he would look to Airnin who would respond, "Again." Finally, by sheer luck, Fearn was able to connect with the rock and sent it sailing towards the heavens. He cheered in excitement. Airnin merely replied, "Again."

"Are you still mad?" Fearn asked.

"Again," was the only answer Airnin would give. Sighing, Fearn returned to practicing. He had to switch hands back and forth when his arm would get tired. As the night wore on, Fearn felt like he was getting worse, not better. Between the fatigue and growing frustration, Fearn wanted to give up, and whenever he told Airnin he was done trying, the only response he received was "Again." It seemed to carry more weight than one word should, as though he was actually saying, "Go ahead. Test me one more time and see what happens." Fearn could also feel the energy he was creating had less power each time he pulled back.

Finally, just before first light, Fearn started to connect with the rock more consistently; each time he hit it, though, it flew a shorter distance. He was still losing a lot of energy, but he felt like he was finally making progress. After a while, instead of the word coming from Airnin, he heard, "You are done. Go get rest. You will need it. Archery practice tonight." Fearn kicked the rock he had set up for his next swing, then headed to bed, grateful the night was finally over. As he reached out to Dainua before he headed up the barrow, she seemed like nothing but a shadow of herself.

The next few nights slipped into weeks that rolled into years. Fearn practiced every night. Some nights, he learned the powers of the Tiller; other nights, they focused on archery, trapping, or creating leather. For a few months, he ran every night; at that point, Fearn had suspected that Airnin had run out of things for him to do. His only break from lessons came when he took leather and furs to market once a season. Each time, he worried that he would be recognized, until he realized that no one thought to look for someone they assumed was dead.

Mouse

In the last days of spring, Fearn, now a man at sixteen years old, made ready for his night of training. He placed some meat from the previous night's kill, root vegetables, and herbs into a metal pot. He dropped in a wooden spoon, picked up the pot and his oska, then headed out.

Leaping from the tunnel onto the blackened hill, Fearn strode into the forest. The black on the barrow had spread like a cancer into the surrounding forest. The training ground, unlike the barrow, still maintained small patches of green and brown interspersed throughout the black. Some of the trees had also been affected by the years of training he had done. They were either dead or slowly dying. It had bothered him at first, but now he barely noticed the blight he was slowly spreading.

Fearn arrived at the current training ground, set down the pot, and went about gathering firewood. He found a tree with a few branches still within reach. He swung his oska at one of the larger branches, releasing the energy just before it made contact. The branch snapped off with a hollow crack, echoing in the clearing. Fearn picked up one end of the branch and dragged it back to the clearing. He retrieved the hatchet he had embedded in a nearby tree the night before and went to work chopping the branch.

I really need to get an ax next time I'm in the village, he thought. He stacked the majority of the cut wood, placing the rest into the firepit. He rubbed his fingers together, then used the flame he created to light the wood in various places until the fire started. He waited until the fire took hold, then added a few more logs, grabbed the pot, and hiked into the woods. As he walked, he pulled suls from his oska into himself and consumed them until he built up the necessary energy. At the brook, he placed the pot in the middle and focused his energy into the stream of water, creating a gently sloping invisible barrier that dammed the water and caused it to start flowing over the bank before slowly moving off the ground and into the pot. When there was enough water, Fearn released the energy and let the water crash down and continue on its way. He gathered the pot and his oska, then walked back to the fire.

Fearn placed the pot next to the fire to warm, then wandered about fifty pebbles into the forest with his oska in hand. It was too short now to use as a walking stick, so he twirled it in his hand as he strolled along, pulling bits of sul he found along the way and storing them in his oska. He consumed most of the suls once he arrived at a small grove of trees. He then knelt on one knee and focused the energy. He peered through the dark at the tree in front of him before sprinting forward, pushing with the captured energy to increase his speed. A few paces from the tree, he leapt, twisted, and landed on the trunk of the tree. He shifted the energy, using the oska to push energy to his left and right so he could stand balanced upright as he ran up the trunk. The power of Telgog rippled around him. He stopped as he reached the branches and focused the energy to hold himself in place. When he closed his eyes, he could see the tree's sul around him. He pulled a little of the sul and consumed it, then leapt from the tree and rolled over in the air until he was perpendicular with the ground. Pushing behind and below himself to move at an upward angle towards the nearest tree, he watched for the sul in its branches to know when to change his trajectory in order to dodge them, feeling the leaves brush against his face as he rushed past. Reaching out a hand, he grabbed onto a branch as he pushed hard in front of him to stop. While Fearn hung below the branch, he opened his eyes to admire the view around him. He was almost at the top of the tree. He could see stars in the gaps between leaves above him. He closed his eyes, glanced down, let go of the branch, and landed on the branch below him, feeding Telgog energy to balance himself. He searched below until he spotted a path down. He dove off and watched the sul of the tree in the branches and leaves pass by. As he exited the tree's canopy, he flipped and pushed down, landing in a crouch with his oska held out, ready to attack or defend. After scanning the trees around him, he opened his eyes and patted the ground next to him. "Thank you, Dainua," he whispered, then gazed up, saying, "Thank you, Telgog." Fearn broke into a run as he headed back to the clearing.

The fire had burned down to coals. Fearn picked up the pot and placed it into the fire, pushing the hot coals around it with a stick. Fearn scanned his surroundings, intently sure that Airnin should be back from his nightly patrol. Airnin had been staying away longer and longer; some nights, he did not appear until just before the first rays of Farkor.

The night air felt refreshing and the stars sparkled brightly overhead. He was leaning forward to stir the soup when he heard a rustling noise from behind. Fearn instinctively dropped the spoon, pulled in a large sul from his oska, consumed it, pushed down hard, and shot straight up into the air, closing his eyes as his feet left the ground. He twisted so his right side was facing his possible attacker while spinning his oska in his hand, surrounding it in energy, letting it flow down and out from the tip just before something crashed hard into the energy shield. Fearn briefly opened his eyes and saw a large ax embedded in the energy field he had in front of him. Releasing the energy, Fearn fell, pushing down at the last moment to slow himself. He landed, ducking just in time as a large rock whizzed past his head, the ax landing head first into the ground at his feet. He kept the oska spinning in his hands.

Airnin stood fifteen pebbles in front of Fearn, with a broad grin rippling across his face. Fearn stopped spinning the oska and opened his eyes. He rushed over and stuck out his hand to Airnin who grasped him at the wrist.

"Oy, I expected the rock, but an ax? Are you crazy? You could have killed me!" Fearn barked, then broke out laughing.

Airnin made a weird shrugging motion, before replying, "Well, you have been whining about needing one, so I borrowed it."

"You mean *stole*," Fearn quipped.

"If a farmer is going to leave an ax outside, they deserve it. I take it you don't want this loaf of bread I *stole*?" Fearn felt guilty, knowing how much a farmer had to give in trade for a decent ax. He tried to laugh it off, "Ay, I do need one."

"You are better than those commoners. I have said countless times that you are one of the finest Tillers I have trained, and being above them gives you the right to take what you want." Airnin then pointed to Fearn's oska. "I enjoyed watching you consume that sul in a heartbeat. It shows me you are going to make a fine ally."

Fearn turned back to the fire to continue cooking his soup. He absentmindedly reached over his shoulder, rubbing his fingers over the scar from Airnin's first surprise attack, which had left an arrow point in his shoulder. Every once in a while, he could feel it scrape against his shoulder bone.

As Fearn stirred the soup, he looked back at Airnin, asking "Am I ready now?" Airnin glided to him, saying. "The time has come to start putting a plan in place. First, though, you need to do something about that oska."

Fearn turned his attention to one thing he truly loved and asked, "What's wrong with it?"

"Well, to start, it is way too short for you. I have not taught you this because walking into the village with a Tiller's oska could arouse suspicions in anyone who was bright enough to recognize an Asinta's staff." Fearn was shocked that there was something Airnin hadn't taught him.

"What is it that I need to learn?" Fearn asked eagerly.

"It is actually something quite simple, and I have been a bit disappointed that you have not figured it out. As you know, your oska is a living thing. It is just a matter of using that sul to make it grow." Airnin held out a hand out to stop Fearn as he started to examine his oska. "Wait until I am gone," he directed.

"There are two things you need to know before you proceed. The next time you walk back to the village, you will shed the cloak of who you have been; there is no turning back from that. The second is that to grow your oska is an art. A tiller does not simply make it longer. The finer and more intricate the twists, turns, or shapes a tiller can put into his oska exhibits to others how well he can wield his abilities, as well as how great his teacher is."

Fearn rolled the oska back and forth in his hands, studying it, angry at himself for not figuring it out on his own. Extending his oska would make some of his abilities easier to do—that was true— but other stances would harder. Uram slipped into his mind. He was the only other Tiller Fearn had met. He recalled the fine lattice work in his oska; he had assumed it was carved. Fearn set his oska to the side to contemplate how he wanted to change it as he finished cooking the soup. Fearn spooned some of the soup to his lips, and it was delicious. He tore a chunk of bread from the loaf Airnin had brought and dipped it into the soup. As he bit into the bread, he wished he had cheese to go with it.

Between bites, Fearn glanced to Airnin, asking, "Tonight is archery practice, correct?"

"Yes, it is. Did you practice in the grove?"

"Yes, while I waited for the coals."

"Go ahead and finish your soup. I will get what is needed." With that, Airnin floated away.

Fearn finished his soup, then headed into the woods to meet Airnin at the clearing where they had practiced archery for the past few weeks.

Airnin stood in the clearing with bow in hand. After closing his eyes, something caught Fearn's attention: the sul in Airnin's chest was fresher. He tried to always look at Airnin's face when he talked with him. He hated to see the thing that kept him alive, a reminder of Airnin's true form. He knew that Airnin had to get a new sul on a regular basis but never broached the subject of how he always managed to find an Asinta or a local who had powers of which they were unaware.

"Airnin, I have never seen you deplete the sul you keep in your chest," Fearn remarked as he studied Airnin's face. He found he could better judge Airnin by his expressions than the words he spoke. This time, his face was still, not a ripple of emotion appeared.

"How easily you forget. Do you not recall a few months back when I was in my tomb resting because I had not been able to find a replacement?" Fearn remembered the month that he practiced alone, waiting for Airnin to recover. He still couldn't recall a time he had ever actually seen it depleted; though, as he thought back, there had been several times Airnin was gone for an extended period.

"Ay, I remember now. It has happened several times, now that I think about it."

"You have to remember, Fearn. Asinta do not simply wander through the forest. I also have to be careful not to draw their attention to the barrow. If my brother found out I had escaped my imprisonment, he would bring his army here. We cannot have that, especially since we are so close to finally being able to enact revenge. I have proven to you through my kindness, caring for and teaching you, that I am not a ruthless killer. Stop being ungrateful. Put those childish thoughts away and let us get back to the task at hand." A look of sadness rippled across Airnin's face, and Fearn felt guilty. Airnin couldn't help who he was. It wasn't his fault he had become a wraith. In many ways, Fearn had come to see Airnin as a second father, but he hadn't been able to say it aloud; something inside him always made him shy away. He knew Airnin had no choice in the horrible things he did in order to stay alive. There were times he still wasn't sure if Airnin wanted him around; though, the stronger he became in wielding suls, the friendlier Airnin grew. It reminded Fearn of when he used to tell tales with his dad.

Fearn finally concluded that Airnin was right. If Airnin was littering the woods with corpses, he would surely have seen them by now. "Sorry, Airnin, I know this isn't the life you chose for yourself," Fearn replied somberly.

Airnin face rippled with a grin. "No need to be sorry. I would be worried if you did not question my nature. Regardless of your common birth, I expect more from you. Let us get back to training. I have tied a mouse to a tree somewhere around here. You must hit it from the spot in which you stand." Fearn opened his eyes and took the bow and an arrow that they had mended together. It had a hawk's sul in the tip and nock. The hawk had taken Fearn weeks to track down. The bow was fused with the suls of young saplings.

Fearn nocked the arrow, keeping the point down. He closed his eyes and examined his surroundings. The smallest thing he had searched for before was a rabbit. He scanned the suls of the trees, watching them flow up and down; he could see through to the trees behind them when their suls shifted. A tree's sul had a rhythm as it flowed and swayed. He allowed it to mesmerize him so that anything which did not flow in the same way stuck out. Fearn slowly turned, sweeping with his eyes. On the third rotation, something finally caught his attention. He waited for it to reappear. Suddenly, a sul shimmered at about five trees away. Fearn kept his eyes on the faint sul, waiting for the suls in front of it to shift again. He kept his ears open for any sound. Airnin had stabbed him in the back several months back while practicing with the bow, leaving a scar that was still pink. The sul in the tree shifted again. Fearn was certain he spotted the target. The sul of the tree flowed and shifted right while the mouse's sul swayed to the left. He reached out to the mouse but couldn't feel it; Airnin had placed it too far away. Examining the suls of the trees between himself and the mouse's sul, he created a visual path in his head. He traced the path from himself to the mouse several times, squared his shoulders, and drew the arrow back. Sighting the tip of the arrow several paces to the right of the mouse's sul, he tightened down on Dainua's sul, pulled a little of it, and consumed it. He let the arrow fly. Focusing on it as it soared, he pushed and pulled on the nock to give it the speed it needed, slowing it down just enough to take a tight turn around a tree. He knew slowing it too much would make it fall, and the manipulation accuracy faded the farther it flew. As he directed the arrow around the last tree, he pushed it hard and let go, feeling it fade away. Fearn turned to face Airnin behind him.

"Looks impressive, but I cannot tell if you hit it or not," Airnin remarked.

Fearn smiled. "Trade you a night off if I did."

"Deal. If you missed, you get to spend all of tomorrow trying until you do."

Fearn sprinted to where he sent the arrow. The tree seemed farther away than when he was pushing the arrow. Finally, rounding a tree, Fearn found a small brown mouse with a string around it pinned to the tree by the arrow.

Airnin glided up to Fearn. "That is impressive. I was certain you would have had to cut the surrounding trees down with arrows before you managed to hit it. You may take the night off; however, if you are dedicated, you will come back tomorrow and try again. This may have been a fluke."

"Really?" Fearn asked, shocked.

"We made a bargain. It was an excellent shot, a fine example of what a wonderful teacher I am."

Fearn grabbed the arrow and slowly worked it out of the tree, then cupped his hand around the mouse and pulled the arrow from it. He wiped the arrowhead on his pants, knelt, set the arrow aside, and dug a small hole in which to bury the mouse. "To Dainua may you return," he prayed before he covered the mouse. He picked up the arrow and turned to see that Airnin had already left.

Making his way back to the smoldering fire, he saw Airnin standing beside it. Fearn added a few smaller logs before asking, "So, I really get a night off?"

"As I said, it was an excellent shot. However, you must practice it again. Besides, I have needed to do a thorough search of the area for any soldiers or Asinta. We have some time left. Why don't you tell me one of your father's tales? You will need to practice them, as they will be needed when we put my plan into motion."

THE LADY OF THE WOODS

Fearn contemplated for a moment before asking, "How about Lady of the Woods? It's a story my dad would tell to the older children."

Fearn turned to face Airnin, but instead of addressing him, Fearn instead pretended he was addressing a crowded tavern. Fearn tried to look taller, and his voice dropped an octave as he began his tale.

"Let's see...

"There once was a boy named Leithadas, the desire of every girl in the village. He was taller and better-looking than the other boys; he bested them at every game they played. He wore the finest clothes, for his parents were wealthy. They owned a mill and several of the farms on which the other villagers lived and toiled. He didn't see the village girls as Dainua's daughters as all boys are taught; instead, he treated them like a cat playing with its prey. He would only give his affection to a girl he thought prettier than the last, and then only keep her around until another girl caught his eye. He left them with a brass trinket, a kiss on the lips, and a promise that he would be back—a promise he had no intention of keeping. Several of the girls dated other boys to try to win his affection back. If jealousy got the best of Leithadas, he would find a way to humiliate her suitor to win her back. However, when he inevitably left her again, instead of bequeathing her a brass trinket, he would give her a silver necklace with a plain golden ring. So all the girls knew whom he favored most.

"One night, on his way to see his newest possession, he was passing the woods that bordered his parents' land. He saw a woman several years older than himself standing just beyond the treeline, wearing a white dress that accentuated *all* of her features. She coyly beckoned for Leithadas to approach. Realizing that she was far fairer than the girl he was going to see, Leithadas hurried towards her. As he neared, he noticed she wasn't any of the girls or women he had seen in either his village or those neighboring. Her skin was a fine porcelain white that seemed to sparkle in the starlight. She didn't say a word but continued beckoning him to follow as she turned and walked into the woods. Her feet were bare and clean despite the dirt she walked across. The trees seemed to glow, their branches swaying in the breeze as if to bow to her as she passed. She entered a clearing, and in the center was a bed; the wooden posts wound up and around, creating a canopy that appeared to have grown directly from the ground. The woman walked over to it, laid down on her side, and motioned for Leithadas to approach. Leithadas gave no heed to the danger of seeing such a sight, too fixated on her beauty. He eagerly entered the clearing. When he was about a pace away, he noticed she smelled like a flowering field and had hair that flowed down and draped her figure perfectly. Leithadas hastily reached out to touch her, but she put up a hand.

" 'I cannot let just any man into my bed. I require his token of affection first. What will you sacrifice for me?' she asked.

"Leithadas desired her above all else and promised her anything; no sacrifice would be too great. She stood and pulled him forward, kissing him on the cheek. Her lips felt like a warm summer day. She snapped her fingers, causing a beautiful chestnut brown horse to burst from the tree line and trot up to them. It had a finely-made saddle on which a bow and quiver were tied.

"The woman whispered into his ear, 'Take flight upon this horse and take down the four white does that roam these woods. Cut out their hearts and return them to me.' The woman's hair felt as soft as rose petals against Leithadas's cheek.

Without hesitation, Leithadas untied the bow, mounted the horse, and headed into the woods. At first, he was unsure which direction to go, but then the horse broke into a gallop with a fevered determination. He clutched at the horn, trying not to fall off; suddenly, the galloping smoothed to a gentle rocking motion. Up ahead, he saw the first doe; it turned to look at Leithadas, and upon seeing him, its eyes widened in fear. Leithadas took an arrow from the quiver and fired. His aim was steadfast and true. The doe crumpled into the dirt. The horse slowed and then stopped without being directed. Leithadas stared in amazement at the doe; it was the most beautiful animal he had ever seen. He smiled to himself, proud that he would be the last to see it. As he dismounted, he realized that he didn't have a knife with him; searching around the saddle, he noticed an elegant silver hilt protruding from a finely crafted scabbard that he was sure wasn't there a moment earlier. He unsheathed the knife and eagerly got to work cutting out the doe's heart and placing it into a leather pouch. He mounted the horse and left. With the horse leading him to each doe, Leithadas quickly found the other three, taking the heart from each.

He rode back as swiftly as he could. He found the woman waiting where he had left her, wearing just a smile. His heart raced. He couldn't believe his good fortune.

"Leithadas quickly dismounted, pulled the pouch from the saddle, and laid it at her feet. He made a grand gesture and opened it, removing the first heart and offering it to her. She gingerly accepted the gift then bit ferociously into it, devouring it in several bites. She daintily held out a bloodied hand for the second heart. She quickly ate each one, her porcelain skin becoming a deeper red with each. Leithadas did not care, too mesmerized by the body beneath the gore. Once done with the last heart, she pulled Leithadas forward and, with blood still on her lips, kissed him deeply as she pulled him onto her bed. Thick nettles quickly grew up and over them.

"Leithadas awoke the next morning to find himself in a dirt hut, the smell of dung and blood hanging in the stale air. He rolled over to see an old woman laying bare beside him. Her skin hung loosely, pock-marked with sores and wrinkled. Dried blood covered everything, including himself. Panicked and disgusted, Leithadas fell onto the floor, desperate to get away and search for his clothes. A cackle rang out; horrified, he looked up to see the old woman glaring at him.

" 'You said you would sacrifice anything,' the old woman chided, before cackling again.

"Leithadas gave no response. Instead, he grabbed at the clothes he could find, opened the door, and dashed out, stumbling over his own feet.

"The warm spring air brought him to his senses. Leithadas looked back and saw a hut made of brambles and lull weeds. As the rays of Farkor fell upon it, the vision shrank and faded away, until he stood in an empty meadow. Leithadas dressed and ran towards home, so quickly that he tripped and fell along the way. After what felt like a day had passed, Leithadas emerged from the trees in front of his parents' field, right into a group of men on horseback.

"The men looked at Leithadas in horror, though satisfied to have found him. The men encircled him; pinning him between their horses. One called out, 'We have found the killer!' Leithadas tried to push his way through, but the circle of horses tightened. Leithadas spotted a thin gap between two horses; desperately, he pushed his way through and sprinted into the open field beyond. The men gave chase. Leithadas ran, but there was no place to hide. He heard the thundering sound of the horses drawing closer, a storm about to break. A sharp pain flared in Leithadas's side, pushing him forward and causing him to stumble and fall. As he scrambled to get to his feet, he noticed a broken arrow shaft protruding from his side. Fear drove out the pain as he regained his feet and tried darting around the horse. Another arrow struck him in his back, causing him to fall again. Leithadas gasped for breath as pain wracked his body; he struggled to stand as the men encircled him again. A rider threw a rope around Leithadas's neck and dragged him forward. He stumbled to keep up and felt like he walked for ages until he was brought before a large tree. Something lay at its base, though he was still too far away to make it out. The rope yanked him still closer to the tree. He collapsed onto his knees, screaming in fright at what he could now see lay at the base of the tree: four beautiful girls, each with their hearts cut out. The hands of each rested across her stomach and, from each neck hung a golden ring from a silver chain. A sharp tug around Leithadas's neck lifted him to his feet, then slowly off the ground. The old woman's cackle rang in his ears before everything went black.

"So, my friends, beware of loving only the flesh, for a deamhon it will make of you." Fearn smiled. Telling his dad's tales always warmed his heart. As a tear rolled down his cheek, he turned his head so Airnin couldn't see.

"Your dad was an exquisite teller of tales, Fearn, and taught you well. Now, I have an errand to run before the night is gone. We need to start putting the plan into motion." Airnin turned and disappeared into the night.

OSKA

Fearn picked up his oska, thinking of his dad. He closed his eyes and focused on the power of Dainua, directing and isolating her sul into the wood and forcing it to grow and take the shape he wanted. He stood to make sure the oska had grown to the desired height, then sat down to work on shaping the oska itself. Opening his eyes after every change, he rotated and held it up to the fire, scrutinizing how the light danced across or through it. Fearn stood abruptly and slammed it against the ground, shattering the top, yelling "Arr, you, grrr... just do what I want you to do!" Fearn paced for a bit, wiping the sweat from his brow before sitting to try again. Farkor's tendrils of light broke the horizon in the East, stretching across the landscape, black fading into a deep purple. Fearn didn't notice. The King's army could have marched by, and he wouldn't have taken heed.

He opened his eyes to inspect his work. At the base, life-like roots expanded out about a palm's width, twisting and turning like a real tree, wide enough for the oska to stand on its own. Satisfied, he traced his fingers further up. The oska had an intricate bark pattern, the color fading to give it the weathered look of a tree that had been standing for generations. Burls stuck out in a few places. Marks below the leather strap looked as if a miniature woodpecker had scarred the tree in search of even smaller insects. The wood curved inwards to meet the leather wrapping, then back out again at the top of the leather where a black slash cut across the oska like an ancient lighting strike. About two hands from the top of the leather grip, the tree ended. The top resembled a mushroom. Its base was made of miniature tree trunks randomly spaced apart. They grew to the base of the mushroom cap, where branches grew out of them to the edge of the mushroom and then changed and grew over the cap, looking like a forest canopy. When Fearn held it up to the first light of Farkor breaking through the trees, the top of the oska looked like a miniature forest; in the center of it stood a large oak tree.

Utterly pleased with himself, Fearn stood the oska on the ground, reached for the pot, and walked to the brook, skipping and turning in circles along the way, humming tunes he had heard as a boy in the tavern. At the brook, Fearn rinsed and cleaned out the pot with small pebbles and dirt.

As Fearn returned to the clearing to get his oska, the exhilaration ceased; no tune left his mouth as he stared at the sight in front of him. The oska stood off-centered in a small circle. It reminded him of the grove he had planted, but instead of the vibrant green grass, this grove was blackened and scarred from the previous night's work. Airnin kept reminding him that blackening the land was simply part of learning to be a Tiller. Fearn hated it. He hurriedly dumped the supplies from the night before into the pot, leaving the ax buried in the dirt and the hatchet cast aside. Fearn quickly snatched up the oska, averted his eyes from the ground, and briskly walked back to the barrow without a single skip in his step.

BONES

Fearn awoke the next night and called out to Airnin but heard no response. He dressed, then picked up his oska and turned it over in his hands, examining the details in the wood. He felt selfish for not thinking of Dainua when he crafted it but pushed the guilt aside as he exited the barrow into the warm spring night. He placed the oska and lantern down on the blackened hill and leapt onto the largest standing stone. It was a place he had discovered the summer before while training. From here, he would often look out over the trees to the Spine of Meron to the south, where loomed a large, impassable mountain range. It ran as far as Fearn could see to both the east and west, completely unbroken, except for an immense gap to the southwest with perfectly vertical walls—the only place to get through. When the wind blew, he would close his eyes and stick out his arms, pretending he was a bird in the sky.

Fearn lay down on his back and dangled his legs off the edge of the standing stone. He gazed into the night sky and watched as the stars twinkled, as Telgog's constellation looked down on him. He waited to see if he could find a star falling, giving the power of Telgog back to Dainua, balancing the power between them.

A rustling sound came from the trees below. Fearn turned his head and peered down to the treeline that ran around the barrow. He spotted a deer darting through the trees, skirting the blackened ground before leaping back into the forest. Suddenly, near the foot of the barrow, there was a shimmer in the air—like heat on a hot summer day. As the shimmer dissipated, Airnin appeared. He never appeared or disappeared in this way unless he was next to his tomb. Quietly, Fearn turned to get a better look and closed his eyes. Airnin stood there, looking around intently as if searching for something, or perhaps to make sure he wasn't being watched. Airnin glanced up the hill. Fearn froze and studied Airnin's face but couldn't make out any facial expressions at this distance. Airnin apparently didn't notice Fearn; he turned back to gaze into the woods again. After a few moments, Airnin slowly faded until he vanished. Fearn tried to wait for Airnin to reappear, but, having the attention span of a squirrel, he turned and slowly lowered himself until he hung from the stone by his fingertips, slowly counting to see how long he could hold on. When he reached seventy-five, he grew bored and let go, letting his hands slide down the rock face, feeling the bumps and cracks speed by his fingers as he fell. He pushed down with energy he had stored and landed lightly on his feet.

Fearn retrieved his oska, lit the lantern, and scrambled down the barrow to where Airnin had shimmered away. He searched around but found nothing of interest; it looked like any other spot around the barrow. A rumbling sound broke the silence as he gave up his search. Fearn patted his stomach, and it seemed to gurgle back, "Get some food!" He was convinced he wasn't going to find anything near the barrow, so he sprinted off into the woods.

He ran towards the farm, staying just within the treeline, then skirted its perimeter and headed towards the grove. He made sure to avoid entering the grove with the hanged man, turning instead towards the village. As he ran, he pulled tiny bits of Dainua from the ground and consumed them, using the energy to push himself forward, leaping into the air with each stride. As he neared the village, he turned left. A few moments later, Fearn slowed down, blew out his lantern, and stepped to the edge of the woods. In front of him lay the village graveyard. He scanned the grounds, hoping to run into another sul like the baker. He crept along the border until he reached the road that ran south from the village. Looking both ways to make sure he hadn't been seen, he ran across the road and into the woods on the other side.

Being at the limits of where Airnin could travel and therefore provide protection if needed, he walked more cautiously and used the light of the stars filtering through the trees to guide his way. It was slower going, but he was afraid the lantern would be spotted by the king's men. He zig-zagged west through the forest, then turned right until he reached a small clearing. In the clearing sat a small house no larger than the one in which he had grown up. It had a tiny garden with a well in the center. Fearn walked north along the forest's edge until he found what he was searching for. On the ground, wrapped in a white cloth, was a loaf of bread. The husband of the baker he had met in the graveyard died a few years past, at which point the daughter moved here, further than Airnin's tether to his bones would allow him to go. Fearn could only get fresh bread if he retrieved it himself. Airnin voiced his disapproval at his wandering so far when he came home with a loaf one morning but never forbade him from going or used any words that strongly implied his dislike. So, Fearn snuck out this way whenever he had a night free from training. He picked up the bread, put it to his nose, and inhaled deeply; he loved the way it smelled. It reminded him of the baker he met in the graveyard and how sweet she was to him. Fearn walked the way he had come along the edge of the forest, collecting dead suls and storing them in his oska as he partook of the bread. He noticed that there was more room to store suls in his oska now that it was a proper size. He reached the end of the baker's clearing, turned, and continued to walk the perimeter until his oska was full. Fearn closed his eyes and studied the woods around him; not seeing anyone, he set down the lantern and slowly made his way across the open field to the garden. It was small—barely big enough to support the family. The garden appeared newly tilled; not a single green leaf poked up from the ground. Silently, he closed his eyes, reached out, and pushed the suls from his oska into the soil, watching tiny sul seedlings in the soil wriggle and grow. He walked around the perimeter of the garden, working as quickly as possible, only pausing to listen for the sound of someone moving in the small house. Once done, the garden was full of vegetables, most of them taller than his knee, far larger than he should have grown them. The bread was especially good, however, and Fearn wanted to look after the baker's daughter now that her parents had returned to Dainua. Fearn carefully made his way through the garden to the well, sat down, and finished eating the bread. He had started helping those from whom he took food a few years back, noticing the quality and quantity of the food left out improved greatly. He carefully folded up the napkin and set it on the lip of the well. Still feeling hungry, he grabbed his oska and headed back to the woods to retrieve his lantern.

After fading back into the darkness of the woods, he trekked north, keeping to the edge of a path in the woods that led from the baker's house to the Bitveen's; he collected the suls of the dead and decaying things along the way. Eventually, the path opened to a large farm. After some searching, he found a piece of leather beneath a bowl and a plate near the edge of the woods. The plate held some sort of meat and was covered in flies. Fearn gingerly picked up the meat and flung it into the woods. He uncovered the bowl underneath, hoping for something more appetizing. It was a large bowl of stew that appeared edible. Fearn withdrew into the woods and found a rock to sit on. The stew was good. Like most stews he found, it was mostly whatever that family could grow with the occasional piece of meat thrown in; however, this stew was made by the Bitveen brothers, who hunted and always had large chunks of meat in their stews. As Fearn finished, he wished he had kept some of the bread to soak up the liquid at the bottom. He placed the bowl back on the leather, scanned the property, and, confident he wasn't being watched, headed across the path that bordered the farm. The plants here already reached his ankle. It was a large field—about twice the size of his dad's. Ducking to make himself smaller, he hurried across the field, weaving back and forth, oska in his right hand and lantern in his left. He pushed the suls from the oska into the plants in patches as he went. When he reached the woods on the far side, he stopped and looked back to admire his work. He hated that he couldn't feed all the crops, but he didn't have the time.

As he turned north to hike to the next farm, a loud noise caught his attention. A dog was barking. The sound grew louder as he peered into the field towards the two houses that sat at the northern edge of the farm. He spotted several lanterns swaying. Something silvery reflected the starlight and was moving quickly in his direction. Fearn turned and fled towards the baker's house. The barking grew ever louder behind him. Realizing he wasn't going to outrun the dog, he closed his eyes and started to draw in Dainua and consume her as he darted to the nearest tree, ran around it a few times, and leapt onto a branch above him. He pushed and pulled to keep his balance as he swayed, judging the distance to the nearest tree, and jumped, pushing behind him, crashing through the foliage of the neighboring tree onto a broad branch. The dog's barking was still getting louder. Fearn crouched and peeked through the branches, surveying the tree he had just left. A large and angry dog appeared, sniffing the ground around the tree. It circled the trunk a few times, stopped, sat down, and let out a loud and mournful howl. Lights appeared through the trees up ahead, and a few moments later, the Bitveen brothers appeared and approached the dog. Both were thin, one of them slightly shorter than the other. They were dressed in a patchwork of the furs Fearn had sold them, which made him smirk. The shorter one patted the dog on the head and fed it something from his pocket. He held up the lantern and peered into the tree above him.

"Oy, you think whatever ran across the field up there?"

The taller man timidly approached the tree and held up his lantern.

"Ay, it a deamhon. Should let it be."

The two men waved the lanterns back and forth as they searched the tree above them. The taller man looked to his brother, saying, "We safe. We have special furs. Oy, I's know—it leapt on another tree maybe?" He turned in a circle as he held up his lantern and examined the nearby trees. Fearn closed his eyes and reached out to a branch right above the brothers; he grabbed the sul in the branch, pinching it off from the rest of the tree as footsteps drew closer.

"Big cheers and ale at the tavern if we catch the deamhon!" the shorter man suggested.

Fearn continued to pull the sul from the branch and consumed it as it streamed into him, giving him the power he needed to balance on his branch. A loud crack echoed off the nearby trees. Fearn opened his eyes and looked down at the men below him who were frozen in place, staring back at the tree; the dog growled quietly, hackles raised. The tree groaned, and its leaves started to shake. Another booming crack like the sound of bones breaking rang out; the tree shook violently as a huge branch crashed to the ground. The taller man gave a sharp yelp, turned, and ran east into the woods, the dog running after him. The other man seemed rooted in place and unable to move. He finally noticed that he had been left behind and ran off in a different direction.

Fearn waited until he felt sure that they weren't coming back. He still looked around cautiously before he dropped from the tree. At his feet, he found an abellio. He picked it up and thought of Uram and how neither he nor any of the other Asinta ever came to investigate the barrow. He hoped Uram was still alive and wasn't a victim of Airnin. He walked, lost in thought until he came to the baker's house. Then, he skirted into the woods and headed towards the graveyard. At the main road, he quickly searched the area before dashing across the road and into the woods on the other side. He followed the edge of the graveyard until he reached its northeastern edge and sat down. As Fearn reached to light the lantern, something shimmered in the graveyard; it was Airnin. Fearn was confused because he knew Airnin couldn't travel this far from the barrow. Airnin was searching around just as he had been earlier that night. Suddenly, he stopped, faced the barrow, and disappeared.

Fearn waited to see if Airnin would reappear, keeping his eyes fixed on the spot where Airnin had last stood. After a few moments, Fearn felt he had given it enough time and walked out to where Airnin had appeared. He lit the lantern and examined the ground, finding nothing but a plain patch of dirt much like the graves next to it, though with no grave marker. He expected there to be something that explained how Airnin traveled this far. He walked through a couple of rows and noticed a few graves without markers, but they were always next to graves whose markers were old and worn away. Returning to the spot where Airnin had stood, he noticed the grave markers around it were newer. Getting on his hands and knees, Fearn brushed the ground where he thought the marker should be but found nothing. Perplexed, he retrieved the lantern and walked towards the barrow. When he arrived at the barrow, only an hour or so remained until first light. Standing at the edge of the barrow, he let Dainua flow into him, and he trapped part of her in his oska before dashing up the hill.

Fearn leapt down into the crypt and looked around but didn't see Airnin. He walked over and tapped his oska on Airnin's tomb, yelling, "Come out, Airnin. We need to talk." Nothing happened. Fearn paced back and forth, waiting. Agitated, he yelled at the tomb again. "I saw you at the graveyard tonight. Why have you been lying to me?" He waited impatiently, feeling a little irritated that he could be yelling at an empty tomb. Slowly, a smoky, misty shape appeared until Airnin came into focus. Fearn closed his eyes and looked him in the face. All he could see were his lips, pursed in a thin, hard line. Fearn didn't feel like this was a wise decision anymore; it was a lot easier yelling at an empty stone tomb. He gripped his oska so tightly he could feel his knuckles pop; the sul of Dainua flowed from his oska into him and back. He tried to calm himself enough to stand his ground. Airnin's lips slowly widened into a grin, a predator just before it pounced. Fearn reacted by pulling all of Dainua from the oska into himself, took an offensive stance, and was ready to devour her if needed.

Airnin spoke carefully. "You have always been very bright, and I knew you would figure it out soon enough. Put away the sul, and I will tell you the rest of the tale about my brother."

Fearn contemplated what to do. They had had arguments before, but it had never led to this. Airnin had been mostly good to him, and Fearn was grateful, so he pushed the sul of Dainua back into his oska. Fearn slowly moved to his right, leaned the oska against the tomb and stepped away, holding his hands at his side; palms up, to show he meant no ill will. He prayed to Dainua that he made the right decision. Airnin walked over to Fearn's oska and inspected it.

"I have seen some interesting designs and details before, but never a tree. The craftsmanship is exquisite. However, I can see you do not want me rambling on about that. I suppose I should have said something earlier." Airnin placed the oska back against the tomb, further from Fearn than it was before. "I told you how my brother outwitted me—that I was outsmarted and framed for the murder of my father. The thing is, I was power-hungry in my own way. When I joined the Asinta, I was seen as someone handed a position for which others had toiled. If I was going to lead them, I needed to gain their trust. I spent hours reading and looking for ways the powers of the tillers and menders could be stretched and better used. I soon ran out of people to ask and books to read, so I set off for the sacred grove, much like where we stand. The most trusted and learned Asinta were buried there so that the knowledge they had would never be lost. I implored them for anything I could do to make myself more powerful and raise the Staff to new heights." Airnin started pacing. "I never sought the power to overthrow the kingdom; the governance of the land was the last thing I wanted. It would have been a hindrance to my ambitions. However, I was not completely blind to what was going on around me. I have my father to thank for forcing me to take lessons with Cial. If I had not, I would not have recognized the look in his eyes when we talked about growing old and the things we wanted to accomplish. I saw what I saw in myself: an intense desire for power. As we grew and learned, I came to the realization that he saw me as an obstacle to his goal of taking the crown. I could not condemn him for wanting it. I did not even try to change his mind. If I had, I would have had to stop seeking my own ambitions because I knew that if I could see the fire in his eyes, he could see it in mine. I had to hope that being a good brother to him would show him that I meant no ill will and that we could both have what we wanted. At the same time, I searched for a way to foil any plan he might have against me.

"I found the solution while studying under one of the masters at the sacred grove. He mentioned a time long ago when the masters could move freely about the kingdom to teach. That changed when one in their ranks named Eolas massacred a village because they had hanged an Asinta for killing a man. Eolas did not care if the man was guilty or not. He knew, as we do, the Asinta are superior above all others. This caused the masters to turn on one another, for there were those who agreed with Eolas and others who did not. At the time, the Asinta decided that their purpose was to help the people not rule them. They removed the means by which the masters moved freely. Once the masters were isolated at the sacred grove, the ruling Asinta dragged the bones of those who opposed them into the light of Farkor, where the masters had no power and burned them. Only the masters who agreed that Asinta should be servants remained. A law was passed declaring that no new Asinta could become a master and that those who remained would be forever isolated from the world. Of course, I pressed the remaining masters for information on how they were able to move about before their isolation. Thinking enough time had passed and no harm could come from it, one of the masters entrusted me with the knowledge. As you know, Fearn, I am tied to my bones and can only travel a short distance from them. When the master Asinta died, their sul was sealed into their bones by a mender. They then placed small pieces of their bones five stones apart, with the majority of the bones buried at the sacred grove. This allowed them to go out and teach other Asinta by moving from bone to bone, using each as an anchor for their sul. They had to return every night because the bone fragment they were anchored to was not large enough for their sul to reside."

Fearn interrupted Airnin, asking, "You need another sul to stay alive as a wraith. How did they get around that?"

"It was quite simple: those most devoted gave their lives to the masters. It was a matter of pride, and to be chosen was thought of as one of the highest honors you could receive. There was never a time when someone did not seek this honor. When there were multiple volunteers, a mock duel was held and the most powerful Asinta was chosen for this honor; the stronger the sul a wraith consumes, the less often he needs a new one."

"Airnin! Are they still doing that?"

"No. Once the masters were isolated, the practice was stopped, causing them to be more shadow than wraith when I went seeking them out. After I had learned all I desired, I put them to rest by pulling down the pillars holding up the roof of their crypt, trapping them forever. Having dealt with them, I went about ensuring that if I was to die at my brother's hands, I would have the means to seek revenge. I had a young apprentice at the time, but he lacked the gifts and talents that you possess. He was, however, a marvelous mender. I had a Tiller stand in a closed-off room so he could not see what I was doing, though he was close enough I could use his powers. I sealed as much of my sul as I could into each of the two bones in my toes and cut them off. My apprentice took the bones and mended them, sealing the sul inside. Walking was difficult at first, but within a week I hardly noticed. We took the bones and, with a stone marker's tool, placed each bone four stones away from each other. That allowed me to cover eighty stones of land. The last part of the plan was to make a pact with my brother: if I ever die, he would bury me in a barrow. This barrow, to be exact. I had it built and readied for the day I would be entombed if it came to that. This is the farthest point I could be from the line of my bones."

Feeling comfortable now that Airnin wasn't going to kill him, Fearn walked over to his bedroll, sat down and continued to listen. "Unfortunately, my plan failed me in the end, when Cial killed all of my men, including my apprentice."

Fearn closed his eyes and looked at Airnin. Airnin's face was sad and distraught. Fearn was sure he was telling the truth, but it didn't answer all of his questions. "I'm sorry. That doesn't explain everything. What have you been doing out there?" Fearn gestured wildly.

"Fine. You will not like what I have to say, but if you are patient, you will see why I did it. I have been using the anchors to search for the clothes you have on your back and the supplies you need. You have to know that the fine cloaks I brought back obviously could not have come from your village—"

Fearn interrupted. "You said that you stole from travelers passing through here."

"Fearn, you have lived here your entire life, and you know people avoid coming here. Why do you think I chose this place for the barrow?" Fearn knew Airnin was right and that he had been lying to himself when he had accepted his past explanations. "You have to realize that, in order for us to kill my brother, we cannot just walk up to him. He has an army of soldiers and Asinta. I have been graciously killing the Asinta and taking their suls, always attacking from different locations so they could not deduce what was going on. When I come across the king's soldiers, I kill them as well." Airnin stopped. Fearn looked into his face, and not a single expression rippled across it.

Fearn had been so focused on learning and training that he never thought what it would take to kill the king. He felt conflicted. He had vowed to himself that he would help Airnin for all he had done for him.

"I don't know what to say, Airnin." Fearn paused, letting his thoughts coalesce. "I know this means a lot to you, and you have done so much for me." He paused again, thinking to himself: *With Airnin being able to travel, he could have easily found a better person to train or even could have killed me, using my sul to enact his revenge.* He thought back on his life with his dad and all of the pain he had caused, starting with his mom's death and ending with his dad's. Fearn's heart broke over the killing Airnin had done—not necessarily for the men, women, or children whose lives were destroyed but for the fact that Airnin was forced to do it. If Airnin's brother hadn't killed him, those people would still be alive.

Finally, Fearn focused back on Airnin and spoke. "I don't like the fact you have killed but understand that you had no choice. Your brother forced it on you." Fearn stood and walked over to Airnin, sticking out his hand. Airnin grasped it by the wrist. "Airnin, what do I need to do?"

"It is growing late; we will discuss this tonight." Airnin faded into a mist before finally disappearing into the tomb.

ᛞEPARTURE

Fearn awoke the next night to find Airnin waiting. Before Fearn could even sit up, Airnin spoke: "This is your last chance, Fearn. Are you certain you want to go through with this? I will be honest; I cannot do it alone. Furthermore, by doing this, you will be able to kill the man who killed your father and bring lasting peace to the kingdom."

Fearn sat up, closed his eyes, and looked at Airnin's face. A look of hope and eagerness rippled across it. He replied, "Ay, you have been like a father to me, Airnin. I owe you. I will be by your side until the end. I made that pact as I shook your hand last night."

Airnin laughed, then held up a hand. "I wanted you to be sure; this will be difficult, and I want you there because you decided to be there. I am grateful that you want to go through with this. I need you to hurry; pack lightly for the road. I have supplies stashed along the way."

"Are we heading to the palace, then?" Fearn asked with excitement.

"No, we have things that need to be put into place first. I want my brother utterly alone before he meets his end. I need you to weave tales like your dad did. Do you think you can do that?"

"Is that why you have been asking me to retell his old tales?"

"Yes. We need a tale to disguise our deceit. Your dad was an expert craftsman, and I see that in you. Let us take a walk, so we can discuss the details."

As the two of them walked through the woods Airnin laid out his plan.

"Airnin, I can't do that! I know I said I was with you but... but isn't there another way?" Fearn asked, his worst fears realized.

"Tell me, then, what do you suggest?" Airnin calmly remarked. Fearn was taken aback, expecting that no matter what he said he was going to be forced to go along with Airnin's plan. He thought back to when he last saw Uram, then to times sitting in the tavern with his father, and finally to the grove he planted. An idea came to him, born out of the hopes and dreams he'd had as a kid.

Fearn leaned against a tree and slowly described his plan. With each step he outlined, he found that the next step became crystal clear to him. When he was done, he looked up at Airnin, who had not interrupted him once. Airnin's face rippled in concentration until his eyes locked onto Fearn's. "What if your plan doesn't work? Will we then continue on with mine?"

Fearn thought his plan over; it *could* work. No, it *had* to work, he told himself. He slowly breathed out and hoped he wasn't making a mistake. "Yes."

"Good. This will be more work since we will need to plan for both; luckily, they are similar in some ways."

For the next five days, Fearn worked on crafting the tale he needed to tell. He also packed the items needed for the short trip west. Fearn became more nervous as each day closer to his departure passed. Airnin stayed out longer and longer each night. The night before Fearn was to leave, Airnin returned with a package. Inside was the finest cloak Fearn had ever seen. It was deep hazelnut brown on the outside and clay red on the inside, thick and heavy. Wrapped in the cloak was a hard piece of leather with leather straps that crisscrossed the back and sides. "What's this?" Fearn asked.

"It is a breastplate—I need you to look the part," Airnin replied. Under the leather breastplate, Fearn found a pair of pants that

211

matched the clay color from inside the cloak and four more pieces of leather. Before he could ask, Airnin said, "Those are for your arms and legs."

The last thing in the package was a supple and soft pair of leather boots. Concerned, Fearn asked, "Where did all of this come from?"

"No need to fret. Those were actually mine at one time. This was meant for my apprentice upon my return. I think they will fit you nicely."

That night, Fearn dressed in his new clothes. They fit perfectly. The armor made movement a little difficult as he moved his arms; it bit into his chest. He reached out to the sul in the leather, isolated the portions at the edges, and pulled. The leather softened, making maneuvering easier.

He slung the quiver of mender arrows he had made with Airnin over his left shoulder, along with the bow, then swung his pack over his right shoulder. There was a shimmer, and Airnin appeared in front of him.

"I scouted, and your path is clear. Are you ready?" Fearn's stomach tingled, and his heart raced.

"Ay, as ready as I'm going to be. You're not going to kill anyone, are you?"

Airnin shook his head. "I have not killed this past week, and I will not tonight if I can help it; though, you have to know that by the time this is all done, there will be blood on both of our hands, regardless of whose plan we use."

Before Fearn could respond, Airnin shimmered and disappeared.

Fearn packed the last of his belongings, then grabbed his oska and lantern. He lifted the lantern and looked around the tomb one last time; his heart sank, and he was confused as to why he hated leaving it behind. Finally, he blew out the lantern, set it down, and made his way out into the night. The warm spring breeze felt good as he entered the shaft. He looked up into the starry night sky and then turned in a circle, admiring the starlight reflecting on the walls around him before leaping out onto the barrow. He walked over and ran his hand over one of the standing stones, hoping to always remember the rough texture and chisel marks, then headed down the hill and into the woods.

Hiking farther south than he normally did before turning west, he carefully made his way by the light of the stars that filtered through the canopy above. He reached a clearing, sat down, and removed his boots to walk across the lush grass. The power of Dainua felt as strong as the day he had created that grove. He walked around the tree, gazing up at the shiny black statue of the hanged man, noticing that someone had been trimming the vines. He knelt in front of it and closed his eyes, opening himself up and letting Dainua flow through him.

"Dainua, please bless me in this journey and be by my side. Thank you for leading me to Airnin and his teachings. I know I have killed much of the land by the barrow, and I hope that you can forgive me." Fearn stood and took in the hanged man as the starlight sparkled over the shiny black features not covered by vines. It reminded him of looking at the reflection of the night sky on water or the walls of the barrow. He walked back to the edge of the glade and put his boots back on. He stared at the clearing, wondering if he would ever lay eyes on it again. Taking a slow deep breath, the smells of the forest assaulted Fearn's senses, and he felt he was on the precipice of something larger than himself. Turning west, he wondered what fate Dainua had in store for him.

Fearn walked until the woods ended at the road that ran north to the village. He looked north and south to make sure no one was watching, closed his eyes, and searched for any suls. He watched the way the suls in the trees swayed to catch if anyone was hiding behind one. Feeling confident he was alone, he clutched his oska tightly, stepped onto the road, and left the days of hiding in the shadows behind him.

Fearn strolled north towards the village, trying to keep a casual pace. As he passed the cemetery to his right, he slowed down and admired how the starlight illuminated some of the headstones. He stopped midway past the cemetery and glanced into the woods on his left, watching and waiting.

Time seemed to stretch on as Fearn stood there waiting for the sounds he expected. He worried that he had spent too much time in the clearing and had arrived too late. He focused on the power of Dainua in the ground below him to calm himself.

Finally, faint cries broke the silence to his left. He squared his shoulders, brought Dainua into himself, and waited to consume her. The screams grew louder as the sound of branches breaking echoed through the woods. Fearn turned to face what was about to burst through the trees, devouring Dainua. He held up his left palm and focused; a small ball of fire appeared and swirled in his palm.

A man carrying two kids, the oldest looking no older than eight, and a woman carrying a toddler burst from the woods and skidded to a halt, almost crashing into Fearn.

The toddler burst out crying, slipped from her mom's arms, and clutched her leg. The parents looked back as if trying to decide which death they preferred the least. Before they could decide, Fearn yelled at them, "I'm here to save you—get behind me!" The man acted first, grabbing the woman by the wrist and pulling her forward. "Come on! We don't have a choice," he shouted. The small child hurried after them like a baby duck. The trees behind them began to glow an intense grayish light that quickly grew brighter. Fearn stepped back, and the family moved to keep pace with him. A loud, spine-tingling scream came from the woods, followed by a large roar like boulders smashing into one another. A wraith burst from the tree line onto the road. Fearn, ready for it, threw the fireball, taking it by surprise, hitting it square in the chest and wrapping around it, enveloping it in flames. The wraith shimmered in the fire briefly and disappeared. The fire also hit the trees behind the wraith, scorching the trunks and searing the green leaves.

Fearn called to the family behind him, "Is there a village nearby?" The woman stammered out, "N-n-north of here." Fearn looked back at them, then directed them up the road. "Hurry! There will be more of them coming."

The family dashed towards the village with Fearn easily keeping pace behind them. Just before they reached the northern edge of the cemetery, there was a shimmer in the starlight as a wraith materialized from the darkness. It looked around and, as soon as it spotted Fearn and the family, made straight for them. Fearn swung his oska in a circle several times on his right side, then stopped, pointing it at the wraith. A ripple of starlight could be seen in the air as the energy rushed out to meet the wraith. It moved to its left, but it wasn't fast enough; the energy struck it on its right side. It shimmered as it spun into the air and faded out just before it hit the ground. Fearn turned to tell the family to hurry on, but they were already a ways down the road, still sprinting as fast as they could.

The group was attacked four more times before reaching the village outskirts. Each time, Fearn struck down the wraith. The man turned to Fearn and asked, "Where do we go from here?"

Furtively searching the area around them, Fearn answered in a hushed voice: "Is there a tavern around here or someplace we can barricade ourselves in?"

The father replied quickly. "Yes, in the middle of this village."

"Be quick. I don't want to have to face several of these deamhons at once."

The family hurried into the village with Fearn following closely, reaching the tavern without further attack. The family burst through the tavern door into the brightly lit room with Fearn on their heels. Fearn slammed the door behind him and braced against it.

Moments later, he turned to look at the room and noticed every eye was staring at him. A man in the back of the room spoke up as he hurried across the room, pushing patrons and chairs out of his way. Fearn recognized him right away; the man had changed very little since last he saw him. Only his hair was thinner and whiter.

"Oy! What is the meaning of this?" Cromm bellowed.

"These folks can fill you in. I need to listen for any deamhons." Fearn turned and put his ear to the door.

Cromm turned to the man and demanded, "Baker, what is going on?" The baker's husband cleared his throat. "After my family and I finished dinner, I went outside to leave food for the deamhon like I normally do. When I reached the edge of the woods, it was dead silent. I strained to hear anything, but not even a cricket could be heard. Then, a howl broke the silence. Not the howl of a dog or wolf;

it was deeper and chilled me to the bone. I dropped the plate and ran for the house. Once inside, I quickly barred the door. The howl changed into horrible laughter. The door shook as the deamhon beat against it, causing the bar clasps to break free. The door burst in, and wood splinters flew everywhere. We huddled together, staring into the cloud of dust that covered the doorway. Not a sound came from outside. Suddenly, the house started to shake. We grabbed the kids and ran through the door, expecting to be devoured at any moment. As we burst free from the cloud of dust, we thought we were alone, but then a low growl came from behind. We turned to see a smoky grey image with eyes as bright as hot coals. We ran, sure our end was near, until we came upon this man." The baker's husband gestured to Fearn. "He conjured fire from his hand and threw it at the deamhon and killed it. We ran towards the village and were attacked five more times before getting here. Each time, this man saved us."

Fearn finally asked, "Do you have a way to bar the door?"

Cromm hurried over as he answered, sounding out of breath, "Yes." Cromm gestured to a bar at the side of the door behind Fearn. Fearn grabbed it and swung it down into place, noticing it was much thicker than the bar they used to have at his farm. Fearn let go of the door and turned his attention to the room. The place hadn't changed at all since he was last there. The only addition was a long shelf next to the fireplace on the right side of the room. A small cough brought Fearn's attention back to Cromm, who was standing with his arms crossed, scowling.

"Would you like to say what you are doing here, Crop Burner?" Cromm motioned towards Fearn's oska. Fearn looked at Cromm dismissively and addressed the entire room: "I am Luwayth. I was with the Asinta until the king killed our imbiber and took control. He corrupted our works and deeds, which had been focused on helping those in need. Instead, he used us to fill his insatiable lust for power. Those of the upper-ranking Asinta who spoke out against him vanished, causing the rest of the Asinta to quickly obey. I ran, knowing that I could never give in and help the deamhon the king had become. I know there are at least a few who felt the same way as I did since I was never hunted down and brought back." Luwayth paused, thinking briefly of Uram and felt shame at tarnishing the Asinta start to creep into his consciousness. Quickly, he brushed it aside, telling himself he couldn't let such ideas cloud his thoughts and impede the task at hand. He checked the bar on the door, and keeping his head held high and shoulders squared, he walked to the right around the edge of the room. The sound of scuffling followed as everyone in the room turned their chairs to see where he was going or quickly moved to make way for him. Cromm walked across the room to cut him off at the fireplace. They stood face to face. Cromm's hands were in fists at his hips, ready for a fight. He spoke first and made sure he was loud enough for the entire room to hear. "So, you're a deserter, and these deamhons are after you? Shouldn't we just open the door and throw you out to them?" Luwayth smiled, then replied, loud enough so his response was heard by all. "Oy, no, they aren't here for me. They attacked the baker's family who ran into me on the road, out in the open, not hiding in some hole. I was on my way here to rid you of them." Luwayth turned and addressed the room. "I may have left the Asinta, but I have allies on the inside that gave me and others information. We were told that the king found an ancient form of conjuring that needed a Crop Burner's blood." The words "Crop Burner" came out thick and slow as he forced himself to say it. "We gathered together and tried to stop them, but we were too late. A rift from the opposite side of Mehron was opened, and out of it poured the deamhon Dainua had trapped. We were lucky. Many of the Asinta, seeing what was done, joined our side and fought alongside us. We killed many brothers and sisters of the Asinta who opposed us until finally, we managed to close the rift; sadly, the damage was done, and hundreds of deamhons had been released. We lost many in the fight and had to retreat or be slaughtered by those foul deamhons. As we fled, the deamhons didn't pursue us but scattered in every direction. They killed whomever they came across, and unlike the deamhons that live in the forests, these feast on suls."

A male voice cried out, "What're we supposed to do?" The rest of the room broke out into questions, some fretting about loved ones they had left at home. Luwayth couldn't yell over the commotion.

Instead, he held out his left hand. A fireball started to form in it and swirled from an unfelt wind. The room grew still as attention was drawn back to him. Luwayth let the fireball dwindle until it was as small as a lantern flame before finally dying out. He continued, "There is a way to protect yourselves. That is why I came—to teach you how. These creatures cannot come out in the day because something that is conjured by the dark can never dwell in the light of Farkor. You must carve oak to look like this." Luwayth dropped his pack on a nearby table and dug into it, pulling out a piece of oak carved in the shape of a circle. "It's simple enough to make," he said as he held it high so everyone could see. "Hang this above your door." Luwayth tossed the carving to a table nearby to allow them to inspect it. He stepped back until his back bumped the mantle of the fireplace, then put his left arm behind his back, created a small fireball in the palm of his hand, and quickly glancing around to make sure no one noticed, he shot it up the chimney.

Luwayth caught something out of the corner of his eye that seemed familiar. He turned to his right and concentrated on the shelf on the wall; it held an old leather mug, a chipped clay plate, and a piece of white cloth.

"Oy, you noticed our collection from Dainua," Cromm said from behind Luwayth. Speaking over his shoulder, Luwayth replied, "Dainua has given you gifts?"

"That she has. People around these parts leave out offerings to keep the deamhon away. Some of them have been blessed by Dainua, waking the next day to see their crops had grown overnight. It started with a good friend of mine who, sadly, is no longer with us."

Luwayth smiled and turned to Cromm. "You must be good people then. It's an honor to be in your presence." Luwayth stuck out his hand.

Cromm looked at it for a moment, scrutinized Luwayth's face, then grasped him by the wrist. "Thank you for helping the bakers; however, we don't want any Crop Burners around here." The rest of the tavern broke out into agreement behind him. A villager, too afraid to approach Luwayth, handed the carved oak to Cromm, who gave it back to Luwayth. As he did, a loud and terrible scream erupted from outside. Everyone turned to look at the door. They all knew the sound was not made by any living thing. The door shook violently, but the bar held. The door started to darken and rot. The Bakers grabbed their kids and pushed past everyone to the back of the tavern. Luwayth consumed some of the suls in his oska and leapt onto the nearest table. He dashed from table to table, knocking over cups and kicking plates to the floor until he reached the table nearest the door. The villagers scrambled to get out of Luwayth's way and as far away from the door as possible. The door started to crumble and cave in. The deamhon crashed into it one last time, scattering bits of wood and dirt across the tavern. In the doorway loomed a grayish form, wearing a long black cloak. Luwayth lifted up the circle of oak, as if to thus ward off the deamhon. The deamhon shrieked in pain and cowered back into the street. Luwayth twirled his oska in a circling motion, and as he did, fire began to appear around it. He flung the fireball through the doorway; it slammed into the deamhon and engulfed it in flames. A horrible wailing came from the deamhon as it shimmered and disappeared.

Luwayth turned around to face the villagers. They were all huddled against the far wall. Each looked like a lamb just before the slaughter. Even Cromm, who stood in front of them ready to protect those behind him, had a fear in his eyes that Luwayth had never seen before.

Cromm bravely strode towards Luwayth. A few paces in front of him, he stopped and stuck out a hand. Luwayth stepped forward and grasped him by the wrist. "Thank you," Cromm said, then gestured to the open doorway. "Will there be more of them?"

"No, that was the last of the ones I tracked here," Luwayth replied, then handed the circle of oak over to Cromm. He noticed that the villagers had crowded closer to hear what was being discussed. "Hang this on the outside of your door. If others come this way, it will prevent them from coming in—for now."

"What do you mean 'for now?' You said earlier this is all we needed," Cromm said, irritated.

"I hope you don't need anything more, but this is part of the reason why I came. These deamhons are searching for something, and we suspect it is a way to reopen the portal and conquer this world. There is only one way to stop them, and I need all of your help." The villagers were slowly making their way back to the tables but making sure to keep clear of the open door. Cromm held up a hand. "I think I should get another round of ale for those that need it before we continue." Cromm looked at the circle of oak in his hand. "I should also grab a hammer and nail while I'm at it." He hurried off.

Luwayth turned and stared out the empty door into the pitch black of the night. He pulled a chair over to the open doorway and sat down, hoping to calm some of the villagers' fears. Every so often, they would look back at the door in sudden fear, then relax upon seeing it was empty. Luwayth turned and looked out the door, trying to catch a glimpse of the starlight above. A hand came down on his shoulder. Luwayth jumped and turned to see Cromm standing there with a large mug of ale. Taking the mug from Cromm, Luwayth smiled at him. "Thank you, Cromm."

"No problem. It's on the house. Thank you again. Beware. These folks don't take kindly to Crop Burners, regardless of what you've done for them tonight. You'd probably be best moving on as soon as possible." Cromm nodded and patted Luwayth on the shoulder, causing the ale to splash over the side, then left Luwayth to himself.

Taking a swig of the ale, he realized it didn't taste any different from the weak ale Cromm used to give him as a kid. Luwayth opened his mouth to call him out on it, then stopped. His mouth hung open as he realized he wasn't Fearn anymore. He closed it, thinking of a life to which he could never return but for which he suddenly yearned.

"Ay, everyone," Cromm yelled. They all stopped their conversations and turned to look at Cromm. "Luwayth here still needs to tell us what he needs from us." Cromm gestured to Luwayth, who held his mug to his lips. He lowered it, wiped his mouth with the back of his hand, then flicked his hand, spraying the ale onto the floor.

Standing, he turned to look at the room. Raising his mug, he said, "First, I want to thank *you* for the hospitality you've shown me tonight, and Cromm, who told me the next round was on him."

The room erupted in cheers. Cromm glared across the room at Luwayth, who just smiled and winked. *That's what you get for watering down your ale*, Luwayth thought. Lowering his mug, Luwayth continued. "What we need you to do is very important. These deamhons have their power tied to the king. The only way to stop the deamhons is to stop him. We need you to take down the circle of oak you nail to your door and bring it to the king's castle a week after Dainua's stars appear. We also need you to spread the word about what you witnessed tonight."

Someone in the back yelled, "Why should we fight the king? He's done nothing to us."

Another called out, "I'm not helping a Crop Burner!"

Luwayth yelled back, "Look around you at this village. After the Asinta came through here, did the king come back and help you rebuild? No. And that's because he was the one who sent the Asinta through here. After the deamhons were released, did he send his men out to kill them? No! If you want to bring peace back to your village, you must stand and fight with us. I need your pledge before I leave tonight. There are other deamhon out there that must be stopped. I cannot stay here, as much as my weary bones long to take a break. I will step outside and let you decide." Luwayth turned and walked through the rubble that once was the tavern door, into the fresh spring air.

Pacing back and forth in the road, Luwayth looked around to see if Airnin was still nearby. It was getting late. "Farkor will probably rise soon," he thought. The sound of footsteps caught his attention. He turned and looked back at the tavern. Cromm appeared in the doorway and proceeded to hang the circle of oak above the door. Luwayth stood in the road and watched. Cromm strode over and stared at Luwayth's face, illuminated by the tavern lights.

"I don't know if your circle will work, but I have to place it or some of my patrons won't come back. They should have their votes wrapped up in a moment. I can tell you now, though, they won't vote for you, Fearn."

At the mention of his name, Luwayth's face went slack, and he found himself unable to give a rebuttal.

"I've no idea where you've been, and I don't have a mind to know. All I know is that your actions led to your father's death and, after you were gone, peace finally came back to this village."

Luwayth's shoulders slumped. He turned and started to walk away. Cromm walked after him and grabbed Luwayth by the shoulder.

"Fearn, I'm sorry. It's just that I miss your dad."

Luwayth turned and looked up at Cromm.

As Cromm looked back, the hatred that he had been carrying seemed to slip from his shoulders as he saw eyes burdened beyond their years. "I'm sorry. It's not your fault, Fearn. The villagers who killed Dair are to blame."

"Wait!" Luwayth spurted out. "Who were the villagers who killed my dad?"

Cromm peered closely at Luwayth, "Why would I tell you that? So you can kill them?"

"Yes!" he shouted.

"Killing someone doesn't fix a killing. Now go, and don't come back."

Luwayth turned and didn't look back as he walked away. His stomach tightened at the idea of facing Airnin and having to go through with his plan.

"There will be more killings. I'm sorry," Luwayth muttered to himself as he headed out of the village.

Just as Luwayth walked into the clearing that bordered the village to the west, Airnin appeared.

"So, did they go along with your plan?"

With Cromm's words still echoing in his head, Luwayth replied, "No. No, they didn't." He closed his eyes to look at Airnin and saw a small grin appear that quickly grew into a menacing sneer.

"We move on to my plan then. You are still going to help, correct? You did promise."

Luwayth glanced back at the village and sighed. He thought to himself, *I have no place to turn back to. I can only go forward from here.* Aloud, he said, "Yes, Airnin, I will help you with your plan."

"Head to the farm as we discussed, and I will meet you there in a few nights. Do not do anything stupid." Airnin then shimmered and disappeared.

Adjusting his pack and setting his sights to the west, Luwayth started down the road, leaving everything he had known behind him.

Ten stone from the village, Luwayth found a simple wooden house on the side of the road, much like all of the other houses he had seen; however, this was dark and unlived in. He turned south from the road towards it. At first, he wasn't able to make out any of its details, but as he drew closer, he noticed a small field covered in lull weeds and a house in disrepair. The front door sat at a queer angle and wasn't square with its frame. The hair on the back of Luwayth's neck stood up. With a trembling hand, he pushed on the door; it wobbled as it swung in. A scraping noise echoed throughout the room as it dragged across the dirt floor. Luwayth couldn't see clearly inside as the light from the stars only lit the threshold. Staring into the dark, Luwayth trembled, waiting for something to happen. After a few moments, he raised his hand, and a small flame sprang from his palm.

The fire reflected off the walls, making them appear as though they too were on fire. Luwayth's memories flashed back to seeing his home ablaze and having to watch as his dad died. Forcing himself back to the present, he looked around the room. If it wasn't for the musty smell of wet wood, he would have thought he was looking into his old house. Cautiously, he walked into the room and made sure he was the only one there. He dropped his pack onto the floor and placed the bow and quiver on the table next to a bowl of dried beans. Finding dry wood next to the fireplace, he quickly stacked the logs, and then reached out a hand and started a fire. He constantly looked back at the door, expecting some unknown assailant to appear. Once the fire was lit, Luwayth wedged the door closed and realized the bar was missing. It looked as if it had been forcefully removed. He then took off the princely clothes that Airnin had given him and slipped back into his rough tunic and pants. Untying his bedroll from his pack, he laid it on the floor against the wall, adjusting it so it lay where it would have in his childhood home. Once he was satisfied it was where he wanted it, he sat down and laid his oska across his lap. Sighing, he let his head fall back and rest against the wall, watching the fire dance in the fireplace while monitoring the door out of the corner of his eye.

Luwayth studied the room, wondering where its occupants ended up. His first thought on what might have happened to them sent a chill up his spine; he convinced himself that if Airnin had done something to them, it must have been deserved.

He thought it was still an hour or more till morning, but he was overcome with drowsiness. It had been a long night. He laid down on his bedroll and stared into the fire. He recalled his days on the farm and cold winter nights by the fire with his dad, though they felt more like a tale than actual experiences. He closed his eyes as his memories spilled into dreams.

As he finally awakened, the waning light of day lit up the mantel of the doorway. Sitting up, he watched as the color changed from an unwashed yellow to red, then pink, and finally faded into a deep purple.

Luwayth stretched his arms and legs as he rose. He felt it best to spend his free time exploring since he didn't have anything to do for a few days. Leaving his pack on the table, he grabbed his bow and quiver and headed out into the twilight as the stars began to appear. Luwayth walked west to explore, his stomach rumbling in discontent. The thought of cheese came sharply to mind, so he turned around towards the grazier's home. He walked north across the road and into the woods, and once he felt comfortable he couldn't be seen, headed back towards the village, following the road. It became harder to make his way through the woods as it got darker. Luwayth spotted the path on the other side of the road that led south to the Baker's farm and turned north, carefully making his way through the woods, closing his eyes, and searching every so often. Luwayth didn't know what Airnin would say if he caught him so close to the village. After a quarter stone, the woods began to thin, and Luwayth saw a large field in front of him surrounded by a wooden fence. He looked for the cows and found that they were currently penned up by the house. Past the field to the north, he could see the top of the old stone mill sitting on the bank of the river. Turning in the direction of the village and staying in the cover of the woods, Luwayth made his way to the far corner of the field.

Set on the corner fencepost was a plate. Luwayth closed his eyes and made sure no one was around, then slowly crept up and grabbed it. Instead of the rough clay plates most of the villagers had, this one had been fired and its glossy white surface sparkled in the starlight. In the center of the plate sat a wedge of cheese and a small bowl of milk. Luwayth quickly grabbed the cheese and left the milk alone—the thought of drinking from a cow disgusted him. As he held the cheese to his nose and inhaled, a small part of him was bitter. Airnin had always made the excuse that he couldn't come out this far. Knowing now that Airnin could have easily traveled here all along made Luwayth mad he had missed out on all of the cheese. Tamping down his anger, he quickly moved back into the cover of darkness the woods provided. He took a small bite of cheese and savored it while he continued back the way he had come. As he drew close to the road, he thought of the baker. After being saved the night before, she surely had to have put out one of her best loaves. He couldn't think of anything better to go with the cheese.

Once Luwayth arrived at the road, he closed his eyes and made sure he wasn't being watched, then ran across the road and into the woods next to the path that led to the Baker's home.

As he approached the farm that belonged to the Bitveen brothers, Luwayth closed his eyes and surveyed for the dog. He didn't want to be chased up a tree again and was sure that the ensuing commotion would draw Airnin's attention. Not seeing anything, Luwayth crept slowly down the perimeter of the property, stopping every so often to check for his four-legged nemesis. Once he reached the southern end of the property, Luwayth searched for what the Bitveens had left out and found two plates, one upside down on top of the other, with a piece of leather under them. Uncovering the plate, he found a sizable piece of meat that didn't have flies nesting in it. Looking out into the field, Luwayth wished he had time to grow their crops. Feeling guilty for taking the meat, he instead left a small piece of cheese in its place. "That should really confuse them," he thought as he smiled to himself, imagining their faces at seeing meat turned into cheese. Placing the plates back where he found them, he hurried on.

Continuing south, still sneaking along and keeping a keen eye out for anyone else, he finally made it to the Baker's house. He spotted the plate sitting on the well's ring. Relief washed over Luwayth, knowing the Bakers had made it home safely. Standing still, he carefully scrutinized the yard, giving extra care to examine every tree in sight. Crouching low to the ground, he cautiously stepped out into the clearing and made his way to the well, pausing every few feet to close his eyes and look around. About halfway there, he felt like it was going to take all night going at this pace, so he stood and sprinted to it, having to jump over and dodge crops along the way. He took the plate from the well and pulled back the white cloth; sure enough, just as he expected, there was a full loaf of bread. He held his oska in one hand and the meat and cheese in the other. Unsure what to do, he dropped the cheese and meat onto the bread and wrapped the cloth around the entire bundle. Once it was secure, he looked around and pushed a few suls into the surrounding crops before sprinting back to the safety of the woods.

Luwayth confidently walked back towards the Bitveens, sure he was truly alone. As he reached the Bitveen's farm, his stomach started to growl in eager anticipation. Continuing along the perimeter of the property, he found a tree stump that sat in the dark of the woods but afforded a vantage point of the field. He sat down, leaned his oska against his knee, and opened the cloth on his lap. He tore off a piece of bread and cheese, then gnawed off a piece of meat. It felt like he was trying to bite into leather. Chewing the meat until it was soft and pliable, he popped in the bread and cheese. The meat was more manageable with the flavors of the bread and cheese mixed in. He paused briefly to observe his surroundings, then repeated the process. About four bites into the meal, a noise softly echoed through the woods.

The noise was so faint that it felt like it was coming from every direction. Luwayth closed his eyes and looked around but didn't see anything. The sound grew louder until he recognized it—the barking of a dog. Or was it yelping? He couldn't tell, as the two sounds seemed to mix together. His body froze and every muscle tensed. Desperately, he searched back and forth, trying to see where it was coming from, straining to pinpoint the source of the noise. Finally, two suls directly across the field from him broke through the tree line and headed to the farmhouse. Opening his eyes, he could make out vague human figures. Their voices started to cut through the sound of the barking and howling. As the men ran, he could see that they kept looking back into the woods. One of the men kept yelling a word, but Luwayth couldn't make it out. Something seemed to be moving at the edge of the woods where the men exited. Closing his eyes, Luwayth saw a smaller sul moving closer to the ground. As the sul exited the woods, he could tell it was the source of the barking and baying. Instead of following the men, the dog appeared to be heading straight for Luwayth.

Luwayth quickly stood and let the meat, bread, and cheese fall from his lap onto the ground, hoping it would distract the dog. He turned and dashed north, as quietly as he could. Upon reaching the road, Luwayth looked back. He couldn't hear the dog but felt it best to hurry quickly back to the farm.

He opted to run down the road, knowing the woods would slow him. He finally slackened his pace when the farm came into view. Leaving the road, he hurried into the house and closed the door behind him, wishing he had a bar to place over it. He lay down, wrapped his blankets around himself, and stared into the empty fireplace. He was afraid to start it and possibly have the smoke draw attention to the old abandoned farm. There he remained, anxiously waiting for the bark of the dog to give away his location until sleep overtook him.

ᕼATRED

Luwayth awoke abruptly, hands pressed forcefully down on his arms, pinning him in place. As his eyes opened, he could only see the rough wooden wall of the house before he was turned over and a dirty hand covered his mouth. The smell of dirt, stale ale, and body odor wafted from the man's hand, forcing Luwayth to choke down a sudden urge to retch. Looking up, Luwayth saw two faces sneering at him; it was the Bitveens. The one with the scar held Luwayth's mouth and spoke first: "I told you it was no deamhon that left the track. I bet he is the one that ate the food we left out last night. What you think we should do with him?"

The other man, who had a lazy eye, held Luwayth's hands in place and replied. "I not know Haych, he looks like the Asinta that showed up at the tavern the other night. If not, he killed him. Those fancy clothes are on the table, there."

"I not care, Druth. I say we string him up now and take the supplies." The pressure on Luwayth's arms from Haych lightened some. The idea of stringing up Luwayth seemed like it didn't sit well with him.

"If he Asinta, why he eat our food and leave a trail? I say that he is deamhon, and I told you we should have brought Dog." Druth's face twisted as if he was concentrating really hard.

Luwayth's attention turned to evaluating his situation. The table was just in sight with the bow, quiver, and oska lying on top of it. Not recalling placing them there the night before, he wondered if the two men had moved them before accosting him. Druth appeared to have finally come to a solution.

"Even if he the one from the other night, we could slit his throat and take his stuff. You know it would fetch a good price. Get us another hunting dog. No one will know we was here." Haych glanced over his shoulder at Luwayth's supplies on the table.

"Ay, those some nice things, and he said so the other night: he be all alone." The full weight of Haych pressed down on Luwayth again.

Closing his eyes, Luwayth felt the sul of Dainua course through him slightly stronger than the night before. There was only one thing he could do. He reached out and probed the men's suls. Opening himself completely to Dainua, he concentrated on latching onto both suls at the same time. He pulled hard, forcing the suls down into Dainua. His grip on them was tentative since he was trying to pull two suls at once, and they didn't flow as fast as he had hoped. As their suls flowed past his, their anger and hatred washed over him, drowning out every other emotion.

The men screamed out and fell away from Luwayth, who leapt up to get away from the men but stumbled as his legs caught in the blankets. He reached out to the wall to support himself until he regained his balance. He looked down at the men who were staring at one another. Haych's dirty, matted brown hair was mostly gone; a sparse patch of grey-white stood in its place. Druth's scraggly beard was peppered with white. The skin on their faces showed dark brown spots and hung sallow. Turning, they looked up at Luwayth. A high-pitched whimper came from Haych. He pleaded for his life as he held up a hand as if to ward off a blow he felt was sure to come.

"It not my idea. I told Druth not to follow the tracks. Please spare me. I tell no one what happened. If you have to kill one, kill him!"

Druth lunged at Haych, screaming, "You would have brother killed to save your worthless life?" Druth was at Haych's throat trying to strangle him; but with the strength he'd had moments earlier gone, he couldn't subdue his brother. Haych twisted and rolled his brother off him. Dirt flew in the air as the two men desperately fought as if their lives depended on it.

Luwayth tried suppressing the rage and anger he felt from the men's suls, but it overrode his impulse to hold back. He reached out towards the sul of Haych, who was currently on top of his brother desperately trying to pummel him into submission. Haych stopped and looked at his hands as they started to tremble, his skin getting thinner and paler. Druth stared in horror as he watched his brother's face age in front of him. A few teeth dropped from his brother's mouth onto his chest; his jaw started to protrude while his lips shrank back over his gums. The eyes that once were so full of life turned a milky white. Haych reached up and clawed at his face as if he thought he could stop what was happening to him. He fell off of his brother into the dirt. The thin bony fingers he now had dug into the dirt floor as he struggled to push himself up to look at Luwayth. He pleaded with a weak whine, "Stop. Please, stop." Falling back onto the floor with his left hand trapped under him, his right arm reached out and continued to claw at the dirt.

The fear Luwayth felt from Haych's sul fed the hatred roiling inside, but he fought back against it, stopping himself from pulling all of the man's sul and leaving an obsidian statue in his place.

Suddenly, hatred flooded over him again and he found himself at the table. His hand grabbed the oska and swung it into the side of Haych's head. A dull, cold crack echoed through the room. The hand clawing at the dirt twitched then stopped. Luwayth tried pulling the oska away, but the roots he had so carefully grown were firmly embedded in the side of the man's head. He pulled harder until a slurping, sucking sound emanated from Haych's head as the roots tore free. Blood, bone, and brain leaked onto the floor and dripped from the end of his oska. Luwayth was now one with the hatred and anger, eager to satiate the blood lust it craved. He looked over to Druth who was lying on his back, staring at his brother in shock, his mouth agape as if silently screaming. The hatred was eager to feed on Druth's emotions. Luwayth struggled, afraid that if he fed the deamhon growing in him more, he would lose control forever. He stepped over Haych's corpse, raised his oska, and drove it straight down onto Druth's face. He turned away just before it struck. The oska shuddered as it impacted bone and then softly sank in. Druth's hand grabbed at Luwayth's leg, pulling at his pants, then loosened and slid to the floor. Letting go of the oska, Luwayth stumbled back until he hit the wall and slid down, his eyes filling with tears. His body shook violently, causing him to gasp for air between loud sobs. Falling to his side, Luwayth clutched at the blankets on his bedroll, pulling them tightly against himself as he wished his life would end. He blubbered, again and again, "I just wanted cheese." Exhaustion finally overtook him and he slipped into nightmares of a dark mist in which the hatred that controlled him earlier transformed into a hulking beast, relentlessly stalking him.

When Luwayth awoke, the hatred had abated and he felt more like himself. The events of that morning seemed unreal. He slowly started to push himself up; his eyes were swollen, making everything blurry. He rubbed at them, wiping away the crusted tears. The oska finally came into view. It leaned awkwardly, like a tree ready to topple over after a heavy storm. Blood and gore were spattered down the carved trunk. Finally, Luwayth summoned the courage to look at the base. It looked oddly like a tree had grown out of an old man's face as he slept. As his vision cleared, that image changed into a man whose remaining features were pain, fear, and anguish. There was nothing peaceful about it.

Luwayth's stomach churned as he gaped in horror at the carnage in front of him. He rushed outside, stumbling over the bodies, and falling to his hands and knees just outside the door. He retched up dinner from the previous night as tears started to stream down his face once again. The tears fell, not for the men he had killed, but for how easy it had been. After finally gaining control of his body, Luwayth crawled sideways a few paces before collapsing into the dirt and rolling over. He looked into the sky above and noticed there had to be a few hours still left of daylight. He turned his head and looked at the open doorway; the shadows inside hid his crime. Luwayth balled his hands into fists and pounded the dirt in frustration. "This isn't who I am," he told himself.

Luwayth closed his eyes and reached out to Dainua. She wasn't as strong since he had used her power earlier that day, but he was grateful it was enough to help calm him.

Realization seized him as he came to understand that these would be the first of many deaths required to enact Airnin's plan. He steeled his nerves, stood slowly, and brushed the dirt and sick from his clothes. Looking back into the house, he knew what he had to do.

He strode over to his oska and yanked it out. The face made a bubbling noise in protest before the oska tore free. The base was covered in brains and blood. Setting it aside, Luwayth reached down and grabbed Druth's leg, dragging him out the door and into the nearby woods, leaving a grayish-red trail. Once in the woods, he dragged the body to a small depression near a tree. Next, he dragged Haych's body out and dumped it next to Druth's. Luwayth pulled a small bush from the ground and planted it between the bodies. He hurried back to the house to grab his oska, reached, out and pulled all of the small suls he could feel across the floor. The blood and gore turned a glossy black. Then, he kicked the black mess out the door and tried to spread it as evenly as he could across the ground. He followed the blood trail, pulling all of the suls and scattering the blackened dirt as he returned to the bodies. Luwayth reached out and made the bush grow and spread until the bodies couldn't be spotted by a passerby. Farkor had set by the time he finished.

THE PLAN

The next few nights, Luwayth kept to the house and used the meager supplies he found to feed himself; boredom and hunger grew each day. It was the fourth night since he had seen Airnin. He paced the treeline looking for suls to replenish his oska. A shimmer appeared a few feet in front of the door to the old farmhouse. As it faded, Airnin appeared and went inside. Hurrying to the house, Luwayth found that Airnin had left the door open. A small fire was burning and gave off a faint light. Airnin was standing in front of the table.

"There you are. I take it you have been hunting or setting traps to feed yourself while I was away?" Thinking of the stale beans he had been eating the last few days, he didn't want to admit he had been too afraid to venture out. Stammering, Luwayth replied, "Y-ye-yes and replenishing my oska." Luwayth closed his eyes. A look rippled across Airnin's face—the one that showed he knew Luwayth was lying—and he briefly furrowed his brow.

"What you have been up to does not matter. I have scouted along my path of bones. It is time to head south towards the palace. You will stop at the taverns along the way as planned."

"Yes, Airnin. You can trust me. We are partners in this to the end."

Airnin didn't say a word but shimmered and disappeared.

The room still felt chilly, even after Airnin left. Moving a chair from the table in front of the fire, Luwayth grabbed a few logs and some kindling and coaxed the fire back to life. Suddenly, fear gripped him. He felt trapped by his promise to Airnin, knowing the horrors he would be forced to face next. Trying to distract himself, Luwayth held his oska and began twirling it between his hands, watching the flames glimmer through the carved forest. Visions of fleeing and leaving everything behind played out in his mind. *Though, where would I go?* he thought. The barrow came to mind. Living in a hole for the rest of his life was something he just couldn't do. The last six years seemed like a lifetime, and in some ways, they were.

"No, the only way I'll be free is if I kill the King. Then Airnin will *have* to let me go," he rationalized. He wasn't really sure where he would go once they were done, though.

The next day, he awoke an hour before first light. Luwayth hurriedly packed the things he would need, including his bedroll, and left the house. The cool morning air felt amazing.

He walked back towards his village, wanting to skirt around it before anyone was up and recognized him. From previous discussions with Airnin, Luwayth knew there was another village due south of his. Vague memories of being there once or twice with his dad when they were traveling and telling tales passed through his subconscious like a mist.

Once Luwayth reached the path that led to the baker's farm, he turned and headed south. As he neared the outskirts of the Bitveen's farm, he could hear the howls of their dog from inside their house. Luwayth couldn't stand the thought of leaving it there to die. *Maybe the Bakers will hear it and come let it out*, he thought. He started to walk away but knew that he couldn't just abandon it.

Luwayth decided to go to the Bitveen's house. He paused as his hand rested on the door. He worried the dog would bite him as soon as he opened it, so he consumed a few of the suls in his oska and readied it in front of him. He slowly pushed the door open, and as soon as there was enough room, a large brown fuzziness lunged at him, bowling him over before he could react.

The dog began to lick Luwayth's face as its tail wagged feverishly back and forth. Panic quickly gave way to laughter as Luwayth tried to pull away, but the dog pursued him and continued to bathe him in slobber. After a few moments, the dog put its nose to the ground, howled, and took off, heading in the direction Luwayth had come. For a moment Luwayth sat in the dirt, astonished that he had been so afraid of the dog. He finally picked himself up and continued on, hoping that the dog would find a new owner.

As he exited the woods near the cemetery, he glanced around, and not seeing anyone, turned and began the journey south.

About midday, Luwayth came upon the next village. It was similar to his, having also been attacked by the Asinta and now showing scars on the buildings and surrounding land. Before he entered the village proper, he searched the nearby trees, and, finding one he felt suitable, he dropped his belongings except for his oska, consumed a few suls, and leapt into the branches, climbing and jumping his way to the very top. Once there, he found a place he felt was safe for his oska and wedged it there before returning to the ground. After picking up his belongings, he brushed the dirt from his princely clothes and headed into the village.

The tavern was empty except for a few locals who looked like they had been there all night. Luwayth ordered food and sat at a table to eat. The tavern owner was the exact opposite of Cromm— short and heavy set.

Luwayth conversed with the owner, telling him he was a teller of tales passing through and asked for any news.

"We don't get many strangers unless they're from the neighboring villages. We haven't had a teller of tales in here in quite some time. If you wouldn't mind telling a few tales tonight, I could arrange a room and a meal."

"That seems like a fair trade, though I do have to be off in the morning," Luwayth replied. He put out his hand and grasped the owner by the wrist.

That night, Luwayth told his dad's tales, and in return, not only did he get a hot meal with meat but also a mug of ale that seemed to never empty. He was cautious not to drink too much and accidentally reveal who he really was.

Towards the end of the night, Luwayth excused himself and headed out of the tavern to use the outhouse. Once he was sure no one was around, he snuck out of town and waited.

After a few moments, Airnin appeared as though he had been waiting for him.

"I take it there were no Asinta or soldiers?" Airnin asked as soon as he appeared.

"No. I plan to leave in the morning and continue south."

"Good," Airnin replied, before vanishing as quickly as he appeared.

The next morning, Luwayth arose, finally feeling used to getting up in the morning again. He ate the meager meal the tavern owner offered before heading to the woods to retrieve his oska and venturing south.

It was a two-day journey to the next village. This one appeared less damaged and more populated than the last. After hiding his oska, Luwayth found the tavern on the outskirts of the village.

As he entered, he found it busier than other taverns he had seen at midday. Spotting an empty table near the back of the room, he walked over and sat down. Eventually, the tavern owner came by and asked Luwayth what he wanted. After introducing himself as a teller of tales, the tavern owner didn't seem very interested. It took some haggling, but Luwayth eventually managed a free meal that night for his tales, though he would have to find lodging elsewhere.

Once Luwayth had things in order at the tavern, he spent the day wandering around the village. It wasn't as exciting as he expected. He found several shops, instead of stalls, where goods were sold; however, not having anything to barter with made it feel like an empty prospect.

He had almost forgotten his reason for being there until he came around a corner and spotted a man in a cloak with an embroidered patch of golden hands clasped at the wrist on the left side. The man also walked with an intricately carved walking stick.

An Asinta, Luwayth thought.

The Asinta tucked a small box into his robes as he closed the door behind him. Luwayth froze in his tracks and watched as the Asinta walked down the street away from him; the people in the street gave a wide berth as the man passed by.

Coming to his senses, Luwayth slowly followed the Asinta who wound his way out of the village towards the nearby woods. Luwayth closed his eyes and tracked the Asinta's sul through the trees. When the Asinta had gotten far enough away that Luwayth felt it was safe, he followed after him into the woods, stopping frequently to make sure he was still going the right direction and was a safe distance away.

About a quarter stone into the woods, the Asinta arrived in a clearing where a horse was hobbled near a small tent and a few supplies. Luwayth stopped and watched. After feeling confident the Asinta was not packing up for the day, he slowly made his way back to the village. Once free of the woods, he relaxed, grateful for all the training Airnin had given him.

That night, after a decent meal of mutton, Luwayth stood on a low stool so the patrons could see him and told his tales. Once he was done, the tavern owner thanked him for his work and offered free meals the next day if Luwayth would tell his tales again. Luwayth agreed and bade the owner good evening before heading out into the night to find a place to bed down.

After Luwayth had gotten partway into the woods looking for a good hollow near a tree where he could lay out his bedroll, he noticed a shimmer in the starlight a few trees away. Luwayth closed his eyes and realized it was Airnin. Airnin cautiously made his way over to Luwayth once he felt safe that he was alone.

"So, what news do you have for me?" Airnin asked

Luwayth pointed in the direction of the Asinta's camp. "There is an Asinta camped in that direction, alone except for a horse," Luwayth replied reluctantly.

"Good," Airnin replied in a silky tone, then glided off in the direction Luwayth had pointed.

Luwayth sat down on his bedroll, his stomach twisting as he thought about the fate he had given the Asinta.

A few moments later, a far-off scream pierced the air, causing a chill to crawl up Luwayth's spine. He strained to hear anything more, but the woods were dead silent.

The air in front of Luwayth shimmered as Airnin reappeared. "My work is done; go and finish yours," Airnin instructed before vanishing.

Luwayth stood and grabbed his bow, quiver, and oska before he trudged in the direction of the Asinta's camp. As he arrived, he saw the horse was still hobbled and grazing in the clearing. Lying next to the fire was the Asinta he had seen, gutted from navel to sternum, his blood pooled against the stones of the fire pit. Luwayth's stomach lurched, and he became light-headed. After steadying himself with his oska, Luwayth pulled the knife from his belt and gingerly walked over to the Asinta. With his head turned away, he fumbled at the man's bloody cloak while he hurriedly cut away the embroidery of the clasped hands.

Luwayth freed the horse and sprinted from the camp back to his bedroll. Once there, he collapsed onto it, his hands shaking as he stared at the sticky red embroidered hands. He wanted to scream and run to the farthest corner of the land. Instead, he gazed glassy-eyed into the dark, resigning himself to the fact that he was a killer and no better than Airnin.

He awoke heavily the next morning, not recalling how or when he had fallen asleep. As he sat up, he saw the bloody embroidery lying in the dirt. He stuffed it into the bottom of his pack and washed his hands with water from his leather bottle. He then lay back down and stared into space, imagining what life would have been like if he wasn't an Asinta.

As Farkor started to set, Luwayth finally picked himself up, hid his oska and supplies, and walked back to the tavern in the village to tell his dad's tales.

The company, food, drink, and retelling of his dad's tales lightened Luwayth's heart and put him in better spirits, almost causing him to forget the events of the previous night, until he was alone again in the woods.

Luwayth camped at the edge of this town for several nights, telling his tales each night, grateful he didn't stumble upon any more Asinta. Airnin only showed up but once, to tell him that it was time to move on to the next village.

The next several weeks were a blur. After visiting a few villages, word started to spread ahead of him that a master teller of tales was on his way. When he arrived at the next tavern, the owner was expecting him and, in most cases, had lodgings, if available. He would scout the village by day and tell tales by night. When he spotted an Asinta, he would report it to Airnin, who always seemed to know where Luwayth was. As he was packing to leave the most recent village, he pulled out the bloody embroidered rags he had cut away from each Asinta and laid out all six in front of him. As his eyes passed over them, he forced himself to recall the image of each lifeless body—carrion left to fester, never seeing a proper burial.

Luwayth hated that each murder felt easier than the last. He was certain he would have gone mad by now; instead, he was becoming accustomed to it. He recalled the look Airnin had after each killing, how he showed no remorse. He never recalled Airnin showing any emotion other than anger, though this made him recognize that perhaps Airnin's face couldn't display those emotions. Surely, he felt as tormented as Luwayth. He couldn't stomach any other explanation. He quickly packed away the rags, pushed the thoughts of killing away, and focused on the day ahead of him.

The weeks continued to pass, and the scraps of cloth continued to pile up in his bag. Luwayth felt like he was reliving the same moments of his life over and over again: tell his tales by night and hunt the Asinta by day. The only thing that changed was the scenery.

TAVERN

Everything changed when he walked into a tavern and saw a familiar face sitting across the room; it was Uram. Also at the table sat a female Asinta, sipping ale and staring into the room. Whenever he saw a female Asinta, Luwayth couldn't bring himself to tell Airnin. For some unknown reason, each one reminded him of his mother, or maybe he pictured her as Dainua. Airnin didn't seem to notice, or at least never commented, that all of the victims Luwayth led him to were male.

Luwayth walked over and introduced himself to the barkeep and, once a trade was negotiated for his tales, sat down at a table where he could watch Uram.

Nothing happened between Uram and his companion that was out of the ordinary. They ate, drank and talked awhile. Then, Uram stood and headed for the tavern's door. Without thinking, Luwayth rushed over and grabbed Uram's cloak. Uram stopped and cast his eyes on Luwayth. Luwayth saw a look of recognition pass over Uram's face before Uram looked down at Luwayth's left shoulder and arm. Luwayth, however, wore long-sleeved shirts to hide his scars.

"Do I know you?" Uram asked, quizzically.

"Uh, no, I, uh, just wanted to say to be careful," Luwayth stammered.

"What should I be careful of?" Uram asked, becoming more interested in Luwayth.

Luwayth's eyes darted around the room as he spoke in a low voice: "The villagers here don't care for the Asinta. That's all I wanted to say."

"Don't you mean *Crop Burners*?" Uram retorted as he studied Luwayth for a reaction. "Are you sure we haven't met before? I feel like I know you from somewhere."

"No, we haven't met before." Luwayth then lowered his head and returned to his table.

He kept a low profile the next few days, telling Airnin when they met that no Asinta were in town. Luwayth also never crossed Uram's path again nor saw his female companion.

A week later, the second part of Airnin's plan fell into place. As Luwayth scouted the village for Asinta, he came across the king's soldiers, dressed just as Airnin described them: blue uniforms with a sword piercing a crown emblazoned on their chest.

The soldiers were coming out of a tavern singing a bawdy song about a barmaid. They stumbled down the road using each other for support.

Luwayth easily followed the soldiers to a small camp just outside the village, then he hurried back to retrieved his bag. He returned to the soldiers' camp but stayed far enough away as to not be spotted and awaited Airnin.

After Airnin materialized, Luwayth pointed to the camp and whispered, "Soldiers." Then, Luwayth turned his back on the camp.

"Are you not coming?" Airnin asked.

Luwayth sighed, thinking back to what had happened with the Bitveens before replying, "No, I can't."

"This is as much your revenge as it is mine. I was too soft in sheltering you from killing the Asinta. You must bloody your hands. It is your final test. You must show your loyalty to me. You did promise."

Luwayth slowly turned to face Airnin. "I have already killed, Airnin, and I can't do it again. Their emotion—it took over. I couldn't stop myself." Luwayth paused briefly, then explained everything that happened with the Bitveens.

Disdain rippled across Airnin's face. "You have discovered the limits of your powers. You are no use to me." Airnin turned and glided silently into the soldiers' camp. A few muffled screams broke the silence of the night but not the torment Luwayth expected. Time seemed to stretch on forever as Luwayth waited for Airnin's return. Finally, a grey form broke from the blackness of night, gliding up to Luwayth.

"It is done. I have left you a task a child could handle. I will not accept failure," Airnin rebuked, then faded away.

Luwayth crept over to the camp and found it eerily quiet. The soldiers were strewn about. It looked as if a fight had broken out amongst themselves. Airnin had staged it perfectly. Luwayth silently moved through the camp, depositing the torn embroidery onto the soldiers until he came across the few left alive. They were obviously inebriated and had passed out. Luwayth cautiously deposited the remaining rags around them. He had one task left. He walked over to the fire pit, grabbed a dry branch, and lit it. As he walked back out of the camp, he touched the lit branch to the tents, until the camp illuminated the night sky.

Luwayth discarded the branch and leapt into a nearby tree overlooking the burning camp. As he crouched on a large branch, he waited for signs of alarm from the village. A few men emerged and, after discovering the fire, called for more help. Luwayth dropped from the tree in the ensuing commotion, blended in, and lent a hand. The villagers put out the flames and found the evidence he had left.

As Luwayth reached the next village the following day, he was relieved. It was the last village he needed to visit before he finished his trek south towards the King's palace. The village was small, like all of the villages he had seen along the way, though it had none of the disfigurement from the Asinta that the northern villages bore.

According to Airnin's plan, he would have to wait here until the discovery of the soldiers' treachery reached the village. That day came and went, but Airnin hadn't appeared.

Luwayth hurried to the tavern and was shown to a room upstairs where he could place his belongings.

The din from the tavern below grew as Luwayth descended the stairs from his room above the kitchen. Making his way to the bar, Luwayth motioned to the barkeep who filled a wooden mug and plopped it down in front of him before disappearing through a door into the kitchen. He returned with a plate of what looked to be a cooked bird and some beans. After placing it next to the mug of mead, the barkeep turned to the next customer.

Luwayth grabbed the plate and mug, then searched for a seat. He found a table with a few empty chairs by the stairs and sat down to enjoy his meal. The men across from him nodded in greeting, then continued on with their conversation.

The room quieted down when an older man stood on a low stool by the fire. Once he had everyone's attention, he started to tell a tale.

"There once was a boy who lived by a village much like this one. After a day with his father at the market selling the last crops from that year, he was sent home to his mother while his dad stayed back to visit the local tavern. The boy took the horse, empty wagon, and the money purse, which was heavy and full. His dad didn't want to get drunk and have the money they earned stolen off him yet again and felt it was wise to send the money home to his wife.

"It was a dark night and the lantern that hung from the horse gave off strange shadows as it swayed back and forth. A few stones away from home, the boy heard a rustling in the trees. He stopped and peered into the woods. After a few moments, he heard nothing more, so he continued on his way. Soon, he found the road blocked by a large man.

" 'Hand over the purse and I won't kill ya,' the man said, reaching over and patting the hilt of the sword that hung from his belt. A wry smile crossed the man's fat face.

"Now, this boy wasn't stupid; he didn't want to die. However, the money he had on him was necessary to feed his family that winter and to buy needed seed for the following year. So, the boy untied the pouch at his waist and held it out to the man.

" 'Ahh, I see that you're smarter than you look,' the portly man said as he stepped forward to take his prize. The boy watched as the man approached with his hand outstretched. Without thinking first, the boy threw the bag into the air and over the man's head. Confused, the man looked up to see where the money was thrown, but his weight got in the way as he tried to quickly turn. Dainua was on the boy's side that night as the boy was smaller and quicker. He darted around the fat man and caught the bag, then turned and fled down the road, with the man giving chase. Suddenly, he saw a large clearing to this right; turning, he fled across what he realized was the graveyard. A few paces in, his foot caught on a grave marker, sending him sprawling through the air. He landed hard and his foot felt like it was on fire. He rolled over but found the man sneering down at him, his jowls flapping like an injured bird from exhaustion.

" 'Was going... to let you go... if you handed me... the coins,' he panted. 'But now... I have to kill... you out of spite... ' He grabbed the hilt of his sword and pulled the long blade from its sheath, leveling the point at the boy's chest. As he drew the sword back, a faint glow illuminated everything around them. The man looked past the boy, and the tip of the sword dropped.

" 'I... I... killed you!' the man yelled. A blur of bluish light flew over the top of the boy and through the man, who staggered back a few paces. The sword slipped from his sausage-thick fingers as he fell to his knees, gasping. He clutched at his throat before falling face down into the dirt, dead. The boy looked up and saw what had killed the man: a woman who he could see through, glowing faintly blue.

" 'Well, that was very satisfying!' she proclaimed, stepping through the dead man's body and reaching out a hand to the boy.

" 'Oy, come now, I wouldn't hurt a fly—unless of course, you killed me.' She giggled at her own joke. The boy raised a shaking hand to her. After helping him to his feet, she stood back and looked him over.

" 'Yes, I think you will do just fine.' The boy stepped back, scared about what she had in mind for him.

" 'You silly boy, nothing like that! I figure that now that I've saved your life, you owe me a favor in return.'

The man telling the tale stopped.

"Speaking of favors," he proclaimed. "Barkeep—another ale." The crowd in the tavern yelled in reply, "Give the man a drink!" After the teller received his ale, he took a long, slow drink before setting the mug down and continuing.

"The boy looked at the deamhon in front of him. She *had* saved his life, he reckoned. It was the least he could do. 'What is it that you want of me, deamhon? Why do you look so familiar?'

" 'Well, you've come into my shop once a month since you were able to walk,' she said, winking. Then it dawned on him.

" 'Oy, you are the baker who died last week. A cart accident, wasn't it?' The boy glanced at the fat man at his feet before saying, 'Well, apparently not.'

" 'That's why I need you to do me a favor. The baker in the next village was losing customers due to my new bread recipe.' The boy scrunched up his face in confusion.

" 'Someone killed you for a recipe?'

" 'O yes, our recipes are our most guarded secrets. If anyone had them, then no one would need a baker.' Nodding in agreement, the boy replied, 'I guess that makes sense. So, what do you need me to do? Steal it back?' The lady smiled, and her blue glow seemed to brighten.

" 'Yes, but there's nothing like a little revenge first. After all, he did hire someone to kill me. I need you to ask him to make this for me.' The woman pulled a translucent piece of folded paper out of her bosom and handed it to the boy. He timidly took the note and found it became as solid as any other paper once in hand.

" 'I need you to take that to him and tell him you want him to bake it. He will refuse and, when he does, hand him this.' Reaching into the apron she had tied around her waist, she pulled out a translucent pouch. As she placed it into the boy's hand, it had no weight to it; as she let go it became as heavy as the pouch he was holding in his other hand.

" 'I can trust you, yes?' the lady asked. Weighing both pouches in his hands, he decided the one the lady had just given him felt considerably heavier.

" 'So, I just need to give him the recipe and then pay him?'

" 'That's all you need to do. Oy, and whatever you do, *do not* eat anything he bakes.' She winked and then vanished.

The boy headed back to the horse and then hurried home, not telling his mom a word about what happened. He briefly considered switching the pouches but thought better of it when he remembered what she had done to her murderer. The next day, he slipped off after chores and cut through the woods to the next village. Approaching the baker's shop, he noticed it was quite busy. He patiently waited until it was his turn to order.

" 'Sir, I have a special request. Can you make this recipe?' The boy handed the recipe to the man, not knowing what was on it because he was too afraid to look at it. The baker unfolded the recipe and read it.

" 'Is this some kind of joke? There's no way I'll make this,' the man huffed. The boy held out the bag of coins to the baker. He took it and peered in.

" 'All of this for this loaf of bread?' he asked.

"The boy nodded in reply. The baker poured a few coins into his hand and inspected them before putting them back and handing the pouch back to the boy.

" 'Oy, you have a deal. Come back tomorrow and I will have the loaf of bread for you.' The boy turned and hurried out.

"At the end of the day, the baker went in back to start preparing for the next day. Looking at the recipe the boy had given him, he decided he should work on that first since he didn't know how long it would take. Plus, the bag of coins the boy promised was good for at least a month's worth of bread he would normally bake. The recipe was like any other he had made—until he got to the end. It read:

Before you let the dough rise, do the following:

Cut the tip of one finger off and fold into dough 5 by 5 times. (The ingredient must come from the one who prepares it.)

"The baker placed his hand on a cutting board. The sack of coins was worth a fingertip, he surmised. Then, before he could change his mind, he picked up a knife and swiftly cut the tip off his little finger on his left hand. After wrapping his hand in a rag, the baker placed his finger into the dough and folded it 5 by 5 times. With the last fold, the blood and finger disappeared. As he filled the pan with the dough, he noticed that he still had another pan's worth of dough left. As he filled each pan, he continued to find more dough when he returned, until every one of his pans was full. Not wanting to waste the dough, he decided to cook all of it; his customers wouldn't notice, he told himself.

"The next morning, the boy returned, retrieved the loaf of bread, and left the pouch of coins behind. As he headed home, he tossed the loaf into a pig's trough.

"The baker sold his loaves faster than ever with a few customers fighting over the last of them. He did not notice, however, that none of his customers that day were people he knew from the village.

"That night, the baker looked at the recipe and thought of how fast the bread sold out that morning. He could have easily sold twice that. "What are two more fingertips?" he thought. The next day, he raised the price of his bread and still sold every loaf he had, with customers clamoring for more. This went on every day until every fingertip was gone. The following night as he looked at the recipe, it had changed; instead of asking for a fingertip, it now asked for an entire toe. The baker didn't delay as he glanced at the pile of coins sitting on the opposite table and how fast it had grown.

"As the weeks passed, the more the recipe called for, the more profits he made. With each new request from the paper, the baker never hesitated to oblige. After the toes, the recipe called for his ears, followed by his lips, nose, teeth, and finally feet.

"That night, as he dragged himself to the kitchen, he lay there wondering how he was going to bake the next day's loaves. Looking down at his disfigured body, he didn't see himself—he saw profit. He heard the front door of his store open then shut. He called out that they were closed but that he would have more loaves the following morning. The stranger didn't answer and his footsteps grew louder.

As he came into view, he looked like any other man—until he smiled that is: his teeth came to points and the baker noticed his ears were pointed, as well. 'My people have enjoyed your bread immensely and we want more,' he said softly, his voice silky and smooth.

" 'Will you pay me for it?' the baker asked. Pulling a knife from his belt, the deamhon smiled wickedly: 'No, no. You will.' Bending over, the deamhon grabbed the man's leg and started to cut just below the knee.

"The next morning, as the boy left to start his chores, there sitting in front of the door was a large sack of coins along with a recipe for bread.

"Remember: beware of greed, my friends, or it will eat you alive."

The man telling the tale bowed with a flourish and stepped off the stool. Luwayth stood and walked over to meet the teller of tales. Holding his hand out to the man, Luwayth proclaimed, "That has to be the best version of that tale I have heard yet." The man grabbed Luwayth's wrist.

"Thank you, and you must be the master teller of tales that everyone speaks of, correct? You seem very young to possess such talent." Luwayth nodded.

"Yes, I was lucky to have a wonderful teacher." The man returned to his seat across the tavern, clasping wrists and taking compliments along the way.

Luwayth went back to his seat to finish his mead before he took his turn to tell his tales. As he sat down, a woman across from him spoke up. "I overheard your conversation with Paighon. Is it true you are the teller of tales that has been traveling down from the north?"

"Yes, that would be me."

The woman had two cups in her hands and pushed one of them across the table to Luwayth.

"Let me be the first to give you a drink in thanks for the tales you will tell tonight."

"Thank you. You may call me Luwayth," he said, graciously.

"You're welcome. I am Nioni." She then lifted her mug. Luwayth picked up the mug she had given him and held it up in front of himself. She nodded and then started to drink. As her head tilted back, he noticed her long slender neck that flowed nicely into the rest of her contours; it awakened something within him. Nioni slammed the mug down on the table, empty.

"Well, what are you waiting for?" she demanded. Coming to his senses, Luwayth put the mug to his lips and tipped it back. He felt there was something different with this ale. It tasted a little bitter compared to the last mug he'd had. However, it didn't stop him from finishing it and slamming his mug down next to Nioni's, trying to impress her.

Nioni leaned across the table, beckoning Luwayth to come closer. Leaning forward, Luwayth could smell the ale on her breath, mixed with the scent of leather and dust. He found it strange how much he liked it—maybe it was because it came from her. Nioni leaned closer to Luwayth, her cheek brushing against his. He desperately wanted to do something but didn't know what it would be, having never been this close to a woman before. She spoke two words that caused a deep chill to shoot right through him:

"I'm sorry." Nioni leaned back, crossed her arms, smiled, and stared at Luwayth.

A sudden urge to flee and get as far away from Nioni as possible took hold. Luwayth stood and tried to escape upstairs, but the world around him shifted. His legs wouldn't keep him up. He grabbed for the nearest table but missed it and stumbled forward. The sounds around him were drowned out by a high-pitched whistle. Something grabbed him by the arm, lifted, and steered him towards the tavern door. He tried to yell out for help, but the words were garbled and incoherent. He became dependent on whoever had him by the arm, unable to do anything but follow. A faint, refreshing, ale-free breeze hit his face before darkness swallowed him up.

CAPTIVITY

When Luwayth awoke, the world around him was black and sounds were muffled. As he tried to sit up, he realized he had a hood over his head and his hands were bound behind his back. He was also trussed to something that moved slowly up and down. The sound of a horse's hooves broke through the haze in his mind. He struggled back and forth but was firmly tied down.

"Stop moving back there unless you want to fall off," a voice called out. It was Nioni's voice, Luwayth was certain.

"Oy, I didn't do anything wrong! You made a mistake," Luwayth slurred, then closed his eyes and reached out, but nothing was there; he was completely cut off from Dainua.

"What did you give me to drink? What did you do to me?" Luwayth stammered, as he started to panic.

"Calm down, just gave you something to make sure you didn't try to have me grow old without any of the fun that goes with it," Nioni quipped. "You can't use your powers on me, boy, and you can't escape. So, just lie there, enjoy the journey, and, if you behave, you'll get food and a blanket for the night. If not... well, you can starve until I hand you over." Nioni's hand patted him on the back. Giving in, Luwayth stopped squirming and began contemplating what to do.

"What is it that you have covered me in?" Luwayth asked, baffled at what could be blocking his powers.

"It's obsidian cloth. Playing the foolish villager isn't going to get you anywhere."

Luwayth wanted to know more but knew he wasn't going to get the answers he wanted. "Airnin will come for me. Just have to wait it out," he told himself. He still felt drowsy, and the swaying motion of the horse soon lulled him back to sleep.

A jostling motion shook Luwayth from his stupor.

"Oy! Wake up! I'm not carrying you again." A hand grabbed his back and pulled him backward off the horse. Luckily, Nioni helped him up stay upright long enough after his feet hit the ground to keep him from falling over.

"You steady?" Nioni asked.

"Ay, I'm fine," Luwayth grumbled. Nioni guided Luwayth a few paces before directing him to sit down. Luwayth did as he was told. Nioni tugged at the hood he was wearing, and a piece of fabric fell away from his eyes, leaving holes just big enough to peer through. He was sitting in a clearing. In front of him sat a circle of rocks with ashes of a long-dead fire. Next to it, supplies were laid out, along with a bedroll. The horse stood off to the left, grazing. Judging by Farkor, Luwayth suspected a few more hours remained until last light. Looking down, he realized he was wearing a thick black shirt that had small, fine stones sewn into it that looked like fish scales. The scales were similar to the stone from which the barrow was made. There were also matching pants that tied to loops in the shirt. Cloth boots covered his feet and attached to the pants in the same manner. He closed his eyes. He could see the suls around him, but he couldn't feel them. Searching the area around where they sat, he saw no one.

Luwayth sat quietly and watched as Nioni set up camp and started a fire. She pulled some dried meat from a pack, along with a water skin. Coming over to Luwayth, she untied another flap around his mouth.

"I don't want to feed you, but I have no other choice." Nioni then held a piece of meat to his mouth. Having learned his lesson from the previous night, Luwayth refused to bite until Nioni took a bite and dramatically chewed it before taking a large swig of water in front of him. Luwayth reluctantly opened his mouth and let her feed him. After she was done, she tied the cloth back around his mouth, then turned and sat by the fire to eat her meal.

"Where are you taking me?" Luwayth asked.

"I am taking you to the king. You are accused of killing Asinta, so a hefty bounty was placed on your head. I don't normally track down Asinta, but Uram said you would be an easy catch—and he was right."

"Wait!" Luwayth blurted. "If Uram knew who I was, he would know that I didn't do it. I have committed no wrongs against the Asinta! Why would he think... " Luwayth's voice trailed off, feeling foolish to dispute something that was true. He stammered, "Well... the king... is evil." Snorting, Nioni replied, "The King keeps my purse full and that's all that matters."

The sound of a galloping horse came from behind Luwayth. Nioni jumped to her feet and walked over to meet the rider. Luwayth turned his head, but the hood didn't move and blocked his view.

The dried grass crunched underfoot as the rider approached. As he came into view, Luwayth recognized him immediately; it was Uram, carrying Luwayth's oska.

"So, you call yourself Luwayth now. Didn't you go by Fearn when we first met?" Uram asked as he tapped the top of Luwayth's oska on his hand.

"I don't know what you're talking about," Luwayth replied, trying to act innocently.

"I'm not naive, Fearn. When you warned me in the tavern, I knew I had met you before. It wasn't until that night that it dawned on me who you were. I went back the next morning, but you were gone. At first, I couldn't figure out what you were warning me about. I couldn't fathom you being the one behind killing the Asinta. I traveled north, retracing your steps, and discovered that Asinta had been killed in every village where you told tales. The last village I stopped in, I asked after a boy whom I taught and was told he was killed along with his father." Uram paused and looked down at

Luwayth's oska. "I think that boy survived and somehow managed to find a mentor."

Luwayth didn't say a word. He just stared at Uram, uncertain of what to do or say.

"Almost fifty Asinta have been killed in the past six years. An additional dozen were murdered these past few months. Then, there is the matter of evidence found on the king's soldiers." Uram stopped and looked at Luwayth.

"Fifty Asinta?" Luwayth asked, horrified. "Are you sure?"

"Yes. That doesn't count the scores of villagers killed who either wielded the power unknowingly or were growing into it."

Luwayth thought to himself for a moment. "Are you saying kids were killed?" Luwayth asked, stunned at the idea that Airnin could do such a thing. "He's not the kindest person, but he would never do that," Luwayth muttered.

"What did you say? Do you know who has been killing us?" Uram said angrily, then stepped closer to Luwayth.

"It's your fault!" Luwayth spat.

"How is this my fault?"

"You never came back! You left me and you promised you would come back." Luwayth started to cry in anger.

"So you are that boy?" Uram paused. "That hill—you went back to it?" he asked, dismayed.

"You promised you would come back and investigate it but you didn't, and because of that, my dad died and it's all your fault," he said petulantly. Luwayth wished he could stand and strike Uram.

"I wanted to but there has been an ongoing war with Soyer. The imbiber and those who would make decisions on what to do in regards to the hill were away, trying to broker peace. I was reassigned elsewhere and promised it would be looked into."

"Well, it wasn't!" Luwayth yelled, his voice straining.

"You must tell me what was under that hill. The destruction it has caused in the last few years has fractured the Asinta. With the discovery of the soldiers' guilt, many more fled into hiding, despite many of us knowing the evidence must have been planted."

Luwayth contemplated what Uram told him, then thought back to Airnin and the many nights he was out alone and how the sul in his chest never seemed to deplete. Why didn't Airnin tell him? Surely he would have understood; it wasn't Airnin's fault that he lived the life he did.

"It isn't his fault. It is his brother's."

"What do you mean?"

"The king killed his father, blamed his brother, and then buried him in that barrow."

"Tell me everything," Uram demanded.

Luwayth told the entire tale, knowing that if Uram knew the truth, he would understand. After he was done, a panic overcame Uram.

"Nioni, take him to the capital and be quick. Take this with you." Uram tossed Luwayth's oska to her.

"I need to leave now; I need to verify this." Uram dashed to his horse and galloped off.

Nioni clicked her tongue, set aside the oska, grabbed a second bedroll, and unrolled it. The fabric was thin, with large holes scattered throughout. She walked over to Luwayth and picked him up under an arm, guided him to the bedroll, and set him on it. She pushed him back so he would lie down and moved one of his legs, while instructing him, "Don't even think about kicking me." Her finger pointed at his face. Grabbing the other leg, she tied them together. She took a blanket that was just as weather-worn as the bedroll and tossed it over him.

"Airnin will be out searching for me tonight," Luwayth speculated. A deep dread slowly spread through him. The image of Nioni in Airnin's embrace, twisting and breaking, flashed across his subconscious. Fear chased after the dread like a hunter bearing down on its prey.

"Nioni, you need to get out of here before it gets too dark. You can't stop what will be coming for you. I don't want to watch you die," Luwayth pleaded.

"Now, that was more convincing than that tale you spun for Uram; however, you cannot scare me with foolish tales of the deamhon. The thieves and murderers I track down have more bite than any tale you can weave for me. Now, be quiet. It's been a long day. Another word out of you, and I will stick my sock in your mouth." There was a rustling sound as Nioni lay down for the night.

Not being able to move, Luwayth stared into the flames of the fire. The way the flames danced used to soothe him, but now every muscle in his body was as tense as a bow string.

A twig snapped in the trees behind Luwayth, causing him to jump. "No, no one would hear Airnin approach unless he wanted them to," he assured himself.

It was a long night. Fear of Airnin's coming gave way to weariness, and, finally, restless bouts of sleep. The next morning came without rescue.

Nioni awoke just after first light. She fed Luwayth the same dried beef they had the night before, then packed up camp. Luwayth sat there, sullen, wondering why Airnin hadn't come for him but glad he didn't have to see Nioni die at the wraith's hands.

Not trusting Luwayth to have his hands in front of him, Nioni tied him down over the horse, his head hanging over the horse's right side. "If we ride hard today, we should be at the capital by nightfall," Nioni proclaimed before getting into the saddle.

Luwayth stared, mesmerized by the dirt and the horse's legs until drowsiness finally overtook him. Fitful dreams of shadowy figures came and went as he awoke on occasion to the ache in his arms or the sounds of a village they were passing through. Nioni stopped when needed to change horses or eat a quick meal.

As Farkor set, Nioni was still riding. Luwayth stared down the road behind them, desperately hoping for Airnin to appear. Only the fading light and an empty road stretching out into the darkness stared back.

His mind kept drifting back to the night he last spoke to Airnin. *Did Airnin truly have no more use for me? Is that why he hasn't come?*

Hours passed until Nioni finally slowed the horse down. Looking forward, Luwayth could make out a large wall of stone that stretched as far as he could see. It stood taller than any trees in the forest. They approached a small wooden door recessed into the wall with two men standing at either side, both dressed in identical uniforms. Luwayth assumed they were the king's soldiers or guards.

The guards approached Nioni as she pulled up to a stop in front of them. Getting a better look at them, Luwayth saw they wore chain mail shirts with a thick leather shirt underneath, dark brown trousers, leather boots that came halfway up their calves, and a helmet with an embossed crown with a sword through it. Each wore a dark green cloak with a hood draped down the back. The one on the horse's left side questioned Nioni about her business and whom she had trussed up. The other man came over and lifted up Luwayth's head.

"Are you who she says you are? Even if you say no, I'm still going to throw you in prison until we sort it out. Best be out with it."

Not being able to look up far enough to see the man's face, Luwayth just nodded his head in agreement at the man's boots before speaking: "I am who she says I am."

Both men returned to the door and spoke through a slit to someone on the other side. Whoever it was seemed to have stepped away, leaving the soldiers on this side to wait. After a while, the person returned, speaking at length to the guards. Finally, the doors opened and Nioni was let in. As they walked through, Luwayth realized the road beyond was paved in stone, appearing identical to the stone that made up the walls and floor of the barrow.

As they entered the capital, the clopping of the horse's hooves echoed between the buildings. Suddenly, the most peculiar thing came into view. It was a house with a hole cut into the side of it. Luwayth peered into it and saw people staring back, then realized they were large dolls wearing clothes. The image of a horse with a black sack appeared briefly in front of it. Confusion slowly gave way to understanding; there was some sort of barrier between himself and the dolls that he could see through. Luwayth wondered how they kept deamhons out.

The streets were mostly empty. Those folks who passed by ignored them. The road constantly made turns as it meandered through the capital towards its center. Luwayth noticed the buildings had similar holes to those in the shops but smaller. Occasionally, he would catch a glimpse of a person through one. Nioni made a left turn, and in front of them loomed a wall at least half the height of the capital's outer wall. They walked up to it and then turned left again, following it as it curved around. Luwayth searched but didn't see a single door or passage through the inner wall.

Nioni finally slowed the horse and pulled to the left as a stone building came into view. It had a small door with large metal bands just big enough for a man to enter. Two guards stood on either side of the door. The guard on the left went to the door and knocked as the other guard marched up to Nioni. "Was told you have a bounty for us; an Asinta by the looks of it. Haven't had one of those in ages." The guard slapped the back of Luwayth's leg. "Don't worry, we have a cell just for you."

The horse shifted as Nioni dismounted. Then, a small portal opened up in the middle of the metal-banded door just big enough for a man's face to peer through. The man on the other side conversed with the guard. A few moments later, a hand grabbed Luwayth from behind and started to untie the ropes that held him in place.

"Oy, going to slide you back," a coarse voice said. Then, a hand grabbed Luwayth and pulled him back, steadying him as he slid off the horse. Once on his feet, Luwayth turned and started to squat to get some feeling back into his legs.

"Don't move!" the guard in front of him shouted, raising a crossbow at Luwayth. Luwayth slowly stood, doing everything he could not to move.

"Sorry, it was a rough ride," Luwayth said apologetically.

A loud clanking noise echoed off the walls around them as the door slowly opened. Six guards filed out, some holding swords, others crossbows—all aimed at Luwayth. Three of the guards approached and roughly seized him.

One of them yelled, "Ready! Churl, start moving forward." Luwayth stumbled forward, his legs still stiff, and passed through the entranceway. In front of him was another door, identical to the outer one, and each side contained wide openings that recessed into a narrow slit. Luwayth spotted arrow points behind the slits. The door shut behind the group with a loud clang, then a guard stepped forward and knocked on the inner door. A small hatch in the door opened up; a guard on the other side peered into the room. He seemed satisfied by what he saw, shut the hatch, and opened the door. Luwayth was pushed forward into a small room with the guards crowding in around him. One of the guards to Luwayth's right said, "We have the skamelar who brought him here. She's waiting outside for payment." The guard then moved to a door on Luwayth's right, which opened up from the other side.

"Come on, churl, get going," a guard to Luwayth's left barked. Luwayth walked through the door and, after hesitating a moment, passed the guard on the other side. It was a narrow stone corridor that ended in steps. Once Luwayth reached the stairs, he looked down them; with his hands behind his back, his balance wasn't good. Something sharp pricked him in the back, then a hand grabbed him from behind. For a brief second, Luwayth was certain that he was going to be pushed down the stairs.

"I got you. Head down," a rough voice said behind him.

The stairs spiraled in a wide circle as they descended, with only the occasional lantern hanging from a hook to light their way. The smell hit Luwayth first; it was the smell of the barrow when he was younger and didn't understand the need to wash regularly until he stunk the place up so badly that even he didn't want to go back in. That was when he realized that Airnin couldn't smell in the same way a living person does. The smell here was more fetid and foul. The stairway ended in a hallway lit on both sides by lanterns with rows of wooden doors running down each side. The stone was different here. It looked natural. Closing his eyes, he saw what appeared to be lines of dirt under the stone, though it was lacking the usual flow of the power of Dainua. He could see about fifteen suls crammed into each room. He spotted smaller suls that slowly dripped into the dirt beneath the stone and rushed away, seemingly pulled by an unseen force. The sharp object that was pressed against his back pushed further into him causing a sharp pain.

"Come on, churl. This isn't your cell." Staggering forward, Luwayth opened his eyes and continued down the hall. It ended in a staircase that descended even farther. Waiting for the hand to grasp him again, Luwayth continued into the depths. They continued this crossing two more times with cells that stank just as bad.

As they descended after the third corridor, the air began to smell fresher. The stairs ended in a small room. A guard was seated on a chair that was carved out of sul-blocking stone. Unlike all of the other guards, this one was dressed in black from head to boot just as Luwayth was. Closing his eyes briefly, Luwayth was surprised to see that not only did it block the wearer from feeling or seeing suls, it also prevented others from seeing their sul. This room didn't have any normal stone like the floors above it but was carved completely from the sul-blocking kind. Straight ahead of Luwayth stood a large door inlaid with the same obsidian stone.

"Here is your churl," one of the guards said behind him. The sharp object jabbing into Luwayth forced him to jump forward a bit.

"Oy, this way," the guard in black said, his voice muffled, as he walked over and unlocked the obsidian door. A small hallway lay beyond, though this one ended at a wall instead of stairs. Luwayth walked forward. As he passed the guard, the guard barked instructions to him: "Enter the first room to the left." Luwayth did as he was told and found himself in a small, empty room. The door clanged closed behind him.

"Stick your arms through the hole," a voice called out. Confused, Luwayth searched and eventually noticed two small holes about the size of a man's face next to the door. The hooded guard's head could be seen in the upper cut-out. Turning, Luwayth backed up to the holes. The man tugged on Luwayth's restraints until they came free.

The guard continued, "If you don't do exactly as I say, I will kill you. Take off all of your clothes, including boots, and pass them to me." Luwayth pulled the black cloth off. He found that it tied up the back in thick leather straps. After pulling all of his clothes off, he handed them back to the guard. Once he was completely naked, the masked guard pushed a cloth back to Luwayth without saying a word. The guard carried away his clothes, then came back and grabbed the lantern that was hanging in the corridor. The light faded as the door to the corridor closed, leaving Luwayth alone in the dark.

HORDE

Luwayth picked up the cloth and found it was a heavy blanket, for which he was grateful; the air around him was frigid. He wrapped the blanket around himself, then sat in the corner of the room, wondering what was going to happen next. He was extremely frustrated that Airnin hadn't come for him, telling himself over and over, "Airnin wouldn't leave me. This has to be part of his plan." All he could do was wait. Wait and wonder. He closed his eyes, feeling for any sign of a sul. The blanket he wore had a faint sul, but not enough to use.

Luwayth stared off into the darkness, wondering what he was going to do if Airnin didn't come for him.

"I have to come up with something. But what?"

The only plan he could muster was pulling the suls from the food he assumed they had to bring him. "They can't give me sul-less food, can they? Would I even be able to eat that?" he asked himself. It was something Airnin had never taught him, but he was beginning to think that perhaps Airnin hadn't taught him everything.

Luwayth paced back and forth, tracing the boundaries of the room. In the far corner, his foot fell into a hole. He just managed to catch himself by hitting the wall that ran up from one side of it. He bent down and felt around inside. It was about the size of the holes that looked out into the corridor. Putting his face closer, he instantly regretted it as he was overcome with the pungent smell of human waste. Luwayth backed up and wiped his hands vigorously on his blanket without thinking, then realized his mistake. He scrubbed the soiled blanket against the rough stone walls.

An idea struck him. Carefully, he walked forward, closed his eyes, and peered down the cesspit. Just as he suspected, there were indistinct splashes of sul; not enough to pull or use, but they were there. As he started to lean back, a faint squeak came from somewhere down the shaft. *Oy, there's a plan*, he thought.

He explored a bit more, being careful where he stepped. He found nothing else of interest, so he sat and waited for something to happen.

Luwayth awoke, startled by someone barking, "Time for breakfast, churl." He had apparently fallen asleep. Luwayth saw a dim glow of light from the corridor. As he stood, another order was given: "Drop the blanket and stand in the middle of the room." Luwayth found it odd but did as he was told. As he looked out the hole into the corridor, it appeared as if the guard in black shifted away and was replaced by another guard in black, who bent down to peer through the bottom hole.

"His sul is clean," the second guard remarked before stepping away. Something was then deposited through the hole.

"Eat up. Don't try to take the sul from it; we will know if you do." The weak light in the hallway shifted and vanished as the guard left the corridor.

Luwayth closed his eyes and searched for the food. He found two piles: crumbs of stale bread and, by the smell of it, rotten vegetables. He scooped the bread into one hand and vegetables into the other. Hesitantly, he put his tongue to the vegetable mush. His stomach instantly tried to prevent it from going any further. He spit the foul-tasting trash out of his mouth and tried to not let anything else follow it. Once he regained control of his stomach and throat, he returned to the corner in which he had been laying, since it had retained some of his body heat. Hoping for better luck, Luwayth stuck out his tongue and placed it to the glob of bread. Thankfully, it just tasted stale, which was delightful compared to the vegetables. Taking a bite and chewing, he started to contemplate what the two men had said.

"What did he mean by I was 'clean'? How would they know if I took the sul from the food?" He glanced across to the hole. "Is there someone mucking around at the bottom of that shaft?" he asked himself. Airnin came to mind—Luwayth could always see the sul that Airnin carried. If he took a sul, could another Asinta see that? It made sense, he thought, though he had never asked Airnin. He was able to see the suls in his oska and when he drew them in before using them. This revelation was going to alter his plan slightly.

After eating some of the bread, Luwayth pressed the remainder of it into the rotting vegetables and rolled it into a gelatinous ball. He walked over to the cesspit, pulled some of the food apart and dropped it in, then left the remainder just outside on the edge. He walked back to his blanket and waited.

Luwayth tried to keep his eyes open in the dark, surrounded by silence, but it was proving more difficult than he suspected. His head lulled forward onto his chest as he started to drift to sleep, then snapped back up. A nearly imperceptible chittering echoed in the room, pulling Luwayth from his stupor. He closed his eyes and focused on the faint sul of the food. A few moments later, a small sul appeared in front of the ball. He focused on the rat's sul and pulled as fast as he could, controlling it so that he left some behind. A loud mournful squeak reverberated in his cell. Luwayth discovered the rat hadn't had time to dart back down the tunnel. It lay just inside the hole, writhing. He grabbed the rat and struck it hard against the floor; a dull thud and the rat lay motionless. Luwayth prayed to Dainua, hoping that his plan would work. He pushed the rat's sul he had trapped in himself back into its dead body. When it was in the barrow, his oska would never lose the suls trapped inside. He now hoped the rat's carcass would do the same. He set the rat down next to the remains of the food and watched as its sul swirled around the dead rat; it didn't escape. Satisfied, Luwayth returned to the other side of the room and waited.

He did not have to wait long; the temptation of eating one of their own was stronger than that of the mush he had left out. Two rats appeared. One nosed at the mush while the other immediately turned to cannibalism. Not wanting to risk losing both, Luwayth pulled the sul out of only one of the rats. Its screams scared its companion down the sewer. Luwayth trapped the sul in the second rat like he had done the first. He continued his rat-catching scheme until he had a small mound of dead rats. It was starting to become a problem: the bigger the pile, the more rats it attracted. Rats streamed out of the tunnel, swarming over and feasting on their brethren, bringing with them the odor of the cesspit. Luwayth pressed himself against the wall away from the growing horde as they continued to pour out, filling the room with brown fetid bodies eager for food. They pressed in on Luwayth; he kicked out as they started to bite at his bare feet. In desperation, Luwayth pulled the suls from a few dozen and then spun his hands in a circle in front of him, focused the energy, and pushed it out. The rats in front of him were swept off the floor by an invisible wave and dashed into the wall across from him. The rats in the center of the focused energy exploded into small pieces, while those on the periphery were crushed or maimed. This briefly helped turn the tide of rats from Luwayth as the remainder fed on the newly found food source. Realizing there was no way to stop the stream of rats, Luwayth did the only thing he could do: scream for help.

The door in the corridor opened. "Oy, stop that... " The guard's voice trailed off as he tried to make out what the large moving mass in the room could be until several rats climbed out of the lower hole in Luwayth's cell and scurried past the guard. Without thinking, the guard thrust his key into Luwayth's cell door and opened it. The horde, finding more space and another meal source, swarmed over the guard. Muffled screams came from beneath the multitude as he backed down the corridor, batting away rats. Suddenly, he found himself trapped, his back against the wall. He realized his mistake too late, as he slipped down and disappeared into the sea of rats.

Luwayth waded through the rats, kicking and pulling their suls as they fought back with fang and claw. He reached the hallway and spotted the guard whose body swayed back and forth with the motion of the burrowing rats. Horrified by the sight, Luwayth averted his eyes.

The rats flowed out the corridor door and up the stairs. Luwayth continued to kick the rats out of his way as he followed. He spotted a sword and lantern on a stone table next to the guard's post. He grabbed the sword, pushing forward through the now thinning trail of rats, and headed up the stairs. As he exited onto the next floor, he discovered two guards hacking at rats with their swords. Not wanting to feel the emotions of the men, Luwayth consumed the rats' suls he had trapped inside himself. An odd feeling of insatiable hunger briefly washed over him. He pulled the men down onto the rats and held them there until the rats subdued them. As Luwayth stepped onto the plain stone floor, the suls and energy he had stored pulled downward harder than he had ever felt before, trying to escape back into Dainua. He strained against the pull as he rushed down the corridor and up the next flight of stairs, losing several suls and some of his energy. The rat horde grew thicker as he ascended. Luwayth almost ran headlong into a guard preoccupied with kicking the rats back down the stairs. Luwayth slid to his side, pressed his back against the wall, and hit the guard's legs with the flat of the blade, tripping the guard down the stairs. The man yelled in surprise as his arms flailed, trying to break his fall; instead, his head hit stone. He crumpled and rolled out of sight, leaving a spattering of red and grey behind him. A few rats turned to chase down their new meal.

As Luwayth reached the next corridor, he could see what appeared to be the leading edge of rats as three guards came into view in the stairway ahead. Shocked upon seeing Luwayth naked, the men paused before charging past the rats. Luwayth didn't have time to pull enough suls from the rats to face three soldiers at once, and his instincts kicked in. He grabbed the sul of the guard in front of him, and the ecstasy of killing bathed him. He consumed the man's sul, then reached out and slammed the remaining two guards into one another, pressing them together. Their screams of agony fed Luwayth's bloodlust. The chain mail the men wore ground into each other as they wailed and desperately tried to push away. The air rippled around them as Luwayth continued to pour energy into Telgog until the crackling of broken bones echoed down the corridor as the men's chests flattened, expelling their viscera out of their mouths and nostrils. Luwayth dropped the two bodies onto the floor, sweating from the exertion, bloodlust partially satiated.

Luwayth ran past the first guard, who was weakly batting away the rats around him, and stopped next to the two men he'd just killed. Luwayth forced himself to stare into the men's faces as he repressed the remaining lust for death.

"I'm sorry," he said; it was all that he could think to say. He glanced up at the next flight of stairs, knowing he would have to kill again. *How much of me will be left when this is done?* Luwayth wondered.

He steeled himself and continued on. He crept up the stairs, but upon arriving, he found the last corridor of cells empty, save for a few rats nosing around for scraps, unaware of the feast he'd left behind. Luwayth moved on and started up the last flight of stairs. He pressed his back to the outer wall as he slowly moved up. Occasionally, he closed his eyes, searching for any guards ahead of him. Finally reaching the top of the stairs, Luwayth found it too was empty. Only three heavily banded doors remained between him and freedom. He now noticed there were two loopholes in the walls on either side that he hadn't seen on his way in. Cautiously, he edged down the corridor, trying to work out his next move, when a voice rang out.

"Oy, churl! Turn yourself over and we won't kill you!"

Luwayth saw that the loopholes were offset so that the archers couldn't shoot one another. The lesson Airnin taught him using the mouse in the tree came to mind. He glanced around and found a few rats. He pulled their suls and consumed them, closed his eyes, made sure he had enough energy and placed his back against the opposite wall of the first loophole. He slowly slid sideways into view. A faint sul rushed towards him. He pushed some energy on the cross bolt, causing it to curve to Luwayth's right and into the adjacent loophole. He heard it ricochet off the walls then a shocked cry. The guard through the loophole in front of him started to duck to let a second guard behind him fire. Using the last of the energy, Luwayth pulled the first guard up just as the second man fired; the man in front grunted, and then Luwayth let him drop. Before the second guard could reload, Luwayth pulled on the man's sul, causing fear and panic to grip Luwayth in a vice of paranoia. He fell to the ground; everywhere he looked, he saw the faces of those he had killed staring down at him. They opened their mouths in unison, revealing row upon row of fanged teeth. Luwayth scrambled away, but the deamhons pursued, closing in for the kill. He closed his eyes and multiples of Airnin appeared all around him, stretching out clawed hands. Luwayth could see his sul start to flow towards them. He jumped and fled down the corridor, looking back as he ran, seeing his sul trailing behind to the duplicates of Airnin as they effortlessly glided after him. He glanced ahead just in time to see the metal-banded door. A crash followed; blackness granted him the escape he desperately sought.

INTERROGATION

Cold water splashed over Luwayth, abruptly waking him. He groggily looked around. He was in a large room. There were guards lining two walls, and each held a crossbow pointed directly at him. He tried to move an arm and found he was tied to the chair. Someone had cut a hole in a blanket and placed it over his head to cover his nakedness.

The door in front of Luwayth opened, and a man dressed in a fine red tunic with matching pants walked into the room. The man reminded Luwayth of an average tavern patron. He had blonde hair that was combed to one side, his face showed no emotion, and he looked past Luwayth, not at him. Panic still gripped Luwayth; he fought the urge to close his eyes and take the man's sul. Instead, he slowly inhaled and exhaled, trying to purge the emotion. The man approached cautiously, studying Luwayth.

"So, you are the Asinta who was captured and thought he could break free. You are not yet dead because I need information from you. The longer that you are useful, the longer I stay these men's hands." Squaring his shoulders, Luwayth looked the man dead in the eye, replying, "I have done nothing wrong. You have no right to detain me here." The man in red raised an eyebrow.

"All of those men you just killed, the families you left fatherless—they do not matter? That is extremely arrogant, even for an Asinta." The man shook his head in disgust. Luwayth knew he had treated the guards as obstacles, nothing more. He thought of the empty chairs he created next to the hearth in each of the guard's homes whom he had killed. What was he supposed to have done, stayed in his cell until they killed him? Lost for words, Luwayth decided not to respond; instead, he stared at the man, focusing on not displaying any emotion.

"Shall we discuss this like men? Or should I just kill you now?" the man in red asked.

Luwayth didn't respond. He nodded his head slowly, keeping his eyes locked on the man, who snapped his fingers. Two guards rushed into the room with a small wooden table, which they placed in front of Luwayth, and a third man entered with a chair and placed it opposite him. The man in red slowly pulled the chair back and sat down. The guards moved in unison until they were repositioned behind the man in red. Each one looked eager to pull the trigger on their crossbow.

The man in red began, "First, let me introduce myself. I am Bealtane, the king's mouth. I am here to find out why the Asinta have left and where they have gone. We need to send an emissary to them right away." Luwayth looked to Bealtane in confusion, then to the crossbows aimed at him, then back to Bealtane.

"I'm not with the Asinta. Have you not spoken to Uram?" Luwayth asked. Bealtane held out a hand, and a guard stepped forward, handing him a leather satchel from which he drew a piece of paper.

"It says here that you have been going from village to village telling tales and killing Asinta you encountered. But for what cause? Why kill the Asinta?"

Luwayth weighed his response as he studied the man. He couldn't tell Bealtane that it was Airnin who drove the Asinta into hiding. He needed more information from him.

"Let me understand: you woke up one day and decided to kill Asinta? No specific reason?" Bealtane eyed Luwayth closely, trying to determine what he was up to before continuing. "This has not been the only occurrence of Asinta being hunted. However, this time it happened in villages you were in. The king sent out soldiers to track down the one responsible, but these soldiers were ambushed—only a few survived. Evidence was found pointing to these men as those responsible. We both know that is a lie." Bealtane glanced down at the paper in front of him again, as if searching for something, then pulled out a stack of papers from the satchel. Glancing up briefly at the guards surrounding him, he casually remarked, "Kill him if he moves." He returned to the stack in front of him until he found what he was searching for. He read the paper several times before holding it up to Luwayth. "Can you read?" the man asked. Luwayth nodded his head and read the fine penmanship. It was an accounting of every village he visited, how long he was there, and the number of dead Asinta.

"I believe you murdered the Asinta or know who did." The man dropped the paper onto the table and glowered at Luwayth, who shifted in his seat uncomfortably. He felt that he was slowly being backed into a corner from which there was no escape.

"Apparently, we have an Asinta who is pretending he is not one, killing off his own, and then planting the evidence on the king's soldiers. Why? Some sort of vengeance? Or is there a darker plot?" Bealtine drummed his fingers on the table as he evaluated Luwayth's responses, both spoken and unspoken, to each question. Mentally piecing together each response, he arrived at a logical conclusion, though he still needed more information.

"If you do not come from the Asinta, where are you from? No one comes from nowhere. You have proven that you have trained under another Asinta, but whom?" Bealtane snapped his fingers again and a guard brought forward Luwayth's oska. Bealtane twirled it in his hands, admiring the craftsmanship, before continuing, "An Asinta of great renown by the look of this."

Luwayth was scared of Bealtane but admired his intelligence and realized he would eventually uncover the truth. He had to protect Airnin; that was the one thing that he must do at all costs. He owed it to him. It appeared that no one suspected Airnin yet. The only thing he could think to do was tell the truth—well, parts of it. He needed to be able to hide the lies well enough to make them plausible. Licking his lips, Luwayth crafted his tale: "I grew up on a farm with no mother and a father who had no love for me. I was shown my powers by an Asinta who came to my house in my tenth birth year. That was the Uram I spoke of. My father and I were attacked by the king's soldiers; my father died at their hands. I fled into the woods and used the skills my father taught me to live off the land. I spent the last six years training and experimenting with my powers. I never stayed in one place long, afraid of being caught. In my travels, I found something that finally gave me purpose: the fact that the king had cruelly murdered his brother. What kind of king would attack a farmer and his son and kill his own brother? A king who does not deserve to sit on his throne. How many more out there were killed by that tyrant's hand, I asked myself. So I trained harder so that I could rid us of him."

Leaning back in his chair, Bealtane eyed Luwayth, taking in the tale he was told, knowing that some truths had to reside within. The boy knew of the king's brother, but how? The king had ensured that all records of that man were destroyed, going so far as to cut out the tongues of those who dared utter his brother's name. Could the boy be bluffing? There was only one way to find out.

"You speak of the king's brother as though you know the truth of his tale. If you are so wise as to what happened, tell me the name of King Cial's brother."

"Airnin," Luwayth replied flatly.

Bealtane tried to keep the look of shock from his face, but a sharp hiss escaped his mouth. He looked directly into Luwayth's eyes and asked, "If you knew the tales of Airnin so well, why would you fight in the name of a traitor who committed patricide? Who shattered the kingdom, creating a rift between the crown and the staff and driving us into a never-ending war with Soyer?"

What is he trying to get me to say? Luwayth wondered. Perhaps turning the words back on Bealtane would force his hand. Sighing, dropping his head slightly, and closing his eyes, Luwayth grabbed some of the sul that lay in the wood of the table and consumed it while speaking. "So, the king destroys the truth about his brother and makes him the murderer of his father? Doesn't sound like someone that I would be following." Luwayth opened his eyes and looked up, speaking to the guards. "Who hides their past? Only someone who doesn't want the real truth to be uncovered." Luwayth glanced back at Bealtane briefly, before continuing to address the guards in the room. "Why would there be a divide between the crown and the staff? Why would the Asinta turn their backs on the crown unless they knew the truth and refused to work with the real murderer and traitor? Those very same people are now hunted by the king's soldiers and forced to flee." As Luwayth paused, most of the crossbows dropped slightly.

Luwayth knew that the more he talked to Bealtane, the closer Bealtane was going to get to the truth and uncover that Airnin was alive. Luwayth dropped his head and reached out to the rope that bound his hands. A voice rang out, "He is using his powers!" Something hit the back of Luwayth's head and the world spun around him.

Luwayth slowly forced his eyes open. His skull felt like it had been torn in two. He tried to blink the pain away while his head rested on the table. As he sat up, he noticed the guards had closed in on him. A voice from behind warned, "Try that again and it will be a cross-bolt."

Luwayth could hear snippets of Bealtane's voice arguing with someone else.

"He...escaped...risk...danger..."
"...want... King...no..."
"...understand...he...is..."
"...deliver...message...dead..."

"Fine! Guards, hood the traitor, dress him, and bring him this way."

The guards walked over to Luwayth and put a black hood with the eye holes still covered over his head, untied his arms, picked him up under each arm, and dragged him forward. A rough tunic was forcefully pushed over his head while burlap pants were pulled on and tied around his waist. Luwayth couldn't even muster the strength to fight back; the word *dead* lingered in his subconscious. He heard a door open, then his feet hit stairs as he was dragged down, out a door and to the left; a turn to the right; a faint breeze; more stairs up this time; the smell of grass; doors opening; doors closing; more turning; a door opening; and finally, a command: "Drop the traitor there." Luwayth fell face-first onto something soft but firm; a boot kicked him in the side and rolled him over onto his back. Several hands held him down while someone tied his hands.

"Ah, you are the cause of all the commotion in the North. You even managed to escape your cell tonight. Each one of those offenses is punishable by death," said an unknown voice. Paper crinkled before the man continued. "Is this the full account?" More sounds of paper and then the sound that Luwayth was sure was Bealtane's voice, "Let me see... yes, that fits the accounts of our conversation."

"Even the name of my brother?" The word *brother* caused Luwayth to gasp, as he realized he was in the presence of the King.

"Yes. I suspect he found someone whose tongue wasn't removed and decided to start tales of him. Being that the boy is from the North, he would at best only be able to read rudimentary words; he feigned the ability to read earlier. I doubt that he came across any written account. Regardless, I have sent men north to find anyone telling tales and to search his last known locations for any documents. He also spoke of an Asinta called Uram. I have sent men out to search for him, as well."

"Well done. Thank you, Bealtane. Luwayth, tell me what you know of my brother," the King demanded. Luwayth lay in the darkness of his hood and thought out his response. He decided to stick with half-truths before replying. He told his tale: leaving Airnin out of it, he said he found a wandering teller of tales and recounted the tale that Airnin had told him. After he was done, there was no immediate response. The only sound was a faint crackle of a fire somewhere in the room. The king finally spoke: "Someone has made my brother the martyr in this. Bealtane, are you sure that all of those who witnessed what happened are dead or were truly loyal to the crown?"

"Yes, I am certain of it. And those who would have told such a tale have been rooted out since then."

"I am going to tell you the truth of the matter before I send you to the executioner; not out of kindness, mind you, but so you can wallow in the torment of knowing you were played the fool."

Luwayth wondered at the King's pretense. There was no reason not to play along. "Tell your tale," he replied.

"Ah, this, unfortunately, is not some tavern tale but the sad truth of things. You see, you have most of the story right, but it was Airnin, not I, who killed my father. He betrayed both the crown and the staff. When my brother ruled over the staff, he realized the immense power they held and, unlike his predecessors, saw no reason why it should be kept in check. He went to my father and made a grand display about how powerful we could be uniting the crown and the staff and placing himself on the throne. My father counseled him against such foolish thoughts, telling him it would break the staff, causing the Asinta to join forces with Soyer. Sadly, my brother was not swayed; instead, he plotted with those within the Asinta who shared his ideals. Once Airnin had gathered a strong power base to move against my father, he approached him one last time, hoping to convince him to see his way was right. My father stood his ground. Airnin interpreted our father's refusal as proof that he loved me more than him. He lashed out in anger, striking my father down, then used a tiller to slowly drain his sul, waiting for my father to give in. He did not; instead, he begged Airnin to see the path he was putting himself on. Those who witnessed this moment say he said with his dying breath: 'I always loved you.' " The king paused, sounding like he was trying to choke down a sob before he carried on. "It was quickly found out what my brother had done, so he fled to meet those who would rally to his cause. They planned to return to take the capital and the crown. I assume he also would have killed me if I stood in his way. Dainua was on our side; many of those who had pledged fealty to him did not rendezvous, having turned away from him upon hearing what he had done to our father. My brother fled north, knowing that I would rally the army and the staff who were still loyal. Airnin razed everything in his path to slow us down. They went into villages, burned the houses, and killed innocent men, women, and children, not sparing a single person who pleaded for their life. The fields they passed were destroyed, leaving not a single living thing in their wake. We eventually cornered them. Those who followed Airnin realized that they had no place to hide and turned on him. They brought him to me in hopes that I would spare their lives, but I could not show mercy after witnessing what they did to the land and my people. As punishment, I cut off their eyelids and burned them alive, then had my men scatter their ashes to the wind. I was set to do the same to Airnin; however, his crimes deserved a far greater punishment. He pleaded with me not to lock him up in the tomb he had built many years ago for Asinta who committed crimes such as his. I consulted with the Asinta about this tomb, and once I learned of its purpose—to lock away a sul never to be joined with Dainua—I felt it a just punishment for his crimes. I had Airnin sealed in the tomb alive, preventing him from ever being joined with Dainua in death. I had every record of the events burned to prevent anyone from following in Airnin's steps. We will track down whoever convinced you of Airnin's innocence and put them to the sword. As for you, Luwayth, for your crimes against the staff and the crown, I will have you killed as I once killed Airnin's men. I will finally rid the world of my brother's treachery."

THE CROWN

L uwayth lay in the darkness of his hood with his mind racing. *Could the king be right? Did Airnin lie to me?* He recalled his time with Airnin and the tales Airnin had told. *If Airnin was the deamhon the king is making him out to be, why didn't he kill me the first night? If the king is going to kill me tomorrow, why tell me his tale? How do I know who to believe?* Luwayth pondered. He felt truly lost, knowing that there was no one he could turn to—no one to tell him what to do or whom to believe. He lay there, staring into the darkness, wishing he could escape into it.

A gasp broke the silence. "How did you get in here?" the king yelled.

"Brother, do you not recognize your own flesh and blood?" Airnin said sweetly.

"Lies! You are not my brother. He lies in a tomb. You are not made of flesh and blood. Get back to where you came from or my guards will kill you." The sound of chainmail clinking came from all around Luwayth.

"Do you mean the tomb I built and tricked you into putting me in, brother?" Airnin said, still sweet but each word carrying a dreaded weight.

There was a brief silence broken by the sound of crossbows firing. This was followed by the crash of wood splintering and pottery breaking all around the room. A voice screamed in agony to

Luwayth's right. He heard a bone snap, followed by a heavy thud as something, or someone, dropped to the floor. Another wail pierced the air; then, the sounds of padded footsteps running drowned out all other sound. Suddenly, there was heavy banging on what sounded like a door, yelling for reinforcements, pleading, and the constant sound of gasps and gulps as the men around Luwayth drew their last breaths.

"Well, you have killed my guards. I suppose I am next," the king said flatly. "I do ask that you think twice before doing this. Think of the kingdom. Your prior actions caused the staff to split from the crown and drove us to war with Soyer. Kill me and we will certainly lose everything."

"Still thinking that everyone will be lost without you, brother? I will unite the crown and the staff, then bring Soyer to their knees. I will create a kingdom more powerful than you or Father could ever have imagined. Kingdoms are not built to help the poor and lowly; they are built so those like us can dominate. We are not here for our subjects; they are here to serve us. You agreed with that vision once, before you turned on me."

A gurgling sound like that of a babbling brook suddenly filled the room.

"Ah, brother... watching you squirm like a rat as I slit you open is so much more satisfying than it was when we watched Father die. I wish I could devour your sul, to feel your anguish as I fed upon you."

Not being able to stay silent any longer, Luwayth blurted out "Stop it! Just kill him and get it over with! Please!"

"I suppose you are right," Airnin sighed. "There is a lot that needs to be done before daybreak. Such a pity; I wanted to watch him writhe until he finally begged me to end it, knowing that I truly broke him before snuffing out his life."

A sharp cry broke out in the room, and, just before the king died, a small whimper broke from his lips: "Stop... please." Then, silence slowly crept over the room.

An icy presence crawled over Luwayth's ankles and then the ropes holding them fell away. After Luwayth slowly sat up, the same icy presence swept across his scalp and sent shivers down his spine as the hood was pulled away. Everywhere around Luwayth were corpses, each face frozen in death. The ropes holding Luwayth's hands came free as Airnin slid his sharp fingers through the rope. Luwayth closed his eyes and studied Airnin's face, seeing a child-like glee flicker across it. Luwayth knew then that everything Airnin had told him was a lie.

Luwayth cautiously stood up; the world tilted some, and the blow to his head still hurt. He looked around at the carnage he had helped create and walked over to a gutted body. Luwayth glanced at the body briefly before studying the man's face. He had eyes of deep blue, forever frozen in sadness. His dark hair, speckled with the gray of age, mixed with the blood beneath his head. The body was dressed in a fine dark green tunic, with golden stitching outlining the collar and a golden crown with a sword embroidered on the left breast. Luwayth felt his face flush in anger as he stared at the king. He was unable to take his eyes from the man's face.

"Drinking in the revenge you so desperately sought?" asked Airnin from behind.

"No!" Luwayth bellowed. "You lied... and... and... used me. I... I... trusted you!"

Airnin grabbed Luwayth by the neck and slammed him into the wall. "You are but a tool to be wielded. You were nothing when you came to me; everything you are now is because of me. You would be wise to remember that or I will devour your sul," Airnin growled in Luwayth's ear.

"Airnin, was the king right? Were you the one who killed your father?" Luwayth croaked out.

Airnin then turned and tossed Luwayth across the room. His body crashed into the floor and rolled into the foot of a large bed. He gasped in pain.

"It does not matter," Airnin spat.

Luwayth pushed himself up and glowered at Airnin, thinking of all the people he had killed for him, before wheezing, "Just kill me. I can't live with what I have done."

"No. As much as I wish that I could be done with you, you still have a part to play in this," Airnin said, irritated. "If you become a thorn in my side, I will simply have to find another who will obey." Airnin turned his head to look at Bealtane who was crouched down next to the door, staring agape at the king's lifeless body.

Tears started to stream down Luwayth's cheeks. "I trusted you, Airnin. You were the father I thought I never had. I thought you loved me. Instead, I'm something that is either unwanted or to be used and tossed aside." He wiped the tears away as he stood. "I killed people, manipulated and used them—for what?" He gestured around the room. "I became everything my father feared that I was. I hate you! I'll kill you for this," Luwayth sneered, teeth bared.

"Still merely the scared boy who came running and begging for my help that first night, are you not? I am superior to you in every way. I am the royalty in this room: you are only the dirty serf placed here by Telgog to do my bidding. Do not forget that. You live because I allow you to live. The training and teachings I gave to you because you are a tool to be honed and used as I see fit." Airnin's voice boomed throughout the room.

Luwayth smiled broadly. "Don't forget: I know where your bones lie and, unlike you, I can walk in the light. As you lay there trapped, huddled, and afraid of Farkor, I will seal your tomb and make sure that you never have a chance to escape again." Luwayth felt sure that he had the upper hand, but a deep and throaty laugh erupted from Airnin—a laugh that made Luwayth shrink back, his heart feeling like it dropped to the floor. It took everything he could not to drop to his knees and quake.

"You truly believe I would be so foolish as to not anticipate that? You would be amazed at what motivates someone—when you hold their infant in front of them and slowly cut out its sul; even more so when you threaten to do the same to the rest of their children."

He was interrupted as the only door to the room burst open, narrowly missing Bealtane. Airnin raised a hand and used his powers to sweep the man off his feet and bend him backward. A sharp scream broke from the man's lips before his spine snapped as easily as if it were kindling. He fell to the floor, mumbling soft horrible moans mixed with pleading until he fainted from the pain, his chest still rising and falling raggedly. The guards in the corridor, planning to follow the first guard into the king's chamber, stopped abruptly but remained just outside the door.

Turning back to Luwayth as if nothing had happened, Airnin continued: "Let us assume my bones have been moved to a safe location and that I killed the ungrateful wretches afterward, for good measure. I could not have them telling people where the bones are located. I still have work to do tonight. You will stop your whining and do as I say. I am going to give you something every dirty, disgusting serf out there would kill to have: you are going to be the next king. Well, you will be the face of the king, as long as you do as you are told."

Airnin turned and directed his attention to Bealtane, who had started backing into the hallway.

"Bealtane, go and send a guard out to every official in the city, including the captain of the guard. Bring them to the throne room immediately. Complete this task and I will let you live." Bealtane didn't say a word; he nodded and gave a small bow before leaving the room.

Airnin instructed Luwayth: "Go to the wardrobe over there and put on clothes befitting a king. You have subjects to attend to tonight, and I will not have you looking like that." Taking in his surroundings for the first time, Luwayth realized he was in an immense bedroom. The bed itself looked as big as the farmhouse in which he grew up. He felt he had no choice. He glared at Airnin as he walked over to the large wardrobe, which seemed to take up an entire wall, and did as he was instructed.

The king's clothes were a little big but fit well enough. Once Luwayth was dressed, Airnin left. Luwayth went to follow, then spotted his oska in the corner of the room. He picked it up and felt whole again, then ran after Airnin. As he approached him from behind, he whined, "Airnin, I don't want to be king. Can't you find someone else?" Airnin continued gliding ahead and didn't say a word. A few guards rushed them, but after Airnin tore off the arm of one and crushed another, the rest they passed pressed their backs to the walls, letting the wraith and his lackey pass without saying a word. Every stare seemed to express that the guards wanted nothing more than to kill them.

After a few twists and turns, they came to a small door and, once through it, Luwayth saw they were in a long room. The ceiling was vaulted, and there was a towering chair in front of them that looked down onto the room, which was empty, save for a few substantial lanterns hanging on the walls. Immense windows capped the high walls; faint starlight illuminated a long green and white rug that ran down the center of the hall. At the far end stood two massive doors.

"Take a seat," Airnin instructed.

"In that chair?" Luwayth asked, shocked. "Aren't *you* going to sit in it?"

"No. No one will follow one such as myself. I need someone who will do as he is told. So, sit."

Reluctantly, Luwayth stepped onto the soft footrest in front of the throne and turned around. As he sat back, the throne seemed to swallow him, making him feel like a small child in his father's chair. Shifting back and forth, Luwayth tried to find a position that felt comfortable but finally gave up. He looked up and to his right where Airnin stood, staring down into the empty hall.

"Airnin, how did you know I was with the king?" Luwayth asked. Without looking down, Airnin replied, "Remember the first time I shot you with an arrow?"

"Yes," Luwayth replied, as he subconsciously reached over and felt the scar on the back of his shoulder through the fancy green tunic he wore. The small arrow point could still be felt against his shoulder bone if he pressed hard enough. In a nonchalant voice, Airnin replied, "When I withdrew it, I slipped in a shard of my bone so that I could keep track of you. How do you think I managed to find you when you were traveling to the various villages? I thought you would have figured it out by now—your stupidity truly has no bounds. Now listen carefully: when your subjects are brought in, I will instruct you on what to say. Make sure to say exactly what I direct you to say. Failure to do so will lead to immediate consequences." Shrinking back from Airnin, wishing the chair would truly swallow him, Luwayth nodded and then deeply studied a stone on the floor in front of him—anything to avoid further conversation with his keeper.

The doors at the end of the hall opened loudly, and a stream of armed men marched in. Airnin flew down the stairs and effortlessly began to dismember or crush each man. The men in the back fled quickly, leaving the large doors open. Airnin left the bodies and returned to Luwayth's side.

A short time later, a man appeared in the open doorway; it was Bealtane. He slowly trudged down the carpet towards the stairs that led up to the dais, ignoring the guard's bodies. He stood there a moment, looking conflicted before he fell onto one knee and bowed his head. "Your Majesty, I have done as you asked." Bealtane remained in his pose, not looking up. Airnin's voice whispered to Luwayth, "Tell him he may arise."

"You may arise," Luwayth squeaked out nervously. Bealtane rose but kept his eyes down as he spoke: "I have the magistrates outside the door along with the captain of the Guard. Would you like me to direct them inside?" Luwayth looked up at Airnin quizzically.

"Say yes, you dolt! Do I have to do everything for you?" Airnin growled.

"Uh, yes, let them in," Luwayth stammered, more a suggestion than a command.

Bealtane hurried back through the doorway and returned with an entourage of men and women mostly dressed in night gowns, except one who had thrown chain mail over his nightshirt and strapped a sword around his waist. They gawked at the dead guards in horror as they approached the dais. Bealtane returned to his bow while the others looked up at Luwayth and Airnin in disgust.

"What is the meaning of this?" one of the men bellowed. "What is this about the king being killed? You cannot simply assume the throne because you killed the king." Airnin slowly glided down the stairs as the man glared defiantly at him. Airnin casually thrust his hand into the man's stomach and emptied the man's bowels onto the floor. One of the women next to him screamed and turned to run. Airnin grabbed her from behind after she had taken only a few steps and tossed her casually into the wall. Her screaming ceased immediately as her body fell limply to the floor. The rest of the group froze. A few fell to their knees, bowing and visibly trembling. One woman stood defiantly until an unseen force pressed down on her, pushing her to her knees. Sweat beaded on her forehead as she strained against it.

"I will not bow to you!" she rasped.

Airnin thrust a finger into her abdomen and gently slid it up. The woman screamed as she aged. It wasn't fast like Luwayth had seen before; instead, she aged slowly, almost imperceptibly, until wrinkles appeared across her face. Luwayth looked up at Airnin and closed his eyes. The sul from the woman was streaming into Airnin's chest, the fangs clasped around it shaking it like a rabid dog.

Not a whisper escaped the woman's lips as her hair turned silver and she finally collapsed in a heap. Her body now looked frail and shook slightly before death released her from her anguish. The magistrates around her bowed lower.

She must be an Asinta or have had the powers unknowingly, Luwayth thought, not shocked at what Airnin had done.

Without a word, Airnin returned to Luwayth's side.

"Tell them I will speak on your behalf," Airnin instructed Luwayth. Luwayth turned to the magistrates below him and instructed them to listen carefully to Airnin, who stepped forward and explained briefly who he was. As the King's brother, he was the rightful heir, and Luwayth was going to be Airnin's proxy and all instructions would be coming directly from Luwayth. No one was to speak a word regarding the king's death; if word of it was heard beyond the walls of the palace, they, along with their families, would be put to the sword. There was some arguing, though no one pushed it as far as the first man who had spoken up. Airnin then instructed the captain of the guard that Luwayth was not to be harmed. Once Airnin was sure that they would comply, he dismissed all of them but Bealtane.

"Bealtane, you were loyal to my father and brother. I will keep you on to assist Luwayth in becoming kinglier while I am away. If anything goes wrong, I will hold you personally responsible, regardless of fault. You can, of course, turn this generous offer down; however, I will kill you if you do," Airnin said, tauntingly.

Bowing until his head touched the ground, Bealtane spoke so Airnin could hear: "Of course, anything I can do for the crown." He sat on his heels and gestured to Luwayth. "May I point out that as soon as you are gone, the puppet King will be killed. There is no one in the palace who will stand by his side without your presence."

"The captain of the guard will not be able to stay everyone's hand, and I don't have enough time to kill more people until the rest comply. Let us proceed to my old chambers."

Bealtane stood and bounded up the steps and past the dais. Airnin followed with Luwayth in tow. After ascending a few flights of stairs, they came upon a room almost as big as the king's chamber. Once inside, Airnin searched the room, knowing all of its secrets. Feeling satisfied, he turned to Luwayth.

"Stay here tonight and do not leave this room until I get back," he directed. Airnin then instructed Bealtane: "You are dismissed. Remember, if anything happens to Luwayth, I hold you personally responsible. I will not only kill you but every servant as well." Once Bealtane left the room, Airnin shut the door and dropped several bars across it before locking it from the inside.

"This will keep anyone from entering. If they do, kill them." Airnin pointed to a small portal in the door about the size of a face at eye level. "If someone knocks, you open this to see who is on the other side." Airnin then shimmered and was gone.

Luwayth went to the small hatch and opened it. Bealtane was still standing on the other side.

"Airnin will be gone until last light. Will you please talk with me?" Luwayth asked, feeling better now that Airnin had departed. He knew he needed to do something clever if he was going to get out of this alive.

ALONE

Bealtane stood and stared at Luwayth through the door's portal. "So, what is the story between the two of you?" Bealtane asked, finally breaking the silence. Feeling he had no alternative but to trust Bealtane, Luwayth explained at length everything that had happened to him since he and Uram first laid eyes on the barrow. Bealtane stood frozen in place the entire time, only nodding on occasion. Once Luwayth was done, Bealtane turned and paced up and down the hallway, occasionally asking Luwayth for greater details or to retell a particular part again. Bealtane finally stopped and looked at Luwayth.

"Well, I can see how one as young as yourself could have been swayed by him, but that does not fix the situation we are in now. You have not said anything about your life before Airnin. Mind telling me that as well?"

Luwayth spilled out everything about his dad and how, in retrospect, life was easier before Uram had arrived.

Bealtane thought over what the boy said. He knew he needed to drive a wedge between Airnin and Luwayth if he was going to keep the country from falling apart. The boy's father felt like the key to that. In his mind, he went over the boy's story again before carefully crafting his words: "I did not know your father. These are only conjectures based on what you have told me. I have seen many cruel things in my life as the mouth of the king. Your father may not have outwardly told you he loved you, but I believe by teaching you to be a teller of tales, he showed his love for you. The act of sacrificing himself out on that road while he had you hide in the trees is proof enough of how much he cared. Would the Airnin you thought you knew before all this have done such a thing if he was still a man?"

Luwayth was completely shocked by this question. He had never considered it. *There is no way Airnin would sacrifice himself,* Luwayth decided. Aloud, he said, "You're right. Airnin would never do such a thing. I don't know why I hadn't thought of that before. I'm shocked you don't hate me for what I have brought upon you and the kingdom," Luwayth said, miserable.

"Oh, do not get me wrong. I hate you and always will for what you did tonight. You may have been led down a dark path, but the murders you committed are on your hands. I am only here because you may be the only way we get out of this. If I did not consider that a possibility, I would have thrown my life away for my king, hoping that, without any guidance, the two of you would fail in this endeavor. However, I know this kingdom would have been torn apart in the process. Before you decide to work with me, know one thing: if we get out of this, your life is forfeit. There is no walking away from that." Bealtane sighed, hoping that showing the boy the truth in his actions may help sway him to his cause. This was a risky endeavor. *If the boy is playing me for a fool, I will be dead before this day is over,* Bealtane thought.

Luwayth turned away from the door and studied the room while he thought over what he should do. He reflected back on the years he was with Airnin, from the night he had arrived at the barrow. If he hadn't shown up, everyone Airnin had killed in the last six years would still be alive. Those murders were on his own hands, Luwayth decided, and there was nothing he could do to redeem himself. *If I can stop at least one more murder, my life will have been worth the cost,* he concluded.

Luwayth turned back to Bealtane and stated, "I don't deserve to live because of what I have done. I don't know if I can trust you, but I have simply no other choice. Please help me. My life is yours."

Bealtane scratched his chin. *It appears I have the boy on my side, but how do I use him to get rid of Airnin?* Bealtane wondered. *First, I need to get him to trust me completely. Maybe there is something he has not divulged.* He then replied to Luwayth. "That is very brave. Now, before we discuss what we should do, I am sure you have questions for me. I promise to answer them to the best of my abilities." Bealtane's tone had a fatherly air about it.

"Before I ask about what needs to be done, I want to know about the walls that you can see through," Luwayth said, his curiosity winning out. Seeing Bealtane look at him oddly, Luwayth continued describing them. "The ones that appear to be walls but no air passes through. They are in the throne room, and here, and, well, lots of places in the capital." Realization finally dawned on Bealtane. "Those would be windows," he said. "They are made of glass; sand that is melted down. I forget how you extreme northerners fear the deamhon that supposedly lurk in the woods and build without windows to protect yourselves."

"How odd," Luwayth said. It was all he could think of as a response. He paused, then continued with his questions.

"I do have a few more important questions. First, where are the Asinta? Though, I think I know part of the answer to that. Like I told you earlier, Airnin had been hunting them down. Why were you so eager to find them when you questioned me?"

"After Airnin was killed, the staff broke away from the crown. Soyer, to the south, saw it as an opportunity to strike at us. The only thing that saved us was the fact that the Asinta in both countries act as one. They swore to have no loyalties to either Soyer or Salare and refused to fight on either side. After what Airnin had done, they refused to be used as pawns in the shaping of what was to come.

"Cial left the North in ruins after tracking down his brother. He had to focus his efforts to the South to prevent Soyer from overrunning us. He assumed he could easily defeat Soyer and return his attentions to rebuilding the North soon after. However, Soyer has always had the larger army. Cial was able to push them back into the mountain pass that connects our lands, though he was unable to drive them completely back into their own land. Cial is... " Beltane paused and wiped a single tear away before continuing. "He *was* a great tactician and the only reason why our smaller force was never beaten. The war has lasted far longer than anyone expected. We have so few men left that we are at the very brink of losing this war. Cial refused to conscript the men in the North into the war on account that he never fulfilled his promise to rebuild it. No matter how much I argued with him, he believed he had made the right decision. Instead, in an act of desperation, Cial returned here, hoping to persuade the Asinta that having Soyer overrun us was not in their best interest, only to find that they had gone into hiding due to your actions. I fear that it is now only a matter of weeks or even days before Soyer will break through our lines without Cial to lead them, especially when word reaches the army that he is dead. The king was greatly loved by his men, and many fought only because he was the one leading." Bealtane walked back and leaned against the wall as tears started to fill his eyes.

"I loved Cial like a brother. I was raised from birth to help counsel him and be a trusted confidant. Many in my position have had kings who tested and argued with them. Not me. I quickly learned that Cial had a pure heart and put his subjects first. It tore him apart when he saw what Airnin had done to the North and even more so when he could not focus on rebuilding it." Tears streamed down Bealtane's cheeks. "You knaves took away the best, and quite possibly, the only defense against Soyer when you killed King Cial. I know you are a pawn in this, but thinking of Cial makes everything in me want to tear that door from its hinges, throw you to the ground, and slit your throat for what you have done." Bealtane's head drooped. Small gasps could be heard as he tried to hold back his sobs. Not knowing what to say, Luwayth spoke just loud enough for Bealtane to hear: "I'm sorry."

Turning away, Luwayth paced the room, giving Bealtane space, knowing from personal experience that nothing he could say would comfort the faithful servant. After a few moments, Luwayth, knowing that some sort of plan had to be put in place soon, returned to the door to intrude on Bealtane's grief.

"Bealtane, we need to find a way to kill Airnin. However, hearing what is going on with the war, I think we need to focus our efforts there first before we can sort out the mess here. What would happen if a lone Asinta showed up to help out in the battle? Would other Asinta rally to Soyer's cause?" Bealtane reached up and scratched his forehead, his eyes still red and swollen. "Well, if that Asinta was able to destroy Soyer's army and then the other Asinta arrived, they wouldn't have an army to rally behind. I doubt they would go at it alone. Hmmm," he mused. "It is hard to say what would happen with the Asinta loyal to Salare in hiding. If Soyer's Asinta decided to attack, we could easily be overrun. However, with things on the brink of collapsing, I am afraid we may have no other choice. I am assuming you are talking about yourself. Do you think you can take on an entire army?"

Luwayth thought back on all the training he had gone through. His biggest fear was absorbing the men's emotions and what would happen if he panicked again. Knowing his life was forfeit regardless of which path he took, he felt like it was the only option available to him. The thought of taking a path he chose rather than being manipulated by the wraith caused a firm determination to rise within him.

Luwayth confidently replied, "If everything you say is true, I have no choice. We lose if we don't do this. If I fail, we are no worse off. It is the least I can do; now, we'll just need to convince Airnin."

"I have plenty of letters from the commanders explaining how dire the situation has become over the past few months, which should help. I can bring the idea to him, then you could rally behind it. If Airnin wants to rule both countries, this would fit into his plans. We just have to hope that this doesn't backfire and give him what he needs to succeed in that endeavor."

A loud and long yawn broke from Luwayth's mouth. "I'm sorry, I haven't been up this late in a long time," Luwayth said, trying to stifle yet another yawn.

"We have both had a long night. I need my rest, as well," Bealtane replied, then yawned.

"Can you make sure the king and all of those who died last night get a proper burial? Is there anything I can do for the families of the soldiers I killed?" Luwayth asked solemnly.

"Our coffers are pretty low due to paying for the war. I will see what I can do about giving some money to those who had families, which might give them some time to find work as a serf for a magistrate. You will have no guards outside your door; you will be alone until I return this evening." Bealtane turned and left.

Once he was all alone, Luwayth felt he could breathe easier. He pulled off his outer garments, climbed into bed, and sank deep; it felt like an unwanted hug. Luwayth climbed out and dragged the blankets from the bed. He curled up in them on the floor, staring at the barred door, wondering if it could hold back everyone who wished him dead. The idea of dying in his sleep felt comforting as he rolled over and fell asleep. He dreamed of his childhood, sitting in the back of the tavern, listening to his dad's tales.

Armor

A loud and gravelly voice boomed through Luwayth's dream, yanking him from his casual stroll barefoot through a field of lush and vibrant grass. He rolled over onto his back and saw Airnin standing over him. His mist-like transparency shifted, the faceless haze beneath his cloak seeming to pierce straight through him. The bitter cold that Airnin brought to everything chilled Luwayth to the bone, causing him to pull the blankets closer.

"Why are you sleeping on the floor?" Airnin demanded.

"The bed was too soft," Luwayth stammered, groggily, then stumbled to his feet, pulling the blankets tightly around himself. He looked for his clothes, then found them laying in a crumpled heap.

"What are you doing?" demanded Airnin from behind him. Unsure what he was doing wrong, Luwayth replied casually, "Getting dressed. Is there something else I should be doing first?"

"I should have taught you better manners and how a King should act. I did not realize you would be this dense. Listen closely: you are the *king*. The King doesn't wear the same clothes he wore the day before—especially soiled clothes. When Bealtane arrives, he will bring someone to dress you."

Not sure what to do, Luwayth shivered in the cold of Airnin's presence, pulling the blankets tighter around himself. He timidly asked, "Can I start a fire?"

Airnin shook his head. "No! A proper King has a *servant* do that for him."

"Oy," Luwayth replied as he rubbed his arms, trying to warm them up.

Luwayth recalled his conversation with Bealtane and, before he could talk himself out of it, he looked to Airnin and closed his eyes. "Airnin, I was thinking last night. I hate that you lied to me. I really don't want to be king; however, your guidance hasn't steered me wrong. I haven't always understood your ways. I guess what I am trying to say is that I trust you and your direction for this kingdom. I told you before we left the barrow that I was in it with you all the way and I still am. I will do what is needed to be the king you need on the throne and heed your guidance." As he spoke, Luwayth looked into Airnin's face, waiting to see what emotions rippled across it, and found a slow, menacing smile.

"I am glad that you have come to your senses; however, that does not mean I will think any better of you. Knowing your place and realizing that I am your superior will make this unwanted relationship easier on both of us," Airnin replied with an air of satisfaction.

A few moments later, a knock came at the door. Luwayth opened the hatch and saw Bealtane, along with a host of other men; none appeared armed. Luwayth lifted the bars, unlocked the door, and let them in.

Bealtane and an older man entered, Bealtane dressed in red and the man dressed in the same green tunic most of the staff wore, followed by several similarly dressed men carrying clothes draped over their arms. Luwayth stood and tried to impress Airnin by bellowing, "Why is this fire out?" The old man leading the procession bowed low.

He snapped his fingers, and a servant in the back dashed over to the fireplace, doing his best to stay clear of Airnin. Luwayth, seeing the fear of Airnin on the servants' faces, stepped closer to him to show he had no such fear. The old man turned around, and the men behind him formed a tight semicircle, holding their arms out. The man walked by each one and finally chose a green tunic from one of the men. He held it up as if to decide how it would look on Luwayth. To Luwayth, the tunic looked similar to the servants' uniforms. Not wanting to disappoint Airnin, he remarked, "You choose to dress the king as a servant?" Then, knowing what Airnin would say next, followed this up with: "You do realize the king is not your equal." It dawned on Luwayth that all he needed to do was act like the men in his tales whom the villagers booed.

"Yes, your highness. I apologize, your highness," the old man remarked, then tossed the tunic aside as if it was trash and turned to look at the remaining garments. *Was that a test?* Luwayth wondered as the man turned, holding a bright blue tunic. Before he could hold it up to Luwayth, one of the servants dropped the clothes in his hands, revealing a dagger, and lunged at Luwayth. Luwayth spun to his right; the dagger found only empty air. The servant was swept off his feet and hurled across the room, hitting the far wall; he appeared to be pinned against it by something unseen. Airnin glided over to the servant.

"Did Bealtane or the Steward put you up to this?" Airnin hissed.

"I did it for the king," the man spat at Airnin.

Airnin put a finger against the man's stomach and started to cut him open.

"I give you one more chance. Tell me: who was behind this?"

"No one!" the servant yelled in defiance as he squirmed from the pain.

Airnin shimmered and disappeared along with the servant. Everyone looked at one another, unsure what to do. A few moments later, Airnin reappeared—alone.

"I put him someplace safe where I can question him until he gives me what I want," Airnin remarked coldly. He looked over Luwayth and demanded, "Why are you not dressed? Hurry."

The dressing went on longer than Luwayth thought it should. The old man, whom he now knew was the steward, insisted on helping Luwayth dress. At one point, after getting particularly close, he remarked softly enough so that only Luwayth could hear, "May I suggest a bath for your highness tonight before bed?" Luwayth subtly nodded his head. When the ordeal was over, Luwayth found himself dressed in a bright blue tunic, soft leather leggings, knee-high boots that were easily the most comfortable he had ever worn, and a cloak, which he thought was odd because it hung from only one shoulder. Luwayth figured the man knew more about dressing to look like a king than he ever would, so he didn't comment on it. The entire time, Airnin stood behind Luwayth in silence. Once he was dressed, Luwayth dismissed the men without a word of thanks, then wondered to himself why he couldn't be courteous.

After the men left, as if on cue, another entourage of men and women entered, each holding aloft a covered plate. They placed the dishes on the table and, with a flourish, revealed a feast such as Luwayth had never seen. It seemed like enough food to feed an entire village. A plate was made with a bite from each dish, then a young waif of a boy was ushered in, wearing nothing but rags. Upon seeing Airnin, he started to visibly shake and had to be forcibly pushed towards the man holding the plate of food. With eyes transfixed on Airnin, the boy slowly started to eat what was on the plate with a great display of chewing and swallowing. Once done, a mug of water was poured from a pitcher on the table and given to him. With as much drama as he could muster, the boy made great big gulping and swallowing noises. He then wiped his mouth with the back of his hand and stood there, obviously waiting for his next instruction.

Bealtane went over to the boy and patted him on the shoulder, then addressed Airnin. "I oversaw the preparation of the meal myself but, to help put you at ease, I found this beggar and promised him a free meal to prove it wasn't poisoned." At the word *poisoned*, the boy turned visibly green. Luwayth had a hunch that the poison part was left out when they went looking for volunteers. Bealtane dismissed everyone but the boy, then turned to Luwayth and Airnin.

"Should we take council here or move it to the council room once the king has eaten?"

Airnin glanced out the window then responded, "The council room would be better suited for our needs." Bealtane turned to the boy, who hadn't moved from his spot next to the table.

"Your Highness, are you comfortable enough with the food that I may dismiss the boy?" he asked.

"Yes."

Bealtane nodded and ushered the boy out of the room.

Luwayth sat down at the table as Bealtane created a plate of food for him, asking for extra portions of cheese. Luwayth dug into the food, not realizing how hungry he was. It was the best breakfast he had ever had; though, if he thought about it, most of his breakfasts had actually been dinners. Most of the foods were foreign to him, but none disappointed. Partway through his meal, Bealtane began to speak. "Airnin, while we wait, may I bring up an important matter that may take some time to think over?" Airnin nodded for Bealtane to proceed. Bealtane then explained in great detail the war that was going on with the country of Soyer, laying out a stack of papers for Airnin to read which explained troop numbers, both Salaran and Soyerian and the current budget. As Luwayth enjoyed breakfast, he was eager to see what would happen. When Bealtane was done, Luwayth closed his eyes and stared at Airnin. A look of grave concern rippled across his face.

"My brother always was the fool. He should have put this war to rest years ago. This puts my plans at risk and is too far south for me to assist." As Airnin spoke, a troubled look undulated briefly across his face followed by another that Luwayth hadn't seen before: fear. Instead of bringing hope to Luwayth, it slowly churned a dark unease deep inside him, though he didn't know why. Airnin turned and paced the length of the table, his head down, face roiling like a raging storm as he pondered how to handle this unforeseen disaster.

Luwayth took a deep breath, steadied himself, then spoke up: "I have an idea that might work. I could go alone and turn the tide of the war. You have taught me how to fight and anticipate attacks from unknown assailants." There was a moment of silence in the room. Then, a deep laugh started low and escalated into a thunderous boom. Luwayth held his ground and stared at Airnin, trying to ignore the sounds of his laughter.

"Are you serious? You believe you can go off and win a war single-handedly? You would not even attack a small camp of soldiers," Airnin mocked.

"Airnin, if we are to fulfill your vision, I have no choice. I will only learn how to deal with the emotions of the sul I absorb by practicing. You have taught me how to master the bow and arrow. I know your ambitions are to unite both kingdoms; this could deal a serious blow that would aid you in your conquest."

"I need to think upon this. In the meantime, you have indulged yourself enough. We have more important matters to attend to." Airnin glided to the door. Bealtane glanced to Luwayth and gave a small, hopeful smile before turning to follow Airnin. Luwayth wiped his face and followed them.

As they entered, there were several magistrates already sitting around the large table that sat in the center of the council room. The magistrates spoke in hushed tones and quickly ceased as Airnin entered. The roof of the room was vaulted; large exposed beams of wood held a curved ceiling. Sizeable windows sat just below the eaves. Where the lanterns cast no light, the room was faintly illuminated by starlight. Airnin went to the head of the table where a chair larger than the rest was placed. As Luwayth followed behind, he wondered why everything the king owned had to be bigger than everything else. He sank into the massive chair, feeling very small. The magistrates in the room fidgeted as they stared at Luwayth and Airnin.

Airnin brought the meeting to order. He did all of the talking, taking care of issues as small as squabbles over a farmer's tree that was encroaching on his neighbor's land and as important as raising taxes to help fund the war. Airnin was level-headed through all of it until he was notified that the North had not been taxed since his flight there. Bealtane seemed satisfied when Airnin decreed that the North would be taxed like everyone else and commanded that taxmen be sent immediately.

Luwayth watched Airnin closely, trying to learn how a king should act. *I need to fit the part until I can figure a way out of this*, Luwayth thought, then noticed something almost imperceptible. Airnin would tilt his head ever so slightly up at the windows as if waiting for something to happen.

A few magistrates complained that it was getting late and that such meetings should be held during the day. Airnin was quick to rebuke them and reminded them what would happen if they disobeyed. The black in the windows lightened some. Luwayth watched Airnin out of the corner of his eye to see what he would do once he noticed. As soon as he did, he called the meeting to a close and ordered the magistrates out of the room. Then, he addressed Bealtane, "If we send Luwayth south, do you have trusted guards who can escort him safely?"

"Only if we disguise him as someone else," Bealtane replied.

"Good. Send a letter along and make it from my brother. Tell the general that negotiations with the staff are going well and that they will aid us. As a good-faith gesture, they sent one of their best to aid the army until the rest arrive. Now, leave and wait for Luwayth outside the room." Bealtane bowed low and then left. Airnin said, sounding almost fatherly, "I need you to remove the bone you have in your shoulder and leave it someplace no one would dare look. I will need to keep things in order here while you are away and the fragment must remain in the palace. You have not told anyone of it, have you?"

"No. I would not betray your trust," Luwayth replied staunchly, staring into Airnin's misty face. Airnin appeared to believe his response and faded away. Fearing that Airnin was still somehow in the room watching, Luwayth waited until a soft purple color appeared in the windows before standing and leaving the room to find Bealtane.

Luwayth immediately found him standing directly outside the door. Bealtane's eyebrows rose as he approached.

"How did it go?"

"Good. You will need to attend to Airnin while I am gone. When do I leave?"

"I already sent attendants ahead to ready the horses and pack the needed supplies. Follow me. I have something that I think will be of use." Bealtane walked briskly down the corridor, looking back over his shoulder. "Come on, hurry up." Luwayth ran to catch up, following Bealtane down a few corridors before reaching stairs that led down. At the bottom of the circular stairs was a room full of armor and weapons. A group of soldiers sat at a table talking and barely looked up as Bealtane and Luwayth entered.

They walked past the guards to the far end of the room, where Bealtane pulled a key from his pocket and opened a large, heavily banded door.

Beyond the door, Luwayth saw a wall lined with armor. In the center of the room stood racks with swords, bows, and crossbows. Bealtane walked over to a set of chainmail armor. "We don't have time to properly fit you for plate, so this chainmail will have to do. It was crafted by menders specifically for tillers." Luwayth gawked in amazement before blurting, "Wait! You know what powers I have? And you didn't call me a Crop Burner?"

"It was pretty obvious what powers you had when you tried to escape from prison. I am aware of the slang the Northerners use, but we are better educated here," he replied, derisively.

Walking over to the armor, Luwayth closed his eyes and observed suls flowing in and out of the armor. Looking around the room, he saw the walls and floor were made of the glossy black stone.

"Bealtane, I have a question. Why are the streets made of this stone? What is it called?"

"The Asinta built this place. It used to be much different before Airnin's attempt to take over. The city was built so that menders could craft things run by suls; building the road out of obsidian prevented anything they crafted from losing the suls trapped inside. You hardly saw a horse in the city back then. Horseless carriages carried goods and people. Grain mills worked without a water wheel. They had many other contraptions as well. Many folks refused to have anything to do with those things when word reached us of what Airnin had done. The staff was blamed for what happened and, from then on, people were looked down on for doing business with the Asinta. Eventually, their contraptions fell out of use," Bealtane explained, looking wistful. Luwayth's mind reeled at the idea of a horseless carriage and was lost in thought until Bealtane snapped him out of it. "I would love to discuss it more, but we must get you ready. I want you out of here before Airnin returns. We do not want you around if and when he changes his mind."

"Wait, you said the stone was called obsidian?"

"Yes, and it is very fragile; however, with the help of menders, it can be made as hard as steel."

"Bealtane, before I put on the armor, I need you to do something." Luwayth then told Bealtane about the bone in his shoulder and made him swear never to mention it.

"Why did you not tell me of this earlier? We can cut it out and destroy it, be rid of him, and stop this whole charade!" Bealtane snapped, agitated.

"No. I have learned that Airnin has plans within plans. This could be a test of our loyalty. We have to do as he says," Luwayth insisted.

"I suppose," Bealtane grumbled, then directed him to turn around.

Luwayth took off his tunic and turned his back to Bealtane. He gritted his teeth as the knife cut into him. Sharp pain shot down his arm as he felt the tip of the blade dig out the bone.

"Done." Bealtane handed the small fragment of bone to Luwayth before putting a small folded cloth over the wound, then carefully dressing Luwayth in armor and a chain mail coif. The armor was like a giant oska strapped to his chest; the metal shin and arm guards also held suls in them.

Bealtane then pulled a bow and quiver from the rack, remarking, "These have mender arrows." Bealtane threaded the quiver onto a belt and then buckled it around Luwayth's waist.

Luwayth looked from the bow to his oska, unsure how he was going to juggle them in battle.

Seeing Luwayth's dilemma reminded Bealtane of the last piece of equipment. He went over to a shelf and picked up some leather straps. He attached a wide leather strap to the armor across Luwayth's chest and wrapped it around his back.

"May I have your oska?" Bealtane asked.

He handed it over and watched as Bealtane carefully held the oska up to Luwayth, measuring before wrapping two pieces of leather around the oska: one towards the top and the other below the leather grip. Bealtane then held the oska to Luwayth's chest. There was a faint click of metal as the oska attached itself to the strip of leather. The top of the oska came almost to his shoulder; the rest hung awkwardly to his left.

"There are spots on the back as well if you want to attach it there," Bealtane instructed.

Luwayth pulled on the oska and realized that, when enough force was applied, the oska came free. Then, as the oska came near, it pulled itself onto the leather, clicking into place.

"Try your bow," Bealtane directed.

Luwayth held the bow in his right hand and drew back. The oska felt awkward but it didn't hinder him.

Bealtane stepped forward and pulled the oska off, then stepped around Luwayth and attached it to his back. "This is too recognizable. You will need to hide it," he explained.

"Thank you, Bealtane," Luwayth said. He turned to face him, then offered his hand. Bealtane grasped him by the wrist and replied, "You are welcome."

I am putting too much trust in the boy, Bealtane thought, as he tied a green cloak with an embroidered crown with a sword through it around Luwayth's neck, hiding the oska, then pulled the hood up, trying to obscure the boy's features.

"Most people here do not know what you look like, but we better be safe. Keep your voice down. Remember—you are just an Asinta going to help, nothing more."

Bealtane led them back into the main room. As they walked past the guards, they nodded again in their direction and went back to playing cards.

Luwayth whispered to Bealtane as they left the room, "Are they supposed to be playing cards?"

"No, but we don't want to draw attention to ourselves by bringing attention to *them*."

Partway up the stairs, Luwayth asked Bealtane to stop. Then, in a hushed voice, he asked. "Can you do something for me while I'm away?"

"Depends. What do you need?"

"I have a plan to defeat Airnin. First, let's head to the throne room, so we can be sure we are alone."

Bealtane nodded and then continued up the stairs and down the corridors to the throne room. The few guards they encountered barely gave them a cursory glance as they walked by.

Once safely inside the throne room, Luwayth asked Bealtane in a hushed voice, "Is it safe to talk here?"

"Yes, but we need to make it quick."

Luwayth proceeded to lay out his plan on how to defeat Airnin and was surprised when Bealtane gave no rebuke to it.

Bealtane thought, *I will put the boy's plan into motion as a last resort if I cannot rally the staff here before he manages to return.*

"Now, hurry. We need to get going," Bealtane urged.

"I will meet you outside the door. I have one last thing to do."

Bealtane nodded. "Hurry!"

Once Luwayth was sure he was alone, he walked to the throne and wedged the small bone from Airnin between the cushion and the arm of the chair, then dashed out.

THE PASS

Luwayth squinted as he exited the palace into the bright morning light. In front of him stood four horses, packed with supplies. Guards held the reins. A stable boy walked up to Luwayth with a horse in tow and held out the reins. Taking them, Luwayth thanked the boy and mounted the horse, then looked up at the building from which he had exited. It was a very plain building that seemed as large as a village; nothing ornate ordained its walls on the side that Luwayth could see—except for half-circles jutting out in even intervals that made it look like waves in a pond.

The guards mounted their horses, and a man wearing a red sash over his right shoulder took the lead, directing Luwayth to follow closely behind. The remaining guards took their positions: one on each side of Luwayth and one to his rear. As they rode away from the stables and main building, Luwayth saw many smaller buildings scattered about. Lush green grass surrounded the buildings and ran up to a large wall that encircled everything Luwayth could see. The guard in front led them down a small gravel path towards the wall. Looking back, Luwayth could see the longer side of the palace come into view. It had a wave pattern to it as well, and Luwayth wondered if each of the semi-circles might be a staircase. In the front of the palace stood a large semi-circle of stairs that grew smaller as it led up to two massive wooden doors. The top of the palace looked like it was riddled with arrows. Chimneys stuck out at various locations all along the roof. At the end closest to him, a section of roof rose up, lined with large, clear glass windows.

Luwayth directed his attention to the path ahead. It appeared to lead straight into the wall, but no doors could be seen. As they got closer, the road started to descend, and loopholes soon appeared, staggered along both sides of the road. Luwayth could see guards posted at each one as he passed. The wall loomed over them until they passed underneath into a long underground tunnel that continued to descend. They passed guard posts and then, after a quarter stone, the tunnel began to ascend. The tunnel spiraled to the right until they came to two large doors with thick metal bands. As they approached, the doors swung inward and a large metal grate slowly rose up.

They exited into a large courtyard with high walls topped by a walkway on which guards patrolled. In front of them stood another set of wooden doors that began to open. There was another metal grate outside that lifted as they approached. As they rode through the second set of doors, Luwayth found himself in an immense plaza. Throngs of people passed, and vendors lined the walls and spaces between storefronts. Luwayth had never seen this many people in one place before; as they passed, not one seemed to notice them.

The leader of their group turned right and headed to an exit in the plaza that continued into a busy street. The crowds slowly thinned out the farther they traveled from the plaza. They wound back and forth through the capital until finally approaching a main gate, which stood open. Guards on both sides questioned those coming and going. As they approached, the guards ordered everyone to the side, leaving a gap through which they could exit. The leader in front of Luwayth nodded to the guards at the gate as they passed.

The lead guard picked up the pace once outside the capital. Luwayth overheard small conversations between his guards, but no one spoke or even looked in his direction. The land surrounding the city was full of farms with pastures and fields so large that numerous people were working them, pulling lull weeds or harvesting. Ahead, a vast mountain range loomed: the Spine of Mehron. Everyone they approached on the road stood to the side to give way. The journey that day was uneventful; Luwayth did all he could to stay awake.

As Farkor set, the lead guard guided them into a clearing across from a small farm. The farmer, upon seeing them, fled into his house. As Luwayth dismounted, he was unsure as to what he should do. Finally, he turned to the head guard and asked; the man nodded and told him that he and his men would manage just fine. Luwayth wandered to the edge of the clearing and explored a bit; the forest here wasn't as wild as it was back at the barrow. As he meandered along the forest's edge, he pulled the suls from the dead things he found along the way, filling his oska and armor. As he approached the road on the other side of the clearing, he looked across to the farmer's field. It was about the size his father had had, full of crops of average size that appeared ready to harvest. Since Airnin wasn't there to stop him, Luwayth walked across the road and hopped over the small fence that bordered the field. The farmer was nowhere to be seen, so Luwayth closed his eyes and walked through the field. Feeling Dainua course from the ground through him was restorative; it felt like coming home. He took the suls he had stored, reached out to the crops, and pushed the suls into them. He was easily able to grow the entire field to twice its original size.

After Luwayth was done, he began to return to the clearing but stopped in the middle of the road. The four guards were lined up on the other side, staring at him in wonderment. When they realized Luwayth was done, they returned to setting up camp. As Luwayth approached, the leader said, "I apologize for speaking without permission. I've heard tales of the deeds of the Asinta but I've never seen it first-hand. May I ask why you did it?" The other three guards paused what they were doing to eavesdrop on Luwayth's response. Seeing the attention the guards were giving him, Luwayth carefully considered his answer; as he thought of Airnin's deeds, the response was clear.

"I did it because if we have the power and ability to help those around us, it is our responsibility to do so. For the greatest harm that one can commit is hiding those talents or, even worse, twisting them to do evil."

"Those are wise words coming from one so young," the lead guard replied as he nodded his head.

Luwayth turned and glanced back at the field, knowing that he could never do enough good to offset the pestilence he and Airnin had unleashed on the kingdom. He walked into the makeshift camp and found a tree stump out of the way to sit on, wondering what he was going to find and do once he reached the army encampment.

A short while later, the lead guard came over and bowed to Luwayth, telling him that dinner was ready. Luwayth took a plate of food and sat by the fire, looking carefully at each man, wondering who they were and where they were from, wanting to get to know them better. The images of the guards he killed played out in his head. These men were seated here because they were paid and not because they wanted to be here, Luwayth realized. Any friendship that they gave him was because they felt an obligation. *I'm destined to walk alone and apart from others*, he told himself. After finishing his meal, he handed his plate back to the guards.

"Would you care to hear a tale?" Luwayth asked.

"Yes," a guard to Luwayth's right replied, so Luwayth told his dad's favorite tales. The guards cheered and applauded when he was done.

Luwayth thanked them for their hospitality and went to the bedroll that was laid out for him, noticing that it looked much thicker and cleaner than those the guards had laid out for themselves. One of the guards came over and helped Luwayth strip out of his armor, and as he did, he spoke in a soft voice so that only Luwayth could hear.

"My parents were farmers and life was never easy. That was a kind thing you did for those folks. Thank you, and thank you for the tales." Luwayth nodded his head in reply. Once the armor was off, Luwayth lay down on his bedroll, staring into the fire and watching the guards banter amongst one another until he drifted off to sleep.

The head guard awoke Luwayth early the next morning, just as Farkor was cresting the horizon and bathing the land in a soft yellow glow. Most of the camp was already packed. They had a quick breakfast consisting of salted beef and water. As they headed out of the clearing and back onto the road, Luwayth noticed the farmer and his wife were outside staring awestruck at their field, the farmer scratching the top of his head trying to puzzle it out. Neither seemed to notice the small group of armed men as they passed.

This day was just as uneventful as the last. They only stopped to water the horses and eat their midday meal. The mountain range ahead was an immense rock that jutted through the clouds above, steep and unclimbable. It ended abruptly at its foot with no rolling hills. The mountain appeared to grow larger the closer they got to the pass, a large gap in the seemingly unending mountain range. The pass rose in sheer cliffs on each side, shooting straight up to the white snow-capped peaks above. As evening approached, the lead guard brought his horse to a stop and gestured for Luwayth to come alongside him.

"Over the following rise, you will see the army's encampment. I was told not to go in with you. Here is a letter that Bealtane gave me to have you deliver to the general; his name is Leonin. Good luck." Luwayth took the letter, thanked the men, and headed off on his own. The guards turned their horses and started their journey back.

As Luwayth drew near the ridge, he saw a large mass of black moving to and fro in the pass. As he studied the movement of the mass, he soon realized they were large black birds circling and occasionally landing out of sight.

Luwayth crested the ridge and reined in the horse. The view ahead of him was like nothing he had imagined in all of the tales he had told or heard. The road he was on switchbacked, sloping gently to a large bowl that sat at the entrance to the pass. Inside the bowl was a large encampment of tents, with rows of wooden structures facing him lining the outer perimeter. From each, a man's body was hanging. The encampment ran to the base of the pass, in which lay churned earth dotted with odd shapes, some glinting in the light of Farkor. The birds above seemed to be attracted to the shiny objects. Not a single speck of green could be seen beyond the encampment. As he surveyed the far end of the pass, he could just see the Soyer camp. Luwayth was dismayed that the pass looked to be four to five stone across. The mountains rose to their immense height and back down again in that short a distance. He hoped he hadn't overestimated his ability to carry out his plan.

Letting the horse lead itself down the road to the camp, Luwayth studied the immense encampment. It was twice the size of a village. Men walked amongst the tents, most in armor. Large patrols were marching just inside the pass.

Partway down the road, a group of armed men on horseback rode up to meet him, demanding to know his business.

"I am here by order of the king," Luwayth responded, holding out the letter that Bealtane had forged for him. The lead soldier took it and examined the seal, then handed it to another soldier, who then turned and rode back towards the camp.

"Follow us," one of the soldiers commanded, then started towards the encampment. Half of the soldiers followed; the remaining men gestured to Luwayth to start and then followed him. Once they arrived at the edge of the encampment, Luwayth was ordered to wait. The soldiers left to resume their patrol. Two of the wooden structures that Luwayth saw from above sat on each side of the road. The one to his left held what appeared to be a fresh corpse, and the body to his right appeared to have been hanging for quite a while.

A few moments later, a soldier approached on foot. Upon seeing Luwayth studying the hanged men, he casually commented, "Deserters." He directed Luwayth to follow. Luwayth nodded and led his horse after the man. The stench of unwashed men and excrement filled the air. The ground was muddy, and the tents closest to the road were splattered with mud and filth from riders passing by. The men who walked by looked defeated and down-trodden. Many bore scars or fresh wounds, and some even had missing limbs. Not one man looked up at Luwayth; all stared at the ground as if awaiting their turn to finally be embraced by it.

They passed a tent with a line of men out front, each waiting their turn with a plate in hand while a man with a large pot slopped something unrecognizable onto the plates.

The ground started to take on a reddish hue. It grew more intense until small rivers of watery blood ran through the mud, collecting in boot and hoof impressions made by passersby. It was immediately apparent where it had originated; the next series of tents showed blood-stained mud at the bottom and shadows of blood spray on the walls. Next to the tent nearest them stood unwashed buckets with partial limbs sticking out. Flies buzzed about and feasted on the now rotting flesh. Muffled screams of pain came from within the tents.

The road finally became a little less muddy, and the tents, instead of a bland dirty white, were vibrantly colored, though the mud and filth showed no prejudice and clung to them like the others the group passed. A small stable came into view to which Luwayth was led. A young boy covered in dirt ran up and grabbed the bridle of the horse while Luwayth dismounted. The boy led the horse to the stable. The soldier Luwayth had been following gestured for him to continue to follow. The ground was less muddy but still squelched as he walked, occasionally pulling at his boots.

They approached a vibrant green tent with white pennants bearing the King's symbol. To Luwayth's estimation, it sat in the exact center of the encampment. Unlike the other tents, this was well cared for; there was much less mud and filth splashed against its sides. Two soldiers stood guard outside and stepped forward and to the center, blocking their path. The soldier leading Luwayth continued forward, conversed with the soldiers, and then was allowed to enter, leaving Luwayth outside.

A few moments later, the soldier reappeared and spoke to the soldiers blocking Luwayth's way. They parted, and as they did, they pulled the flaps of the tent open. Luwayth stepped into the tent.

The first thing Luwayth noticed was the smell of burning herbs. The tent was lit inside by flaps in the roof that had been pulled back, along with a few lit lanterns hanging around the room. A large table surrounded by older men in clean but severely dented armor stood at the center of the room. Everyone stared in Luwayth's direction. Another tent flap behind the men led into another room. A strange, sinking sensation crept over Luwayth. Breathing out slowly, he played over in his mind what Bealtane had told him he needed to do.

He stepped forward and bowed, then addressed the men: "I am here as an ambassador and gift from the king. I know I am only one man, but the rest of the Asinta should be here in two to three days' time."

A man came around the table and stuck out a hand. Luwayth grasped it by the wrist and shook. The man's wrist was thick and muscular; his grip around Luwayth's wrist was calloused and rough.

"I am Leonin, the general of this rabble and mess. I fear that you have come too late. We are due to ride out in the morning and surrender. We don't have enough men to fight, let alone defend our position anymore. Soyer knows this and has given us an ultimatum: surrender or die by the sword. The remaining soldiers are loyal to the crown, but they do not deserve to die for a lost cause. If you had all the Asinta with you, Soyer would still outnumber us three to one." The general's voice was sullen and low; it held an inflection and tone that made Luwayth feel as if he would follow the man anywhere.

"I am sorry, Leonin. Are you sure there is nothing I can do?" Luwayth couldn't think of anything he could say to sway the man.

"No, unless you know when the king will return. We need him to help negotiate an agreement that will not lead to our being swallowed up by Soyer."

The image of the king's dead eyes seeped from Luwayth's thoughts and across his face.

"What's wrong?" Leonin asked. Luwayth, suddenly aware of his mistake, quickly composed himself and answered as confidently as he could, "I am sorry, Leonin, there is no way the king is going to arrive in time."

Leonin was crestfallen. "Then all of our efforts were for naught. I will have a soldier show you to a tent you can use for the night. You will leave first thing in the morning before we surrender. There is no telling what they will do if they find an Asinta in our midst."

"No, Leonin, I came to support you. If that support is in the surrender of Salare, then I will be there by your side," Luwayth responded.

"I appreciate that, but you must be off before first light," Leonin commanded, then turned to the soldier who had led Luwayth to the tent. He instructed him where to take Luwayth, then remarked, "I will have a soldier come get you for dinner tonight." Luwayth stuck out his hand and grasped Leonin's wrist again, thanked him for his hospitality, then left the tent.

The soldier walked only a few tents away and pulled the flap aside. "This was the general's second in command's tent before he fell in battle last week," the soldier remarked as he walked in, lit a lantern, turned, and left.

ᒣHE ᗞEAD

Standing alone in the tent, Luwayth paced, trying to decide what to do. The situation appeared to be already lost, and he hadn't even had a chance to help.

An irrational idea came to him. He walked over to the tent flap and pulled it back slightly. He didn't see anyone nearby. He returned to his tent, sat in a chair made of animal hides, and waited. As twilight approached, he cautiously opened his tent. Soldiers patrolled the well-lit area between Leonin's tent and the stable. The pass beyond was heavily shadowed, as the last light of Farkor was fading. Luwayth searched for any soldiers near his tent and, upon seeing none, darted from the tent in the direction of the pass, moving between the shadows of the tents. The occasional patrol passed by but didn't seem interested in searching; instead, they were focused on getting to the end of their shift. This allowed Luwayth to quickly sneak to the edge of the encampment where he found the largest patrols, all of which actively searching for deserters and signs of the enemy. The walls of the cliffs glowed faintly in the growing starlight. Staying to the shadows, Luwayth waited until a patrol passed by; then, consuming a sul trapped in the armor around him, he pushed down, flying up and over the path of the patrols into the pass.

The ground was uneven and trampled from the innumerable battles that had been fought here. He closed his eyes and saw flecks of small suls all around, as well as a few human-shaped suls. Quickly making his way across the field, Luwayth found broken swords, crossbow bolts, and arrows shafts littered about the occasional body of a fallen soldier—from which side Luwayth couldn't determine—some still wearing armor, though most were stripped bare. They all bore signs of carrion feasting. Luwayth braced himself and pulled some of the remaining sul from one of the bodies he found. The feeling of anguish and longing was deeply felt but dissipated quickly. Feeling confident that the dead man's last emotions wouldn't hamper him, Luwayth pulled the remaining sul, creating a black statue in its place. He watched the starlight sparkle across the glossy black surface, then looked around him at all of the men left and forgotten. He pushed some of the sul out to grow the grass around the newly created monument at his feet, hoping that life would return. He strolled towards the enemy's encampment, stopping at the soldiers' bodies he passed to pull all of the remaining sul and create a monument to the fallen soldier. After he pulled the suls of ten soldiers, Luwayth realized he could be in the pass for a week and still not have found all of the bodies. He had to pass many of the fallen; instead, he focused on soldiers who died reaching out for help, grasping limbs that had been brutally hacked off or trying to pull out arrows or bolts in their final moments. He hoped these monuments would put fear into the hearts of the next troops who passed by, giving them something to reflect on before waging another war.

Luwayth wondered as he worked: if he had been conscripted to be a soldier, could he have fought after seeing what devastation war wrought? The chaos that led to this land of the dead was worse than he had ever imagined. The tales he had heard in the southern villages had made war out to be so glamorous, but nothing could have prepared him for this reality.

The pass was longer than it first appeared. He had to resort to pushing down and leaping far into the air in order to cover more ground. Eventually, he found himself on the other side of the pass. Soyer's side didn't have bodies strewn about, but flecks of suls were still present all around him. Soyer's camp was far larger than the one he left. Lanterns and flames lit the encampment, men milled back and forth or sat around large fires. Patrols carefully monitored their surroundings. Sitting in the darkness of the battlefield, Luwayth wondered what he could do to stop such an innumerable force. The only thing he had on his side, he realized, was that no one was expecting someone with the powers of an Asinta.

Upon spotting a patrol about fifty pebbles away, Luwayth crept forward near the western cliff face and ducked behind a large boulder near the wall. Grabbing two rocks, Luwayth pounded them together, and the sound echoed off the cliff face. The men turned and slowly started to walk in his direction, swords unsheathed and lanterns held out in front of them. Luwayth pushed down and landed a bit farther back in the pass, then pounded the rocks together again, drawing the men deeper into the pass. As the men drew closer, Luwayth pushed up and out so he hit the cliff face, pushing the power out to hold himself in place. He looked down and waited for the men to walk by. As they passed, the light of their lanterns didn't illuminate high enough for them to see Luwayth, as they were designed to cast light out in every direction instead. As the last man passed, Luwayth snapped his oska to his chest, slid his bow from his shoulder, and unsheathed an arrow from the quiver that hung from his waist at an odd angle. He aimed up and to the rear of the patrol and fired. He pushed the arrow into an arc at the last soldier and then shoved as hard as he could. The small pointed tip of the arrow pierced through the chainmail and leather. The soldier staggered forward, called out for help, and dropped face down in the dirt. The patrol effortlessly broke into an offense position and searched for the unknown assailant. Another arrow emerged from the darkness and turned to find its mark. The second soldier stumbled as he clutched at the arrow in his throat which had found the gap below his helmet. As the patrol started to switch its offensive position to face the threat, an arrow came from above, striking a soldier in the back and piercing clean through to the front. Chaos erupted as the patrol broke ranks and fled. Regardless of what direction the soldiers ran, the arrow always struck true.

Luwayth silently dropped down amongst the dead men and retrieved his arrows. Sweat dripped from his forehead, the strain of concentrating on both keeping himself in place and directing the arrows beginning to take its toll.

He breathed in and out, closed his eyes, cleared his mind, and pulled the suls of the men. The fear and anger from them washed over him. He envisioned the soldiers' camp on fire, blood pooling everywhere, and found himself consumed by the desire to kill. He focused on allowing the anger and fear to feed his desire to maim and murder, savoring the men's anguish. The bitterness of the fear became sweet, and he desired more.

The faint noise of armor moving caused Luwayth to glance back to the encampment. He spotted two patrols headed in his direction. He wanted... no, needed... their pain and anguish. He slung his bow over his shoulder, pulled his oska free from his chest, leapt into the air, and latched onto the cliff face. Pushing himself against it as he sprinted towards the patrol, he had to jump over gaps in the rock face from previous rock slides. The patrols were spaced apart with a swath of unlit ground between them. Luwayth pushed off and twisted in the air, directing the energy in himself to the bottom of his oska. He stretched the oska above his head as he started to land head first into the midst of the first patrol. He released the energy, and it shot out in every direction, knocking the soldiers off their feet. The energy pushed Luwayth back into the air. He flipped forward and landed on his feet. He grabbed the sul of the nearest soldier, causing the emotion of confusion to flair inside himself. Instead of letting it affect him, he laughed out loud and yelled, "Your suls are mine. I will feed on them tonight." He devoured the man's sul and used the energy to grab the next soldier and fling him straight into the air. Luwayth charged a third man and swung his oska at his chest as the man stumbled to his feet. His ribs cracked as he was hurled into the darkness. Luwayth heard the shuffling of feet, ducked, and shifted sideways. The sword narrowly missed him. The man sneered, showing crooked teeth. A loud, crashing noise came from behind the soldier. He glanced back briefly, seeing his comrade laying in a broken heap from his fall. Luwayth snatched the opportunity, grabbed the man's sul, yanked on it, and gleefully watched the man age. The yells of the second patrol rushing Luwayth's way stopped him from turning the man to stone. He pushed the sul into his armor and used the remaining energy to leap into the darkness, leaving the old man behind. He pushed down, landing softly near the mountain's face, then studied the patrol as it quickly formed rank upon discovering the bodies. Luwayth searched around, needing a quicker way to dispose of the men.

He noticed large rocks and boulders that had fallen from the rock face. The soldiers had grouped tightly together, searching around for the unknown assailant or assailants. Luwayth stepped behind a large boulder about the width of four men and then slowly took each of the suls he had stored and consumed them. The energy coursed through him, trying to escape, but he continued to devour more. His mind strained under the pressure, and his muscles felt as if they would rip from the bone. He stopped and focused on his oska. He twirled it in a circle as he pushed the energy to the base; the energy crackled and hissed as some escaped into Telgog. Sweat poured down Luwayth's face as he strained to keep the energy in place. He focused on the boulder to time it just right, then released. The cracking of energy boomed, and the boulder flew forward at a tremendous speed. The soldiers had no time to react as it smashed through them and into the darkness beyond.

The release of energy was so immense that it shook the mountain face, causing parts to sheer off and crash to the ground. A large boulder hit Luwayth's left side; he jumped to the right, realizing too late that he had no energy left. Another rock crashed down just behind him. He sprinted forward, trying to outrun the avalanche of rocks. He dove behind the next boulder he came across and felt the rush of rocks and stone blow past him.

As the dust and debris finally settled around Luwayth, he found himself in a small clearing surrounded by rocks and boulders. The sound of horns could be heard in the distance from Soyer's camp. They would soon be on him.

The answer to his problem became clear. He ran over to where the soldiers had been. The boulder he threw had crushed a few men, but most had been pushed away by the force of the rolling stone. Luckily, the debris from the avalanche had ended just before the scattered bodies.

Luwayth pulled suls from the soldiers he could find, steadying himself with each emotion he encountered: pain, fear, hate, shock, dismay, anger. With each one, he forced his own nature aside, making himself feed on it and hunger for more.

He hurried towards the cliff face, searching for any remaining suls until the rubble became too thick. He consumed a few of the smaller suls and leapt onto the broken cliff face. He ran up the cliff, jumping over large portions that hadn't fallen and now jutted out like steps for his personal use. He scrutinized the pass; soldiers' fallen lanterns glittered like starlight until one by one, they sputtered out and died. He turned and ran towards Soyer's encampment, around the edge of the cliff face to the side that sloped down to the enemy's tents and troops. Luwayth noticed the side of the mountain had cracked in many places from rainfall, but no large boulders had broken away. He took suls one at a time from his filled armor, consuming each until the energy that coursed through him was at its limit. He made sure to hold a few suls in reserve. He noticed he couldn't hold as much in as before; his muscles were weary, and his head ached. He searched until he found a large crack and released energy deep into it. The mountain shook as fractures spread like a spider's web around him, and then a thunderous boom erupted from the mountain. The ground shifted under Luwayth's feet and slowly started to fall away, gaining momentum rapidly. Luwayth jumped away from the shifting rubble beneath his feet and then pushed in every direction around him as he watched the avalanche sweep through Soyer's encampment, each fire and torch snuffed as the wave roared through the camp, destroying everything in its path.

As the rocks came to rest, Luwayth relaxed and fell; he consumed the remaining suls, concentrating on the darkened landscape below, and as soon as he saw the starlight reflect from the rubble, he pushed, landing lightly on his feet.

The enemy encampment exploded in a panic like a bees' nest dropped from a tree. Luwayth dashed towards it. The rubble from the mountain cut a wide deep gash through the center of the encampment, but the tents on the periphery were still intact.

He pulled the suls around him but struggled to store them. *Oy, I'm exhausted*, he thought. The remaining soldiers were too busy rushing to aid their brethren buried in the rubble to pay attention to Luwayth. As Luwayth neared the closest tent, he consumed the stored suls and moved his hands in a circle until a large fireball appeared. He hurled the ball of flame into the tent, catching it on fire. Luwayth quickly spun his oska and threw a wall of energy towards the tent, which broke apart, flinging pieces of burning debris across the camp. Fires ignited, quickly spreading as they burned the strewn rubble of the encampment.

Completely exhausted and nearing collapse, Luwayth hoped what he had done was enough. He tried to run back to the mountain pass, but after a few paces, his strength gave out and he slowed to a walk. As he approached a boulder, a man, disheveled and covered in rock dust, came into view.

"Apparently, the Asinta decided to take arms against us right before we dealt the final blow to Salare?" the man said in a smooth, calm tone.

"No, I am not with the Asinta. I am here alone," Luwayth said out of breath.

The man surveyed the area and laughed at the devastation around him before remarking, "I apparently underestimated Cial. You may have defeated my army, but I will not flee this fight." The man withdrew a sword from its scabbard and stalked towards Luwayth.

Luwayth took a step backward, closed his eyes, and reached for Dainua, but her energy recoiled. He glanced back at the approaching soldier who started to swing his blade. Luwayth held up his oska and the blade bit into it. The two of them struggled, then the man's eyes went wide and he dropped to the ground, an arrow protruding from his back.

The army of Salare had arrived and was quickly overwhelming the remaining forces of Soyer.

A Salaran soldier on horseback pressed forward, diverting his troops to pursue their fleeing enemy through the burning encampment. As the soldier on horseback approached, the light from the flames lit his face. It was Leonin.

Feeling there wasn't more that he needed to do, Luwayth watched as Leonin directed his men to chase down and kill Soyer's soldiers as they fled.

As the commotion around Leonin died down, Luwayth wearily walked over and called out, "Oy, it's Luwayth! What brought you here?"

Leonin turned in his saddle to stare in Luwayth's direction, then motioned for him to approach. Luwayth stumbled forward until he reached the horse's side. Leonin addressed him: "When my men came to get you for dinner and you weren't there, we searched the camp. On the outskirts, one of the patrols came across a black statue. Upon inspection, they found a line of them leading into the pass. Once I was informed, I knew that whatever you had done or were about to do jeopardized our surrender in the morning. I rallied the troops and force-marched here, following the trail of statues you left for us. When we saw the mountain give way and wipe out the camp, I assumed it was you. An interesting tactic. I can't condone what you did, but now isn't the time to argue over it."

When morning finally came, most of Soyer's encampment was ash, flickering with a few lingering flames. Leonin's men had regrouped at the encampment's northern edge near the pass.

Standing by Leonin's side, Luwayth watched as he directed men and received news from the battlefield. There were still small attachments of soldiers that had not returned after pursuing Soyer's men. Runners had left to catch up with the pursuers to tell them to turn back; Leonin didn't want any men killed in an ambush.

After seeming to be content with the current status, Leonin turned to Luwayth; the leather in the saddle creaked as he moved.

"Well, it seems we are victorious. This will deter them from regrouping and striking back. The reports I have received say that we now outnumber any who are left that still want to fight. Your actions last night were reckless, and I will have words with the king when he returns regarding his decision to send someone so foolhardy. For now, I have no more need for your assistance. You are dismissed." Leonin turned back to watch the proceedings around him.

Not sure what to do, Luwayth began to trudge towards the pass, then stopped and turned back to Leonin. Luwayth struggled for words. He wanted to tell Leonin about the king. He felt like he owed it to the man but didn't know why. Unable to find the words, Luwayth dropped his head and continued through the pass. It was time to turn his attention to Airnin.

The Road Back

A few stones into the pass, Luwayth glanced back and spotted soldiers on horseback returning from the battle with a few ownerless horses in tow. Word had gotten out about what Luwayth had done, and as a thank you, one of the soldiers handed over the reins of a horse.

Luwayth mounted the horse and rode until he found an undisturbed patch of grass. He dismounted, fell to his hands and knees, and closed his eyes. Dainua was faint, so Fearn pushed out his sul into her power and then quickly pulled it back in dismay. He looked down at himself and studied his sul. It was cracked—marred by a web of fine black lines. Luwayth recalled the previous night. At the thought of the men's emotions, something deep inside still hungered for more. Tears filled Luwayth's eyes, and he fell to the ground. He reached out to Dainua while whispering between sobs, "I'm sorry, Dainua. I had no other choice." He watched as Dainua's energy reached out to soothe him but recoiled when it came across one of the faint cracks.

"Why didn't Airnin warn me of this?" Luwayth questioned. The image of the wraith pulled him back to the present. "I need to get back to the palace. You can't wallow here," he scolded himself. As he stood, every muscle ached in agony. He gingerly got back into the saddle and continued on his way.

He inspected his oska on the way. It had a large chip on one side along with a small crack, but he felt confident that it would hold up when he faced Airnin.

Once back at Leonin's encampment, he rode around until he scrounged up enough supplies to get him back to the palace. Most of the supplies he took without permission, figuring that now that the war was over, Leonin wouldn't care. He was stopped a few times by patrolling soldiers, but as soon as they saw his oska, they quickly apologized and went on their way. Finally, Luwayth stopped off at the stable near Leonin's tent to swap the horse for the horse that had borne him from the palace. Not a single soldier was in sight. After stowing his supplies, Luwayth went into Leonin's tent. It looked just as it had the previous day. Hurrying, Luwayth looked for a quill and ink, which he ultimately found on a small desk next to a large table in the center of the room. The quill sat on a tall stack of papers next to what appeared to be notes from prior meetings. Luwayth picked up the quill and a blank sheet, sat down, and slowly penned a note to Leonin. It had been many years since he had written, and when he was done, the sheet was full of crossed-out words and others he was sure were misspelled. He read it over one last time; it bore the message he wanted to convey. It was a hurried account of what had happened to the king, which Luwayth took full responsibility for despite Airnin's involvement. After he placed the letter in the center of the table, he turned and left the tent. He mounted his horse and rode north across the encampment, finding fewer and fewer soldiers along the way.

By midday, Luwayth was exhausted but knew he had to push on until nightfall. He let the horse walk at its own pace while his head bobbed, trying to stay awake. Abruptly, a voice called out to him, forcing him out of his stupor. On the side of the road stood an elderly woman. She had a head of deep grey hair with streaks of white. Her back was bent, making her appear like a turtle walking on its hind legs. She held a cane in one hand and a basket in the other. Her clothing was worn and showed signs of being mended on more than one occasion.

"Oy there, boy!" the old woman croaked, waving her cane to get Luwayth's attention.

Luwayth pulled on the reins, bringing the horse to a stop. He looked down and greeted the old woman, whose face appeared oddly young. Then, he looked up the road and back the way he had come.

"Looks like you are far from home. Where are you headed?" Luwayth asked. The old woman strained her neck to look up at Luwayth. "Just picking berries. I am old and alone and without a horse. Would you be kind enough to let me ride the rest of the way home? It isn't far." The old woman's voice was dry and cracked. After she spoke, she smiled widely, revealing quite a few missing teeth. Luwayth knew he needed to get back to the palace as fast as possible, but just as he was about to tell the woman he was too busy, his dad's tales came to mind.

Instead, Luwayth dismounted the horse and held out a hand for the old woman. She curtsied before taking his hand, gave Luwayth her basket and cane, then let him help her into the saddle.

"Thank you so much for your kindness. Home is just over the rise there." The old woman then took the reins and headed off at an easy pace with which Luwayth could keep up.

Feeling he wanted to know more about the old woman, Luwayth introduced himself.

"Hmm, Luwayth is it? You don't strike me as a Luwayth. I met a Luwayth once, and he wasn't a very nice man. You don't seem like a bad person; you should find a better name."

"Well, you can't go about changing your name just because someone else with the name was a bad person. I did have another name not so long ago, but it belonged to a better man. I feel that Luwayth is a name more suited for me, especially if it is a name suited for those of ill repute." The last words that Luwayth's dad spoke to him bubbled to the surface of his consciousness.

"... your mom was right. Fearn was a good name... "

The old woman reached out a hand and patted Luwayth on the top of the head. "You seem like a fine boy to me. You shouldn't be too hard on yourself."

"If you knew who I was and the things I have done, you would ride off on my horse and leave me here. I have spent my life either struggling for the love and affection of my father or finding that devotion in a man who used it to twist me into the wretch you see before you. My hands are stained with the blood of the innocent. Instead of being who I wanted to be, I let others choose for me; I discovered that too late. I would have done anything to hear the words 'I love you' from my father. I chased those words from a man who used that need to manipulate me. This morning, I rode away from a man who truly loved his king. I know that as soon as he hears who killed his leader, he will hunt that murderer down. I expect the doomed man will be waiting eagerly to be freed from the torments he has caused." As Luwayth spoke these words, nothing he had spoken before rang truer in his own ears and he felt relieved that all of this would finally come to an end.

The woman reached out and ruffled Luwayth's hair. "Such despair from one so young. Take it from someone who has been around long enough to tell you that it is never too late to be the person you want to be. We all make mistakes. It is how we learn and grow from them that shapes us. Certainly, there will be those who see ill deeds in others and, despite any changes that person may make, will only see those deeds instead of the person they have become. You seem so focused on how others see you. If you want to be a better person, then be a better person! Do not let others deter you from that. There will be actions in our lives that we cannot take back. Some will forever haunt us, reminding us of the person we were and could become again. Instead of thinking that you can be no better than your most heinous deed, use that experience instead as a guide to walk a different path. The blackness is out there waiting for everyone. But so is the light—neither discriminates. Remember: we are our own worst deamhon. You are young. In front of me, I see a man who, at a young age, has learned something that others take a lifetime to learn. Do not throw that knowledge away, and you will do just fine."

Luwayth looked up at the old woman, whose smile now radiated a sense of warmth. Her brilliant steel-blue eyes didn't look back at him with pity or disgust but with hope.

The rest of the walk was silent. Luwayth pondered the things that the old woman had said, and the old woman enjoyed the fact she didn't have to walk.

About a hundred pebbles down the road, a small hovel appeared. The old woman clapped her hands and exclaimed. "Ah, home! What a wonderful sight. Thank you again, my young friend, for your help. Would you like to come in? I plan on making a cobbler with those berries and have fresh rabbit as well." The tales that Luwayth's father told echoed through his head. Besides, he didn't recall seeing the hovel on the way to Leonin's encampment.

"Thank you for the invite, but I have an urgent matter to attend to and must be on my way. If I am ever back this way, I promise to stop and partake of your hospitality." Luwayth hoped that if the woman was some sort of deamhon, his answer might appease her. The old woman just frowned. "Well, I suppose another night alone will not hurt, but company would have been so nice." The woman sighed, "Goodbye, Not-Luwayth."

Once back in the saddle, Luwayth kept the horse at a steady pace until he felt he was far enough away, then urged the horse into a gallop to distance himself before nightfall, just in case she was something more than a kind old woman.

The small farm across from which he had spent the night with the guards came into view. Feeling this was as good a place as any to stop, Luwayth led the horse over to the clearing opposite the farm and set up camp for the night, which really only consisted of a bedroll. He let the horse wander around the clearing to find grass. After gathering wood for a fire and suls for his armor and oska, Luwayth built a small fire. As he sat and watched the flames, he knew that this may be his last fire, especially if things with Airnin didn't work out the following night. He reached out to Dainua and hoped that his scars would mend; her touch was timid and recoiled from the dark parts of his sul.

A sound came from across the road. Luwayth saw the door to the farmhouse open and someone step out with a lantern in hand. The person headed in his direction, and as the person drew near, Luwayth could see it was the farmer and he had something in hand.

"Excuse me for interrupting, but my wife insisted on having me come give this to you. We were blessed the other night by Dainua. Our crops grew threefold. My wife was insistent that we pass those blessings on to others, so here is a warm bowl of soup she made with those vegetables." The farmer held out the bowl of soup to Luwayth, who took it graciously and thanked the farmer, who then hurried back to his house. The soup was good and helped fill a stomach that had wanted more than dried meat.

The following morning, before daybreak, Luwayth packed up and left the empty bowl by the farmer's door. He mounted the horse and continued on, hoping that it wouldn't be his last morning.

TREACHERY

Luwayth arrived at the capital gates a few hours before nightfall, the horse on the verge of collapsing from exhaustion. Upon seeing Luwayth's oska, the guards sent a man ahead to find someone to verify his identity.

A little while later, Bealtane arrived on horseback.

"That was too quick. We will start preparations for a siege."

"No, I was able to defeat the army. I need to get back to the throne room before Airnin returns. I can give you details on the way."

Luwayth followed Bealtane into the heart of the capital. Along the way, he recounted the battle and its outcome. Bealtane sat in silence, listening, not wanting to interrupt. Once the account was complete, Bealtane nodded. "This ended more quickly than I expected. That rock fall must have been a sight to see."

Bealtane thought to himself: *Perhaps I underestimated the boy. I will need to send out a rider to verify his tale. If he is lying, we will need to prepare for a siege.* Aloud, he remarked, "I was able to make the preparations you requested. Do you intend to put your plan into place tonight?"

Luwayth looked around to see if anyone was listening. "Yes, it must be tonight. As soon as Leonin finds out I killed the king, I suspect he will be riding here as fast as possible." Bealtane pulled up hard on the reins, bringing his horse to a stop. "Wait. You told Leonin you killed the king?" Bealtane looked horror-struck.

"Well, no," Luwayth replied, "but I did leave a letter recounting what happened. If things don't go well with Airnin, then hopefully Leonin can come and finish what I couldn't. And if I do manage to defeat Airnin, I will wait for Leonin and accept the fate that comes from my actions. Maybe then the kingdom can return to peace."

Bealtane didn't respond but urged the horse forward again. "That forces our hand. We will have to move things into place more quickly than I expected. Having more time to put things in place would have been to our advantage, though Leonin would have found out eventually."

Bealtane explained that Airnin hadn't done much in Luwayth's absence and everyone was growing more resentful at having to be subject to a deamhon.

Once back at the palace, Luwayth hurriedly bathed at the insistence of the steward and asked that the armor that he was wearing be cleaned so he looked presentable once Airnin arrived. After he was clean and dressed, Luwayth walked to the throne room carrying his oska. The guards he encountered along the way gave menacing looks but allowed him to pass. Upon arriving, Luwayth reached between the throne's cushions. The piece of bone was where he had left it. He pulled it out, clutched it in his hand, and waited for Airnin. Bealtane stood at the base of the dais, hands clasped behind his back. Luwayth glanced up at the windows; the overcast sky looked black.

Finally, a shimmer appeared next to the throne and a hooded figure shrouded in mist appeared.

"Back so soon? I take it things did not go well. I should have suspected. Bealtane, have you started preparations for a siege?" Airnin's voice grated with contempt.

Luwayth cowered back against the opposite side of the throne from Airnin before saying, "On the contrary—everything went well. Leonin was about to surrender, but I was able to sneak into Soyer's camp and turn the tide. By the next morning, the war was over." He closed his eyes as he finished to see Airnin's reaction.

A look of surprise flickered across Airnin's face before a look of satisfaction replaced it. "My teachings all those years paid off. Tell me the details."

Luwayth told of the rock slide, burning the camp, and Leonin's defeat of the remaining Soyerian troops. Airnin smiled wickedly with each description of a soldier's death.

After the tale was told, Airnin turned to look down at Bealtane. "First, I want you to send word to Leonin to hold his position. We are going to conscript every able-bodied man and send them to the pass. He will then march south to crush any remaining forces until Soyer surrenders to us. Then, send in the magistrates. Let us get to tonight's business... " Airnin's voice trailed off, his eyes flaring red as he studied Luwayth.

"You tainted your sul? I did not think you had it in you," Airnin exclaimed in surprise.

"I had no choice, Airnin. Will it get better? Dainua recoils from me now."

"It will not. You seemed too timid to ever take your powers that far. You will be weaker but you have shown your true devotion to me."

Luwayth slumped, hoping that Airnin was lying to him.

Once the magistrates arrived, Luwayth tried not to nod off while listening to the affairs of the country play out as the night dragged on. Every now and then, Luwayth watched as Airnin glanced up, waiting for the sky to lighten.

After bringing in the latest pair of squabbling merchants to have their protest heard, Bealtane reached up and scratched his head with two of his fingers. At that signal, Luwayth barked out, "Bealtane! I have not had my dinner yet. Where is it?" The room grew silent. The merchants stopped bickering, appearing aggravated at being interrupted by something they felt was trivial. Airnin turned and looked at Luwayth, who shrugged his shoulders before replying, "I was in a rush to get back, and Bealtane never gave me my meal I requested. I am not going to let him think my needs are less than his." Closing his eyes, Luwayth looked Airnin in the face.

Only a thin line of lips briefly appeared before he spat out, "Fine. Bealtane, get the brat his food while I finish with these ingrates." The merchants' disposition turned from aggravation to anger at the word *ingrate*, until they glanced back at Airnin and realized to whom they were talking.

Rushing up the dais, Bealtane darted around the throne and exited. The merchants came to a compromise quickly, trying to get out of Airnin's presence. Once they had left, Airnin looked up at the window again. It was still overcast, and the starlight hadn't broken through the clouds. He turned back to Luwayth. "All of this unimportant business has made this night feel never-ending. I need to teach you how to deal with this squabbling so I can focus on more important things," Airnin said, irritated. The door behind them opened, and Bealtane reappeared with a silver tray in his hands, another servant following on his heels. The servant placed a tray with a black cloth down next to the throne. Bealtane then placed the tray on top of the cloth. It was a plate of scrambled eggs, mushrooms, and a single wedge of cheese.

"Is this all the cheese you brought? "Luwayth asked Bealtane irritably. "I asked for two." Bealtane gave orders to the servant before rushing down the dais and across the room to get the new pair of merchants to have their plea heard. Luwayth noticed Airnin was staring at him.

"What? I asked for two pieces of cheese. I am going to get two pieces of cheese."

"You best remember you are not the real king," Airnin snarled.

Airnin turned his attention to the next pair of merchants crossing the room towards them. Too nervous to eat but knowing he had to, Luwayth reached for the plate. Once the food hit his lips, the hunger won out over his anxiety.

The plate seemed empty for ages before he heard the door behind him open and then the shuffling of feet as a servant quietly walked over and replaced his current plate with a new one holding a single wedge of cheese. Looking over to Airnin, who didn't seem to notice, Luwayth took the piece of cheese and shoved it into his mouth.

As the two men who stood before them left, Bealtane followed after them to the door and didn't return with anyone else.

"Is that it? Are we done for the night?" Airnin asked Bealtane. But, before Bealtane could respond, Airnin turned to see that Luwayth was standing on the throne, his hand outstretched and holding a small piece of bone between two fingers.

"What is this?" Airnin demanded.

Luwayth didn't say a word. His eyes closed and the bone in his hand darkened, then burst into flames. Airnin dully watched as the bone slowly turned to ash in Luwayth's hand.

"You think you are smarter than me, boy? Do you think I would let you control the only piece that ties me here? I do not need that bone. My bones are close enough now. That accident of a victory has made you arrogant. I see that I will need to find a replacement for you—someone more compliant. All those years wasted!" Airnin's face was full of rage.

"Not so fast," came Luwayth's reply. "I have one more surprise. According to the cheese, it is two hours past first light." As the words 'first light' crossed Luwayth's lips, he let out the energy he had consumed and pushed against the windows. The glass burst outward revealing it had been painted black. The light of Farkor now flooded the room.

Airnin back away from the light, his misty form starting to shrink.

Luwayth held out his oska. The figure in front of him bore the resemblance of a man more than it had ever done before. Anger burned in Airnin's eyes that filled Luwayth with fear.

"I may be weaker," Airnin growled, "but I am still more powerful than you will ever be. I will feast on your sul while I burn down the rest of your village. But first, I will kill everyone in this palace. Someone aided you, and all will suffer because of your actions."

The throne lurched forward and tore free from its anchors, forcing Luwayth to leap to the side. It swung around the back of Airnin in an arc before coming straight at Luwayth, who pushed back as hard as he could. The throne stopped in midair. The force of Airnin and Luwayth pressing from opposite sides caused the throne to buckle and deform. Luwayth jumped to the side, crouched low, and altered his force, causing the throne to fly past him and into the stone wall. Pieces of wood and metal flew in every direction.

Luwayth noticed the sul that was writhing in Airnin's chest had grown fainter and weaker.

Airnin flew towards the door at the back of the dais. It burst out into the hall just before he reached it and he disappeared through it. Luwayth sprinted after him. In the hallway, the bodies of two guards lay on the floor. Screams came from his right. Luwayth turned and ran in that direction. It was not hard to follow Airnin; bodies of guards and servants lay dead in his wake. Luwayth grabbed their suls and filled his armor and oska, letting their emotions take over and drive his rage. He then consumed a few suls to build up energy. He spun the oska in front of him as he ran letting the energy flow around it.

Luwayth rounded a corner, and a blast hit the shield he had created, causing him to slide backward on his feet. Luwayth stopped the spin of his oska, pointing it at Airnin who stood down the hall from him. The energy crackled as it coursed through the air and grew to fill the hall. It hit Airnin as he fled backward. Airnin turned sideways to try to avoid it but was spun and pushed onto his back. Airnin slid down the hallway. Luwayth seized the opportunity, sprinted after him, and spun his oska on his right side, ready to strike again. As Luwayth neared Airnin, the deamhon lunged at Luwayth, grabbing the leather strap across his chest and tossing him down the hallway. Airnin pushed hard against Luwayth, whose speed increased drastically. Luwayth noticed a wall fast approaching, turned his feet towards it, pushed down, and created a shield beneath his feet. The force of the impact blew the stone in the wall outwards. Luwayth lost control of his energy as it sputtered into the air around him. He spun in the air, landing hard on the grass outside. Taking quick stock of himself, Luwayth realized he was bruised but nothing seemed broken. He felt relieved until he looked down and saw one of the fingers on his right hand stuck backward at an odd angle. He studied the hole in the wall but couldn't see Airnin. He grabbed his finger and quickly pulled it forward. A loud popping sound was followed by a sharp pain that ran from his finger down his arm. "Ow," he cried out, then readied his oska.

Airnin was just on the other side of the hole, staring daggers at Luwayth before floating through and into the light of Farkor, which stripped away the wraith and left the shadowy form of a human whose arms and legs could now be seen. The mist that was his face was replaced by a man's. Luwayth tried to pull some of the power from Dainua around him. She recoiled, but Luwayth persisted, and she slowly flowed into him. He consumed some and threw a force of energy at Airnin, who shifted to dodge it. The energy slammed into the palace wall, pushing several stones in.

"Give up. Even in the light of Farkor, you cannot best me," Airnin jeered.

Luwayth consumed more of Dainua's power, then reached down into the ground and surrounded Airnin in a bubble of energy. He focused the energy to throw Airnin up and over his head in an arc. Just before Airnin hit the ground behind him, Luwayth released the bubble, slamming Airnin hard into it, creating a small crater. After a few moments, Airnin slowly emerged, seemingly unharmed, though the sul in his chest looked weak and fragile.

"I have had enough of this," Airnin growled.

An unseen force pushed from beneath Luwayth, throwing him high into the air. He looked down and watched the palace fall away as he flew over the wall surrounding it and into the capital. As he came hurtling back down, he quickly pushed out to slow himself before hitting and then rolling across a roof. As Luwayth glanced in the direction he had come, a blur streaked towards him. Luwayth crouched and started to swing his oska around himself, but the shield wasn't strong enough. Airnin slammed into him, forcing Luwayth to fall back against the roof. He felt a sharp twinge in his back as the impact pushed him through the roof into the room below. Luwayth rolled over, his back spasming in pain as he desperately searched for Airnin. The only source of light, however, was from the hole above; the rest of the room was sheathed in darkness. Luwayth consumed a sul in his armor and created a barrier around himself. A shadow fell over Luwayth as Airnin appeared. The sul in Airnin's chest was all but gone.

"You are broken and beat. Give up. Your sul is mine," said Airnin with a sneer.

"Never! I will fight you until you have no power left," Luwayth spat back.

A shadowy fist came down hard onto the shield Luwayth had around him. The force pushed him into the floor, and the pain in his back flared out. "Rrrraaaaa!" he yelled in pain. His vision dimmed, and the shield fell away.

Pain became the only thing Luwayth could experience as Airnin picked him up. He struggled to find the strength to fight back, but the agony overwhelmed him. No matter how hard he tried, he couldn't focus through it. The shadowy form of Airnin's face loomed in front of him. With the little strength he had left, he spit into it, which passed through Airnin and hit the floor behind him. "You insolent brat!" Airnin hissed as he tossed Luwayth across the room and through a covered window. The world spun around Luwayth, and for a brief moment, there was no pain, until the shiny black street came into view. Luwayth pushed out with the last of the energy he had just before he hit the road. The blue of the sky was above him, and his world consisted of only pain and agony. It was so intense that he couldn't remember what it was like not to be plagued by it. The sounds of screams could be heard around him and footsteps running.

Holding Luwayth's oska, Airnin landed next to him. The sul in his chest was just about depleted; Farkor was further sapping its strength with every moment that passed.

Luwayth turned his head from him. Out of the crowd stepped Uram with several Asinta by his side.

"You are too late. I have the sul I need right here," Airnin yelled as he twirled the oska in his hand. Energy shot from it into the building to his right; two large chunks fell into the street, blocking the Asintas' path.

Airnin roughly snatched up Luwayth. The air around him shimmered. The houses and streets faded and shifted until they were replaced by the image of a cavern entrance.

Airnin pulled Luwayth close to his face. "You may have depleted my power but your sul is mine now.".

A sul! Luwayth thought. *I need a sul! Wait...* Luwayth focused on Airnin, and with every last ounce of strength he had, he drew Airnin into himself. Airnin was caught off guard but managed to fight back, pulling himself away. Finally, the sul that gave Airnin his strength winked out.

Luwayth could feel Airnin's sul swirl in himself, and when it passed by his sul, he wrapped around Airnin and bit into him. Suddenly, a vision flashed in his mind:

An older man was standing in front of him, dressed elegantly. He turned to his right and saw another man beside him. He felt himself reach out to the man on his right and attach his sul to his before turning his attention to the old man in front of him. The man began to age slowly. The old man didn't beg; instead, he said, "Son, do not do this. This is not who you are. If I failed you as a father in some way, I am sorry, but this is not the answer. I love—" The man's words were cut short when the rest of his life was pulled quickly from him. He collapsed onto the floor. His mouth moved, but no words came out. Only his deep blue eyes conveyed his grief before he died. A door opened to his left, and he turned to see another man enter the room.

"Is it done, brother?" the man asked.

The vision faded as the energy in Luwayth surged beyond anything he had experienced before. It felt like it ripped him apart. A bolt of lightning shot out of him into Telgog, and the ground rumbled in pain as the rest pushed into Dainua's power below.

A COST

Luwayth opened his eyes. The ground in front of him was midnight black. He moved his arms and then his legs; everything still worked. He felt the heat of Farkor on his back. He tried pushing himself up, but his back screamed in protest, so he slumped back into the dirt, tasting the dust around him. He peered through blurry eyes into a narrow periphery. He spotted his oska lying next to him in the dirt; he reached out, but it was beyond his grasp.

Fighting Airnin in the capital seemed far—as if it had happened in a dream. He reflected on the fight, wondering why he wasn't dead.

Did I pull in all of Airnin? Or did some of him escape? I can't feel him anymore. The emotions before have always lingered, he thought.

Hesitantly, he asked out loud, "Airnin, are you there?"

Silence.

"Airnin! Are you there?" he yelled.

Again, only silence.

He pushed down with his left hand and fought through the pain as he rolled onto his back. Above him appeared to be the entrance to a cave. He turned his head in both directions, straining to find anything that could explain how he was still alive or where he was. He could only glimpse blackened dirt. He used his elbows, then his hands, to slowly sit up. The pain was excruciating. Ahead of him lay the entrance to a shallow cave, faintly lit by the light of Farkor. Sitting in the middle of the small alcove was a sack. Next to it lay the bodies of several men.

Forcing himself upward, he grunted through the pain until he was on his feet. He stumbled forward, bracing himself against the cave's entrance. He glanced back to his oska and noticed that the ground where he had been lying was a large, oblong-shaped patch as black as the barrow. Blackness flowed out in every direction like streams from a lake.

Luwayth stumbled over to his oska and kicked at it, hoping he could get it to stand without bending over. Just as he was about to give up, his foot caught one of the roots at the base and tilted it up. He caught it just before it slipped free from his boot.

He used the oska to steady himself as he walked into the cave. In the center was the burlap bag surrounded by several bodies, all gutted. He searched the room and found a man slumped against the wall near the entrance wearing the green of the King's servants. The clothes were all but rags now. The man showed signs of a severe beating, cuts running across all of his visible skin. Luwayth shuffled forward and kicked feebly at the man. There was no response. Luwayth returned to the middle of the room, picked up the bag, and felt something rattle inside. He stumbled into the light, his back spasming in pain with each step. He could see the walls of the capital in the distance and, to his right, the Spine of Mehron on the horizon.

Luwayth turned the sack over and spilled the bones onto the blackened ground. The longer he stared at them, the more anger welled up inside him. His pain forgotten, he swung his oska at the bones, shattering them. As rage overtook, Luwayth swung again and again at the bones, destroying the top of his oska. A scream boiled to the surface as he swung harder and harder. Finally, he turned the oska around and pounded the roots that grew out of it against what was left of the skull until there wasn't a piece left he could break apart.

Exhausted and back screaming in pain, Luwayth dropped his oska and collapsed in the dirt. He laid back, tears streaming down his face. He tried to open himself to Dainua but felt nothing.

He struggled to turn himself over and crawled through the dirt to a patch that wasn't blackened, desperate to feel the comfort of the only mother he knew. She wasn't there. He closed his eyes and saw her energy all around him, just out of reach. He clawed at the dirt, pulling himself closer, but her energy pulled away. It seemed to crash into an invisible barrier all around him.

He hesitantly looked at his sul; the black cracks had widened into deep gashes, and the parts that weren't cracked had grayish boils.

"I'm sorry!" Luwayth screamed as he dragged himself towards Dainua, desperate to feel her love.

"I had no choice! I'm sorry. Please, I need you," he sobbed, pleading. Silence was his only companion.

He lay in the dirt and stared at Dainua, feeling tormented to be able to see her but not able to feel her loving embrace.

"Please, just take my life," he whispered. Desperate to be joined with her, he lay quietly, tears clouding his vision until he drifted off.

Luwayth opened his eyes, unaware he had fallen asleep, and saw starlight above. Having no strength left, he closed his eyes and fell back asleep.

The next morning, Farkor blinded Luwayth as he opened his eyes. He still felt the absence of Dainua. He glanced at his sul and saw that nothing had changed. He crawled back to his oska which he had left in the dirt behind him and used it to stand. He stared at the shattered top; it was as broken as he was. His back still hurt with every movement. He slowly walked over and studied the broken bones of Airnin. He closed his eyes and noticed the bones were empty. He opened them in confusion. He had never seen anything without a sul that wasn't black. Feeling confident that Airnin was truly gone, he kicked at the bones one last time before slowly hobbling down the hill.

He looked through the trees towards where the capital lay. Oddly, the words the old woman had spoken came to mind. He turned away from the capital and slowly made his way through the woods, determined to do some good before his death.

After trudging a few painful and agonizing stones' distance from the cave, Luwayth stumbled onto a road that came from the north and headed west in front of him. Before he left the safety of the woods, he turned to the nearest tree to take in some of its sul to store in what remained of his oska. He closed his eyes and reached out to the tree's sul. It recoiled from him. He cornered some of it in a branch and pulled. It wouldn't flow out.

"Of course," Luwayth muttered, defeated.

No longer caring if anyone was near, he stepped from the trees, slowly stripped off the armor and dumped it onto the road, then made his way west.

A few stone further down the road, Luwayth's back spasmed in pain so badly that he couldn't take another step. He feebly crept into the woods near the road and lay down in some fallen leaves. The exhaustion was greater than the pain that wracked his body, and he was soon asleep.

Awaking to the sound of horses galloping down the road, Luwayth struggled to his feet, and stumbled out of the trees but only found dust in the air.

His back had started to feel a little better, so he walked along the road's edge, searching for food to forage. He found a handful of berries and a couple of mushrooms.

At about midday, he came across a farm; the farmer was busy harvesting his field.

"Oy, Farmer!" Luwayth called out.

"Oy, Traveler!" the farmer called back.

"You in need of a pair of hands in exchange for a meal?" Luwayth asked as he drew near.

"Sounds like a fair trade," the farmer agreed.

He walked over to Luwayth and stuck out his hand. Luwayth grasped him by the wrist. The Farmer instantly pulled his hand back as if shocked by the touch, and his eyes went wide as he searched the boy's face.

"Uhh... I just recalled a few hands are on their way this afternoon. You will have to be on your way," the farmer said, his voice dripping with fear.

Luwayth nodded and continued down the road. After he was out of sight of the farm, he looked down at his hand. It didn't look any different.

"Could the man feel my diseased sul?" Luwayth wondered.

Luwayth spent that night in the woods and was back on the road at first light.

"Where are the riders?" Luwayth pondered, certain that they would have headed back in his direction.

As he started down the road, he heard a mournful crack as his oska split in two. He inspected the wood and realized the cut from the soldier's blade had spread.

Luwayth walked to the side of the road and used a stone to dig a shallow grave. His eyes filled with tears as he gently laid his oska down, lining up the two halves. He gently caressed the wood as his tears watered the ground. When he couldn't cry anymore, he carefully covered the oska, thinking of his father.

As he leaned back, grass grew from the grave; flowers stretched up to Telgog, then bloomed spectacularly. Luwayth closed his eyes and saw Dainua's energy flowing through the oska, feeding the tiny grove. Telgog's energy whirled and danced around it.

"My deeds have cost me everything," Luwayth confided to the grove, feeling utterly broken. He glanced down the road, saying, "My life isn't even mine."

He sat in the dirt, hoping for death to ride up to take him. When it didn't arrive, he slowly stood and continued on in search of it.

By midmorning, he came across another farm. His stomach growled at the thought of food. This farmer, just as the last, was busy harvesting his field.

"Oy, need a pair of hands?" Luwayth called out, hesitantly.

"Ay, I could use a pair. Give you a meal in exchange," the farmer said as he walked over and stuck out his hand. Luwayth shied away like a frightened animal.

"Timid? Nothing to fear from me," the farmer said innocently, then he noticed the boy's swollen eyes, the bruises covering his face, and the rips in his soiled clothing. There also was an invisible weight of torment that seemed to press down on him.

"Made some bad choices," Luwayth quietly replied.

"Ay, I see," the farmer stated as he scrutinized the boy. Then, out of pity, he pulled two strips of cloth from a pocket. "Mind pulling lull weeds?"

Luwayth shook his head and carefully grabbed the strips of cloth, making sure not to touch the Farmer's hands. He wrapped one around each hand and walked into the field, then slowly bent over to start pulling lull weeds, grateful to finally be doing some good.

"Oy, what's your name, boy?" the Farmer asked with deep curiosity.

Without hesitation, Luwayth replied: *Fearn.*"

ACKNOWLEDGMENTS

I want to start off with the sappy thank you that you see in every book: a huge thanks to my parents. To my father, who provided inspiration to sit down and write this book, and my mom, for letting me live long enough to grow into a functioning adult. Without their support, I don't know if this book would have ever made it into your hands.

A thank you to my wife, both for encouraging me along the way and cheering me up during the times I lost hope in my writing. I don't know what she sees in me but I'm grateful that she has decided to stick by my side. She was my first editor and turned what was initially 125,000 words of streaming consciousness into something a human could read and understand. She is my greatest love. I can't think of another person I would have wanted on this journey.

I have a wonderfully dysfunctional "reading group with an eating problem" of which I have been a member since high school. Crickhollow has become our second family and were instrumental in getting this book to the state it is in. If you didn't like it, I blame them. Many of them read this book from the horrible first draft and stuck with me through all of the rewrites, giving me brutally honest feedback along the way. Dave Riske was brave enough to lead a discussion on what I thought was close to the final draft, which helped me step out of my role as an author and understand the issues I needed to address. Steve Gaddis, a man with an encyclopedic knowledge of fantasy, mythology and armor, was wonderful in reading everything I threw at him and showing me the Hollywood-esque flaws I had in the book.

To the test readers who read and reread the manuscripts and gave invaluable feedback, including those of you who sent along cheese as a thank you (and if you were wondering - no I am not a cheese fanatic - I just couldn't find a way of making chocolate fit into the story!), I'm humbled by your encouragement and assistance.

Lastly, I want to thank everyone at Global Book Publishing for all of the hard work they put into my novel. Sush, who worked with me every week, and the art department for the beautiful work they did in bringing Fearn to life. Lastly, a huge thank you to Maxwell, my editor, who took what I thought was going to be an experience from the deepest bowels of hell and instead made it a journey of encouragement.

About The Author

Gavin Black lives with his wife and two boys in Reno, Nevada. Growing up, he spent his formative years in the hospital due to a congenital lung malady. He found an escape in fantasy and science fiction novels, beginning with the books of David Eddings and followed by so many of the greats: Tolkien, Heinlein, and Asimov, among others. He was always drawn to stories with deep character development and that defied readers' expectations. When not writing, he can be found playing board games with his family and friends, reading, or discussing the varied merits of many a pop culture franchise.

Gavin and his wife, Ann, met at Renovation, the 2014 WorldCon. Together, they enjoy attending numerous conventions – always in cosplay! – including D23, WorldCon, Wizard World, and any others that come within 100 miles of Reno. Gavin's favorite panels always include learning more about the creation process in any media form. He's also attended courses by Neil Gaiman and Brandon Sanderson on the ins and outs of writing fantasy.

Before he began writing, Gavin imagined up dozens of worlds and characters, often inspired by the unique folks he met traveling while working as a systems engineer for different gaming companies. Although only a few have found their way into his first novel, he swears he has a never-ending supply for future tales!

www.gavinblackwrites.com

Made in the USA
Columbia, SC
01 December 2021